FROSTBITTEN

DIETRICH STOGNER

To Horace Stogner

Who taught me how far I could go by taking one step at a time.

Thanks, Dad.

CONTENTS

FROSTBITTEN

PROLOGUE

Nothing sharpens the focus like trying not to vomit. This battle to swallow the lump rising steadily up his throat had begun at the point at which Tomas Greenleaf had climbed the first two hundred steps of the Ascent To The Empress. Unfortunately for him, those were only the first of five thousand.

A few days before the evaluations began, Greenleaf had expressed some apprehension to his father about the climb to the arena. He'd climbed the Ascent before, but never with the promise of such a grueling challenge at the end. As they sat outside his parent's home in a lower district, the summer sun gently warming their skin, his father had listened to Greenleaf's concerns. "It's a lot," he acknowledged with that deep, rich voice Greenleaf had always loved. "Just remember. You're not trying to climb the entire Ascent. You're only responsible for your next step. Just take one more step."

"And then what?"

The older man grinned, white teeth against his dark skin. "Do it again."

The polished granite steps were lined on either side with throngs of cheering people, their faces a blur as Greenleaf's deadened legs climbed one step after another. Greenleaf had stood on those steps himself as a child, cheering as the handful of men and women to survive the grueling five years of training to become an Imperial kaviak jogged past, light gleaming off their armor as they climbed through the six levels of the city to the arena at the top of the hill. He'd been told that his cheers inspired them to even greater heights once they reached the trials at the end of the stairs.

The reality was somewhat less glorious. Sweat stung his eyes. His chest heaved like bellows. Cramps gnawed at his roiling guts. That shining armor hung like a millstone on his shoulders, and the only inspiration he drew from the cheers was the realization that if he fell to his knees and spilled his breakfast over the hard stone stairs, he'd do so in front of a few thousand disappointed onlookers. Word would spread faster than the grey fever through the city that a candidate fell before reaching the top, and that would be his story. So he kept planting his foot, lifting himself up one more step, and doing it again, gasping humid Kaani air with each seven-inch tall victory.

He hadn't passed any of the other candidates. That wasn't a surprise; the instructors sent them up in ten-minute intervals, and each of the others was just as physically fit as Greenleaf. He'd been the last to begin the climb. He'd be the last to enter the arena. Theoretically, that meant that if he was able to reach the top of the Ascent faster than the others, he'd have more time to rest, but Greenleaf had been warned several times that had yet to happen in the history of the Trials.

The first sign that he was close to the end of his climb was the sound of the crowd in the arena, shouts and cheers punctuated by groans marking an error or misstep by a candidate. He wiped the sweat from his eyes, trying to make out the water clock at the entrance to the arena through blurred vision. As he mounted the last step, several attendants rushed forward, one carrying a tray with a clay mug. Gratefully, he drained the cool water inside as two others worked to unfasten the armor straps.

"Did you stop for noodles on the way up?" Sergeant Illyn Ash's wooden leg thumped on the granite slabs as he emerged from the entrance to the arena, his bushy eyebrow raised as he approached. "I could have made the climb faster, and I've got half the legs you do."

His heart was still pounding as he gulped air, but Greenleaf made a weak gesture back to the stairs. "Be my guest," he mumbled, his speech slurred. He accepted another cup, dumping it over his inky black hair, cut close to his scalp. His uniform was soaked through with sweat. Another attendant began removing the iron weights from around his ankles, and Greenleaf winced as he saw the skin chafed raw.

"It's fine. The anatomists will fix you up afterwards," Ash said, impatiently tapping his cane against the ground as he waited for the attendants to finish. As the last weight was removed, he grabbed Greenleaf's arm. "Come on. You've got maybe four minutes, less if Seena shits the bed. I heard hoofbeats in there. Doesn't bode well."

They made their way through the doors into a dark room, lit only by the ghostly glow of cinderstone spheres mounted to the wall. Benches lined the sides, with basins of water in between. In the center were elevated cots, upon which sat several other men and women, all wearing the same uniform as Greenleaf, and all in various states of abuse. One soldier winced as an anatomist gently prodded at a clearly broken nose. In the closest cot, Oriana Halfsdotir was wheezing, clutching her stomach as she held a bowl of vapors beneath her nose. A deep cut over her eyebrow had been hastily bandaged, and another anatomist was preparing a needle and gut. Halfsdotir spotted Greenleaf as he entered, offering a weak smile.

"You still among the living?" he said, making his way over.

She offered a weak nod. "Heavy infantry. Two of them. Gave me a rapier to deal with them," she rasped. "Bastards."

Greenleaf winced. "Least you walked out."

"I did at that. Put both the fuckers in the dirt, too." She tried to lean in, and gasped in pain, her lips white. "Gods, this hurts. I think I broke all my ribs. Feels like I found a few extra to snap as well." She shook her head sharply. "Dina got carried out. In the infirmary now. Don't know if she'll make the Elevation."

A bell chimed three times, and the crowd inside the arena roared, the deafening sound traveling through the long hallway to the staging room. Greenleaf swallowed as Ash gestured to the end of the hall.

"Don't die, candidate," Halfsdotir rasped.

"I'll do my best." Greenleaf reached out and grasped her shoulder, following the sergeant down the hall. The staging room gave way to a long, dark hallway, lacking any decoration. Dirt crunched under his aching feet. The noise from the crowd had subsided to a rumble, and Ash slowed to walk next to Greenleaf.

"If they're mounted, you have to keep moving," he said. "Don't let them line up, and don't try for the horses. They'll be ready for that."

Greenleaf nodded. His heart had slowed when he finished the climb, but it now drummed out a frantic tempo in his chest.

"You know how to deal with archers or crossbowmen. Think. You'll have a few precious moments before the bell sounds. Use them. Know where you're going to step." They reached a plain wooden door, and came to a halt. The sergeant turned to face him, looking him over. "You good? Your head straight?"

His legs were dead posts underneath him. The abrasions from the ankle weights were starting to burn. There was a pressure behind his eyeballs, and his wool uniform clung to his sweat-soaked skin. His hands were trembling slightly; whether from the exertion of the climb or nerves, he couldn't say. Despite all this, Greenleaf offered a short nod. "Two minds, sergeant."

"Two minds." Footsteps sounded on the other side of the door as someone approached. Quickly, Ash said, "Ignore the crowd. Only thing that matters is your enemy. Deal with them quickly, and I'll see you on the other side."

The doors opened. The noise swelled as the three Imperial soldiers looked over Greenleaf. One with legionnaire stripes on his sleeve said, "Candidate. Fall in for evaluation."

Greenleaf pulled himself upright. "Yes, sir." He fell in behind them, feeling Ash's eyes on the back of his neck.

Light began to fill the tunnel as they approached the end. The noise poured into the space like water flooding a ditch. Greenleaf took a deep breath into his aching lungs, counting his heartbeats, willing them to slow.

The end of the tunnel opened up onto the broad, oval arena, and they paused just before the threshold. Dozens of attendants were raking the dirt back in place. He spotted the telltale rust coloring of blood on the ground. A high wooden wall rose around the sides of the arena, dozens of War College instructors seated before it with a clear view. His eyes lingered on two faces: that of his parents. His father gave Greenleaf the tiniest of nods. Beyond the wall, row after row of broad benches were packed full with hundreds, thousands of faces.

The legionnaire turned to face him. "Do you enter this evaluation willingly?"

"I do, sir."

"Your weapon." One of the other soldiers stepped over to a table, and picked up a spear. Greenleaf's expression didn't betray the relief he felt as he accepted the hickory shaft, topped with a blackened spearhead. He knew the point was dulled, but the familiar weapon felt comforting in his hands.

"Step forward, and may the Empress lend you strength."

The roar from the crowd as Greenleaf emerged into the light was almost a physical thing. People stomped their feet and shouted encouragement as he stepped into the arena. Three men were waiting for him. All wore light infantry armor, leather jerkins with steel panels sewn above the vitals. They wore no helmets, but their gloved hands held longbows, arrows nocked. The stunner arrowheads were blunt spheres of iron, but he knew they could easily smash bone and teeth on impact. Short swords hung to the right of their hips, a quiver to the left. The three stood in a wide semicircle, thirty feet apart from one another, watching him impassively.

Someone was speaking loudly, but Greenleaf wasn't listening. His waking mind had fallen silent. The soldier's mind had stepped forward.

Three opponents, ranged weapons. Too far apart to engage at the same time. They won't loose at the same time; they'll coordinate. No matter how I move, one will have a shot. Can't slow down, can't give them a chance to aim. Twenty feet. Have to close within twenty feet.

The soldiers watched him as he approached the wooden circle in the center of the arena with hard eyes. He knew they weren't trying to kill him. He also knew that soldiers in the Imperial army competed for the right to stand against the candidates, and should one successfully disable him, they'd earn six months pay. He came to a stop, gripping his spear. The three archers each stood thirty feet away.

Right one is big. Strong arms, strong back. Older. Other two are younger. Hands are shaking. They're nervous. Right isn't. He's the threat.

At the far end of the arena hung a long brass cylinder. The speaker shouted a command, and an attendant struck the brass bell with a hammer, the low tone reverberating through the stadium. The two younger archers drew their bows back, sighting in on Greenleaf. The older archer waited.

Impulsive. They'll fire. He'll wait.

A second chime. The noise of the crowd fell away. Greenleaf's knees bent, his grip on the spear loose and ready. The point came up into ready position. He fixed his eyes on the center archer. He could hear the creak of wood as bowstrings strained, could feel the dirt shift beneath his soles.

Twenty feet.

The span between the second and third chime seemed to stretch like taffy. When the bell sounded, Greenleaf leapt.

His spear snapped back against his chest as he tucked into a roll, diving between the two younger archers. As his shoulder struck the ground, he heard the hiss of a stunning arrow before he felt the air move. The iron head flashed only inches over his shoulder, and as he came up, he spun to face away from where the shot had been loosed.

Greenleaf turned his back on the soldier that had loosed early, darting to put the middle archer between him and the older archer. The spear came up just as the middle archer loosed. Some distant part of his brain noted the angle of the bow, their relative positions, and he sidestepped before the arrow had flown. Thanks to the missed shot, the archer had to choose between reaching for a second arrow or drawing his sword. The second of indecision was enough time for Greenleaf to close the distance, and the blunted spearpoint slammed into the archer's guts with enough force to fold the man around it with a gasp of pain.

Two left. Might have a second, maybe two before the one behind me can draw and loose again. Have to take out righty.

Reaching out, Greenleaf grabbed the man's collar, pulling him close as he ducked down. There was a fleshy *thump*, and the already injured archer cried out again as the stunning arrow smashed into his back. As he tumbled to the ground, Greenleaf planted his feet, and threw his spear with a grunt. The blackened steel point flashed through the air, and struck the older archer in the hip with enough force to spin him around as he fell.

A second arrow zipped past his head from behind him, hissing as it missed his ear by a few inches. Without thinking, Greenleaf reached down, tearing the short sword from the leather sheath on the insensate man's hip. He spun, eyes widening. The other archer already had his third arrow nocked, and was sighting in. There was still about thirty feet between them. Greenleaf glanced down at the short sword in his hand.

Close range weapon.

He mentally shrugged.

Says who?

The archer's eyes widened as Greenleaf threw the thirty-inch steel blade as hard as he could. Not designed for flight, the sword tumbled haphazardly through the air, flashing in the bright midday sun. The leather-wrapped hilt struck the archer on the shoulder before the blade clattered to the ground. It wasn't enough to injure, but the impact caused the archer's fingers to reflexively loosen. The arrow flew, missing Greenleaf by nearly a meter as he charged forward, dirt spraying from his boots as he ran towards the archer. His hands balled into fists as the distance between them melted away.

Twenty feet.

The archer dropped the bow, reaching for the hilt of his sword.

Fifteen feet.

The blade began to slide from the scabbard, the archer's other arm coming up to block the onrushing attack.

Ten feet.

Greenleaf's eyes were locked on his target. The archer was too slow, too close to react before Greenleaf could get his hands on him, and once that happened...

Five feet.

His boot came down, and the dirt slipped beneath his sole. His fingers brushed over the archer's wrist before slipping away.

The archer didn't try to slash at him. Instead, he shifted his angle, and as he drew the sword, he drove the pommel straight out, striking Greenleaf in the chin. His teeth snapped together so hard he feared they would break as the blow landed, and he felt blood as the skin on his chin tore. A heartbeat later, Greenleaf crashed into the archer, the pair falling to the ground in a tangle of limbs. For a few brief seconds, the two of them scrabbled in the dirt like quarreling schoolboys, but Greenleaf had both size and position. The archer landed a few sharp blows to his abdomen, but the question was answered when his nose flattened under Greenleaf's knuckles, a spray of blood hot on Greenleaf's face. Gasping, the archer slapped the ground, and Greenleaf paused his second blow as the bell chimed once more.

Silence fell for one heartbeat, then two, and the spectators roared.

***

The anatomists were the first to reach them, a half-dozen of the grey-robed healers sprinting from the edges of the arena as soon as the fight was over. Greenleaf sat heavily down on the ground as they approached, wiping blood from his chin, the exhaustion of the day finally catching up to him. He looked down at his hands, which were trembling. An older man dropped to his knees next to Greenleaf, taking his chin delicately in hand.

"That's going to need stitches," the anatomist muttered. He pulled a flask of clear liquid from his bag, and tilted Greenleaf's head back as he poured it over the open wound. "How's your head? Hear any bells?"

"Not since the last one," Greenleaf said weakly.

"Funny." He pressed a wad of folded linen to the cut. "Hold this here. It should stop the bleeding for now. We'll sew you up after."

Greenleaf nodded. "The others okay?" The archer he'd just tackled was on his feet, and heard him speak. He offered a weak wave with his right hand. One of the others held a cloth soaked in red to his face.

"No one's dead. Most everything else we can sort out."

Sergeant Ash came to a stop next to him, and offered a meaty palm. Greenleaf accepted it, and the sergeant pulled him to his feet. The older soldier was grinning. "First few moments were very pretty. That last bit, though…"

"I know," Greenleaf said. "Slipped. Had to improvise."

"It'll cost you points. You know that, right?"

But how many? Is it enough?

Greenleaf pushed away the unwelcome thought, and nodded. Ash patted his shoulder. "Don't let it worry you. Suspect you'll make up a few with that trick with the short sword. Quick thinking, that."

More people flooded into the arena as attendants brought out dozens of chairs, arranging them in neat rows facing a dais at the north end. Greenleaf began to say something, but straightened as his parents approached. Ash turned, and came to attention. He pressed his right fist to his left shoulder in salute. "Colonel Greenleaf. Ma'am."

"Sergeant," the colonel said, offering his hand. Ash shook it. "Seems like you've done a fair job these last five years. That was a tricky setup."

"He's not totally hopeless, sir. The three archers... That one's a bit notorious. Knew he was in trouble when they gave him the spear."

"I was hoping for a spear," Greenleaf said.

"Exactly," the sergeant said. "If your enemy ever gives you exactly what you want, you need to worry."

"Well said." His father smiled gamely for a moment, and Ash took the cue.

"I'm going to see if the other candidates need anything. Give you three a moment."

Greenleaf hugged his mother. "Sorry for the smell. It's a lot of steps."

"You did beautifully, Tomas." She smiled up at him.

"Thought you'd ruined your chances when you threw the spear." Greenleaf glanced over at the odd edge to his father's tone. "Nice thought, throwing the sword. Thought you had him." The colonel paused, and asked, "What happened there?"

"My foot slipped."

His father's eyes lingered on his for a long moment. "Slipped."

Greenleaf nodded, trying not to betray the knot forming in his stomach. "Loose dirt, I think."

Devon Greenleaf opened his mouth as if to say something, but closed it, and nodded. "All right. It's done and over." He reached out and gripped his son's shoulder. "If you'll excuse me, I want to give my best to the commissar." His father walked away to a cluster of officials speaking to one of the other candidates.

"He mispronounced 'I'm proud of you'," Leah Greenleaf said, rolling her eyes.

"Yeah, he does that," Greenleaf said. He offered a weak smile, wincing as the movement tugged at his chin. "It's fine, mom."

The bell chimed as several more candidates emerged from the staging room, each in various states of injury. One candidate was carried in by four attendants on a stretcher, her leg wrapped in thick layers of linen blotched with red. An officer raised his voice. "The candidates will take their seats."

Normally, candidates of the Imperial War College were quick and disciplined. Today, their sluggish movement and weariness were forgiven. Five rows of thirty chairs had been set up. The family and spectators all took their positions around the chairs, as Greenleaf and seven other candidates found the chair marked with their name. He knew no one would criticize him if he sat, but he could feel his father's eyes on him, and remained standing.

The spectators were still on their feet, but the cheering had quieted to a dull roar. Greenleaf looked out over the faces. Most were pointing and chatting animatedly, grinning as they lifted children up for a better look at the sea of empty chairs. His eyes lingered on a group of a few dozen near the front, right behind the dais. They stood silently, watching. Each wore a white tunic with stylized broken bridge embroidered on the front. The stands around them were mostly empty, the rest of the crowd distancing themselves.

"Tomas." Jon Greymane was in the row behind Greenleaf, and leaned forward on the cane bearing his weight. He nodded at the silent spectators, speaking low enough that no one else could hear them. "That's the anti-bridge faction, right? The Brehai?"

Greenleaf nodded, glancing over the stone-faced protestors. "That's their sigil. I didn't expect them here."

"They shouldn't be anywhere near..." Greymane trailed off as the bell chimed three times quickly, and came to attention, along with the other candidates. Even the one on the stretcher sat up as best as her wounds would allow.

A quartet of guards took their position on the dais, each clad in plate armor of a dull grey, the light catching the metal and reflecting in shimmering colors. They held halberds, with longswords sheathed at their hips. Once they'd come to a halt, one at each corner of the dias, a general stepped out in full dress uniform, the scarlet stripes bright against the inky black of the tunic. With a voice practiced in echoing across a raging battlefield, he boomed, "Rise and be seen." The crowd all rose to their feet. "Subjects of the Alddarri Empire, rise and be seen. Give your ears, your eyes, and your heart to our defender and mother, beloved by all. Evia Illych Contasia VII, Empress of the Alddarri Empire, Commander of the Imperial Army, Speaker of the Imperial Chorale, and Voice of the Alddarri people. Rise and be seen, hear and attend."

As he spoke, the spectators in the broken bridge tunics all turned as one, putting their backs to the stage. Everyone else fell into a hushed silence as the Empress emerged onto the dais. If she noticed the silent Brehai behind her, she gave no indication. Empress Contasia was in her late fifties, thin and tall. She wore a coal-black gown, glittering with small chips of glowing cinderstone sewn into the fabric, as if someone had cut fabric from a summer midnight sky and wrapped it around her. A thin silver crown sat upon her head, from which a teardrop of emerald hung in the center of her forehead, catching the light in a dazzling display. Even from his seat, Greenleaf could see her brilliant sapphire eyes. Her lips were painted black with a single vertical white stripe in the center, and when she spoke, the rich timbre of her voice carried throughout the arena.

"From the moment my family chose to stand against the chaos and violence that had shattered our continent into pieces, there have been those who have chosen to stand with us. For over two hundred years, they carried our banner, bringing light to those who had suffered so long in the dark, warmth to those who had shivered too long in the cold." Her eyes fell to the eight battered candidates looking up at her, shifting from one after another. "The dream of unification would have remained a dream without their courage, their dedication, and their sacrifice. For those who have been born in a unified nation, a nation of peace and prosperity, the hopes for the future ride on those who exemplify that courage, that dedication, and that sacrifice. And nowhere is this better exemplified than in the kaviaks of the Alddarri Empire."

She extended her hand, waving across the mostly empty seats. "Five years ago, these chairs were full of the most gifted young men and women from across the Empire, each the shining jewel of their family and community. For five years, we demanded perfection. For five years, we demanded dedication. For five years, we asked them to give all that they had, to allow themselves to be heated, hammered, tempered, and forged into the best of us. One by one, those chairs emptied, as candidates found other ways to serve, and cleared a path for those who remained. Eight stand before us today."

Empress Contasia smiled down at them. "In the name of the Alddarri Empire, I name you each kaviak, and charge you with the defense of those who serve the Imperial Family, and who my family serves in kind. I offer a gift to each of you, to carry forth as you defend the people of this beloved empire. I offer my thanks to each of you, to carry forth as you defend the ideals of this beloved empire. I offer my love to each of you, to carry forth as you defend the future of this beloved empire. I name you kaviak, and place the peace and security of our home in your hands."

The general stepped forward. "Kaviaks!"

In one motion, the eight snapped their fists to their shoulders, and bellowed, "For the Empress!"

The empress bowed at the waist. "For the Empire," she said, her voice quiet enough to barely carry. Turning, she stepped away, glancing briefly at the backs arrayed to her before vanishing back behind a door.

Taking the place she had just vacated, the general said, "Each of the kaviaks that join our ranks today have endured years of grueling training. Today's evaluation was the last of a trio of tests completed in the last month, judging their knowledge, skills, and love of the Empire. All have earned the title of kaviak. But only one can be chosen as the First among Equals, and awarded the honor of fulfilling an Imperial Arrogation."

Greenleaf kept his face still, but his heart was pounding.

Was it enough?

Was it enough to fall short?

An attendant stepped up, and handed the general a small wooden box. He raised his voice, shouting, "Subjects of the Empress, give tribute to your kaviaks!"

If Greenleaf had thought the crowd loud before, the roar that erupted from the stands put their previous efforts to shame. To his surprise, the Brehai protestors had turned back around, and while they weren't as enthusiastic as the rest of the spectators, they still applauded. The ovation seemed to last for an eternity, only dying down when the general raised his hands. Greenleaf's fingers dug into his palms as he clenched his fists and held his breath.

Looking down at the graduates, he barked, "Kaviaks, give tribute to the first among equals... Captain Tomas Greenleaf!"

Looking back on that moment, he could only reason that he must have heard the crowd cheer, must have felt Greymane, Halfsdotir and the others pounding his back as they congratulated him. But when he thought back to that day, to the moment his name was spoken, he only remembered that it was the second time that day that he felt as if he was going to be sick.

CHAPTER 1

Three weeks later

Snowflakes drifted past curtains of impossible light to live a brief life on the tip of Greenleaf's nose. He stared up at the luminous ribbons of the aurora in the fading light as the snow fell around him, breathing deep the chilled air. This moment of relative peace was shattered almost immediately by the bellow of a burdened man.

"Move, gods-dammit!" The young soldier wasn't particularly large, but clearly had muscle beneath the thick poncho draped over his shoulders. He shifted the weight of a large crate cradled in his gloved hands, lumps of black coal peeking above the rim. Realizing his comment had been directed his way, Greenleaf stepped to the side as the soldier lumbered past, handing the crate up to another man standing in the open back of the stovewagon.

Relieved of the weight, the loud soldier turned to glare at Greenleaf. "I get that it's pretty, but maybe pick any other spot than in my way to goggle at the lights?"

"Thought all the cargo got loaded last night."

The soldier arched an eyebrow. "You a passenger?" Greenleaf nodded, and the soldier grinned as he inspected the pale grey cloak wrapped around Greenleaf's shoulders. "Hope you don't have a particular fondness for that color. You're going to look like you tumbled through a coal pit by the time we reach the oasis."

"I thought stovewagons vented the smoke outside."

"Most of it, yeah. But more than enough'll bleed into the cargo bay to make your eyes water and your clothes black." He made a face. "No one calls them stovewagons, by the way."

"What do they call them?"

Before the soldier could answer, he spotted someone over Greenleaf's shoulder, and straightened somewhat.

A woman wearing the same dark brown poncho as the soldier walked past Greenleaf to stand before the spearman. She was in her late forties, with a shaved head covered in campaign tattoos. The three silver studs of an Imperial sergeant dotted her nostril. "Finished already, Spearman?"

"Almost, sergeant," the soldier said. He gestured at Greenleaf. "Passenger. Was gawking at the skylights right in my path."

"I see." She peered down at the spearman with deep brown eyes narrowed in irritation. "And you decided this was an ideal opportunity to educate our new passenger on his place?"

"Uh, I thought..."

"Gonna stop you right there, Pyle, because that's clearly untrue. You have no idea who this passenger might be. He could be the Empress in disguise. Maybe a Vetticcian emissary, up from the south." She stopped within inches of his face, her voice growing colder than the wind blowing in from the west. "Or maybe it's our new kaviak. Personally, I'd hope it's the empress or a Vetticcian, because that would mean you didn't just talk to your new commanding officer in that tone."

Pyle's face was rapidly approaching the color of curdled milk. "Shit."

"While an accurate summation of your current circumstances, that's still not what I want to hear come out of your mouth, Spearman."

The soldier came to attention as several others carried crates to the wagon behind him, doing their best to avoid attention. "I'm sorry, Captain. I shouldn't have..."

"Don't you have coal to load, Spearman?" Greenleaf asked.

"Yes, sir."

"Then hop to it."

Pyle beat a grateful retreat as the sergeant turned to face Greenleaf. "Apologies, sir. The message wasn't entirely clear on when you'd arrive, but that still doesn't excuse his behavior." She offered her hand. "Field Sergeant Rosi Idar."

Greenleaf clasped her hand, raising an eyebrow at the poncho his new sergeant wore. "Not exactly regulation, is it?"

"Begging pardon, sir, but regulation uniforms aren't really made for the ice. Command gave us special dispensation a long time ago," she said. "I have two set aside for you. He may have been out of line, but Pyle wasn't wrong. Coal dust'll ruin that cloak pretty quick."

"I'll be fine." Greenleaf gestured towards the wagon in which Pyle and several other soldiers were loading coal. "Am I riding in that one?"

Idar shook her head, pointing. "Yours is the second one, down the road. I'm jamming eight soldiers in the last bakery. Between the company and the smell, don't really think you'd enjoy the trip. We're carrying a team of Chorale to Lahar, just five. I thought I'd put you in with them."

He arched an eyebrow. "Bakery?"

The sergeant nodded. "Yes, sir." She began to say more, but a loud crash from the soldiers drew her attention. Cursing softly, she said, "With your permission?" He nodded, and she turned to head towards the men crouched around the smashed crate, stormclouds building in her glare. Greenleaf began walking past the wagon towards the one she'd indicated.

The stovewagons were massive, each nearly thirty feet long and half again as wide. Slats of blackened wood were fixed together with iron brackets. A iron chimney topped with a conical hat sprouted from the top like a metallic mushroom. The heavy vehicle sat on eight wheels affixed to four thick axels. Instead of wagon wheels, the bakeries rolled on thick discs of blackened oak. At the front, a pair of pale grey animals, each standing nearly six feet tall at the shoulder, snorted and shuffled in their harnesses, chewing their cud slowly. The snow frosting their heads and backs didn't seem to bother them. Greenleaf walked around to look at their faces.

The yaks had big, wet eyes that drooped as they stared back at him with a dull expression. The massive animals were covered in long grey fur, hanging thick over their sides. They had the snouts of cattle, but the similarity ended there. Large black horns coiled out from the side of their skull, and their legs were thick like that of a hippo, broad flat hooves shuffling over the snow-packed road.

Turning towards the second wagon, Greenleaf could see a handful of people already seated inside. As he approached, one turned to face him, and lifted a friendly hand in greeting. "Lieutenant! The sergeant said you'd be riding with us."

Greenleaf nodded as he approached. The man was in his early thirties with thick blonde hair, wearing a familiar set of white robes.

As he offered his hand, Greenleaf saw the key tattooed on the inside of his wrist. "Preceptor Creel, at your service."

"Captain Tomas Greenleaf." He'd only had a few weeks to get used to saying his new rank aloud. It still didn't feel right.

"My apologies!" Creel smiled broadly. "You're awfully young to be a captain, if you don't mind my saying."

"I don't."

"He's a kaviak," another voice boomed. A second man in white poked his head from the wagon. "Different rules, I suppose." He reached down his hand. "Allow me, Captain. I'm excited that we'll be traveling together."

Greenleaf accepted the offered hand, and the man pulled him up with surprising strength, saying, "Preceptor Knoxol. A pleasure."

Glancing around the interior, Greenleaf spotted several others getting settled. "Didn't expect Chorale to be making this trip. Are you academics? Artificers?"

"Masons, actually."

They were interrupted by a burly man peering in. "Ready? Closing up in five."

Creel clambered up, and nodded down. "We're good."

"Take a deep breath, Captain," Knoxol said. "Last fresh air for six days."

"It's all right by me," Greenleaf said, drawing his cloak tight around his shoulders. "It's cold as hell out there."

Knoxol grinned as several of the others in the wagon exchanged a glance. "No, Captain. It's not."

Even after they'd settled into the bakery, it took nearly an hour for the convoy to get moving. The caravan master had methodically walked around every one of his five wagons, checking for gaps or cracks in the wooden shell, counting crates of coal and sparking up a fire in the iron stove in the center of the wagon. By the time he shut the heavy wooden doors with a loud thunk, black smoke was issuing from the chimney, heat radiating from the dull black metal. Ten minutes later, the bakery lurched into motion, and Greenleaf sat back against the padded seat.

The ceiling was only about five feet tall, so Knoxol had to crouch as he made his way to the seat across from Greenleaf. Settling in, Knoxol said, "I expect this is your first time to Lahar?"

Greenleaf nodded. "New posting."

"What was your last?"

"Didn't have one. Graduated three weeks ago."

Knoxol raised a bushy eyebrow. "Three weeks out of the Imperial War College, and already a captain? I thought new graduates were lieutenants."

I should be. "This posting was an Imperial arrogation. The kaviak assigned got advanced to captain, since it's technically a territorial command."

"I suppose Suviev is technically an Imperial territory," Knoxol said. "Granted, one with fewer than four hundred residents, all of whom live in one small village, but it's still a territory."

"It's the fourth biggest territory in the Empire."

"With less than one percent habitable." Knoxol shrugged. "Seems like an odd place to find one of the vaunted kaviaks."

Greenleaf felt a flash of irritation. "The Empress has her reasons for sending me. Just like I'm sure she had her reasons for sending you." The smell of burning coal was already overbearing. "I thought all of the Chorale masons were down south, working on the bridge."

"We were, up until two weeks ago," Knoxol said. "However, the Chorale is dedicated to answering the call to serve the people of the Empire, in the many ways that our humble abilities may allow. The people of Lahar requested our help, and were deemed worthy of our small team of resonants." He offered a toothy grin. "The fairly large donation they made to the Lyceum probably helped foster that perception of worth."

"Is this the first time you've been?"

"Third. Other Chorale masons have gone out several times over the last few years."

"What for?"

"Help on the farms."

Greenleaf frowned. "I thought nothing grew in Lahar."

"That's never precisely been true," Knoxol said. "And it's even less true lately. You'll see once we arrive. The Laharian farms are actually fairly ingenious." Leaning forward, he asked, "May I ask you a question, captain?" Before Greenleaf could answer, Knoxol continued. "You don't seem excited for your new posting."

"That's not a question." Greenleaf wiped the beads of sweat that had begun to form on his brow. When he brought his fingers away, they had faint streaks of black. "I'm honored to serve the Empress in any way."

"That's the exact same answer we've given for the last six years we've spent over the Breaking, growing a few inches of whitestone a day."

"From what I've heard, the bridge was supposed to take six months to complete," Greenleaf said.

Knoxol shrugged. "Having never summoned millions of tons of stone to span a chasm six miles wide brimming with never-ending storms, I think it reasonable that our initial estimates were a bit off."

"That delay isn't making things easy," Greenleaf said. "Once it's finished, the Brehai won't have anything to rant about any longer. As long as it remains incomplete..."

"Rest assured, Captain. Soon enough we'll reach the southern side, and you and your fellow kaviaks will lead our forces to bring stability and unification to the Dominion." Knoxol paused. "Well, the other kaviaks, at least. You'll be busy defending the Laharians against…" He scratched at his beard. "Do you know, I have no idea what you'll be defending them from?"

"Don't be an ass, Knoxol." Creel glared over at his companion. "It's far too long a trip locked in this box for you to start up already."

"I was just asking questions."

"You know exactly what you were doing."

Knoxol opened his mouth to reply, but appeared to think better of it. "Captain. We'll talk again later." He waddled to the front of the wagon. Creel took his place as Greenleaf watched him settle in next to one of the other Chorale members.

"Apologies, Captain. My colleague is a gifted resonant and scholar, but his real talents lie in being a smug bastard."

"I'd imagine a commissar might have a word or two to say about his attitude," Greenleaf said. Before Creel could reply, he asked, "How long will we be in here?"

"Four days to the oasis," Creel said. "Two more after that to reach Lahar."

"I don't suppose there's a chance of getting a bit more air in here. It's already a bit stuffy."

"The bakeries aren't the most pleasant method of travel, I'm afraid," the resonant said. "By this point, we'll have almost certainly crossed the bridge. We're in Suviev, and…"

"I know. I was briefed." He gestured at his cloak. "I came dressed for the cold."

Knoxol snorted, and Creel shot him a look before responding. "With respect, captain, you're dressed for a Kaani winter. Without a frostsuit, you wouldn't last five minutes on the ice."

The next four days were some of the longest of Greenleaf's young life. There were several small cots built into the side of the bakery that the occupants took turns using, but between fitful sleep, there was little to pass the time. The resonants read books and shared quiet conversations that the kaviak couldn't follow. One of the few distractions he had was watching one of the novices practice her craft under Knoxol's judgmental eye. A large cluster of cloudy quartz crystal stretched like taffy in her fingertips as she created impossible sculptures. He'd never seen a Chorale shifter work up close before, but even the novelty of that sight faded quickly.

He hadn't brought a quill with him, but one of the resonants had loaned him a steel nib and a pot of ink, as well as a dozen sheets of paper. Greenleaf hadn't thought that he'd need that many, but after he crumpled up the third attempt at a letter to his father, tossing it on the glimmering coals in the stove, he was grateful for the excess. He winced as a bump in the road sent a scrawl of ink across the page, but he kept writing, hoping his father would forgive the jagged penmanship.

I don't know if it's a coincidence, me being in this stovewagon. The sergeant seemed to have made the decision before I arrived. After meeting Knoxol, I wonder if he's the reason. He's awfully cavalier about the delays in the bridge. I know you always said that Chorale were an odd group, but the entire empire is looking to them to finish the work.

Another bump, another scrawl of jagged ink.

I know you were called away, but I wish I could have seen you before I left. I'm trying to do what you told me. Just one day at a time, one step. But I don't know what I'm taking those steps for. I know she sent me here for a reason. I just need to understand...

The nib jammed straight through the paper as the wheels loudly thumped three times, the bakery rocking as they rolled over the marker bumps. He glanced up at the signal, seeing the others sitting up as the lumbering vehicle slowed.

The wagon jerked heavily as it stopped, but nearly five minutes passed before a loud knocking came at the back door. Creel rose to his feet, drawing a blanket over his shoulders. The other resonants followed suit. He glanced down at Greenleaf. "You should prepare yourself. This can be a bit of a shock."

Greenleaf nodded, and Creel leaned over and repeated the knocks on the inside of the door. Several loud thunks issued forth, and the hinges squealed as the caravan master hauled the door open. Immediately, the wind leapt at the opportunity, carrying a foul stench through the wagon. The icy breeze pulled a gasp of shock from Greenleaf. Outside, he could hear shouting and footsteps crunching on ice. He drew the cloak tight around him as the resonants piled out the back. Greenleaf grabbed his canvas pack and followed, his breath puffing out in clouds before him. His boots crunched into the snow as he leapt down, his hand coming up to block the light reflecting off the ice.

Within moments, his teeth began to chatter as he took in his surroundings. To the south of the wagons was a vast expanse of blinding white snow and ice. A single odd tree stood about half a mile away, gnarled and twisted, a thick trunk with several branches, icicles hanging from every inch, glittering in the sun like crystals. The wind cut through the thick heavy wool of his coat like needles in his skin, and someone tapped his shoulder. Pyle was wrapped in thick layers as he leaned in close to speak to the kaviak.

"Sergeant'll have my ass if I let you get frostbite, sir," the younger man said, his words muffled by the knit scarf wrapped around his mouth and nose. "Follow me, and we'll get you warm."

Falling into step behind the young spearman, Greenleaf fished in his pocket for his scarf, trying to wrap it around his face the way Pyle had. It was a violation of uniform regulations, but his trembling hands and stinging cheeks made a strong argument regarding the unimportance of said regulations in this environment. While the scarf helped a bit against the cold, it did nothing against the smell of rotten eggs that crawled into his nostrils, happily taking up residence in his nose. "Gods, it smells like death."

Pyle nodded. "Not exactly fresh air, sir."

The stench kept intensifying, but the cold began to ease off. Greenleaf could feel the warmth against his forehead and eyes a few minutes before he saw the first patches of sickly green moss. Another of those strange trees stood fifty feet in front of them, below which the sergeant and a corporal with a field anatomist insignia on his sleeve were setting down bags. A stone's throw past them was the rim of the oasis.

From a very, very far distance, someone with terrible vision might think it a small pond, less than thirty feet across. The ice gave way to rock and mud, surrounded by large sections of moss and lichen. The surface was the yellow of old vomit, streaked here and there with ripples of nauseating pinks and greens. It wasn't water, but a thick mud of some sort, bubbles swelling occasionally on the surface to thickly pop. Across the surface of the bubbling sulphur spring, a grid of blackened steel bars was stretched out a foot above the surface, the ends bent at a ninety-degree angle, buried deep in the ground along the shore. The space between the bars was less than a foot, the metal discolored and pitted in several places. The smell coming off it was overpowering, and Greenleaf had to fight the gorge rising in the back of his throat.

"If you don't mind, sir, just step away from the malheur tree if you have to vomit," the corporal said, raising an eyebrow. "Rather not have to deal with both smells for the next few hours."

Greenleaf shook his head. "I think I'll be all right." This close to the oasis, the warmth poured off, and he followed the other soldier's example, taking off his scarf, gloves, and coat. There were weathered wooden posts driven into the ground with hooks on the side upon which he hung his cold weather gear. He stretched, his back and knees popping, and sighed in relief. "It stinks, but a few minutes out of the wagon..."

"Why we stop here, sir," Idar said, nodding. "Three days cramped in there is bad enough. I've done a few runs when this vent is active and we couldn't stop. By the time we got to the valley, I was so stiff I could barely stand up straight."

"What's with the grate?" Greenleaf asked.

The sergeant shrugged. "Been here long before any of us made the run. Supposed to keep anyone dumb enough to get close from falling in. Mud's boiling hot and stinks like rotten eggs, so I'm not really sure who'd do such a thing, but someone must have for them to fence it off like that."

There were old wooden benches built out about twenty feet from where the edge of the grate punched into the frozen ground. Greenleaf sat down heavily on one, setting down his pack. After a few moments, he was able to take a deep breath without the smell threatening to overwhelm him. He glanced up as the corporal approached, clutching his field bag.

"Corporal Sand, sir. Field anatomist. If you don't mind, I'd like to check you over. Make sure the soot in the wagon isn't getting to you," the patcher said, his tone making it clear it wasn't a request.

Greenleaf nodded. The corporal had the captain open his mouth, inspecting his throat with the light from a small chip of cinderstone set into the end of a steel probe. "Been coughing any more than the others? Spittle black yet?"

"No. Is that going to happen?"

"Doubt it," Sand replied. "Happens to us every now and then, but we're in the bakeries a lot more than you'll be. Just making sure, though. Might hear about it if we bring the new kaviak to his posting with blacklung." He glanced up as he began stowing away his equipment. "I've never served with a kaviak. We never needed one here before.

You still don't. Greenleaf stopped the thought from reaching his lips, but the irritation must have shown on his face. Sand didn't seem to know how to respond. Greenleaf didn't look at him, instead studying the empty horizon intently. He pointed at the gnarled tree in the distance. "How can that thing survive? The one closer to the oasis, I get, but..."

"Malheur trees live all over Suviev," Sand replied. "They're pretty spread out, but the cold doesn't bother them. Probably because of their sap." Greenleaf raised a questioning eyebrow, and the anatomist said, "Sorry, sir. Malheur tree sap is hot. Stays hot, too, for months. Keeps the tree warm enough that the cold doesn't freeze the whole thing solid."

"That doesn't make sense," Greenleaf said, frowning. "How does a tree keep its sap hot enough to overcome all of this?"

"Because it's not a tree," Knoxol's booming voice announced. The resonants were milling with the soldiers, but Knoxol had made his way over. Nodding at Sand, he asked, "Corporal, may I have a moment with your new commanding officer?"

Inwardly, Greenleaf wanted nothing less, but he nodded at Sand's questioning glance. Once he was out of earshot, Knoxol said, "I'm claustrophobic."

Confused, Greenleaf rose to his feet. "What?"

"Tight spaces. Hate them. They make me irritable and even more unpleasant than usual, which, to be fair, is saying something. However, it's not a reason to make everyone else miserable. My associates are used to my less appealing traits. You are not, and I apologize. I was unnecessarily antagonistic."

Greenleaf took a deep breath, immediately regretting it as his nose filled with the sulfurous stink. "Why come out here? It seems cruel to send someone who's claustrophobic on a six-day trip sealed in a smoking box."

"I volunteered."

"Why would you do that?"

The resonant shrugged. "I suppose that, despite the trip, I relished the idea of taking on a job that people actually wanted me to do. The work on the bridge... It's difficult to feel like you're doing something noble when half the country is screaming for you to stop. At least no one in Lahar curses my name while I work."

"Ah." Greenleaf kept his face passive. *Guilt?* His mind flashed back to the stone-faced Brehai standing behind the Empress. *Would you have been next to them, Knoxol?* "Well. No need for apologies. I haven't been at my best either."

"Yes. Well." Knoxol cleared his throat. "I will do my best to keep my more difficult traits to a minimum on the rest of the trip. Fair?"

"Fair." The resonant turned to walk away, but paused when Greenleaf spoke. "Knoxol?"

"Mmm?"

Greenleaf spoke quietly. He didn't want his voice to carry. "Lahar. Is it... Do you like it there?"

Knoxol considered him sympathetically for a moment. "It's not a place I'd choose to stay. The Laharians have made a home there, but..." He shrugged. "They built a town on shores of fire to hold the ice at bay. It's never been an easy place."

"That's what I thought."

"How long is your tour?"

"Ten years." The words sounded like a judgement.

"Ah." Knoxol ran fingers over his bald head. "Well." He searched for something positive to say. Greenleaf could see the exact moment in his eyes when he gave it up as a hopeless task. "I'll try not to be an ass on the rest of the trip."

CHAPTER 2

When the three melodic bells chimed outside the heavy oak walls of the bakery, the Chorale resonants with which Greenleaf shared the smoky interior all sighed in relief. Greenleaf glanced over at Sergeant Idar, who had joined him in the second bakery after they departed the oasis. "That mean we've arrived?"

"Ten minutes out," she said, pulling a heavy coat from beneath the bench. "There's a panel set in the road. The bells sound when the first wagon rolls over it. Lets the Laharians know to be ready to unload. We'll want the entire shipment unloaded in a few hours. Gives us enough time to load the shards and weapons for the trip back."

"How long before you head back out?"

"First thing in the morning," Idar said. "We have to maintain a guard on the wagons from the moment the shards are loaded. Sooner we can offload it in Darun, sooner we can take a few days off."

Greenleaf quickly stripped off his soot-covered uniform, pulling a fresh change from his bag. Holding up his heavy coat, he frowned at the black streaks. "I should have brought another coat."

"We can bring one on the next trip out," Idar said. "We'll be back in two weeks."

Nodding, Greenleaf did his best to brush most of the soot from the wool fabric. His uniform sleeves ended just below his forearms, leaving them bare with the exception of the aquasteel bracer. Both his breeches and tunic were as white as the ice outside, blood red piping running along the seams. His captain's chevrons were embroidered in gold over his breastbone. The cotton was thin, designed to breathe and not to hinder movement. When the door was hauled open, he instantly realized how insufficient his uniform was going to be for this assignment.

He could hear a low rumbling in the distance, punctuated by dull cracks. Pulling the heavy coat over his shoulders, he leapt down from the bakery, his heavy boots clicking on stone instead of ice. Straightening up, Greenleaf slowly looked around.

Behind them, the canyon walls rose sharply on either side of the road, which had been cut down through the high cliffs surrounding the village. Lahar looked as if a massive hand had scooped a divot out of the barren arctic landscape, leaving a fiery bloody wound in its wake. Greenleaf's eyes followed the towering cliffs looming over the town to the northern point. "Gods," he whispered.

Cascades of molten rock poured from massive cracks in the grey stone walls to the north of town. He'd heard descriptions of the firefalls of Lahar when he was a child, but nothing could prepare him for the sight of thick columns of lava tumbling hundreds of feet down to crash into a lake of fire far below.

The surface of the lake spit and belched, small bubbles of glowing magma growing to the size of boulders before bursting in a fountain of boiling stone. The southern end of the lake narrowed, extending a glowing finger that wound through the valley. Nearly twenty feet across, the lava snaked between dozens of boxy buildings, the surface the color of lingering coals, dotted with spots of black drifting lazily along, tiny spurts of flame licking towards the grey sky from various points. Tributaries of orange and red split off from the main stream of the Serao, reaching between buildings, small tendrils of lava disappearing beneath the smallest of the grey structures. The fiery glow of the river bathed everything in a dull orange light.

Snow was falling from the sky, but other than the roofs of the taller buildings, the flakes were short lived. They burst into tiny puffs of steam on the surface of the river, and melted into the ground everywhere else. Bursts of green and blue exploded over the ground, thick moss carpeting the spaces between the stone paths that wove between the various buildings. Small orange flowers dotted the expanse, and several dozen malheur trees were scattered throughout Lahar. To the south, a huge pillar of steam climbed into the sky, disappearing into a pale grey cloud looming high overhead. He pointed. "Is that where it reaches the ocean?"

Pyle came up beside him. "Yes, sir. Huge delta of black glass and volcanic rock. Hard to see from here, too much steam."

Greenleaf began to respond, but approaching footsteps drew his attention. He turned to see a cluster of people walking up the stone road from the village towards the halted bakeries. The Laharians wore heavy ponchos made from caribou pelts draped over their shoulders, dark breeches, and boots covered in thick fur. The ponchos had hoods rimmed with grey and white fur, but most had them pushed back. As they passed, most gave Greenleaf a quick inspection, their faces blank.

A pair peeled off from the group heading to the convoy, and approached Greenleaf. The taller one came to a halt, offering his hand. "Captain Greenleaf. I'm Dhrez Edeline, village counselor. We welcome the Eyes of the Empress, and stand ready to serve."

Greenleaf looked over Edeline as he clasped his hand. The man was tall, nearly three inches taller than Greenleaf, but rail thin, his poncho hanging loose over his shoulder. An obsidian disc hung from a leather cord around his neck, and his face was mottled with small pox scars. He wore brass-rimmed spectacles, and had a knife sheathed at his waist. "I offer the protection of the Empress as thanks for your dedication and service, and stand as kaviak and guard to the people of Lahar," Greenleaf recited.

Edeline nodded. "I hope I said it right, Captain," he said, offering a slight smile. "We haven't had to greet a kaviak since my father was a child."

Gods. This really is nowhere.

Outwardly, Greenleaf returned the smile. "Quite right, Counselor."

"I should hope so," the second man said in a deep voice, a broad grin on his face. He thrust out a pudgy hand covered in rings, brass and quartz bracelets clinking softly around his wrist. "I've drilled it on him nightly since we learned of your posting here."

"This is Ayal Proudlake, Imperial liaison and commissar for Lahar Valley," Edeline said, stepping to the side. Greenleaf shook Proudlake's hand. Where the native Laharian's grip had been rough and strong, Proudlake's palms were damp, his skin sticky with some kind of cream. Greenleaf had to refrain from wiping his hands after releasing.

"The Voice to your Eyes, my boy," Proudlake said. Instead of the hide breeches and poncho of the others, Proudlake wore a padded silk doublet of rich blue, gold thread embroidering swirling patterns. The eight white stripes around his sleeve each marked four years of service. A silver chain hung around his neck, disappearing under the velvet collar. He had a full head of greying hair, shaved close to the sides but long on top in the Kaani style, and his blue eyes sparkled as he clasped his hands over his prodigious belly. "I can't tell you how delighted I am to have you here. I have a thousand questions about the capital, the country, all the things I miss here in Lahar."

"Of course…" The "sir" had nearly left Greenleaf's mouth when his eyes caught the rank signet dangling from the commissar's nose, and the words died in his throat. He kept his face even, although his right eyebrow lifted enough that Proudlake noticed.

"Only the third echelon, I'm afraid," the political officer said, his smile unwavering. "Not much opportunity for advancement in such a small community. I suppose that technically, that would make you and I the same rank, correct?"

"Ah, yes. Yes, I believe so." Greenleaf could not remember ever meeting someone with so many years of service with such a low rank. Normally, retirement would be far preferable. He wasn't quite sure what to say, but thankfully, Edeline broke the silence.

"I know how grueling the trip out here can be, captain, but if you're feeling up to it, I'd be honored to take you on a trip through town."

"Thank you," Greenleaf said. "I'll take you up on that, but it's protocol to debrief with the local commissar upon arrival at a new posting."

Proudlake didn't even twitch an eyebrow. "Don't worry, Dhrez. I'll see him brought to you as soon as we're done."

Edeline glanced between the two of them, frowning briefly, but nodded. "Well. I look forward to it, Captain."

"Counselor."

Edeline turned and headed to the wagons, where Laharians were helping soldiers offload heavy crates. As soon as he was out of earshot, Proudlake leaned in close. "I wasn't aware of that protocol."

"We need to talk."

Proudlake's head bobbed up and down. "Yes, Captain, I believe we do."

***

Proudlake made idle conversation as they made their way down into the village. The path was made of slabs of grey stone, the same type of stone that Greenleaf had run on as a boy outside his family's small home in the Canal district of Kaani, the Imperial capital. Most of the buildings were an odd, blocky structure, each nearly twenty feet tall, but at the center of town, straddling the fiery river, was a broad hexagonal building. The light from the lava glinted off flecks of quartz in the huge blocks of granite that made up the walls.

"Welcome to the Castle, Captain," Proudlake said as they headed towards heavy oak doors set in the side.

Greenleaf looked up at the domed roof with a large shifted quartz skylight. "That looks like granite from the northern peaks. Must have taken forever to haul all those blocks out here."

"Long before my time, but I'm led to understand that it was quite the endeavor," the commissar said. "Nothing to be done about it, though. They needed material that could withstand the heat of the Serao."

Glancing over at one of the smaller buildings, Greenleaf asked, "They're all granite?"

"No, they're ice mixed with sawdust." At Greenleaf's quizzical expression, Proudlake shrugged. "I don't know the reasoning, I just know it works. I'm sure Edeline would be happy to tell you more."

As he opened the door for Greenleaf, warm air flowed out, providing a sharp contrast. Stepping through, Greenleaf let out a low whistle. The interior of the Castle was open, paved with blue slate tiles. Through the center, the dull orange glow of the river cast light over everything, heat pouring off the surface. Proudlake led him to a set of stairs leading up to the second floor, a broad balcony with rooms on either side of the river. A bridge connected the east and west sides.

"This building serves as a town square, trading post, seat of government, essentially everything central to Lahar," Proudlake said as he laboriously made his way up the stairs. "Other than the mine and forge, of course. The handful of children in town come here five hours a day for lessons."

"They have a teacher here?"

"Nothing so formal. I teach civics and history. Members of the town teach other essentials." Reaching the top of the stairs, Proudlake walked to the end of the balcony to a pair of doors. "My quarters and office. You have quarters on the other side of the river. An office, too, although I told them that wasn't necessary." He shrugged as he opened the door. "I suppose you could use it for storage."

"Quarters will be fine," Greenleaf said. The office was small. A battered desk sat in the center, topped with paper and an inkwell, as well as a bottle and several glasses. On the wall, Proudlake's Imperial assignation was framed in oak.

The door clicked shut. When Proudlake spoke, his voice had lost some of the warmth from before. "I appreciate the need for security, Captain. But it's traditional to send the local commissar the assignment brief prior to the arrival of any Imperial military forces." He made his way around the desk, settling into his chair. He was trying to keep the irritation from his expression, but wasn't very successful. "There have been six convoys since we were first notified of your posting here. Any one of them could have brought the brief and given me time to better prepare."

Confused, Greenleaf asked, "I'm sorry?"

"An apology isn't necessary, it's just…" Proudlake picked up a cloth from the desk and dabbed the sweat from his brow. "Never mind. Nothing for it. May I at least review it now? It may take me a few days to determine how best to assist…" His voice trailed off as Greenleaf raised a hand.

"Commissar, I don't have an assignment brief for you. I assumed it would have been sent out before I arrived."

"What?" Proudlake shook his head. "If Sergeant Idar had been given a message for me, she would have told me. I thought that meant you were going to bring it in person." Leaning forward, he said, "Captain, with all due respect, what the hell are you doing here?"

Greenleaf stared at him for nearly ten seconds. "I thought… Commissar, I was told I would be briefed on my arrival. As far as I can tell, you're the only one here to brief me."

Proudlake's brow furrowed, and he slowly shook his head. "Sit down, Captain. Please." He uncorked the wooden bottle, filling each glass a quarter full with a rosy liquid. A tart, fragrant scent filled the air. "Have you had cloudberry brandy before?"

"I'm not supposed to drink on duty."

Chuckling dryly, Proudlake gestured to the empty room. The walls were bare, except for a map of the region and Proudlake's framed Imperial assignation. "Well, there isn't exactly anyone to report you to." He slid the glass over, but Greenleaf shook his head. Proudlake sighed. "Sit down, please." Once Greenleaf had settled into the hard wooden chair, Proudlake said, "Captain, I apologize if I was brusque. When I got the message that you were being detached to Lahar, I didn't understand why, but I assumed you had a specific assignment."

"If I do, they forgot to tell me," Greenleaf said. "I haven't been detached to Lahar. I've been posted here."

Proudlake's eyes widened. "You're joking."

Greenleaf shook his head. "Imperial arrogation. Direct from the Empress. She issued it three months before our class graduated. Imperial command informed us that whoever finished at the top of the class would get the honor of the assignment." Despite his best efforts, the bitterness was clear in his tone.

"But they had to tell you why, give you some details about what you were supposed to do here."

"I thought that you would be briefing me about what was happening in Lahar that required a kaviak."

"Captain, I give you my word. I have no idea. I didn't request so much as a two-man guard force. If they'd asked if I thought we needed it, I would have said no." Proudlake set down his glass.

Greenleaf leaned forward. "The Empress had to have her reasons. With the graduation of my class, there are 211 kaviaks in the entire empire. She wouldn't send me here unless there was something."

Proudlake sat back, scratching at his nose. "Captain, I've been here for twenty years. I know my role. I am the voice and ears of the Empress. It's my task to ensure that her will is followed, that the people think and act in accordance with her wishes. It's an important job, even here. This village is small and remote, but it's the only place that has ever produced aquasteel. Without that steel, the Imperial Army wouldn't be a shadow of what it is," he said. "But my job is easy. The Laharians do their duty to the Empire. Aquasteel production has been reliable and steady since long before I showed up. Every convoy carries at least two shards back to the capital for shaping." He tilted his head. "You have to have a few theories about why you're here."

Greenleaf gave a slight shrug. "I know about the aquasteel. I thought there might be an issue with the production, or maybe the forge. I thought maybe Brehai sympathizers were causing issues."

"The Brehai?" Proudlake shook his head. "It's hard to influence people you never meet. No one from Lahar has traveled to the mainland in..." He thought for a moment. "Five years, I think. A woman became ill, past what we could manage. We sent her back with a convoy to see if Imperial anatomists could help."

"Could she have brought back Brehai materials?"

"She didn't make it. They did everything they could, but sent her body back her for funeral rites," he said. "We get the occasional merchant that rides in on the convoy, but they're never here long. The only people who come here on a semi-regular basis are the soldiers who escort the convoys, and the Chorale masons who work on the farms. Neither seem likely as Brehai."

"You sure about that?" Greenleaf asked. "We don't know that there aren't members of the Chorale opposed to building the bridge. They began construction five years ago, claimed that it would take six months. They're less than a quarter of the way across the chasm."

"The Breaking is six miles wide," Proudlake pointed out. "I can't imagine that summoning a bridge two miles wide of whitestone is a simple task. Have they given a reason for the delay?"

"Of course. They say that the storms in the Breaking interfere with their abilities, slowing the process down."

"It could be true."

"Could be," Greenleaf admitted. "But it could also be that members of the Chorale are sympathetic to the Brehai. Maybe even prefects."

Proudlake looked dubious. "I find it hard to believe that the anti-bridge movement has that much influence."

"It's getting more and more popular. There were protestors at the graduation ceremony. They were escorted out."

"Not arrested?"

Greenleaf shook his head. "Imperial command was worried that could touch off riots."

"Gods." Proudlake shook his head. "Protests, riots? I knew the Brehai Movement was growing in strength, but open protests?"

"Their mark is everywhere. Painted on buildings, tree trunks. Some shops and homes have the broken bridge painted on their walls intentionally. They pay the fine, but refuse to remove it." Greenleaf stood, stretching his legs. "Sorry. Still stiff from the trip down here."

"The last convoy. One of the merchants said something about one of the primarchs coming out publicly against the bridge," the political officer said. "Is that true?"

Greenleaf nodded. "Three in total. They've made official requests to stop construction immediately, that the funds and efforts of the Chorale be redirected to other programs. Rumors say at least four others are debating coming out publicly against it as well."

"That would be over half the Convocation." Proudlake ran his fingers over his bald head. "I had no idea it had gotten so bad."

"Two of the Governesses have implored the Empress to reconsider the construction," Greenleaf said. "They posted the request in Kaani Square. The other two haven't joined in, but they're no longer vocally supporting the bridge. From what I've heard, it's even worse outside the capital. Especially east of the Greymare Peaks."

Proudlake snorted. "That's less surprising than anything else you've said. The clans took longer than anyone else to yield, and they've never been the most enthusiastic of the Empress's subjects."

Greenleaf said, "We're not just talking protests. Our last year, we focused our training on mountain fighting. Studied maps of Bolsk and Skroma, heard lectures from veterans of the fighting out there. Command seemed pretty gods-damned sure that we'd be seeing action back out there sooner or later."

Proudlake sat back heavily in his chair, at a loss for words. Greenleaf wasn't surprised. In the twenty-eight years since the Empire had completed its conquest of the northern half of the continent, there had been no fighting, no rebellions. Even the Hoberian clans that had fought for eight decades had begrudgingly accepted the Imperial assistance in rebuilding cities and homes wrecked by nearly a century of constant warfare. That had always been the Alddarri Empire's tactic: ruthless in conquest, generous in peace. It was effective. At least it had been.

"Is there any sign that the Empress is reconsidering the bridge?" Proudlake asked. "Considering the public's response?"

Greenleaf shook his head. "Her word is final. She's commanded the Chorale to bridge the Breaking, and they claim to be committed to that goal. Imperial command has been increasing the garrisons in towns that have a heavy Brehai presence. They're worried that as the bridge gets closer to the south, the Brehai may decide that protests aren't enough." He drummed his fingers against the rough wood. "That's the only reason I could think of that I'd be sent here."

"Don't get me wrong," Proudlake said. "Laharians are reluctant Imperials. They do their duty, send the shipments, but this is a very insular community. Twenty years, and they're only now beginning to look at me like I'm not an invader. You won't see any yellow pennants on Unification Day, and there are definitely a few that don't think of themselves as anything more than Laharians. But if there's anything more organized, more recent, I haven't seen it."

"Then why?" Greenleaf said, his frustration clear. "Most kaviaks are responsible for entire cities, trading routes. Assigning one to a village this small? Even with the aquasteel, there has to be a reason."

"If things are as bad as you say..." Proudlake took another sip as he considered. "The way I see it, the Empress has two choices.

She can acquiesce to the wishes of the Brehai Movement and those who sympathize with them, abandon the construction of the bridge." He shook his head. "Obviously impossible. The moment she allows someone else to dictate the future of this nation is the moment that the Imperial family loses control. Unless you think I'm wrong?"

Greenleaf shook his head.

"The other option, the only option, is that she makes sure that she has complete and absolute control over the most important parts of the Empire. Specifically, the military. That means the cavalry, the infantry, the Chorale, and all of the infrastructure that supports them. Including Lahar's forge and the aquasteel production," Proudlake said. "For a long time, the Empire has had a voice in Lahar. With you here, that voice has some steel behind it. I suppose it could help prevent any issues in the future."

Considering this, Greenleaf shook his head. "You might be right. They might have decided a military presence was a good idea. But a kaviak? Why not send a five-guard garrison? Hell, two would probably be enough for a town this size."

"I don't know. But if she issued the arrogation personally, the Empress must have felt this was crucial," Proudlake replied. "It might not have been your first choice on posting, but you're a captain while the rest of your classmates are lieutenants. From everything I've heard, the competition in the months leading to Elevation is fierce."

Greenleaf didn't trust himself to respond. After a few awkward moments, Proudlake cleared his throat.

"Captain, I feel confident that this is not where you pictured your career as a kaviak beginning," the commissar said. "But you're here. I know I may have been less than welcoming when we sat down, but I really am quite pleased to have you here. As duty postings go, Lahar may not be the most comfortable, but if it's important enough that the Empress sent you here…" He shrugged. "You'll find a way to distinguish yourself here, I'm certain."

"Really?" Despite his efforts, the bitterness slipped through. "I don't even know why I'm here. If it's because of the Brehai, why not tell me?"

"You had to imagine there was a chance you wouldn't get the duty station you wanted," Proudlake said, not unkindly. "We serve the Empress. It's not our place to question her will."

"I know. I just…" Greenleaf leaned forward, picking up the glass. "I worked hard, Commissar. My whole life. My father, he earned a field commission, but he knew that I could go so much further if I could become a kaviak. He started preparing me when I was ten."

Proudlake raised an eyebrow. "That's a lot to put on a child."

"It wasn't, though," Greenleaf said. "My father served during Unification. So did his sister, and my grandfather. They believed in the Empire, and so do I. I didn't work that hard because it was expected of me. I didn't do it for glory or for decoration." He watched the liquid reflect the light in the oil lamps. "I did it to serve."

"You can serve here."

Greenleaf shook his head slowly. "You said the competition is fierce leading to Elevation. You're right. It was. Just not how you think." His fingers tightened around the glass. "There were four of us in contention for the top spot. Less than a few points separated us. When the arrogation was announced, we met in private. Each of us promised to do our best, to keep pushing just as hard as we had for the past four years."

"But they didn't," Proudlake said quietly.

"No. They made mistakes, little ones, on evaluations, inspections. Nothing big, but each was a point deduction. They added up."

"Did you know?" Proudlake asked. "What they were doing?"

Greenleaf shook his head. "The evaluations are done in isolation. I didn't know until the morning of Elevation, when the rankings were posted. By that time, the only thing left was the combat test."

"In front of half the capital," Proudlake said. "It says a great deal about you that you didn't follow their path. That you kept your word."

Greenleaf felt the lump of guilt that had taken up residence in his gut since he'd seen his father's face in the arena.

Slipped.

He finally took a drink. "It's good." Looking up from the glass, Greenleaf said, "All I've ever wanted was to stand and serve the Empire. I never wanted a royal guard position or an instructor job. I wanted to fight in the cavalry, to stand with everyone else risking their lives for the Empress. I did my duty. I did what I was meant to do. And I end up here." Shaking his head, Greenleaf said, "There's a reason the Empress sent me here. There has to be. Something rotten in this place, something that needed the attention of a kaviak."

Proudlake nodded slowly. "I think you're right. I may not know what, but if Imperial command got wind of a serious threat, something worthy of coming to the Empress? That might justify sending you here." Raising an eyebrow, he leaned forward. "And if you find that threat, and deal with it..."

"There won't be a reason to keep me here." Greenleaf rose to his feet. "I believe I'm going to find Counselor Edeline, take him up on that tour."

The commissar nodded. "I'll start asking some questions. Quietly. We're going to figure this out, captain." He offered his hand, and Greenleaf took it, grateful, feeling a bit less alone than he had when he'd walked through the door.

CHAPTER 3

It didn't take long to find the Laharian counselor. Edeline was downstairs, speaking with a burly man in hushed tones. They fell silent as Greenleaf descended the stairs, and the large man muttered, "Forget it. Just forget it." He looked up at Greenleaf, and his jaw worked briefly as he spun on his heel and stomped out into the cold.

"Problem, Counselor?"

Edeline massaged his temple for a moment. "Nothing in particular." He turned to face Greenleaf, offering a wan smile. "Part of the job. Someone's always annoyed about something. I trust you and the commissar had a productive meeting?"

Greenleaf's eyebrow twitched at the clear change of topic, but he let it pass. "We did. I thought I would take you up on that tour."

"Of course, Captain," Edeline said.

They stepped outside the door, and Edeline led the way down the stone slabs streaked with lichen that wound their way between buildings. Pillowy clusters of moss carpeted the ground between buildings. As they approached the first blocky structure, Greenleaf could feel the temperature rising. "Is that heat from the Serao?"

"Yes and no." Edeline pointed towards the building. "Each of our homes is built over a tributary off of the main river which ends inside the building. Provides heat and a source for cooking. We don't need to ship in coal or firewood."

Greenleaf nodded. "How many people live in town?"

"Two hundred eighty-four," Edeline said. "We have two women expecting, though, so that number will go up during the long night."

The door cracked open, and a middle-aged woman peered out. "Dhrez, has the convoy come in? Until we get the wool, we can't make any progress on..." She fell silent when her eyes found Greenleaf. "Oh." A young girl poked her head around her mother's legs, eyes wide, staring at Greenleaf. The woman pushed her back. "I'll find you later. When you're not busy." The door closed before either man could speak.

Edeline glanced over at Greenleaf. "She's not usually..." He cleared his throat. "We don't get many newcomers here. You'll have to excuse everyone if they're a bit cautious around you for a while."

"Any particular reason why? They knew I was coming, right?"

Chuckling, Edeline nodded. "Oh, yes. We held a town meeting a few hours after Ayal and I got the message. About half the town attended. The other half knew before I'd finished talking. Gossip travels quickly."

Greenleaf gestured at the house. "From what I could see, you don't have that many homes. How many people live in each one?"

"Two, three families, usually." Edeline watched as Greenleaf scanned what buildings he could see, counting silently to himself. "Where are you from, Captain?"

"Kaani." Greenleaf gestured to a much larger building with a pair of blackened oak doors, like that of a barn. "Is that the forge?"

Edeline shook his head, pointing north to the firefalls. "The forge is built closer to the lake. But we built the mine further downriver. Gives us more opportunity to spot the streaks as they come in."

"The streaks?"

"The raw aquasteel still in the river."

"Show me," Greenleaf said. "Please."

Edeline nodded, and led the way to the huge doors. The slabs of thick oak sat atop iron rails built into the hard ground. Edeline grabbed a heavy iron handle, and rolled the door open with surprising ease. Instantly, the heat struck Greenleaf with an almost physical force, sweltering air pouring out as if off of a glowing forge. He stepped through, sweat already beading on his forehead.

The rumbling of the river was louder than ever here, dull cracks echoing through the inside of the cavernous building, the walls and ceiling awash in the dull orange light pouring from the river. The Serao drifted slowly through the center of the room. This was no tributary. The bubbling and languid lava spanned twenty feet wide, the air above shimmering and distorted. As they walked into the mine, they passed six slabs of black glass, each nearly ten feet square, sitting atop dirty blocks of stone.

Stretching over the lava river was a bridge hanging from thick chains stretching to the ceiling. The heavy beams of blackened wood that made up the bridge hung fifteen feet over the surface, wrapped in bands of iron. Standing in the middle of the bridge was a man in the strangest outfit Greenleaf had ever seen. He wore a padded wool tunic, draped down to his knees, with a blacksmith's heavy leather apron over the top. His legs were encased in hip-high boots of cracked and dirty leather, the soles made of blackened wood. The gloves he wore reached up to his shoulder, and his face was covered by a woven steel grate affixed to a heavy leather hood.

In his gloved hands, he grasped a cable which looped up to a pulley sliding along rails in the ceiling, stretching the width of the fiery river. He was carefully lowering a strange panel, interwoven bands of blackened steel with inch-wide gaps, down to the surface. As the panel dropped further, an older man standing about twenty feet from the edge of the river bellowed, "To the right! You're gonna clip the edge, Reif!"

The figure nodded, his entire torso moving in lumbering motion, and the pulley squeaked as he dragged the assembly to the right. The older man nodded, waving for him to continue.

"That's Odel Deric, our mine foreman," Edeline said, wiping the sweat from his brow as he pointed at the older man. "He's been running our aquasteel mining operations for sixteen years."

"What are they doing?" Greenleaf asked, taking a step closer. Edeline grabbed him by the arm, and Greenleaf tensed.

"Sorry," Edeline said, pulling his hand back. "It's too hot to get close without protective gear. You could get burned." He pointed to where the Serao entered the building beneath a huge granite archway. On the surface, an oddly colored blob shimmered, rainbow colors coruscating over the length as it drifted closer to the bridge. "They call those streaks. It's raw aquasteel, come to the surface. He's going to... Well, just watch."

The Serao didn't flow quickly. It took nearly three minutes for the blob of aquasteel to travel the distance to the bridge. The miner didn't lower the sieve into the lava immediately. Instead, he halted it five feet above the surface and waited. By the time the streak drew close, the bottom half of the sieve was glowing a dull red. The mine foreman, watching closely, shouted, "Dip!"

The sieve dropped, plunging into the molten rock mere inches in front of the streak of raw metal. The current began to drag the entire assembly downstream, but the cable from which it was suspended struck the edge of the bridge, holding it in place. Greenleaf looked back to Deric, who was counting silently to himself. About thirty seconds later, "Pull!"

Lava cascaded off the sieve as the glowing steel burst up from the Serao. As the molten rock fell away, Greenleaf could see metallic blobs clinging to the grating. Instead of glowing red and white from the heat, the blobs were a dull grey, struck through with blues and greens like the surface of an oil slick. The miner kept hauling the assembly upward, but as he did, he took heavy steps to the edge of the bridge, the pulley rattling along the rails. Two other men waited at the edge of the river in similar heatproof gear, long poles topped with hooks clutched in their gloved hands. They snagged the grating, dragging the sieve over to one of the obsidian slabs as the aquasteel very slowly began to droop like cold molasses.

"Fix it. Reif, take a break!" The miner on the bridge offered a weary wave as the two other miners tied off the grate, which was pinging softly as it started to cool. The foreman turned to his visitors, acknowledging them for the first time. "Second one today, Dhrez. That's six shards this week."

"Odel Deric, this is Captain Tomas Greenleaf, our new kaviak." Deric tromped forward, boots thudding on the gravel, and clamped Greenleaf's hand into an iron grip. Greenleaf did his best not to wince.

"Good timing. Sometimes, we can stand in here scratching our asses for hours without seeing a streak," the foreman said, his voice thick and raspy. "Would have been slightly less impressive. Hang on a moment."

Cupping his hand around his mouth, Defic bellowed, "EARS! EARS!" Each of the miners clamped their gloved hands over their ears.

Greenleaf looked over to Edeline, who was doing the same. Deric said, "Cover your ears, Captain. This next part gets loud."

Greenleaf just managed to comply when the drooping aquasteel came into contact with the obsidian. The moment it did, the entire mass of the molten metal shivered violently, and issued a piercing squeal, like a tuning fork dragged over cracked glass. It was brief, but Greenleaf waited until the others had lowered their hands. "That was unpleasant."

"Never lasts more than a moment," Deric said. "You get used to it."

"What happens now?" he asked, pointing at the grate. The aquasteel was drooping like taffy, beginning to pool on the black glass surface. "Won't it cool in that position?"

"Raw aquasteel doesn't like to change temperatures," Deric said. "Same thing as refined, although refined doesn't change temperature at all. It'll settle on the slab, and over the next five days, it'll crystallize into a shard. Here." They followed the foreman over to another slab. On the surface sat a dull grey crystal, nearly three feet long and six inches wide. It looked like thousands of individual metal fibers, all bundled together to form the whole. Greenleaf could still feel heat pouring off of it. "This one was dipped four days ago. Still hot enough to cook a steak on."

"You ever tried that?" Greenleaf asked, curious.

"Once. Tasted like shit." Deric nodded to the corner of the room as he tugged off his gloves, to a large vat nearly six feet tall. "Tomorrow night, we'll move this one to a quench, and it'll be ready for shipment."

"Hey, boss!" The three turned to look at the miner, who had descended back down to shore and was taking off his helmet. His sandy blonde hair was matted against his scalp, and sweat shone off his freckle-dusted face. His eyes were a bright blue above a strong jawline. He towered over the other miners, nearly seven feet tall with arms and chest thick with muscle. Nodding up at the hanging grate, he said, "I heard a few cracks. I think this one's kicked it."

Deric cursed, walking over to the grate. He peered up at the cooling metal, and shook his head. "Yeah, I see the fissure. Up near the top. Damn sure there'll be a few more in the grating. Okay. Once it's dropped the aquasteel, pull it and send it back to the forge."

"That happen a lot?" Greenleaf asked.

"We can dip you in the river if you like. Pretty sure you'll develop a crack or three," the miner responded, giving Greenleaf a sideways glance.

"Reif." Deric glared at the younger man before turning back to Greenleaf. "The sieves are steel, but they're usually only good for ten to twenty dips before they start to fracture. If they break in the river, we'll lose both the sieve and the streak. We'll send it back to the forge. They can melt it down, make us a new one. We have a few more in the meantime." He shrugged. "Best steel in the world can't handle the Serao for more than a bit."

"Why not make the grate out of aquasteel?" Greenleaf asked.

"Hey, boss, he fucking solved it!" Reif said, rolling his eyes.

"Your shift's up, Reif. Hang up your gear, go get some food." Reif scowled, but walked away. Glancing back at Greenleaf, Deric said, "He's had a long shift. That much time over the river'll make anyone short-tempered."

"I can imagine." Greenleaf watched the miner as he removed his mining suit and stomped out the door, not looking back. "What's his last name?"

Deric held up his hand. "I promise, he's not..." Greenleaf raised an eyebrow, and Deric sighed. "Zdene. Reif Zdene. He's just hot-tempered. Give him some space, he'll calm down."

Greenleaf nodded slowly. "You were saying? About the grate?"

Running his fingers through his hair, Deric cleared his throat, and said, "We never let raw aquasteel come in contact with refined. Aquasteel is memetic. It's how the resonants in the Chorale can make it remember the forms. Unfortunately, that same property means that if raw aquasteel was to touch a refined weapon or piece of armor, it would instantly crystallize, take on the same properties." He tilted his head. "I hear that kaviaks are all issued aquasteel weapons when they finish the Elevation. That true?"

Is there a reason you're trying to get a look at my weapon?

Greenleaf considered the older man briefly, but finally raised his right hand out in front of his body. A dull metal bracer was wrapped tightly around his forearm, extending from his wrist to just beneath the elbow, inscribed with his graduation date and the sigil of the Imperial kaviaks. In a smooth motion, Greenleaf's thumb danced over his fingertips, pinky to index.

The metal surface of the bracer briefly shivered, like the surface of a calm lake under a quiet breeze. In the span of a heartbeat, the metal burst into liquid, pouring forth into Greenleaf's hand as if filling an invisible mold. It flowed above and below his closed fist, forming a shaft extending two feet below his hand and four feet above. A leaf-shaped blade, nearly ten inches long, shaped from the flowing steel glinted, and within a second, the metal shivered once more and solidified.

Edeline's eyes widened, and he took a step back while the other miners stared from over by the slab. Greenleaf spun the spear around, offering the haft to the foreman, who gently took it and examined it with a practiced eye.

"Not bad," he said, nodding. He tilted it, and as the light from the Serao danced up the hilt, a rainbow of color shimmered along the length of the spear. "I've seen a few traditionally forged pieces, the kind they issue regular army. But these resonant-shifted weapons are so much better. Plus, the memetic properties are flashy." He reached back to the table, picking up a scrap of boiled cowhide. Bringing it to the edge of the blade, the steel whispered through the thick leather with no resistance. Deric's eyes widened. "Damn."

"How do you sharpen it?" Edeline asked hesitantly.

"You don't." Greenleaf extended his hand, and Deric handed back the spear. His fingers tapped out a quick pattern on the hilt, and the weapon collapsed back into liquid motion, pouring back down his arm until the bracer settled back into place. "Aquasteel weapons don't lose their edge."

"So long as you don't touch it to the raw stuff," Deric said. He pointed at the thick liquid aquasteel. "If you touched your spearpoint to that, it'd instantly bond and harden. You'd have a blob of aquasteel permanently affixed, we'd be out one shard, and not a damn thing could be done to get rid of it."

Greenleaf nodded. "Never came up in training."

Deric shrugged. "Until you, no one with an aquasteel weapon came within a hundred miles of Lahar. Not since I've been alive, anyway. They probably figured there was no need."

Glancing around, Greenleaf asked, "You keep records? Of the shards?"

"We do." Deric walked over to a bookcase set against a far wall. Wood-bound tomes filled the shelves. Pulling the left-most book from the top shelf, the foreman flipped to a marked page, tracing his fingers down the writing. "Here, you can see. The time we pull the shard, time we do the quench, weight, dimensions, and time and date of loadout."

Greenleaf scanned the rows of neat, black writing. "How far back do your records go?"

"Over a century," Deric said. "We actually make two copies, one for us, and one for the commissar. His are in his office, I think. But we only started doing that when he got here, so his records only go back twenty years."

Nodding, Greenleaf handed the book back to Deric. "Could you please arrange to have the last ten years of records sent to my quarters?"

Deric paused as he slid the book back into place. "Ah, we never take them out of here. It's kind of a rule."

"Whose?"

Deric glanced helplessly at Edeline, who pressed his lips together. "Mine. Those records are very important. The mine is the only building in town that's never unoccupied. Safest place for them."

Greenleaf nodded. "It's a smart precaution. But I need to review these records, and I need a private place to do so."

"Why do you need to..." Deric trailed off as Edeline raise his hand, and frowned as the counselor spoke.

"Of course, Captain. I'll have them in your quarters by tonight."

Edeline was reserved, saying little as they walked away from the mine towards a cluster of homes like the one they'd passed earlier. His body language spoke volumes, though. Greenleaf could see how rigid he carried himself, like a soldier on the parade field under watchful eyes.

"You seem distressed, Counselor."

"Do I." It was not a question. Edeline came to a halt, his breath puffing in the frigid air. Greenleaf came to face him, trying not to shiver. As long as they'd been moving, the cold had been bearable, but he could feel goosebumps raising over his forearms.

The older man weighed his words carefully, as if examining each possible sentence before setting it aside. Finally, he said, "I don't know if there's much point in me asking why you want to see the records.

I'm under no illusion that I have any authority over you, Captain, and as kaviak, you are of course entitled to examine anything in town that you wish." He gestured at one of the mottled houses. The wall facing them was lit up a dull orange from the thin finger of lava creeping beneath. "If you wanted to conduct a home by home search, I don't have the authority to do anything more than file a complaint with the commissar."

"I'm not going to do that," Greenleaf said, rubbing his arms. "Not unless it's necessary."

"And I have no input as to the decision of whether or not it is," Edeline said. His voice was even, but his eyes narrowed. "All I can do is deal with the consequences." Before Greenleaf could speak, he held up a hand. "That's not a threat, Captain, I promise. It's just reality. This community isn't used to outsiders. We don't have a garrison, or Ministry halls. The commissar has, for decades, been the only permanent addition to Lahar that didn't leave a few days after his arrival, and for the most part, he keeps to himself. You, however..." He shook his head. "You're an unknown quantity."

"And that worries you?"

Edeline nodded. "It does. This is a hard place, Captain. It's my home. But if you walk half a mile in either direction without a frostsuit, you'll be dead in an hour. I was born there," he pointed at a building not far away, "and I was raised understanding the work that has to be done for us to simply survive. Every part of this community has been carefully thought through. Everyone has a role. Everything has a purpose, and without exception, that purpose is to keep Lahar alive. It's a very delicate balancing act, and it's my sole purpose to keep this place and the people in it safe and thriving. Unknown quantities are not just concerning. They're potentially existential."

Greenleaf couldn't help the chuckle that slipped free. "Apologies, Counselor. I have no doubt you're sincere, but I'm not here to raze Lahar to the ground."

"Then why?" Edeline asked. "Why? I'm not a particularly wise man, Captain, but I don't think of myself as a fool. I have wracked my brain to try to understand the logic behind assigning a kaviak here."

"Kaviaks are tasked with protecting the people of the Empire…"

"Protect us from what?" Edeline asked, exasperated. "All due respect, Captain, but we haven't had a kaviak stationed here for over a hundred years. There are fewer than three hundred souls living in Lahar. We don't have bandits. No one's crossing the ice to try to rob us. Even if they did, where would they go? There's no front any longer. The war ended over twenty years ago, and even if it didn't, we're thousands of miles from any fighting. Any internal disputes or crimes, we deal with locally, with Ayal's guidance."

He began ticking things off on his fingers. "We haven't slowed down in our shipments. We haven't requested any protection or manpower. The last raid or attempted theft of an aquasteel shipment happened when my father was a boy. We transport the shards back in a bakery that you couldn't open with a battering ram without the key, with a half dozen Imperial soldiers escorting it. It would be unusual if they stationed a small garrison of regular soldiers here, but one of the precious kaviaks? How many kaviaks are currently commissioned in the whole of the Empire? A hundred? Maybe two?" He folded his arms. "There is no sense that I can see in you being stationed here on guard duty, which tells me that you're looking for something."

Came to that realization fairly quickly, didn't you? "And what do you think that is?"

"I give you my word, Captain, I have no idea."

Couldn't make it easy, could you.

Greenleaf cupped his hands around his mouth, puffing into them to try to warm his frigid fingers. "Counselor, if there's a reason that you don't want me looking through the mine's records, it's best for you to talk to me."

Edeline took a breath. "No, there isn't a reason. I just... Please be careful with those records, Captain. We take great care to protect them. They are essential to the people of Lahar."

"So I'm not going to find any discrepancies?"

"Gods." Edeline rubbed his nose. "No, Captain. The mine foreman logs every shard that comes from the river. Our blacksmith logs every arrowhead, spearhead, everything that comes out of the forge. Once a week, I sit down with them and review every line. Once I'm satisfied, I sit down with the commissar, who does an independent inspection of our logs. He signs off on every shipment. And once a year, an auditor with the Ministry of Allocation travels out and goes over every single letter and number with a magnifying glass."

"Then there shouldn't be an issue with me... wait." Greenleaf frowned. "Allocation audits are done every five years."

"Unless a higher frequency is requested."

"Who requested that?"

"I did!" Edeline snapped, his temper finally breaking through. "Captain, please, you have to understand. I don't obsess over every line of those records because I fear the Empire, I do it because we need those records to be perfect. I'm not worried you're going to find an error. There are no errors, no discrepancies. I'm worried that you're going to misplace or damage the records." He took a breath. "I'm not explaining myself well. May I show you something, something that might help you understand?"

Greenleaf nodded, grateful to be moving. The temperature rose steadily as they approached a long building straddling a thick branch of the Serao. A heavy wooden door was set into the side. Edeline grasped the iron handle, and went inside.

Greenleaf followed him through, and came to an immediate halt, his eyes widening.

"Gods," he breathed, his head tracking around slowly, trying to take it all in.

The stream of lava flowed through the center of the building, thick as a log. Large cisterns of water sat next to the edge, drops from wooden taps bursting into steam even before they struck the molten rock. The rest of the interior was a riot of life. Strings of pots hung from the ceiling, leaves spilling over the rims. Raised beds filled every available space, each packed with tomato plants, clusters of ice blue peppers, fat squash resting on dark soil. Beans clambered up poles as workers plucked pods from between the glossy green leaves.

The smell of rich soil and manure filled Greenleaf's nostrils. A buzzing sound snapped his head to the side, and he tracked a fat bumblebee weaving drunkenly through the air to land upon a blossom growing from a zucchini plant. On the far side of the building, a bee-keeper checked one of over twenty boxed hives, a cloud of bees milling harmlessly about. The building stretched nearly three hundred feet in length, every one of those feet packed with plants that had no business growing at the top of the world.

"We don't know each other," Edeline said. "And regardless of why you're here, the fact is, you're here. If you're here to serve this community, you should know who we are. Why it matters so much to us that those records are safe."

Greenleaf looked over strawberry plants dangling out of pots on the wall. "Knoxol mentioned working on farms, but I never imagined..."

"This is our sixth," Edeline said quietly. "The resonants are here to finish the panels on our seventh." He pointed to the ceiling, which was filled with huge transparent sheets on wooden joists, each reflecting the light of the thin creek of lava. Through the panels, Greenleaf could see the crescent moon crawling its way across the arctic sky. He spotted movement, and pointed.

"There's someone up there!"

"Our farmers, sweeping the snow off the quartz panes. They're slanted, so heavy snowfall slides off, but clear the lighter drifts several times a day."

Greenleaf shook his head. "I've never seen quartz so clear. Why not glass?"

"Glass isn't strong enough to hold up to the snow. We have to ship in barrels of quartz crystals, and commission Chorale masons to shift it into the right shape and clarity." Edeline leaned against the edge of a raised bed. "Each of those panels cost this town nearly forty thousand marks."

"That's..." The young kaviak shook his head. "That's a fortune. Who paid for them?"

Edeline shrugged. "The Gift." Everything within the borders of the Empire was the property of the Empress. But for centuries, every community was granted The Gift, a quarter of the value of what they produced, so long as it wasn't requisitioned by the Imperial Army.

Edeline continued, saying, "Ever since the war ended, the Ministry of War cut their allotment of aquasteel. But our production hasn't changed, so they've begun selling shards outside the military, using the money to fund Imperial projects. As it's no longer for the military, we've been granted the Gift, and at the price they charge for aquasteel..."

Greenleaf whistled softly. "That's a lot of wealth for such a small community."

"This is where virtually every mark has gone." Edeline reached out, plucking a fat strawberry from one of the nearby pots. "This was my father's dream. He always tried to grow ice pepper plants in pots in our home. He'd take them outside during the warmest part of the day, try to get them enough light so they'd thrive. Sometimes it worked. Most of the time, it didn't. If they're outside, it's too cold. If they're inside, it's too dark."

He took a bite, wiping away the juice that dribbled down his chin. "He was sixty when he asked a visiting Chorale sorcerer, here to study aquasteel, if they could create clear panels that would hold in the heat, but let in the light. It was doable, but the cost was impossible, a fantasy. He died believing that to be true."

Greenleaf shook his head. "I always thought Lahar survived on hunting and fishing."

"During the war, we did," Edeline said. "But going out on the ice has always been dangerous, and even if they load the sleds with fish and seal, there are just too many of us. So we traded the pelts, the few barrels of brandy we could make, for food. Weevils in the flour, or a bad hunting season? Many who saw the sun set wouldn't get to see it rise again in a few months."

"What you've done here, Edeline..." Greenleaf reached out and touched the soil in a nearby bed. It was damp and rich, nearly black. "It's extraordinary."

"It wasn't me. It was all of us. This entire community has worked for nearly a decade to make these farms a reality," Edeline said, tossing the stem and leaves from his strawberry in a compost pot. "We can't grow during the night. In a month, all of this will be shut down. But every year, a new farm opens, and every year, we grow closer to self-sufficiency, to a day in which we don't have to depend on the

Empire just to keep our children fed. And we're so close. But we need the Gift to make my father's dream a reality."

"The Gift..." Greenleaf nodded, realizing what Edeline was telling him. "If something were to happen to the records..."

"Any error, any issue, and the Ministry of Allocation will freeze the Gift until they finish an audit that could take years," Edeline said. "Years."

Greenleaf turned slowly, taking it all in. Finally, he met Edeline's stare, and said, "The records will be safe. They won't leave my quarters until I've finished my review, and once I've done, I'll ask you to help make arrangements to return them to their storage at the mine. I'll even walk escort as they do." He nodded at the sprawling green farm. "This is worth protecting, Counselor, and I give you my word: That's exactly what I'm here to do."

"I hope so, Captain." The older man looked unconvinced. "I truly do."

CHAPTER 4

Greenleaf closed the door to his quarters behind him, exhaling slowly. His trunk had been left at the foot of the cot. Sergeant Idar had offered to bring a proper bed out on their next trip, but Greenleaf had assured her it wasn't necessary. As he settled onto the rope and canvas frame, he began to regret that choice.

The room was small, the grey stone walls bare. A wooden desk and stool sat against the far wall. Next to them were twelve crates, each stacked with the wood-bound volumes of the mine's records. Rising to his feet, Greenleaf ran his fingers over the top few, noting the dates. Nodding to himself, he walked back to his trunk, lifting the lid and pulling out the flat wooden case sitting atop folded uniforms and several books. As he sat at the desk, he set the case in front of him, lifting the lid. The smell of cedar filled his nostrils as he pulled out the bottle of black ink, and a steel nib set into a polished rosewood grip. He pulled the glass stopper out, and inhaled.

"It smells."

She smiled down at him. "I like it." Her dark hair fell over her face, and she brushed it out of the way. "Be careful. If you spill it, you have to clean it up. And walk back to the scribe to get more."

He nodded, handling the bottle and nibs with care, arranging them just as he'd seen her do so many times. He settled onto the plush chair, the desk coming up to just above his chin. She laughed. He did too.

"That won't do. Here." A few cushions from his bed brought the polished desk to the right level. "Now, do you remember how we practiced?"

"Yes, mother." His tongue slipped out from the corner of his mouth as he clumsily fit the end of the wooden pen between his fingers, the smooth oiled wood grasped between his thumb, index finger, and pinky. "It feels strange. I don't want to drop it."

She kissed his head. "If you do, just pick it up."

He set the paper on the battered pine desk, and picked up the pen, dipping the nib in the bottle. The grip was odd, but after so many years, it felt natural, and the point danced over the paper, leaving the elegant trails as he wrote.

Mother,

It's cold here.

He'd been the only candidate that knew how to write. They were all taught during their time at the war college, but he had written dozens of letters home for classmates, each delighted to send their words home riding the flowing script. He'd always been a bit self-conscious writing his mother. His calligraphy was clean. Hers was art.

He filled two pages, signing the end and dusting the page to keep the ink from smearing. Setting it aside, he pulled out another sheet of paper.

Father,

The pen paused, and he stared at the blank page. His father's face swam up in his mind, eyes fixed on his son, his expression blank. He remembered the empty, cold words as his father said, "Slipped."

Father,

I...

Greenleaf shook his head sharply, as if trying to shake off a buzzing insect. Quickly, he began to write, signing his name only halfway down the page.

The knock at the door came just as he finished sealing the folded letters. "Come in."

Proudlake closed the door behind him. "I wanted to see how you're settling in."

"One moment." Greenleaf finished writing his parent's names on the letters, and set them aside. Proudlake picked one up, raising an eyebrow.

"I didn't know calligraphy was taught at the war college."

"It's not," Greenleaf said, capping the ink and putting carefully everything back in the case. "My mother's a calligrapher. Works for the scribing guild. She taught me."

"Not a common skill for men. Especially soldiers."

"It was my father's idea. Wanted me to have something from her that could never be lost." Greenleaf stood up, gesturing at the stool. "Want to sit?"

"I'm all right," Proudlake said. He set the letter back down, and nodded at the records. "I hear you're already making friends."

Greenleaf snorted. "Edeline wasn't happy. Said he's worried I'll damage them."

"He is quite particular about them." He walked over to the crates. "This will take you quite a while. I've copied every one since I've been here, know them quite well. If you tell me what you're looking for..."

"I don't know, exactly," Greenleaf said. "But the aquasteel is the most valuable resource in Lahar. I want to understand more about it. Whatever the reason I'm here, it's likely to be connected to the mine."

Proudlake nodded. "Want some help?"

"Thank you, but I think I can manage." Greenleaf shrugged. "It'll most likely take a while, but I have the time. I'm not going anywhere." He looked up, remembering. "Oh. Tell me about Reif Zdene."

"He's a pain in the ass."

Greenleaf grinned. "I was hoping for something a bit more comprehensive."

Shrugging, Proudlake said, "He comes by it honestly, at least. His father's even worse. Many people were confused and apprehensive when we announced your arrival. The Zdenes, though…" He shook his head. "They were hotter than the Serao. His father came just up to the line of sedition. Probably would have trampled right over it if Edeline and a few others hadn't dragged him aside, set him straight."

"You didn't detain him?"

"Have to be careful about that, Captain," Proudlake said. "Until you came, it was just me. I could have asked Sergeant Idar to arrest him during one of the convoy stops, but I do try not to actively make things worse. As it was, most of the town just rolled their eyes when Reif or his father began ranting. If I'd tried to bind them, the others may have viewed that as more hostile than anything either of those two blowhards had said."

Greenleaf nodded. "So why were they so upset about my arrival?"

Proudlake considered him for a moment. "You do have a gift for asking interesting questions, don't you? And that's a particularly good one."

"Well," Greenleaf said. "Maybe I should ask him."

***

The sun set early in Lahar. Greenleaf knew they were quickly approaching the long night, the period in which the sun would vanish behind the horizon and remain there for nearly ten weeks, plunging the entire frozen province into darkness. As the long night drew closer, the days grew shorter and shorter, and the Laharians abandoned the rising and setting of the sun as any kind of reliable reference for time. Instead, one of the younger villagers was tasked with spending the day next to a large sand timer, ringing three large chimes hanging on the outside of the castle to mark the time.

When the chimes sounded, Greenleaf carefully marked where he'd reached in the record he'd been reading through. Standing up, he stretched. Downstairs, tables were being set up and food was being prepared. Other meals were enjoyed at home with families and friends, but for the evening meal, the community came together, trickling in over a four or five hour period, sharing a meal and conversation.

His first four nights in town, Greenleaf had eaten alone in his quarters, or with Proudlake in his office. But today, he pulled on a fresh uniform tunic, and headed out to the walkway overlooking the plaza that made up the bulk of the Castle's ground floor. There were a few dozen people already, the low hum of conversation mixing with the scraping of chairs against the floor. He scanned the crowd, and spotted a man in Lyceum robes sitting at a small table to the side. Nodding to himself, Greenleaf headed down the stairs.

It didn't take long for people to notice him. Conversation died and eyes tracked him as he walked over, nodding at stony faces as he made his way through the crowd to the food. A young man was lifting a tray of charred and roasted fish onto the table, and saw him. He offered a slight smile. "Hi. Um, Captain. Hi."

"Hello," Greenleaf said, returning the smile. "Counselor Edeline said anyone was welcome to come join the evening meal. I hope I'm not intruding."

"No!" Leaning over, the young man snagged a chipped wooden plate, and scooped three or four of the small fish, along with a few pieces of dark, flat bread. "No, everyone comes here to eat." He pointed. "Water cask is over there. Do you have a cup?"

Greenleaf produced his steel campaign cup. The boy offered a toothy grin, and Greenleaf chuckled.

He walked over, dipping a cupful of cool, clear water, and walked over to where Knoxol was sitting. As he approached, the resonant set down his fork and nudged the chair across from him out. "Have a seat, Captain."

"Thank you." Greenleaf sat down. "You're leaving tomorrow morning, aren't you?"

Knoxol nodded. "The caravan is scheduled to arrive in a few hours, and we'll be on our way. I'm sorry we didn't get more time to chat."

"You seem to be feeling much better."

"Once again, I offer my sincerest..." Knoxol fell silent as Greenleaf waved it off.

"The trip was a miserable experience, and it didn't exactly leave me in the best mood either." He sniffed the bread, and made a slight face. "It smells like sulfur."

"Like everything else here, it's cooked over the river. Very efficient heating source, but it does have a distinct odor. Doesn't seem to affect the flavor, though."

Greenleaf took a hesitant bite. Chewing for a moment, he nodded. "Different. Not bad, but different."

"One could say the same thing about this place." Knoxol had a clay pot next to him along with several small clay cups, steam trailing from the spout. "Blackleaf tea? One of the villagers made us a pot. It's quite good."

"No, thank you." Greenleaf glanced around, keeping his voice low. "Didn't think the Laharians would give us the time of day."

"Oh, they can be quite pleasant. Just not to you."

"So it's personal."

"Well, from what I've heard, you've done an excellent job establishing your authority over the last few days," Knoxol said, grinning. "No doubt important, but not exactly conducive to making friends. Besides, I can offer them something that you can't possibly."

"I saw the quartz panels in the farms," Greenleaf said. "They're impressive."

"They'd better be. We're charging the Laharians enough for them." Knoxol took a sip of his tea. "But no, that's not what I was speaking of. We offer them the certainty that we'll soon be gone. Our presence here is entirely of their choice, and we linger not one moment longer than we're welcome." He shrugged. "It's easy to be friendly to someone visiting your home. Someone who moves in without invitation? Much more difficult."

Greenleaf glanced back at the few dozen Laharians, who were doing their best not to stare. Quietly, he said, "I don't suppose that it matters that it wasn't my choice."

"If your plan is to inform each and every one of them how much you don't want to be here, I believe that's what they would refer to at that war college of yours as a tactical error."

In lieu of responding, Greenleaf nibbled at one of the fish. It was salty, but the flesh flaked away easily, and the flavor was rich and savory. Swallowing, he said, "I suppose they're more used to resonants here anyway. The first Lyceum was built up here, wasn't it?"

Knoxol didn't say anything for a moment, but nodded. "It was, but that was a long time ago. Nearly half a century." There was an odd tone to his voice.

"Why? I can't imagine a less hospitable place to build a school."

"Long before my time, I'm afraid," Knoxol said. "It didn't last long. The Chorale abandoned it a few years after it was finished."

"Why?"

Knoxol chuckled. "It's still late summer, Captain. When the sun sets in a few months for its long nap, I suspect you won't have any question as to why my predecessors decided to relocate to more temperate climes." He rose to his feet. "If you'll excuse me, Captain, I believe I'll make sure everything is ready for our departure."

"Of course." Greenleaf watched him leave. The Chorale resonant didn't look back at him as he opened the door to leave, but stepped back to allow several Laharians to enter. Greenleaf spotted the tall blonde miner immediately. He was chuckling at something, his eyes crinkled, but the laugh died in his throat as the burly man with him elbowed Reif and nodded in Greenleaf's direction. Scowling, the miner fell silent.

Gods, he's a big one. Greenleaf tracked him with his peripheral vision, slowly eating as he watched the pair pile food on their plates, muttering to each other and occasionally glancing over at the kaviak. They found a table on the other side of the room and hunched over their plates, furiously whispering at each other.

Big and angry. Greenleaf tilted his head. *Let's go make him angrier.*

A few moments later, he settled into the hard chair next to Reif Zdene.

The miner paused, a forkful of fish halfway to his mouth, staring at the kaviak for a few moments. The other man glanced between the two of them for a moment, as if unsure what to say. Reif set his fork back down, and raised his voice. "Friends, mark today in your memory. We've been graced with the Eyes of the Empress, who has descended from on high to dine with us simple folk." He lifted the battered wooden cup in front of him. "For the Empress!"

Someone cleared their throat. Several people murmured behind him, but Greenleaf didn't take his eyes off the miner. He kept his voice even. "Not exactly how that toast is meant to go, but I'll take it in the spirit it was intended." He tipped his cup in Reif's direction. "You going to introduce your friend?"

"If he wants to know you, he'll know you."

Greenleaf glanced over. The other man frowned. "Braddock Hale," he muttered.

"Do you work with Reif in the mine, Braddock Hale?"

He shook his head. "In the forge."

Nodding, Greenleaf said, "I need to come take a look at the forge. Laharian steel is famous."

"Won't that be a treat for everyone," Reif said. Braddock didn't say anything. He just tore a massive bite off of his bread and chewed, staring down at the tabletop.

Turning his attention back to Reif, Greenleaf said, "So I've come to understand that you and your father weren't very pleased to know I was coming to Lahar."

Reif shrugged.

Greenleaf took a sip of his water. "My job is to serve the people of this community, Reif. If you have a problem, I'd like to know more so I can help address it."

"And if my problem is sitting across the table from me?"

"You don't even know me."

Reif nodded. "True. Only know what I've seen. You like the fish?"

"What?" Greenleaf blinked, confused. "Yes, it's good."

"It's one of my favorites. We call them silvers. Catch them off the coast. You drop a chunk of rotting meat in the water, and five minutes later it looks like a glittering cloud around it. Scoop them up with a net, hundreds at a time." He picked one of the fish up. "Of course, it takes thirteen hours on a dogsled to reach the coast. If we're going to make the trip worthwhile, we have to bring back at least two hundred pounds of fish. We lay it out to freeze, wrap it, load it, bring it back. It can be hard to do in frostsuits, but we do it three, four times a month."

"I thought you worked in the mine."

"No one has just the one job here, Imperial. We all pitch in any way we can." He popped the fish in his mouth whole. Swallowing, he picked up his cup of water. "Tomorrow, we're having caribou. Those bastards..." He shook his head, chuckling. "Big fuckers. Arrows don't do much more than piss them off, so you have to hobble them and finish them off with spears. Few years back, Braddock here got kicked by one in the upper arm. We could hear the bone break." He elbowed the man next to him. "Give the man credit, though. He grabbed the spear with his other hand and got right back to it."

Greenleaf raised his eyebrow. "That's impressive."

"What had to be done," Braddock mumbled.

"He said it, right there," Reif said. "It had to be done. It had to be done because if we didn't bring that caribou back, that's a good three hundred pounds of meat that we don't have come nightfall." Greenleaf had lifted his cup to take a drink, and Reif pointed at it. "Know where the water comes from?"

Greenleaf sighed, setting the cup down. "The cisterns. I've seen them, to collect snowfall."

Reif nodded. "Maybe. But it doesn't snow all that much around here. Not enough to fill our casks. We can't dig a well. There aren't any streams or rivers, least not ones you want to drink from. No, every day, a few dozen people put on their frost suits, and walk out of the village to fill casks with snow and ice, and haul it back. The kids go with them. They can't carry a lot, maybe a bucket or two full, but they go. Know why?"

The room had fallen silent. Greenleaf glared at Reif. "All right. I get it."

"Do you? Do you really?" Reif asked. "Because you're still sitting across from me, eating fish that Laharians brought back, drinking water that children hauled in from the cold. Everyone here has a purpose. Everyone here works hard, in every way they can, to make sure that Lahar survives. But you?" He shook his head.

I didn't ask to be here, you... Greenleaf could feel the eyes of the room on him.

Reif leaned back in his chair. "Proudlake tell you he teaches the kids here?" Greenleaf nodded, and Reif said, "I won't say I was a good student. I didn't like him, and didn't really want to be there. Few things stuck with me, though. I liked learning about animals." He grinned at Greenleaf, who felt his face burn with anger. "Remember him teaching us about tapeworms. They get in your stomach, you know? Getting fat and long while you wither and die." He tilted his head. "Funny, the things you remember."

Greenleaf's blood thundered in his ears, and he began to rise.

Two minds.

He shut his eyes for a heartbeat, sinking back into the chair. When he opened them again, he tilted his head and asked, "Are you done? I can wait if you're not done." He took a bite of fish, and nodded at him. "Go ahead."

"Excuse me?"

"You were saying something. I wasn't really paying much attention, sorry."

Reif's fair skin flushed as he shot to his feet, the chair clattering back against the floor. His hands were tightened into fists, his nostrils flaring as he stared down at Greenleaf. "You shouldn't be here."

"And yet, here I am." He shrugged, and took a drink of water.

Reif's jaw worked. Braddock stood up slowly, gripping the miner's arm. "Reif," he muttered urgently. "He's a kaviak."

Shaking his his arm free, Reif snapped, "I'm not afraid of you."

Greenleaf raised an eyebrow. "You sure about that?"

"Gentlemen." All three men looked to the stairs. Proudlake stood about halfway up, his voice carrying. Before he could continue, the door to the Castle came open, and Edeline came through. The young man who'd served the food stood next to him, worry creasing his face.

"Reif." Braddock tugged on his arm even harder. "Let's go."

Edeline covered the distance between them quickly, and moved between them and Greenleaf. "Listen to him, Reif. You're done."

"Captain, perhaps we should speak in private," Proudlake said. "Dhrez, I trust you have this well in hand?"

Edeline nodded. "Go. Please."

Greenleaf rose to his feet, touching two fingers to his forehead. "See you soon, Reif."

"Captain." Proudlake's voice was hard. "If you will."

***

The door hadn't even closed as Proudlake spun on his heel. "Do you mind telling me what the hell that was?"

Greenleaf shrugged. "You said it: He's an ass."

"That's a fact," the commissar said. "It's also a fact that you were deliberately antagonizing him. Were you trying to get him to swing on you?"

"Yes."

Proudlake blinked. "I'm sorry?"

"He's an ass. But there's more to his hostility." Greenleaf leaned back against the wall. "He really, really doesn't want me here. I'd like to know why."

"And starting a brawl in the plaza was going to help you find out how, exactly?"

"He hits a kaviak, he's in a kind of trouble he's not seen before," Greenleaf said. "If the alternative is the sergeant hauling him back for tribunal in shackles, he might be a bit more willing to talk."

Proudlake stared at him for a moment. Finally, he walked around to sit heavily down at his desk. "All right." He pressed his hands against the desk. "Captain, I understand what you were trying to do. And I understand the desire to interrogate Reif. But I don't think you understand just how badly that could have gone."

Greenleaf raised his eyebrow. "You don't think I could handle Reif?"

"Don't be absurd. You would have put him down before anyone realized what had happened," Proudlake said. "But what do you think would have happened next? Do you think Braddock would have watched you thrash a man he grew up with and done nothing?"

"I wasn't worried..."

Proudlake bulled right on as if he hadn't spoken. "Did you know Braddock's brother was sitting two tables away? Two of the men that work with Braddock in the forge were sitting with them."

Greenleaf shook his head. "Attacking a kaviak is a serious offense."

"None of them would have cared. None of them." Proudlake shook his head. "We're not in Kaani. There's no guard force to come back you up. I'd be worse than useless in a fight. It would be you. Alone." Leaning forward, he asked, "How many would come to their feet before you brought that out?" He pointed at the bracer around Greenleaf's forearm. "If your plan had worked, there'd be blood on the floor, and I don't think either of us are prepared for the consequences of that."

Running his fingers through his hair, Greenleaf said, "Well... shit."

The commissar nodded. "A fair assessment." He leaned forward. "I know you want out of here, Captain. Better than you know. I've been here for twenty years. I don't want to see that happen to you, and I promise, I'll do everything I can to make sure it doesn't. But you have to be careful."

Walking over, Greenleaf sat down. "Yeah." He shook his head. "Yeah, all right."

Proudlake sighed. He stood up and poured a finger of brandy in two glasses, sliding one over to Greenleaf. "We will figure this out."

Taking a sip, Greenleaf exhaled slowly. "It's good."

"Mmm."

Watching the light dance through the amethyst liquor, Greenleaf said, "Can I ask you something? Something personal?" Proudlake nodded his assent. "How'd you end up here?"

"Ah." The commissar shrugged. "I requested posting here."

"Gods, why?"

Proudlake didn't answer for a long few moments. Finally, he opened a drawer, pulling out a small wooden box. He slid it across the desk. Greenleaf opened it, and his eyes widened at the pair of teardrop-shaped rubies inside.

"My sons." Proudlake drained his glass, setting it down on the stained wood. "Elgor fell fighting the Hoberian clans. Rober got sick escorting a convoy through the Spine. Grey fever."

"I'm so sorry."

Proudlake nodded. "It was a long time ago. My wife passed a few years after we got the second teardrop. After that, it was hard to be in the home we'd shared, around neighbors who had known our boys." He closed the box, returning it to the drawer. "They died for something bigger than themselves. I took pride in that, and I still wanted to serve, just... somewhere else. This posting came up, and I raised my hand."

Greenleaf stared into his glass. "I don't know what I'm doing here."

"Your job, Captain."

"Tomas."

Proudlake tilted his head. "Pardon?"

"Call me Tomas."

The commissar smiled. "Ayal." He lifted his glass. "It's going to be all right, Tomas. You're not alone here."

CHAPTER 5

Sergeant Ash had taught many things in Greenleaf's five years of training. The old veteran had been Greenleaf's shadow, a hard stare and growling voice following him from when he woke each morning to when Greenleaf fell into bed each night, muscles aching and eyelids heavy. Ash was constantly drilling him, relentlessly pushing him, and always, always lecturing. But his favorite topic, by far, was patrol.

"Patrol is everything. Get it through your thick skull. You have to know your route, know every rock, every cockroach, every blade of grass, and you need to put your eyeballs on every single point as often as you can. It might take you months to patrol every bit, but the moment you stop, the moment you get complacent, the moment you think you have things figured out, something's going to sink a mouthful of teeth into your ass."

Greenleaf looked out over the breadth of his patrol, and shook his head.

"Well, you crusty old bastard, it takes me half a gods-damned hour to walk the entirety of my route," he muttered under his breath.

That route took him through the mine, around the south of the village to the shattered rock and glass of the Serao delta, where the river split and split again before spilling into the frigid water of the Cobalt Sea. The noise was terrific, cracking stone and hissing steam as molten blobs tumbled into the black waters, the surface a boiling froth that never seemed to stop. From there, he wound his way through three of the farms.

Each of the farms the Laharians had built specialized in different plants. One had row upon row of huge clay pots with fruit tree saplings, an orchard early in its life, where another was a combination of root vegetable in raised beds and over two dozen hives buzzing with honeybees. The fourth farm lacked any edible plants whatsoever. Instead, miniature willow trees grew next to feverfew and palmetto, aloe and valerian roots filling pots in every corner. The medicinal farm had an oddly strong scent, but just like the others, they'd packed every inch of space with soil and life. As he left the sixth farm, he reflected that the only things they seemed to have in common were the cisterns and irrigation systems, the buzzing of pollinators, and the immediate and tragic death of any discussion once he entered the building.

Since the incident in the plaza three weeks ago, the Laharians had gone from curious to hostile. Any questions he asked received only short, one-word answers, particularly from the younger villagers. Greenleaf still took his meals in the plaza, but ate alone, reviewing the notes he'd taken on the records he was slowly making his way through.

Two chimes rang from the castle, marking the midday point. Greenleaf glanced at the sun, a fat hazy yellow sitting just above the horizon as he began making his way back to the Castle. The days were getting shorter and shorter as the long night drew closer.

It took him less than five minutes to reach the commissar's office, even after a stop by his quarters. He rapped his knuckles twice on the door, and heard, "It's open, Tomas."

Proudlake was pouring a cup of tea as Greenleaf settled into the chair, dropping the volume he'd just retrieved down onto the desk. "Everything still in its rightful place?"

Greenleaf snorted. "If I climb up on the roof, I can see everything sitting in its rightful place."

Proudlake chuckled, sliding the cup to Greenleaf. "Look at the bright side. It's less time outside in the cold." He poured himself a cup, and sat down. "All right. You said you found something?"

Sipping at the spicy tea, Greenleaf nodded. "I think so." He set the drink down, well away from the records, and flipped to the marked space. "Might be nothing, but it's strange."

Proudlake walked around the desk to look over his shoulder. "Show me."

"Okay. There are two exports that the Laharians keep comprehensive records on. The aquasteel shards, and the weapons from the forge." His finger traced two columns on the page. "In each case, they log them here by weight."

Nodding, Proudlake said, "It's the easiest way. Plus, it keeps them from overloading the bakeries."

"Right. Now, these mining records are permanently maintained, stored forever. They have all the detail about the shards: size, time it was pulled, time it was quenched, I have everything." He pointed at the column for the weapons. "The only detail we have in this log for the forge output is the weight."

"The forge keeps its own records," Proudlake says. "A full inventory of each shipment, down to the arrowhead."

Greenleaf nodded. "I know, I saw them. But they only go back a year. Once the auditor from the Ministry of Allocation signs off on them, they send the previous year's records back to the capital to be stored in the Archives. So at any given time, there's always less than a year of inventories for the forge. Anything before that, all we have is the weight."

Proudlake shrugged. "The Laharians are never going to care as much about the forge as they do the mine. That goes to the army, and doesn't qualify for The Gift."

Greenleaf waved that off. "I get the reasoning. But I found something weird." He pointed at the log. "This is from about eighteen months ago. The forge always ships between five and six hundred pounds of steel." His finger moved from one line to another. "553 pounds." He flipped to a random page. "Four years before, 504 pounds." Another page. "602 pounds. It's always fairly consistent with how much raw steel they get shipped in."

Flipping back to the original page, he said, "But look. 814 pounds."

Proudlake leaned down, brow furrowing. "They were high."

"For just one shipment." Greenleaf flipped the page. "Then, back to 572, and they're at normal weights from that point on."

"Did you ask anyone at the forge?"

Greenleaf nodded. "I spoke with Braddock, Reif's friend. He wasn't too enthusiastic, but he remembered. Said that they collect all the scrap pieces, and once every few years, they melt them all down and make spearheads and arrowheads. Add them to the next shipment."

"Okay," Proudlake said, nodding. "I know next to nothing about forging, but that makes sense."

"I thought so too," Greenleaf said. "But I've gone back fifteen years in these logs. It never happens any other time."

Proudlake frowned. "Huh. That's a bit strange. But if they were hoarding weapons, wouldn't the weight be low?"

"I don't think they're hoarding weapons," Greenleaf said. "I think they stole a shard."

Proudlake's eyes widened. "I'm going to need you to explain that."

"Look." He pointed to the last column on each page. "This is the final shipment weight. It's the combination of the shards and the weapons, right?" Proudlake nodded, and Greenleaf said, "It varies quite a bit, mostly based on the size of the shards that are going out. But look at the dates that the forge supposedly overproduced."

The commissar spent a few moments looking over the entries, his lips moving slowly. Finally, he went back to his chair and sat down heavily. "Damn."

"Tell me I'm wrong."

Proudlake shook his head. "I cross check everything, but for the shipments, I just look at the total weight. The combined weight was in the normal range. But if they were shipping a few hundred extra pounds of weapons..."

"The total weight should have been that much higher," Greenleaf said. "It's not. And guess what the average weight of a shard is."

"I'm going to guess a few hundred pounds." Proudlake rubbed the bridge of his nose. "I don't know how I missed that."

"You've been here a long time," Greenleaf said. "You have a system for checking the records. They figured out a way to get around it."

Proudlake drummed his fingers against the table. "Okay, what comes next? A search?"

"I don't think so," Greenleaf said. "First, it's been eighteen months. That shard's probably been gone for a while. Second, this isn't actually proof." He flipped to a few other marked pages. "Shards normally weigh around 150 pounds, but there's a lot of variation. Here, seven years ago, they pulled a five hundred pound shard. I asked Odel Deric. He remembers it well. Said it took three miners to haul it out, and it broke one of their cooling tables."

"Shit," Proudlake said, nodding. "I remember that. I had to justify the cost of a replacement."

"Other times, they've pulled thirty, forty pound shards," Greenleaf said. "They usually wait to ship them with others so as not to waste the trip, but if they had a lot of extra weapon weight, they may just have shipped one of those small shards instead of a full-size one. This really could be nothing."

"There's another question, though. Why?" Proudlake asked. "They earn the Gift on every shard they send now. Even a smaller one, that's a lot of money."

"I can think of three possibilities," Greenleaf said. "First, they want to make their own aquasteel weapons and armor."

Proudlake shook his head. "Impossible. You need a resonant to shape aquasteel, and a good one at that."

"They do have a group of resonants that visit Lahar every few months to work on the farm," Greenleaf pointed out.

"Those are masons, not smiths," Proudlake said. "Plus, I find it hard to believe that a member of the Chorale would do something like this. And to do so in this town without drawing attention?"

"It's difficult. Not necessarily impossible. But I suspect you're right. It's too high risk."

"What's the second possibility?"

Greenleaf said, "They sent it to the Brehai."

"Even more unlikely," Proudlake said. "The only shipments going out of here are in Imperial convoys guarded by Imperial soldiers, inspected on both departure and arrival. Even if the Brehai wanted a shard, I can't imagine how they would get it."

"That leaves the third possibility." Greenleaf leaned forward in his chair. "They sold it."

"To whom?"

Greenleaf stood up, walking to the map of the province on the wall. "I've been asking around. The Laharians send out hunting and fishing parties, about one every two weeks. This," he pointed at a spot on the coastline, "is one of their main hunting grounds. A hunting party is going out in two days, in fact."

Proudlake nodded. "They would know where the best fishing and hunting is, I expect. Their lives have depended on it for centuries."

"True. But look at this cove," Greenleaf said. "It opens onto open water. It would be difficult, but a ship could make the trip up from Saltai, or Bayan..." He raised an eyebrow. "Or even south of the Breaking."

Proudlake's eyes widened. "That's a long trip."

"It is. But the Dominion and Vetticci both know we're building the bridge. They don't have any aquasteel. To get their hands on a shard?" Greenleaf shrugged. "I don't know if the Dominion has any ships that could make the trip, but Vetticci definitely does. And Vetticci could afford to pay a lot. More than the Gift, for gods-damn sure."

The commissar was silent for a moment, but finally, he said, "There's a young man, Braden Noya. He's been going on the hunting trips to help fish, learning the trade. A few weeks back, he was showing everyone something in the Plaza. I asked to see it, and he got very uncomfortable." He looked back up at Greenleaf. "It was a ducat. A grey coral ducat."

Greenleaf's eyes widened. "He had Vetticcian money?!"

"He said a trader in one of the convoys gave it to him. It's such a small amount, I didn't think anything of it." Proudlake shook his head. "The traders that come up, they sell everything they can carry.

Ducats aren't common, but Vetticcian merchants do make their way up to Tyum and Saltai. Braden could have been telling me the truth."

"Or, he got it directly from a Vetticcian," Greenleaf muttered. He stood up, thinking for a moment. "It's not enough."

"What do you need?"

"I don't know." Greenleaf began to pace as he spoke. "There's not going to be any evidence left in the cove. But at the very least, I need to be sure that it's possible for a ship to anchor close enough to shore to send a boat."

"I don't see how you're going to be able to do that," Proudlake said. "Not without talking to the Laharians from the hunting party."

Greenleaf shook his head. "If they really are dealing with Vetticci, I don't want to tip them off. No. I need to see the cove myself."

"Oh, sure," Proudlake said. "It's just a quick twenty-five mile trip over open ice in weather that will kill you in thirty minutes without a frost suit. Also, you don't know where you're going."

Grinning, Greenleaf said, "No. But the Laharians do. And they're heading that way in two days."

"You want to go with them?" Proudlake's eyes widened. "Tomas, that's very dangerous. There are a thousand ways to die on the ice, and that's without taking into account that you'll be surrounded by people who might be trying to hide something from you."

"I can handle myself."

Proudlake raised an eyebrow. "You don't have a frostsuit."

Greenleaf shrugged. "I'm in the only place in the Empire that they're made. I think I should be able to find one."

CHAPTER 6

Greenleaf shivered despite his poncho as he tromped through the recent snowfall that covered the stone path leading to the southernmost house in Lahar. He had thought that the valley was cold when he first arrived, but as the days grew increasingly short, the temperature continued to drop. Even the Laharians didn't stay outside any longer than they had to. Proudlake had given him a scarf made from yak wool which was wrapped around the lower half of his face, and a caribou hide poncho was draped over his uniform. Both were technically in violation of uniform regulations, but he'd stopped caring about that in short order.

The house he approached was further from the village than the rest of the homes, the thin trickle of lava snaking beneath the stone arch throwing an orange glow against the frozen walls. It was just past midday, but the sun had yet to rise. They'd only have three or four hours where the sun peeked over the horizon, barely tipping over the distant white ice before it sank back below. Reaching the door, he raised a hand, pausing for a moment, then knocked twice.

The door creaked open, and a pair of grey eyes peered up at him from beneath short snow-white hair, tumbling down over an aged and wrinkled brow. "You're early."

"Mistress Elif?" Greenleaf asked.

"Not sure who the hell else it would be," the old woman said, her voice raspy and thin. "Ten minutes early, at least."

"I can wait until you're ready."

Roenne Elif shook her head. "Not gonna leave you to freeze your southern balls off." She turned, and Greenleaf followed her into the house, closing the door behind him. The tendril of molten rock snaking under the far wall filled the house with a stifling heat, and he began unwrapping his scarf as quickly as possible, beads of sweat bursting onto his forehead.

She was short, less than five feet in height, her frame thin and lanky. A knit shawl was draped around her shoulders, covering a light grey cotton dress, two skinny legs sticking out from the hem. Elif hobbled over to a large wooden table, upon which lay several pieces of mottled white clothing. She began fiddling with one of the pieces. "Tea in the pot over the crick. Mugs on the table."

"I'm all right."

"I didn't say it was for you. Sugar, two lumps."

Greenleaf winced as he approached the end of the stream of lava. The heat pouring off the stone sent a shimmer through the air above, and he quickly reached out to grab the cloth-wrapped handle of the kettle hanging from an iron hook. Carrying it over to a small round table ten feet away, he poured the steaming brew into a clay mug, adding two brown lumps of sugar from a bowl. He brought it over to Elif, who accepted it.

"Thanks. Take your clothes off."

His eyes snapped wide, and he found himself at a loss for words. "Ah... excuse me?"

"My back hurts most of the time, my knees aren't worth a damn, but I'm fairly sure I don't stutter, boy." She waved a bony hand in his direction. "Clothes. Off. All of them."

The heat flooding his cheeks had nothing to do with the lava. "I thought I'd change somewhere else."

"They teach frost suit fitting at that school you spent so long at? You're the one who demanded I have one ready this quickly, I thought you'd be in more of a hurry." She raised an eyebrow as she looked back at him. "Don't be bashful, now. My libido's been dead longer than my husband."

Taking a deep breath, he nodded, and began stripping down, folding each piece of his uniform carefully and setting it on a nearby stool. Elif returned to making adjustments, not watching until he stood naked, awkwardly covering himself with his hands. Turning back, she looked him up and down. "Not burdened with an excess of fat, are you?"

Furiously, he tried to will the red out of his face. "They... ah, they train us pretty hard in the war college."

She grunted. "Bit of blubber around your waist and thighs would be better." She picked up an assortment of thin leather straps, and began fastening it around his biceps. "Lift your arms. This is going to go a lot faster if you stop trying to guard that Imperial virtue."

Another set of straps wrapped tightly around his chest, her fingers working deftly at the wooden clasps. His cheeks burned as she began fastening another pair of strips around his upper thighs. Greenleaf tried to focus on a collection of cutting tools and markers hanging from clips on the wall, willing her to finish faster. Grunting as she straightened up, she walked back over to the table, and picked up a stack of small flat bags. "There are loops next to your balls, under your arms, and in the center of your chest. Slide these in and make sure they're fastened snug against your skin."

He took the first one, and grunted in surprise. "It's hot." The bag didn't have any obvious opening, and felt squishy, as if filled with a thick syrup.

"Malheur sap, inside a bag stitched from a seal's bladder. Four months from now, it'll still be about that temperature."

He fastened them in place, one on the inside of each thigh, one in the center of his chest, and one under each armpit. Each bag was as warm as a stone warmed under a blazing summer sun. As he secured the last one, Greenleaf could feel the warmth flooding through his body.

"The malheur sacks maintain your core temperature," she said. "They've got to be placed there, because..."

"It's the blood vessels," Greenleaf said. "They're warming the blood where it's thickest."

She glanced back at him, raising an eyebrow. "I suppose a kaviak would know where the blood flows fastest." She passed him a pair of mottled white breeches. "Put these on."

It took a moment to pull them on. The fabric was unlike anything he'd ever felt, slick and smooth. "I think it might be too small."

"Quite a high opinion you have of yourself, don't you? They're supposed to be snug."

He'd hoped that having some clothing on would make him feel less exposed, but the tight breeches offered little in the way of modesty. A snug tunic followed, sleeveless, the malheur sack on his chest a slight bulge right over his heart.

She circled him, using a long, thin strip of leather to measure a few points on his body. Satisfied, she went back over to the table, and began making some adjustments. "This is your first time, right? Out on the ice?"

He nodded.

"Whose fool idea was it for you to tail the hunters on this trip?"

"Ah, mine." At her incredulous look, he said, "It's been pointed out that I don't contribute to Lahar's food supply. I thought this might earn me a bit of respect."

She raised an eyebrow. "Think that likely?"

He didn't reply. The icy response that had greeted him on his first day in the village had yet to thaw in the slightest.

"Don't take it personally."

"People keep telling me that," he said tersely. "After a while, it's kind of hard not to."

"Fair enough. Just comfort yourself with the knowledge that if the Empress herself tromped into town in a ballgown made of crystals and moonbeams, they wouldn't give her more than a dirty look either. Especially if she spent the first few weeks poking through everyone's business and trying to start fights at dinner."

"I wasn't..."

"I figure you have your reasons. Whether they're stupid or not remains to be seen." She turned back to him, holding out a second pair of breeches. These were looser, made from a soft pelt of some kind. "Caribou leather. Blocks the wind quite well."

He pointed. "Why are there slits?" At several places along the outside of the breeches, long slits were held shut by small leather loop and button fastenings.

"There's no shortage of things in the white that'll end you, but the two you need to be most worried about are the cold and sweat," she said as he pulled them on. "This fabric is as waterproof as I can make it, but nothing's perfect, and if it gets wet, it won't be worth a fart in the wind. So don't fall in the water, and if you start sweating, open up vents to cool off until you stop."

"Hard to imagine that an issue out there," Greenleaf said, raising an eyebrow.

"Try harder. You're going to have four layers, malheur sacks pumping heat into you, and a poncho made from the hide of a snow bear. If you really get to huffing and puffing, you'll start sweating, and the Imperial Army will have to dispatch us a shiny new kaviak."

Next came a jumpsuit, layered thick with cotton padding, also featuring nearly a dozen vents in various places. Over that, a heavy poncho, mottled grey and white, that draped over his shoulders, leaving his arms free, with a heavy hood rimmed with thick fur. Boots and gloves made of heavy leather with thick fur on the interior finished the outfit. Elif walked slowly around him, making adjustments to the belt at his waist and the leather ties that kept the sleeves and cuffs of the legs snug against him, leaving no room for icy wind to slip through.

Satisfied, she nodded. "Remember. A frost suit doesn't make you invulnerable out there. It'll keep you warm enough when the sun is up, and hold the cold back for a day or so during the spring and summer. But if you get caught out there at night, it's not going to buy you more than a few hours." She made a few more adjustments. "You should be able to handle this yourself from now on. Here." She picked up an odd item, handing it to him. It was a pair of discs, rimmed in tightly wound reeds surrounding a circle of bone, set in a wide leather strip. A narrow horizontal slit was in the center of each disc.

"What's this?"

"Eye shields. Protects against snow blindness, not to mention ice crystals from slicing up your eyeballs."

Holding them up to his eyes, he frowned. "I'm supposed to be protecting the hunting party. Limiting my field of vision doesn't seem like the best idea."

She shrugged. "If the wind isn't too bad, and the sun isn't up, you can leave them off as long as you can stand it. But that Imperial anatomist will be a long time coming if you come back blind, and neither he or I will be able to do all that much about it."

Greenleaf nodded. "Thank you."

"It's my job." As he rose to leave, she glanced back at him, and said softly, "You got a bad roll of the dice, captain. If you give it time, and show us that you really are who you say you are, you'll figure out how to live here."

***

The road that came into Lahar Valley was cut down through the cliffs that surrounded the lava-warmed settlement, a gradual decline paved with slabs of whitestone. Unfortunately, that wasn't the way that Greenleaf was leaving the Valley today. He approached the cliffs to the west of the village, eyeing the steep ramp cut into the side of the cliff. It was narrow, less than six feet wide, without a railing or wall to prevent someone from tumbling off. As he made his way up, his boots crunched on gravel scattered over the stone to offer some traction. He could hear barking from the cliffs above. By the time he reached the top, Elif's warnings about exertion had been thoroughly demonstrated. His breath was puffing in the cold air as the top of the cliff came into view.

Twenty feet ahead, a group of six Laharians were gathered around a broad, flat sled, tied to eight snowy white dogs flopped out in the snow.

Several of the dogs wagged at Greenleaf's approach, but the humans all stared at him balefully. He couldn't recognize any of them at first. Each wore a frost suit much like his, their faces masked in wrapped wool, their heads covered by thick fur-lined hoods. One stepped forward towards him, eying him up and down. "You're late."

"I'm not," Greenleaf replied, meeting the green eyes burning in his direction. "Edeline said third bell. Haven't heard it chime yet."

"Fine. You're last. Wanted to leave five minutes ago."

"My apologies."

The man grunted, and said, "I'm Cole. Usually in charge of these things. Guess that falls to you, now."

Greenleaf shook his head, a mild headache already taking root as he looked out over the barren landscape. Drifts of white whirled and spun in the air, dancing through the white fog that covered everything. He wasn't cold. The malheur sacks were warm against his skin, and the only place that felt the bite of the wind was on his brow and eyes. "Cole, I'm here to do my part, but I have no clue where we're going, how we're getting there, what we're doing when we get there, or how we get back. If you really want me to be in charge, my first order's going to be to scrap this hunting party, and form a new one with someone at the head that won't get everyone killed. Far as I can tell, my role is to shut up, pay attention, and stand watch while you and your people do your job."

Cole nodded. "Okay. I suppose I can live with that. Never really needed someone to stand watch, but an extra set of hands can't hurt." He pointed back at the others. "That's Cailyn, Braddock, and Reif. They're the hunters on this trip. Braden and Poyel will run and check the gig lines, and break down the kills. I navigate and keep the dogs taken care of. Questions?"

"I thought Reif was a miner. Braddock works in the forge, doesn't he?"

"No one in Lahar has just the one job. Except you, I suppose. You bring rations?"

Nodding, Greenleaf said, "Enough for eight days."

"Only gonna be gone three."

"I'll have snacks."

Cole grunted again. "Throw your pack on the sled. You'll have to carry it back, but no reason to lug the weight."

"Understood." Following Cole back to the sled, Greenleaf dropped his army-issue pack next to two of the caribou-hide bundles favored by the Laharians. As Cole secured the load, Greenleaf turned to look over the others. Reif was easy to identify. The burly miner was the only one taller than Cole, by at least six inches. His face was exposed, a scarf around his throat. White frost was already forming over his straw-colored beard and mustache, but if it bothered him, he gave no indication. He was leaning his weight against a long spear, six feet of thick hickory topped with a blackened steel point.

"Forget your spear, Imperial?" White clouds puffed from his mouth as he spoke.

"Didn't forget anything." Greenleaf pointed at the spear. "That from the forge?"

"Traded a convoy for it couple years back. They don't let any of the weapons from the forge stay in town, they all go south," Reif said. "Why waste it here?"

"Seems like that'll do the job," Greenleaf replied. "An army pike isn't really ideal for hunting."

Reif opened his mouth to reply, and Cole snapped, "Enough. Time to move. Braddock, Poyel, you bring up the tail. Everyone else fall in."

Greenleaf followed as everyone tromped through the snow to a position behind the sled, forming a loose line. He fell in behind Reif and in front of the last two as Cole climbed up on two wooden pegs jutting out from the back of the sled. Taking a pair of leather reins in his hand, he barked a command that Greenleaf couldn't quite make out, and the dogs clambered to their feet, snow shaking off their bushy tails as they all started wagging. Cole let loose another whistle, and the sled lurched forward as the dogs began walking forward through the snow.

Greenleaf didn't understand at first why they all fell into step in single file behind the sled, but the reason soon became clear. It never moved faster than a walking pace. The front of the sled had a pair of weathered wooden planks affixed to the front, angled in to form a large wedge. As the sled knifed through the snow, the white drifts piled up to the side, leaving a hard packed layer across which the hunting party tromped. Once the sled had begun moving, Cole tied off the reins, and hopped off, walking just behind.

After an hour of walking in relative silence, Greenleaf spoke up. "Is there a particular reason that no one talks?"

"We talk." Poyel spoke from behind him for the first time.

"We don't usually need to watch what we say," Reif said without turning around. "Bit different this time."

Greenleaf raised an eyebrow. "I'll admit to being curious as to what exactly you feel the need to hide from me. But I'm here to help, not to spy on you." He was glad that his face was covered by the scarf. Lying had never been Greenleaf's strong suit.

"Really?" Reif spun off his heel, walking backwards as he faced the kaviak. "Got to say, hard for me to figure out what other reason you'd be coming with us, given that even you admitted to being dead weight."

"I'm here for ten years. I thought I could learn something."

The big man scoffed. "Lucky us. I'm sorry we're not more entertaining, Imperial." He turned his back on the kaviak.

"Who are you talking to?" Greenleaf asked, his voice hard.

"Excuse me?"

"Who are you apologizing for not entertaining? I thought it might be me, but you weren't clear."

"The fuck are you talking about, Imperial?"

"There, you did it again." Reif turned back to Greenleaf, coming to a halt, and Greenleaf snapped, "You might be talking to me, but considering that every single person here, including you, is an Imperial subject, you're a bit vague." He pointed past Reif to Cole. "Imperial." Chucked a finger back over his shoulder to Poyel and Braden, who'd stopped along with Greenleaf and Reif. "Imperial." Stepping forward, he jabbed a finger into Reif's hide poncho. "Imperial. Every single one of us. So if you have something to say to me, you can address me as Captain."

Reif's eyes burned, and he opened his mouth, but before he could respond, Braddock rested a hand on his shoulder. "Leave it, Reif."

His breath puffed in sharp exhalations, and his jaw worked. After a few moments, Reif gave an exaggerated bow. "By your orders, Captain. With your permission, mind if we return to the silence that was so damn preferable to your words of wisdom?" Without waiting for a response, he turned and stomped ahead, putting some distance between him and Greenleaf.

The captain looked at Braddock, who just silently turned and kept walking. Poyel and Braden wordlessly walked around Greenleaf, who sighed and took up the rear, listening to the crunch of his boots and the wind blowing across a frozen wasteland only marginally colder than his companions.

CHAPTER 7

The hunting party stopped three hours later. The sun had set long before, the shallow arc it took over the western horizon brief this time of year, but they continued on, the moon bright and full, spilling silver over the white landscape. They stayed at a pre-built shelter dug into the ground, huge slabs of the frozen sawdust mixture laid over the top, a small hole cut in the center. A large incline down below the surface led to a four-foot tall opening. Greenleaf ducked on his way in.

The dogs had already been brought inside. The interior of the shelter was nearly thirty feet on each side, the ice slabs overhead low enough that the soldier had to stay crouched. In the center was a pit, about six inches deep, dusted with snow drifting in from the hole overhead. Braddock and Cole glanced up as the soldier entered.

"Captain, did you bring a fire kit?" Cole asked.

Greenleaf nodded, dropping his pack and crouching beside it. "Where's the wood?"

"No wood." Cole pointed at a weathered barrel in the corner. Greenleaf peered inside. Reaching in, he drew out an odd clump about the size of his fist. It was hard and grainy, patches of green over a dark grayish brown.

"What is this?"

"Caribou shit." Reif had just entered, carrying several packs that he dropped in the corner.

Greenleaf wrinkled his nose, but gathered up as many chunks as he could carry. He made a small pile in the center, trying to keep some room for the fire to breathe. He dug through his fire kit, finding a few small chunks of fatwood, and used his knife to shave off a few small pieces. One of the others came up beside him, lowering her hood. Red curls spilled out, and she removed her scarf, revealing pale skin dusted with freckles.

"What's that?" she asked, peering at the amber-colored wood in the soldier's hand.

"Cailyn, right?" She nodded, and he handed her the chunk. "Fatwood. From the pine forests near Kaani. Lights pretty easily."

"Huh." She sniffed it. "Smells odd."

"It's the resin. From the sap of the tree."

Handing it back, she said, "You don't really need it. Mash up some of the scat, and it'll take a spark just fine."

"Good to know." Kneeling down, he struck the heel of his knife against a piece of flint from the leather fire kit. On the second strike, a few sparks tumbled down onto the fatwood shavings, and a small orange flame burst into life.

"Oh," Cailyn said, leaning down to watch. "Scat takes a spark, but it takes five or ten minutes of babying before it makes a flame. That works a lot better."

"Here." He handed her the piece of fatwood. "Speed things up for you next time."

"Thanks." She eyed him with a curious expression, and returned back to her bag, pulling a blanket out and setting up her sleeping area.

Within two minutes, the chunks of scat were burning with a merry blue flame, white smoke drifting up to the ceiling. The pungent scent of manure quickly filled the shelter, but once the fire was steadily burning, the Laharians began pulling off their ponchos as warmth filled the shelter. Greenleaf selected one of the only empty spaces, near the dogs, and sat down. To his surprise, Reif tossed his bag down a few feet over, taking a seat. "Hope I'm not encroaching on your space, Captain."

Greenleaf sighed. "Look, I'm not here to tell you what to do, or anything like that. I'm not sure what I did to get on your bad side, but..."

Reif didn't reply at first, pulling a small bundle from his pack, and sitting down on his blanket. He unwrapped the bundle, and pulled out a strip of dried meat. Glancing up, he offered it to Greenleaf. "Never had Imperial army rations before. Trade?"

Raising an eyebrow, Greenleaf nodded. "Your funeral. They're not very good." He handed a square of the hard golden bread over, and accepted the dried meat. Reif took a bite, frowning as he struggled to break off a chunk. He chewed for a bit, making a face.

"You're not lying. That tastes like moldy sawdust."

"We can trade back. Like I said, I brought extra."

"Nah." Reif leaned back against the wall, taking another bite. "It's terrible, but it's different. What's in it?"

"Spearman tears and sergeant sweat."

"Seems about right."

Greenleaf sniffed the dried meat. "Caribou?"

"Black seal."

The meat was salty and tough, with an odd mix of spices that drew tears to his eyes. Greenleaf coughed, reaching for his water skin. He tipped it up, but nothing came out. Peering inside, he saw the block of frozen water.

"Might be a good idea tomorrow to keep that inside your poncho," Reif said mildly, munching on another dry bite of hardtack. "Leaving it hanging outside your pack like that... You're lucky it didn't burst."

"Thanks for the tip," Greenleaf wheezed. "Couldn't have said something before we left?"

"Could have, yeah."

Greenleaf set aside the meat, smacking his lips as they tingled and burned. He loped over to the fire, setting the frozen water skin down near the blue flames, and came back over to sit back down. It was a few moments before the heat left his mouth.

Swallowing the last of the hardtack, Reif brushed some crumbs off his tunic. "That school you went to, the war school. Is it true that only one out of twenty finish the program?"

Taking another small bite of the dried seal meat, Greenleaf delicately chewed, trying to get used to the spice. "About that, yeah. What is on this stuff?"

"Dried ice peppers. We grow them in the farm." Reif pulled his water skin from beneath his arm and took a sip. "What do they teach you?"

"Combat tactics, weapons, survival, leadership skills, strategy... a lot of things." He glanced down at the water skin. "Don't suppose you'd like to trade anything for a drink."

"Nope."

"Didn't think so."

Reif took another long pull. "So four years of being trained by Imperial generals..."

"Five years."

"Okay, five. Five years. How many graduated with you?"

Greenleaf started to take another bite, but the steady heat scorching his mouth convinced him to surrender. Setting it aside, he pulled out another square of hardtack. "There were eight of us."

"So there really aren't that many of you kaviaks, are there?"

Greenleaf shook his head. "A few hundred throughout the Empire. Most serving in command roles."

"See, that's what I hope an educated man like you can help me with," Reif said, tilting his head. "We don't hear much about the rest of the Empire, but even we've heard of the kaviaks. Finest soldiers in the Empire, the best that our exalted Empress has to offer, and rarer than a white stag. So can one of their number please explain to a simple Laharian villager why Imperial command, in their vast and infinite wisdom, would waste such a valuable soldier on us."

The hardtack was bland enough to help offset the spice from the meat, but dry enough to make him regret the lack of water even more. Greenleaf made a face as he swallowed. "I was ordered to come here, to protect the subjects of Lahar. Guard duty isn't uncommon for kaviaks."

"Oh, sure. To guard the Shadowed Path, or the Imperial family, or something that actually needs protection." Reif sniffed the air. "Worst threat to us is the stink of burning caribou shit or an angry tiger seal. Not sure where combat tactics, leadership skills, strategy, all that bullshit comes into play. Unless you plan on using the spear you forgot to bring home a trijjat head."

"Funny," Greenleaf said.

"Reif." Cole looked up from across the room, his weathered face hard. "That's enough."

Holding up his hands, Reif nodded. "Fine." He glanced back to Greenleaf. "Thanks for the food. Tastes like shit, Imperial."

***

It was still dark when Cole shook him awake the next morning. Greenleaf finished rolling his blanket, lashing it to the side of his pack with leather straps. The ice shelter was quiet, with little conversation as the hunting party blinked bleary eyes, sipping a fragrant tea smelling of pine and mushrooms from small wooden mugs they all had hanging from their belt. Cole walked over to Greenleaf, offering his mug, nearly topped off with the tea. He cleared his throat as the captain gratefully accepted it. "Listen, ah, Captain. About Reif..."

The big man, crouched less than ten feet away, didn't look up from his pack at the mention of his name. Greenleaf waved it off. "Forget it."

Cole shook his head, but said, "All right. We've got about an hour before we reach the ice fields. Usually I stay with the dogs at the gig lines, but if you're willing to keep an eye on Poyel and Braden, I can go with the others and give them a hand, maybe see if we can't haul back a bit more."

"You don't want me with the hunters?" *Trying to get rid of me, Cole?*

"No offense, Captain, but you're not familiar with how best to move over the ice quietly. I'd rather not lose a kill until you're a bit more comfortable out here." He glanced over at Reif. "And if I'm being honest, I think you'll get along a bit better with those two than you would the hunting party."

Greenleaf couldn't think of an argument, and after a few moment's pause, nodded. "Fine. Anything I can do to help while I'm there?"

"Braden!"

Easily the smallest of the group, Braden's head came up to just under Greenleaf's collarbone. "What's good, Cole?"

"The captain here is going to watch over you and Poyel, make sure you don't take a nose dive through a gig hole. Keep an eye on him?"

"Both of 'em, that's a promise." Braden's head bobbed up and down.

The smaller man fell into step beside Greenleaf as they trudged behind the sledge, the hiss of the rails against the compacted snow the only sound. Overhead, it looked as if someone had spilled a bucketful of stars over an inky black pool. To the east, a low mountain range poked up into the darkness, the white slopes reflecting silver light from the crescent moon peeking above. To his shock, he saw some small shape scamper out of the path of the sled, darting in a zig-zag pattern off into the darkness. "What the hell was that?"

Braden shrugged. "Probably a snow fox. They hunt in early morning. You ever met a Vetticcian?"

Still staring into the black, trying to spot the animal, the abrupt change of subject threw Greenleaf for a moment. "What?"

"A Vetticcian. I hear that some of them have visited the capital. You're from there, right?" Words tumbled out of Braden's mouth as if each was shoving the previous one out of its way in a desperate hurry. "Kaani. You came from Kaani?"

The hell? Greenleaf nodded. "I did. Uh, I haven't met one personally. Most of the trade delegations don't leave Tyum. The only ones that come to the capital are diplomatic, and they didn't spend much time at the War College. I've seen a few of them, though. One of the Five Families sent a delegation, and they were invited to attend the graduation ceremony."

"Did you see their ship?"

Raising an eyebrow, Greenleaf said, "Kaani is a thousand miles from the coast. Kind of difficult to sail a Vetticcian galleon up the river."

"Oh." Braden seemed disappointed.

"Why so curious?"

He shrugged. "One of the last convoys brought some books. He said they traded them to him for some black ferric wool, but he didn't read, so he let us keep them. One was from Vetticci. It's about their navy. It says they have over five hundred ships."

"I can believe it," Greenleaf said. "I've never been, of course, but I've seen maps of Pallia Bay. It's bigger than any of the islands in the Fingers, and that city lives and dies by trade. I'd imagine that takes a lot of ships to keep things running smoothly."

"He gave me a ducat, too. I have it back home."

Either this kid has a hell of a stone face, or... Greenleaf shook his head. "There are a few of those going around the capital. Not technically legal currency, but it's pretty hard to find someone who won't take coral."

Braden nodded. "When the bridge is done, are we going to be at war with Vetticci?"

Glancing down at him, Greenleaf asked, "How old are you?"

"Fifteen," Braden said.

"Fifteen." Greenleaf nodded. "I wouldn't worry too much about it. Last I heard, it's going to be at least ten years before that bridge is done, and there's still the entirety of the Dominion between the Breaking and Vetticci."

"Ten years." The pair glanced back behind them, where Reif followed. The big man shook his head. "That would make Braden here twenty-five. I would say he should worry very much about the possibility of the Unification starting up again."

"The Unification finished years ago," Greenleaf said.

"Did it." Reif raised an eyebrow. "The Empire conquered every square inch that lay before them. They took every island in the Fingers, every tribe and clan in the west, all the way from the ocean to the Greymare Peaks. Tallest mountain range in the world, impassable. That's what they said, right? Seventy-five years ago, they said the Unification would have to stop at the mountains. But the Chorale bore a road right through the bedrock, right through the heart of those mountains, a road big enough to open everything east of the Greymare to the Empire's armies." He scoffed. "The only thing that stopped us from going south was the Breaking. A chasm, miles wide, impossible to cross. But just like before, the Chorale finds a way."

"The Empress has said nothing about bringing the Unification south of the Breaking." Even to his ears, the official Imperial line sounded a bit hollow, but Greenleaf kept his voice even.

"Do you think she said anything before her sorcerers burst through the eastern walls of those mountains?" Reif said. "When that bridge is finished, when the Empire touches the Dominion, this long rest we've all enjoyed, that comes to an end. You know it, Imperial. So don't feed Braden here a pile of shit about not worrying about the bridge."

Greenleaf shook his head. "The Empire doesn't conscript people essential to supporting the war effort. There aren't that many people in Lahar, and the mine and forge will become more important than ever if we ever find ourselves at war once more. I can't imagine many Laharians will be called up."

"Really," Reif said. "That why Cole here did twelve years with the legions fighting the clans? Edeline spent eight years away from his family working in a weapons depot in the Greymare Peaks." His eyes narrowed. "My father did ten years on an Imperial sloop. He left Lahar with ten fingers and a brother. He came back with eight fingers and a damn ruby teardrop. The Empire takes what it wants. Why should the sons and daughters of Lahar be any different?"

Greenleaf's jaw worked under the wool scarf. Braden's eyes darted back and forth between the two. Finally, Greenleaf turned and began following the sledge again.

The stony silence lasted for a while. The winds were gentler this morning. Instead of hurling tiny knives of ice against his exposed brow, tiny whorls of snow traced lazy spirals above the ground. When the first golden light of the sun erupted over the eastern horizon, it poured over the barren landscape, scattering yellow light across the gentle rolling slopes across which they walked. The sky lightened as the sun began its shallow, abbreviated arc. It would stay close to the horizon as it traced its path to where it would disappear, as if frightened to get too high overhead.

Everything seemed impossibly far. Greenleaf could see a handful of the strange malheur trees, interrupting the empty white expanse like broken fingers poking up through the ice, the needle-like leaves barely visible in the distance. He peered at one, and couldn't tell if it was a mile away or a dozen. The empty landscape defied easy measurement. He looked up to spot the guiding star, but most of the stars had melted into the pale grey sky, only the most stubborn still visible.

Something glinted on the horizon. He thought it just a trick of the light, but it happened again. "Is there something out there?"

Braden nodded. "It's the spire. From the Old Lyceum. The tip of it pokes out of the valley, reflects the sunlight. When it's dark and the aurora is in the sky, it looks like it's glowing purple or green."

"How far is it?"

"It's far. Thirty miles, maybe more? No one goes out there, but it's pretty." Braden pointed past the flickering reflection. "See that?"

The horizon was hard to make out clearly, but he could see one mountain towering high above the others, disappearing into a wisp of clouds. "Is that the Watchtower?"

Braden nodded. "The Serao comes from there. Biggest mountain in the Fingers."

Motion drew his attention, closer than anything else. It took a moment, but he could see a long strip of brightly dyed fabric, the color of flame, gamely fluttering in the weak breeze at the top of a gentle rise to their right, about half a mile away. To the north, a second strip of cloth hung from a long metal pole driven deep into the ice. "What are those?" he asked, pointing.

Braden followed his extended finger. "That's the border."

"The border?" Greenleaf shook his head, confused. "We're in the middle of Suivev. There's no border anywhere near us."

"It's not that kind of border." Braden glanced at the others, then said, "We don't go past the orange flags. It marks where we're not safe anymore."

"What's past them?"

"The ice."

"There's ice everywhere," Greenleaf pointed out. "What's different about out there?"

Braden didn't answer. "I'm going to go see if Cole needs help." Without waiting for a reply, the boy jogged ahead, shouldering his way past Braddock towards the sledge at the front of their strange procession."

Greenleaf could hear Reif's footsteps as he crunched closer, falling into step beside the captain. The big man was scowling.

"I have to ask you a favor," he said, keeping his voice low.

Greenleaf raised his eyebrow so high he thought he'd strain something. "Really."

"Yes, you ass."

"This should be good."

Reif stared ahead, silent for a moment. Finally, he muttered, "I shouldn't have mentioned Cole's time in the war. He doesn't like to talk about it." His jaw worked for a moment. "I'm holding out a very small sliver of hope that might be something that even you can respect."

Whatever Greenleaf had been expecting, that wasn't it. He blinked several times. "Done."

"Really." Reif glanced over at him, frost tumbling down from his hood. "Just like that."

Greenleaf watched Cole far ahead, next to the sled, as he tromped over the snow. Now that he knew to look for it, he could see the hunched shoulders, the eyes scanning the white horizon, the hand never straying far from the long knife on his hip. Greenleaf had seen the same in his father while they walked through the hunting grounds north of the capital in the years before he'd left for training. "Just like that."

"Thanks." Reif walked next to him for nearly three minutes before he spoke again. "Braden's wasn't trying to be rude. Before, about the flags."

"No?"

"No," Reif said. "Braden doesn't know how to be rude, or dismissive. But he also doesn't want to talk about the border. No one does." He shrugged. "We don't go out there. Ever. We have our space. Lahar, and the road in, and the coastline. We have everything we need. The ice gives us that. The rest doesn't belong to us."

Greenleaf stared out at the line of drifting pennants. The white fog that always blanketed the area seemed thicker past this border, the low mountain range in the distance the only thing he could make out.

"When I got this assignment, I asked everyone I knew about this place. I heard that Laharians were primitive, backwards, superstitious. The only place that didn't take in foundlings, a hostile, stagnant community, only valuable for the steel they pulled out of the lava, and the weapons they forged over the heat."

Reif's eyes narrowed. "I've heard things like that before."

"I get here, and see what this village has built. The forge, the homes..." He shook his head. "Those farms. Gods, I've never seen the like. You're not backwards, and you're not primitive. You're more than most give you credit for, and I'll not deny it. But this place, this cold, isolated place, it seems baked into your bones. You're just like your home: Cold and distant. I've been here for months, and only a handful of people will even say hello. You're the only one who's said more than a few sentences to me, and each one of those sentences is carefully crafted to make me feel foolish, or to tear down the things I believe in."

He looked over at Reif, who walked wordlessly next to him. "You're Imperial, Reif. You were born in the Empire, and you'll die in the Empire. You can argue all you want that you're separate, independent, but you're wearing leather gloves and boots, and I don't see any cows. I came in on a road built with granite from the quarries outside Y'Shan, on wagons made from wood that didn't come from a malheur tree. Even those remarkable farms..."

"We built those farms," Reif snapped, his face flushed and eyes narrow. "Laharians built them, mixed the ice and sawdust for the walls..."

"Sawdust from where? You hiding a pine grove up your ass that you haven't told me about?" Greenleaf's gesture took in the empty wasteland. "Seeds from where? Soil from where? Edeline told me that the farms were a dream for a long, long time, but without Chorale sorcerers to shift the quartz for the panels, without the Empire's Gift, without pieces from every gods-damned corner of the Empire you spend so much time shitting on, they'd still be a dream."

They weren't walking anymore, but facing each other, feet apart, their voices carrying over the snow and ice. From the corner of his eye, Greenleaf could see that the rest of the convoy had stopped, Cole moving towards them.

"Lahar was here long before the Empire came."

Somewhere deep inside his head, a voice warned that he was crossing a line, but Greenleaf was tired of the icy winds and icy stares, and that voice was smothered under the cold satisfaction at seeing Reif's face flush with anger. "Lahar was a handful of shivering fishermen, constantly praying to whatever gods are stupid enough to find their way into this frozen end of the world that they'd catch enough fish not to starve." Greenleaf stepped closer, eyes locked with the dark pools of anger peering from under the fur-lined hood. "Lahar barely survived alone. It thrives as one small part of the Empire. Were we to really, truly leave you alone, you'd be back to scrabbling in the ice in a year."

Reif shook his head, snow falling from the stitched hide hood, breath coming in puffs sharp enough to punch through his scarf. "We don't need you."

"Me? Or the Empire?"

"Neither, you sanctimonious sack of..."

"That's enough!" Cole shoved between the pair, pushing them each back a step. "Reif, I can't send him back, but I sure as shit can tell you to drag your sour ass back across the ice until you find someone willing to put up with your bullshit. Another word, and you'll field dress every gods-damned fish and seal we pull out of the ice on your own, and drag the damned sledge back with your teeth. So make no mistake: This is a gods-damned fucking order." Cole's finger jabbed into Reif's chest, punctuating each word. "Shut the fuck up, now."

Before Reif had a chance to say anything, Cole spun on his heels. "And you. I can't give you orders, even if you say I'm in charge. I know that. And I know that this little shit has been a sore on your ass since you met him. But you can't walk around from the moment you arrive curling your lip like you smell some dung, digging through our lives and stirring up shit with our people, and expect hugs and fucking daisies in return. You can't walk around with a polished, rosewood, Empress-issued stick up your ass, then sulk about how no one likes you. You're supposed to be an Imperial kaviak, a soldier bearing the will of a royal family stretching back four gods-damned centuries, not a sullen child."

His shoulders rose and fell as he glared. In that moment, he reminded Greenleaf very much of his father. Cole asked, "You gonna arrest me? Report me to Proudlake?"

Greenleaf felt very, very small. He shook his head.

"Fine. Then do all of us a favor, Captain Greenleaf, and demonstrate how graduates of the Imperial War College shut the fuck up so that he can follow your good example."

CHAPTER 8

For the first hour after he and Reif had been dressed down by the older expedition leader, Greenleaf had fumed silently to himself, reviewing and discarding dozens of scripts for how he would confront Cole upon their arrival at the hunting grounds. But with nothing to fuel that anger, it began to sputter, and behind it lurked the uncomfortable truth about what the man had said. By the time they crossed a rise and the ocean came into view, shame had begun to worm its way uncomfortably underneath Greenleaf's skin.

The sight of the coast did provide a momentary distraction. During his training, Greenleaf's class had traveled to the small coastal city of Avaz, a small port with a handful of fishing boats and a pair of old Imperial junks, used exclusively for training. The waters off the southern coast of the Empire were calm and warm, forgiving of the clumsy efforts of young candidates trying their best not to embarrass themselves in front of the exasperated bosuns. The coastline there had been sand and gently waving reeds, drifting lazily under a warm ocean breeze.

The wind today may have been mild, but the similarities ended there. The ice they traveled on gave way to a rocky shore, dotting with chunks of dirty ice and snow. Instead of waves lapping at the shore, the water was a sheet of solid ice, stretching far out to sea. Several large snow gannets hopped from rock to rock, stretching their black tipped wings and squawking in outrage at one other, while a cluster of grey seals, half a mile away, spotted the oncoming hunting party, and slid through a hole in the ice, disappearing with a distant splash.

Reaching the point where the snowy terrain met the rocky shore, Cole brought the sledge to a halt, and the team wordlessly began to gather packs and gear off as the older man untied the dogs, lashing the sledge to metal spikes he hammered into the ground. Reif, Cailyn, and Braddock dragged a bundle of wooden slats off the sledge, quickly assembling it to the framework of a smaller sled tied to straps. The dogs fell in behind Cole, wagging and lapping at snow on the ground as he approached Greenleaf.

"We shouldn't be gone more than six hours," he said. "These two know how to set up the gig lines, so if you're able to give them a hand, that'd be helpful. Just keep your eyes on the hills. The wolves don't usually stray this far west, but the ice bears haven't started hibernating quite yet. If you spot one, just make a lot of noise. They don't like lively prey."

Greenleaf nodded. "Cole, I just wanted to say..."

"Don't. Either you listened or you didn't. Not much need for a speech either way."

"Right." He glanced over at Braden and Poyel, who were gathering their equipment, pointedly not looking over at the discussion. "Do we need a fire? Something to keep us warm?"

"Nah. We'll get back to the shelter before it becomes an issue. If something goes sideways, there's a hidebound coverall tied to the sledge. Those two know how to set it up." He clicked his tongue. He and the dogs fell in with the other hunters, and began heading north along the ridgeline.

Braden offered him a pair of flat assemblies of twisted metal. "Creepers, for your feet. So you don't slip on the ice." He strapped the creepers to the soles of his boots, and Greenleaf did his best to follow suit.

Greenleaf fell in behind Poyel out onto a large ice shelf jutting out to sea. He expected the footing to be slick, but a layer of oddly pebbled snow crunched beneath his boots, offering more traction than he'd expected. He looked out over the sprawling ice shelf, peering at the black water beyond. It was calm.

"Do you ever take boats out?" Greenleaf watched the pair of Laharians for any indication of alarm as he kept his voice even. "Try fishing in the deep water, instead of just close to shore?"

Poyel glanced over at him, raising an eyebrow. "Would you like to haul a boat out on the trip we just made?"

Not really, but you wouldn't be the ones bringing the boat. Greenleaf shrugged. "I know some of the southern fishing villages make animal hide canoes that are pretty light."

"Don't know how something like that would handle water this cold," Poyel said. "Besides, it wouldn't matter." He pointed out to the water. "See those white pieces of ice?"

"The little ones?"

Poyel nodded. "Yup. But they're not actually that little. You can only see the top of them, but below the water, they're the size of buildings. They bob and crash against each other all year. You find them all up and down the coast. I don't know much about boats, but I suspect dragging the bottom over jagged ice won't be good for it."

Greenleaf eyed Poyel as he spoke, trying to detect any hint in his tone. *If he's telling the truth... shit.* He tried counting the white slivers of ice, and gave up at thirty.

"Plus, Cole yells at us if we get too close to the edge of the ice," Braden piped up. "Further you get from shore, the more unstable it is."

Greenleaf came to a stop, scanning the ocean and the ice shelf upon which they stood. *Any ship big enough to make the trip up here would draft at least fifteen feet. Add in the icebergs and the difficulty reaching shore... Would anyone even attempt this?*

"Uh, Captain?"

He looked over at the pair of Laharians, who had paused to look back at him. "Everything okay?" Poyel asked. "We really do need to get started."

Greenleaf nodded slowly. "Yeah. Just... Not what I expected." He fell into step behind them.

A few hundred feet from the shore, Poyel dropped to a knee, and pulled a large wooden flask from his pack. Uncorking it, he poured a viscous amber fluid onto the ice. It steamed as soon as it struck the surface, pooling to the size of a shield. Greenleaf leaned in, eyes widening, and Poyel glanced up. "Malheur sap. Beats chipping one out with an ice axe."

Over the next fifteen minutes, Poyel poured seven more pools of the sticky amber liquid, melting a total of eight holes through the ice. By that time, Braden had arrived with several bundles of thick sticks, bound with leather cord, a leather bag, and several large metal spikes. Hammering the spikes into the ice a few feet from the gig holes, he assembled a small wooden framework with a tiny silver bell hanging from the side, unspooling waxed hempen line through the loops in the frames. He tied one end to the spike. The other end of the line was wrapped in leather, protecting his hands from the half-dozen barbed hooks lashed to the cord. He baited each with a chunk of frozen meat, and tossed the line into the dark water.

By the time Braden had baited the last of the gig lines, the first two gig lines were softly ringing, the lines twitching and shifting against the edge of the ice. Poyel ran to the first, and began hauling in the lines. Greenleaf jogged to the second, calling out, "Tell me what to do!"

"Pull it in! Don't jerk it, and don't wrap the line around your hands," Poyel said. "If they're tugging too hard, it'll cut your glove. If it's a choice between losing the fish or cutting yourself, let the fish go."

"I can handle a few scrapes and nicks," Greenleaf said, taking the thick line in his gloved hands.

Poyel shook his head firmly. "You get cut, it means your frostsuit got cut, and then we have a whole other problem. Bruises are fine. But you start bleeding, you tell me right away."

Over the next few hours, the trio kept up a steady pace, running from hole to hole as the bells chimed over and over. Within ten minutes, Greenleaf had to pause to unfasten several of the vents on his frost suit, his chest heaving and sweat beginning to bead on his brow. The cool air worming its way through his layers was a relief, but there was no time to enjoy it. He fell into the rhythm of gripping the lines, and hauling them back, hand over hand, foot by foot, until the thrashing body of the fish burst out of the dark water. The orange and grey-striped fish were between two and four feet long, their muscular bodies sending sheets of icy water from the holes as they hurled their formidable weight from side to side.

The gig frames allowed for the fish to be dragged onto the ice, about a foot away from the hole. They would tie off the lines, and using heavy iron hatchets, finish the ice char off with sharp blows behind the eyes. The still-twitching fish would be dragged to a growing pile about twenty feet back. There was seldom time to catch a breath before the soft jingling brought one of the trio running back to the holes, the metal creepers on their boots scraping against the ice.

"This is wild," Braden puffed as Greenleaf helped him haul in a furious char larger than any they'd seen. "Most trips, we pull fifteen, twenty from the water in a day. We've got twenty-five, and they're still running!"

"Must be a school under the ice," Poyel grunted as he reset a line. "Cole's gonna be mad."

"Why?" Greenleaf asked, kneeling down to smash the flopping fish's head. It took several blows before it reluctantly stopped fighting. "This seems like a good thing."

"It is," Braden said. "But if he'd known the gig lines were going to pan out like this, they would have stayed behind to help. We could have really brought in a haul, rather than those four burning daylight chasing seals."

Greenleaf straightened up, stretching his aching back. "How often do you come out here like this?"

"Twice a week in the summer," Braden said. "We slow down as the days start to shrink. When the water gets warmer, the fish head back out to sea. Catch is usually lighter."

"Not today," Poyel said as another line jingled. "Must be a cold water current along the shore. Brought the char into feed."

After three hours of near-constant effort, the pile of fish was huge, nearly the size of the sledge, the cold already freezing the dead char. Greenleaf's arms and back were burning from the exertion. He was trying his best not to show his exhaustion. Every one of the vents on his frost suit were open, and he'd dropped the scarf to expose his face.

It had been nearly five minutes since the last gig line had chimed, and the three sat on the ice, catching their breath.

"Thanks," he panted, and the other two looked up at him in confusion. He gestured at the pile of fish. "For letting me pitch in."

Poyel raised an eyebrow, and Braden grinned. "Not sure I've ever had someone thank me for putting them to work like that."

"Never got to do anything like that before," Greenleaf said, shrugging. "First time since I've been here that I didn't feel like a glorified decoration, like I was actually contributing."

Neither of the Laharians seemed to know how to respond. "Can't be easy, coming here," Braden said. "I've lived around the same people my whole life. Don't know what I'd do if I had to go somewhere I didn't know anyone."

Greenleaf nodded. "I always thought that wherever I'd be posted, there'd at least be some other soldiers stationed with me. Being alone here..." He cleared his throat, shifting uncomfortably. "Not how I pictured it."

Poyel slowly climbed to his feet, trudging over to the pile of char. He drew a small belt knife, slicing a strip of flesh from one of the first few they'd caught. He tromped back over, creepers clicking loudly on the ice, and carved a slice of the raw fish, offering it to Greenleaf. "Tradition. From your first trip. Everyone eats a piece fresh off the first they pull from the water."

Greenleaf raised an eyebrow. "It's raw."

"Yup."

"Did you clean that knife?"

"Nope."

He took the meat, which was partially frozen. Greenleaf sniffed it, and glanced up at the two of them. "You both did this?"

In response, Poyel carved a chunk off, pulled down his scarf, and popped it in his mouth. Greenleaf raised an eyebrow, but took a bite. The flavor was stronger than any fish he'd ever had, and his eyes widened as he chewed. "It's good!"

One of the gig lines chimed, and Braden clambered to his feet, grinning broadly. "Wait until you try seal liver."

"Need help?" Greenleaf asked, taking another bite.

Braden waved him off. "I'll shout if I do."

As the young Laharian trotted away towards the jingling line, about thirty feet away, Greenleaf glanced over at Poyel. "He was joking, right? About the seal liver?"

"Nope."

"Not sure I've got the stomach for that."

The faint sound of barking echoed over the ice from a distance. Poyel glanced to the north. "By the sounds of it, you won't have to wait long to find out."

"Great. I'm sure Reif'll be delighted to watch me vomit on my boots." Greenleaf narrowed his eyes as he peered at Braden, who had just slipped as he struggled with the gig line. "I think he's having some trouble. Should we go help him?"

"Yup. He goes in the drink, Cole will make us go in after him." The pair rose to their feet, and made their way over to the fishing hole, creepers scraping along the ice. Braden was puffing when they arrived, his face red.

"Line'll go slack, then it yanks right out of my hands," he said. As if on cue, the line jolted forward, dragging through his gloved fingers with an alarming speed. "Bastard must be huge, and not in the mood for some fresh air today."

Greenleaf grabbed the coil of gig line behind Braden, which was rapidly unspooling into the black water. He started to wrap it around his hand for a better grip, but thought better of it, and dug his creepers as far into the ice as they could, bracing himself for when the slack ran out. Seconds later, the line snapped tight in his gloved fists, nearly jerking him off his feet. He tightened his grip as much as he could, but the line kept hissing across the thick leather. "Gods. I don't know that we can get this one in."

Poyel was moving quickly, lashing another length of line to the ice anchor and tying it to the existing line, doubling the length. "Big or not, they all get tired sooner or later." He frowned down at the line zigzagging wildly through the exposed water. "Don't know if it'll fit through the hole if it's that big."

"If it doesn't, what do we..." In an instant, all tension from the line vanished, spilling him and Braden back onto the ice. Greenleaf cursed, but Braden was already hauling the line in as fast as he could. Together, the pair pulled until the hooked length at the end emerged from the water. A mangled char head dangled from one of the hooks, the barbed steel jutting out from its upper jaw. The flesh dangling from the bottom of the neck was torn and bloody.

"What the hell." Greenleaf clambered back to his feet as Braden's face fell. "A shark, maybe?"

Poyel shook his head. "Too cold for sharks."

Braden leaned over the ice hole, peering down at the water. "Whatever it was, they owe me a fish."

"We've got plenty," Poyel said. "Come on, we heard the dogs. They'll be back soon." He turned to leave, but paused at Braden's voice.

"What's that?"

Greenleaf walked over to look down in the hole. For a moment, he saw nothing but the frigid water lapping at the melted ice edges, but a shadow darted past once, twice, vanishing back into the water. "Another char, maybe?"

"Maybe. They don't usually come so close to the surface." Braden leaned closer to the water. Something twinged at the back of Greenleaf's mind, a quiet, distant alarm bell.

"Hey, let's get back to the catch."

Braden looked back up at him. "I just want to see what it is."

Greenleaf opened his mouth to make it an order, but the shadow appeared again, a small distortion in the center of the hole that rapidly grew. His eyes widened as something took shape in the water. Reaching out, he grabbed the back of Braden's frost suit, intending to pull the boy back, and began to shout. There wasn't time.

The ice exploded.

The frozen rim around the hole shattered as if struck from beneath with a massive hammer, chunks of white ice flying into the air. The section Greenleaf and Braden stood upon lurched and jolted upwards, hurling the two of them back. The grey skies flashed overhead as Greenleaf flew through the winter air for what felt like an impossibly long time, until the solid sheet of ocean ice came hurtling up to smash into his back. His head smacked painfully back off the ice, and lights popped like fireworks in his vision. He vaguely registered the grunt of Braden smashing down next to him, sliding back over the ice like a thrown toy.

Without thinking, Greenleaf rolled to the side, coming up on his feet, turning to face the remnants of the fishing hole. His eyes widened as he saw the creature thrashing its way up onto the ice. He'd seen drawings of Suviev sea lions before, but nothing like this. The animal was massive, the size of a covered wagon, sleek black fur streaked with golden stripes, two front flippers slamming down on the ice with ear-splitting smacks that echoed across the coastline like cracks of thunder. Its head was jet black, bulging onyx eyes darting around above a snout covered with stubbly whiskers, water spraying as it snapped its jaws at the air. A pair of tusks, gleaming white and half the length of Greenleaf's arm, jutted down, chunks of fish still stuck to the ivory.

Snapping its head from side to side, the sea lion spotted Braden, unmoving, and it roared. The sound was a guttural shriek that rolled over the ice, the maw of the creature stretched wide as it bellowed in fury. There was nothing graceful about its movements. When it charged, it flexed the muscles in its bulk, lifting its massive chest off the ice and hurling itself forward. The ice cracked, but held as the bull stormed forward. The twenty feet between the sea lion and its prey shrank quickly, but suddenly Poyel was there, jumping between Braden and the onrushing bull. He held a gaffing hook in his hands, and swung it as hard as he could. The wood shaft of the hook smacked into the bull's head and shattered, the metal hook spinning off to clatter onto the ice. In response, the bull ducked its head, snapping it up to slam into Poyel's hip, hurling the smaller man in a boneless arc to smash down onto the ice.

Greenleaf pulled the knife from the sheath on his belt, and snapped his hand forward without conscious thought. The knife flashed out, striking the sea lion just over the front flipper, a laughably small splinter in the sleek black flank, leaving a small scarlet scratch as it bounced off. Somehow, it was enough. The huge head whipped to the side, beady eyes fixing on the soldier thirty feet away, and the bull roared again as Greenleaf dropped into a ready stance, ripping off the glove from his right hand, his thumb brushing over his first three fingertips. The aquasteel bracer erupted into liquid motion, and as the bull began to charge, the gleaming spear fell into Greenleaf's hand.

Part of his mind was busily screaming in terror, cataloguing all the ways that he was about to die. That voice fell silent, and a new voice stepped to the front, calmly dissecting the situation.

It's big, strong. Faster than you expected. Keep it occupied, keep it busy. The hunters are coming.

The bull's momentum gobbled up the distance between them in a few quick heartbeats. Greenleaf stood, motionless, until the right moment. The bull dipped its head to smash Greenleaf the way it had Poyel, but when its head came back up, the kaviak wasn't there. The soldier had leapt to the side, creepers skidding for a moment on the ice before gaining purchase, and the point of the spear flashed twice in quick succession. He'd meant to strike the eye, but the slick ice threw off his aim. The leaf-shaped blade kissed the sea lion, once on the snout, once an inch behind the eye. Each time, the razor edge left a deep incision swelling with steaming scarlet.

Thrashing its head from side to side, the sea lion's roar raced up nearly a full octave, howling in pain. When it whipped its head over to try to catch him with those wicked tusks, Greenleaf was ready, diving to the left, landing in a roll and coming up in a crouch. The bull undulated, massive muscles flexing under its skin, and its entire back half whipped in a blur towards Greenleaf like a meaty scythe. He was not prepared for that.

It was like being struck by a charging ram. The tail hit the kaviak just above his hip, and Greenleaf felt something snap in his left side as his feet left the ice. For the second time in only a few moments, he found himself hurtling through the cold arctic air. The spear flew from his hands, skidding and spinning over the ice to come to a stop over thirty feet away. Greenleaf managed to roll when he landed, tumbling over the ice until he came to a stop. Something poked into his side. It was the broken hook from the gaffer, the rusted surface already covered in hoarfrost. Scrambling to his feet, Greenleaf picked it up, the cold steel burning like fire against his bare palm.

He'd apparently been thrown far enough from the bull that the animal decided he was no longer a threat. It had turned back to where Poyel lay groaning on the ice, curled into a fetal position, clutching at his abdomen. The bull wriggled forward, slamming its front flippers down to pull it across the ice, slithering towards the incapacitated Laharian. Greenleaf quickly considered all of his options, dismissed all but one as doomed to failure, and the last as near-certain suicide. Gritting his teeth, he ran forward as fast as he could on the ice, and leapt onto the bull's back, bringing the hook down to sink deep in the flesh behind its neck.

The resulting bellow was deafening this close, and Greenleaf's empty left hand scrabbled at the wet pelt of the sea lion, trying and failing to get a grip. His bare skin was white around the pitted steel of the hook, gripping as hard as possible as the bull bucked violently, trying to throw Greenleaf free. Blood fountained from where the hook had pierced into its back. When the red drops splashed over his bare fingers, it felt like boiling water.

Somehow, he managed to keep his grip. Reaching around, he found the second knife he kept in a horizontal scabbard at the small of his back. Between the writhing bull and the fact that the sheath was designed to be drawn from the right, it took him several tries to wriggle it free. Once he did, he drove the ten-inch dagger deep into the sea lion's flank, less to wound and more to get another grip.

The bull bucked again, and its spine came up, smashing into Greenleaf's jaw. His teeth snapped shut, catching the tip of his tongue, and the bright, coppery taste of blood filled his mouth. His hand slipped off the leather-wrapped hilt of the knife, and the sea lion snapped its body sharply to the side. Greenleaf felt a tearing pain in the palm of his right hand as he was thrown free, spilling onto the ice a few feet away. He rolled onto his back, and saw the tusks of the sea lion rear high overhead, ready to spit him through the chest, but something brought the big head snapping quickly to the right.

Through the disorientation, he could hear the baying of hounds. Just past the bull's massive chest, he saw three of the grey-haired dogs about ten feet away, snarling and growling at the sea lion, ears flat against their head, teeth bared. They were pitifully small compared to the bull, but as its head shifted from one to another, the other five dogs ran up, forming a ring around the animal. Snarling and barking, they hopped back when the sea lion turned to face them, while another darted in to nip at its flanks.

Lifting his head, Greenleaf could see four figures running across the ice, slipping without creepers, spears clutched in their fists. Reif was at the front, and when he was fifty feet away, he planted his feet and hurled his spear with practiced movements. The blackened steel point flashed through the air, sticking deep in the sea lion's shoulder. It bellowed in pain. Moments later, Braddock's spear flew true, burying in the bull's flank, and an arrow struck its forehead. The projectile bounced off, but it left a red laceration over the sea lion's eye.

Between the furious barking of the dogs and the men running towards it, the bull paused, its head bleeding from several wounds as it swung frantically about. It roared once more, and turned to head back to the shattered hole in the ice. The dogs started to pursue, but a barked command from Cole brought them to an immediate halt. They continued to bark and snarl until the sea lion, blood dripping from several wounds and a spear wobbling from its shoulder, slipped back into the dark water.

Braddock skidded to a halt next to Greenleaf, dropping to his knees and helping him up. Greenleaf instinctively planted his right hand against the ice to brace as he stood, but it slipped, and he stared dumbly down at the streak of blood on the ice. He turned his hand to see the palm, and said, "Oh." The flesh of his palm, along with the inside of three fingers, had been flayed, the skin ripped away. He remembered the pain when he'd gripped the steel hook, and the tearing sensation when he'd been thrown free. "That's not good."

"Gods." Braddock pulled his scarf from his face, and began wrapping Greenleaf's ruined hand, bundling the fingers together. "Why the hell would you take off the glove?"

"Couldn't call my spear with it on." Greenleaf took a deep breath, and was rewarded with an agonizing streak of fire up his side. "Braden, Poyel. Are they…?"

"Cole'll see to them." Braddock frowned. "I need to make this tight. It's going to hurt." Without waiting for a response, he cinched the scarf tight around the shredded flesh. Greenleaf frowned.

"It doesn't hurt. Not really."

"Shit." The smith shook his head. "Come on." He took Greenleaf's arm over his shoulder, helping him to his feet. Greenleaf saw Poyel on his feet, still clutching his stomach, but waving Reif off as the miner tried to help him. Past that, Cole was tending to Braden, who lay unmoving on the ice. "Reif!" Reif turned to them, and his eyes widened as the pair hobbled over. "We need a fire. His hand is in bad shape. Frostbite's setting in."

"Where's your glove, Imperial?"

Greenleaf waved his hand idly back towards the shattered ice. "Not sure. Over there, maybe." He could feel his words slurring in his mouth. The adrenaline that had narrowed his focus and powered him through was fading, and he was starting to tremble. The pain in his side was a throbbing fire, but his hand was now completely numb.

"We're not going to make it back to the shelter before sundown," Cole said as he walked up. "You two, go start setting up the hide coverall. We've got maybe four hours before the temperature starts to drop, so hurry."

Braddock began to move, but Reif said, "I don't know if that's a good idea, Cole." He was staring at the ice, about six feet away from where they were standing. Scarlet was streaked across the slick white surface. Cole saw it, and his face paled.

"Is that your blood, or the sea lion's?" he asked, looking over at Greenleaf.

"What?" The kaviak shook his head. "I'm not... I don't know. Mine, I think. I pushed myself up. It's not bleeding anymore. I'm okay."

"We have to make it back to the shelter," Reif said to Cole.

"There's no way." Cole glanced up at the sun. "The hillside. Think we could do a dugout?"

"We have what, four hours at most?" Reif asked. "It'll be tight."

"Go. There are shovels lashed under the sledge." With a nod, Reif jogged over towards the sledge, calling out to Braddock.

Greenleaf limped forward. "The bleeding has stopped. What's the problem?"

Cole glanced over at him. "How bad? Your injuries, I mean."

Prodding gently at his side, Greenleaf let out a hiss of pain. "Two, maybe three broken ribs. Don't think anything's leaking inside. My hand is bad, but it should keep until we get back." He shook his head, trying to clear the fog. "You didn't answer. What's the problem? Why won't the hide shelter work?"

Throwing Greenleaf's arm over his shoulder, Cole took some of his weight as they began to move. "I'm worried about predators. The smell of blood might draw them."

Greenleaf wasn't so foggy that he didn't recognize a deflection when he heard it, but the exhaustion and pain settling into his body left him little strength to argue. The pair made their way over to Poyel, who nodded weakly at Cole. "Just got the wind knocked out of me. I'll be all right."

"Braden?" Cole asked. The younger fisherman was still lying insensate on the ice six feet away, Cailyn crouched over him.

"It's not good," she said. "He's slipping in and out of consciousness. He hit his head pretty damn hard. We need to get him back to Lahar."

"First things first. We need a dugout. In the hillside, over there."

"What?" Poyel straightened up, and winced, clutching his side. "That'll take hours. We can have the coverall up in..."

"No coverall. We need the dugout." Cole tossed his head back the way they'd come. "Blood on the ice. Might be his."

Poyel's eyes widened above his scarf. Quietly, he said, "I'll go give them a hand."

"Your training, it included field medicine, right?" Cole asked Greenleaf, who nodded. "Cailyn!"

The woman glanced over at Cole, and straightened up. Walking over, she quietly said, "His right pupil isn't responding to light, and he's drifting in and out."

"I understand. The captain here is going to monitor him, keep him going," Cole said. "You and I need to go help them with the dugout." Cailyn opened her mouth to object, but Cole said, "No arguments. Reif will explain. If we can get it set up quickly enough, we'll load Braden on the sledge, and I'll send Braddock back with the dogs. They can move quickly without the rest of the load, get back to Lahar faster, bring back help."

She shook her head, but turned and headed towards the others, who had begun digging into the side of the hill leading down to the coast, shovels biting into the snow and ice. Poyel was using a spear to chip at the harder ice. Cole eased Greenleaf down on the ice next to Braden, who was mumbling something under his breath. Straightening up, the old hunter looked down at the captain. "I'm waiting for an argument."

A thousand questions were bubbling in his head, but Greenleaf shook his head. "You're in charge. Go. I'll keep him conscious." He gestured. "My spear, it's over there. Might be better to dig with than what you've got." Without waiting for a response, he turned to tend to his patient.

CHAPTER 9

B y the time red began to bloom over the horizon, the hunting party had dug a cave nearly fifteen feet deep into the frozen hillside, about six feet wide. Chunks of ice and snow were piled on either side of the narrow opening, a two-foot wide slit in the side of the rise, twin frozen walls of discard lining the entrance. The Laharians worked silently, frantically racing the sun's slow descent.

The temperature was dropping. The scarf Braddock had wrapped around his wounded hand wasn't nearly as effective as his glove had been, and the frigid air crept in, slithering up his arm, tugging shivers and gooseflesh as it tried to penetrate the frost suit. Greenleaf tried to focus on his charge. Braden slipped in and out of coherence, but Greenleaf wouldn't let him fall back into unconsciousness. Any question as to whether the boy had a concussion had been answered hours ago. His right eye bloomed with a halo of blood, and floated listlessly as the other darted around. He asked questions in a dreamy, slightly slurred tone.

Greenleaf told him stories, whatever tales from school and the capital that he could think of. He tried to ask Braden questions, interrogating him about everything from his favorite foods to his first kiss. Braden would gamely begin answering, but trail off mid-sentence, confused. When Cole came tromping back over, Greenleaf patted Braden on the shoulder and rose painfully to his feet.

"It's as good as we can make it," the older man said. His brow was flushed, and his voice weary. "We need to get him loaded onto the sledge. Braddock and Reif are prepping it." He crouched down. "How you feeling, Braden?"

"Hmm." The teenager looked up at him, his good eye dreamy and unfocused. "Head hurts, Cole. I'm tired."

He patted Braden's shoulder. "We're going to get you home as fast as we can, boy. It's going to be okay."

"Tired." Braden blinked slowly. "Want to sleep."

"Don't do that." Cole glanced over as the dogs barked. They dragged the sledge onto the ice, the lead pair of grey dogs stopping just next to Braden. One licked his face.

Together, Reif and Cole lifted Braden onto the sledge, securing him with straps and piling several blankets on top of him. Braddock was checking his frost suit, and asked, "How do I keep him awake if I'm running the dogs?"

"You don't," Greenleaf said. They glanced at him. "If you don't get him back soon, won't matter if he stays awake or not. You need to focus on getting him home. Can you navigate in the dark?"

"The dogs know the way," Cole said, scratching one of the Laharian hounds behind the ears. "They eat?"

"Chopped up some of the fish for them. They've all drank their fill of snowmelt."

Cole nodded. "Okay. Don't stop for anything. Wolves won't come near the sledge."

"What about..."

"If they come, they'll come here. Further away you are, the better."

Braddock nodded. "I'll be back with help as fast as I can." He climbed up on the foot boards, and took the leather reins in his hand. He barked out a strange word, and the dogs sprang into motion, their feet skidding over the ice until they gained enough traction for the sledge to lurch forward. Once they left the ice, they quickly picked up speed, until the hiss of the runners over the ice and snow faded into the growing darkness.

"Come on," Cole said. They tromped over towards the dugout. Cailyn and Poyel were outside the entrance, methodically smashing the wood for the collapsible sled into pieces. Greenleaf frowned as they reached them.

"What are you doing?"

"We need a fire, and we need it to last to sunrise." Cole looked over the pile of broken wood. "This it?"

"We have five pounds of caribou scat, give or take," Poyel said, gesturing at a pile of dried dung. "I can scout around for more, but they don't usually come this close to the shore."

Cole looked up at the deepening inky blue of the sky. The first few stars had emerged into the darkness, flashing brightly. A faint green and purple shimmer could be seen out over the ocean. "No time," he said. "We'll wait as long as we can to light the fire. Everyone in."

Greenleaf had thought the established shelter small, but it was a concert hall compared to the hastily excavated dugout. They left most of their gear outside, bringing in only water skins, spears, and a few extra blankets. Cailyn was laying out leather pelts on the ice floor, while Reif began stacking lumps of caribou scat just outside the entrance, piling a half dozen pieces of wood atop in a pyramid shape.

Poyel squeezed in, holding a Laharian spear in one hand, and Greenleaf's gleaming aquasteel weapon in his other. "Can you use this?"

Glancing down, Greenleaf tried to flex his injured hand. The spike of pain and stiff fingers were too much. "I can use my left hand, but not as well." He pointed to the Laharian spear. "Give me that one. You or Reif should take mine."

They all squeezed into the space. Poyel, Cole, and Greenleaf hunkered at the back, shoulder to shoulder. Cailyn and Reif crouched in front of the entrance, clutching spears, and staring out into the darkness. The aurora overhead threw emerald and amethyst light over the ice and ocean, but from his position at the back of the dugout, Greenleaf couldn't actually see the ribbons of light in the sky.

"Are you worried about another sea lion?" His voice was low. Cole shook his head.

"Suviev sea lions are territorial. Never find more than one bull for a hundred miles, excepting mating season." He snorted softly. "Of course, didn't expect to find one here." Greenleaf raised a questioning eyebrow. Cole said, "We see a lot of seals and brown sea lions around here. Suvievs, though…" He shook his head. "They follow the char, and the char don't come this far north. Water's too warm."

Greenleaf frowned. "Weren't those char that we pulled out of the water today?"

Both Poyel and Cole nodded. "That's the strange part. We fish this area for silver salmon. They congregate close to this part of the shore because of the warm water," Cole said. "There's a branch of the Serao, deep underground. It flows into the water under this ice shelf. The lava coming into this part of the ocean creates a hot spot. Perfect for salmon, but char don't like it. No char, no sea lions. There's no reason that bull should have been here."

Greenleaf glanced over in the darkness, hearing the tone in Cole's voice. "It wasn't your fault. From what you're saying, you couldn't have known this would happen."

"I'm in charge." Cole grunted. "Maybe I should have insisted that you take command."

"If it's anyone's fault, it's mine," Poyel said. "I knew the char shouldn't have been there. I was excited about the catch. Never gave it a second thought."

Looking over the narrow entrance, Greenleaf's stomach tightened at the thought of the bull lion returning. His blood was still smeared a stone's throw from where they huddled, and he didn't know whether the wounded creature would be drawn to it. "Cole." The older man looked over when Greenleaf spoke. "Are we in danger? Right now?"

Cole hesitated, then nodded slowly.

"Then we can argue about whose fault it was later. How long will it take Lahar to send help?"

"Assuming Braddock doesn't have to stop for any reason? Seven hours there, at least an hour to put together the rescue party, and seven back."

"Will the sun come up by then?"

Cole shook his head. "This time of year, it'll be sixteen hours before sunrise."

By this point, the only light coming through the entrance was the eerie green and purple hues from the aurora. They sat in relative silence. The dugout was warmer than Greenleaf had expected, particularly sitting so close to the others, and the exhaustion of the day's ordeal was quickly catching up to him. He found his eyes drooping. Blinking several times, he glanced over at Poyel. The fisherman had taken off his scarf, and was sipping from his water skin. His eyes were fixed on the silhouettes of Reif and Cailyn at the entrance. The steel of

Cailyn's spearhead was dull and blackened, but the gleaming aquasteel shimmered with verdant reflected light.

He blinked, and when his eyes opened, the dugout had plunged into darkness. The light from the aurora was gone. He'd been awakened by Cole and Poyel clambering to their feet, trading places with Reif and Cailyn. There was some whispered conversation between them that Greenleaf couldn't make out. Moments later, Cailyn settled down to his left, Reif to his right.

"How's the hand?" the big miner asked in a whisper, tilting his head close so Greenleaf could hear him.

"Doesn't hurt. At all." Greenleaf tried to bend his fingers, but the scarf was wrapped too tightly. "Hoping it's not as bad as it looked."

Reif grunted. "Miss Elif will patch you up."

"The woman who made my frost suit?"

Reif nodded. "She's a halfway decent healer. Not a trained anatomist, but knows quite a bit. She's the one who convinced us to dedicate one of the farms to medicinal herbs." He fell quiet for a bit.

Greenleaf was struck at the silence that swallowed the six of them. The waterline was too distant to hear waves. If there was wind, it made no sound. Every time that Greenleaf had spent time outdoors, the sound of insects and small animals scampering through the underbrush had been a constant drone in the background, but in this place, there was nothing. When Reif whispered again, it felt harsh and heavy, as if it was smashing through the silence.

"I'm not going to apologize for yesterday."

If anyone else could hear the two of them, they gave no indication. "I didn't ask you to."

"Good." Reif's jaw worked for a moment. "What you did, out there with the sea lion... You know how stupid that was, right?"

"That thought occurred to me pretty gods-damned fast."

"There are things out here you can fight. A Suviev sea lion, that's one of the things you run from."

Greenleaf let out a dry chuckle. "Believe me, I'd have preferred that."

"So why didn't you?"

"Braden was down. Not moving. He couldn't run." He shrugged, wincing at the needle of pain the motion sent through his side. "It's my job."

"You really believe that, don't you?" The miner stared at him, his expression unreadable.

Greenleaf nodded. "Eyes of the Empress, right?"

"Huh." Reif looked at him as if he didn't know what Greenleaf was. "I don't..."

They both fell silent as Cole glanced back, finger pressed to his frosted lips, brown eyes wide. He made no sound, but Poyel leaned forward into his crouch, gripping the aquasteel spear tightly in his gloved fists. Silence slammed down once again, and Greenleaf strained to listen. Several heartbeats passed, and then he heard the soft crunch, then another, and six pairs of eyes slowly swiveled to look at the ceiling of the dugout.

Something was walking on the hillside.

The steps were slow, tentative, each just barely louder than the last. Cole slowly passed the spear back to Reif. He turned back to the pile of kindling and dung, scraping his sole along the floor as he did so. The footsteps stopped. Cole dropped to a crouch, silently pulling a piece of grey flint from his fire kit, along with a curled striking steel. Earlier, they'd taken a piece of Greenleaf's fatwood, and a pile of the orange wood shavings sat near the middle of the kindling. Cole leaned forward, took a deep breath, and struck the steel against the piece of stone. The click seemed the loudest thing Greenleaf had ever heard, but no spark lit up the darkness. The snow crunched again and again, the footsteps making their way down the hill towards the entrance.

Cole shook his head sharply, and struck again. This time, a few orange sparks tumbled out, landing on a frozen chunk of caribou dung, winking out of existence almost immediately. Again. This time, a spark landed on one of the resin-soaked curls, and a flickering yellow flame sputtered into existence, eagerly gobbling up the fatwood shavings. The footsteps were loud now, feet crunching into the ice and snow. Something scratched at the wall of excavated ice to the right of the door as Cole leaned forward, blowing onto the weak flame.

There was another sound. Greenleaf leaned forward, his heart hammering in his chest, as he tried to make it out. At first, he thought it was a rattle. As a boy, his father had taken him hunting, and they'd nearly ridden into a golden rattlesnake curled under a rock. He never forgot that chittering whisper erupting from the slab of sandstone, never forgot how it raised the hairs on the back of his neck. Those same hairs were all straining outward now, as if trying to leap from his flesh to avoid the fate that sound prophesied. In between the sound of Cole's desperate exhalations, he heard it again, and realized that it wasn't rattling. It was chattering.

Greenleaf could hear someone's teeth chattering.

The acrid smell of burning dung reached his nostrils as the flame licked higher and higher, blackening the pale wood piled atop, the frost on the dung giving way to allow the shit beneath to smolder. Flickering blue and orange light threw dancing shadows across the white walls, the ice glinting and flashing in the firelight. That same firelight spilled from the entrance, pushing back the darkness. Cole and Poyel were in his way, but as he rose to a crouch, Greenleaf could see just past them. The end of the ice wall was just barely visible, a white barrier vanishing into the blackness, and as his unblinking eyes tried to trace the edge, he saw four long shadows curl around as something gripped the ice, slowly pulling a face around to peer into the dugout.

The fire continued to grow, spilling more and more light over the ruined face that looked in at them. The skin was rough and charcoal black, with splits in the cheeks revealing bloody furrows. Wide blue pupils, the color of sapphires, floated in the middle of ice white eyes, unblinking, lidless. If there had once been a nose, it had long since rotted away. There were no lips, no ears, no hair, just cold blue eyes staring from dead black flesh. The tip of a tongue, pink and thick, darted out like that of a snake, between cracked teeth erupting from grey gums like a rotting fence after a storm. When the tongue retreated back into the mouth, those broken teeth began dancing against each other once more, the chattering slithering in past the flames to fill the dark cave.

Cole and Poyel slowly stepped back into the dugout, blackened steel and shining aquasteel spearpoints trembling in the firelight. Greenleaf's blood was thundering in his temples, but he could hear Cailyn muttering under her breath.

"Please, Goddess, light the shadows... Please, Goddess, light the shadows..."

Greenleaf swallowed. His knife was in his left hand. Both Reif and Caitlyn were gripping their spears, but neither made any aggressive motions.

"Why don't you throw?" he hissed to Reif. The instant he spoke, those wide, unblinking eyes shifted to fixate on him.

"Shut up." Reif's voice was as quiet as he could make it, and he didn't look away from the creature.

"But..."

"It won't hurt it. Only the fire can keep it back." Reif swallowed as those empty eyes darted back and forth. "And it's not alone."

Greenleaf's breath fogged in the air in front of him, sharp hissed exhalations puffing in the cold night. "What is it?"

Cailyn paused her prayers long enough to hiss a single word. "Trijjat."

Greenleaf remembered his mother, sitting next to his bed, telling him the stories that he loved to hear, those that sent delicious shivers up his arms as she gleefully spoke of the fate of children that wandered in the night. The creatures waiting in the dark to reach out with spindly, clawed fingers, the ones he'd feared for several nights waited just outside the window over his bed, she called trijjat. He'd been terrified to pull back the curtains, certain that blue eyes would stare back at him. Those fears had been left in his childhood, but here he was, a world away, and the nightmare had found him.

It took everything he had to look away from the ruined face staring in at them, motionless except for the darting tongue and chattering teeth, but Greenleaf tore his eyes away, looking down at the fire. He had no idea how long they'd crouched, frozen in position, but the fire was now burning merrily, gobbling up the dung and wood, the pile of fuel shrinking every minute. Poyel slowly reached down, picking up another stick, and laid it carefully on the fire, which shifted under the addition, sending a shower of sparks into the air. One drifted lazily through the night, tracing glowing orange trails before landing on the impossibly long, black finger curled around the edge of the ice wall. The piercing squeal that issued forth sounded precisely like the unearthly shriek of the molten aquasteel hitting the frosted stone in the mine, and both the face and the fingers vanished back behind the ice wall.

Cailyn's muttered prayers mixed with the crackling fire and the heavy, rapid breathing hissing out from between Reif and Greenleaf's clenched teeth, but none of it was loud enough to disguise the chattering from out in the darkness. Moments later, the snow crunched again, this time to the left of the shelter.

Again, from further up the hill.

Something clicked against the sheet of ice stretching out into the night ocean, like a nail tapping on glass. A chunk of wood snapped loudly, another shower of sparks filling the entry to the dugout, and the eyes of all six fell to the fire, each willing the wood to burn a bit slower, the dung to smolder just a bit longer.

In the cold dark, broken teeth chattered.

CHAPTER 10

Any possibility of further sleep disappeared the moment those black fingers curled around the ice wall. Greenleaf had no idea how long they'd been huddled in the cave, but the splintered chunks of wood had long since collapsed into piles of coals, orange heat shimmering over the broken surface. The dung still burned with that cheerful blue flame, but while it seemed sufficient to keep the creature back in the darkness, the fire was slowly losing the battle against the cold.

He could no longer feel his arm. The malheur sack tucked under his armpit managed to keep the chill from creeping into his chest, but the numbness had crept past the elbow, the trickles of cold air slipping in the gaps of his makeshift bandage. The others weren't much better off. Reif's face was bare. He'd given his scarf to Braddock to replace the one wrapped around Greenleaf's mangled hand, and his cheeks were a deep red color, his eyebrows frosted white with ice crystals. Cailyn and Poyel were both shivering, taking turns getting as close to the weak fire as possible. Cole had not looked away from the dark entrance to the dugout. His hood was dusted with frost, and his hands kept flexing around the heavy shaft of his spear.

Hours passed with no words. Greenleaf thought that he had identified at least three different sets of footsteps outside. The staccato clicking of rattling teeth was faint enough that it was hard to judge direction or distance. Occasionally, he thought he could see movement out in the dark, but the flames had robbed him of what little night vision he had on this moonless night. The fire shifted again as Cole added the last piece of yellowed wood, not much thicker than an arrow.

"That's it," he said quietly. "That's all the wood. We have a few chunks of dung left."

Greenleaf tried to swallow. It was difficult. His lips and tongue didn't seem to want to work right. "How much longer until sunrise?"

Cole shook his head. "Seven, eight hours. At least."

"The fire won't last that long." It wasn't a question, but Cole answered anyway.

"No." He sighed, his breath hanging in the air, a small cloud drifting up. "Even if we didn't have to worry about..." He gestured vaguely at the darkness outside. "This shelter isn't enough to keep us warm. Even with the frost suits, I don't know how long we'll last."

Greenleaf considered. His thoughts seemed to take their time to form, as if his brain was slogging through molasses. "We need something else to burn."

"There isn't anything else." Cailyn said, glancing back from the fire. Her face was heavily shadowed.

Frowning, Greenleaf gestured at the spear she held. "What about that?"

She glanced down, and raised an eyebrow. "You want to burn our spears? Really?"

Looking over at Reif, the soldier said, "You said that the spears wouldn't help against them, right?"

Reif shrugged, the barest twitch of his shoulders. "The stories say no. I've never tried."

"We have five spears," Greenleaf said. "With that narrow entrance, that's at least three more than we can use effectively in here. The shafts, they're made of oak or hickory?"

"Hickory."

"Burns slow. Hot coals."

Poyel looked down at his weapon, nodding slowly. "We'd have his spear, even if we burned all four of the others."

"I don't like it," Cailyn said, tightening her grip.

"If that fire dies, they don't even have to come in here after us. Two, three hours, we'll be in no shape to put up any fight at all," Cole said. He nodded, and pulled out his belt knife. One edge of the long, blackened steel blade was notched with serrations, and he began slowly sawing at the spot where the haft met the spearpoint.

"Not there." Greenleaf struggled to his feet, and pointed about a foot down from the point. "Cut them there. You can still use them as daggers, and we can get a good amount of wood."

The spear hafts were thick, nearly three inches in diameter. By the time Cole had cut the first shaft into four foot-long segments, the blue flame was flickering helplessly. He threw the last fragment of fatwood onto the fire. It flared bright orange, spitting as the resin burned, throwing a harsh light over the inside of the shelter, and Cole lay the first three chunks in place.

Five minutes later, orange flames were licking at the wood. The hickory blackened and cracked, but compared to how quickly the yellowed pine had burned, the hardwood lasted much longer. The temperature inside the dugout began to rise.

"Do we have enough?" Reif asked Cole, still murmuring. "Enough to get us to the morning?"

All five watched the flames slowly nibble away at the hickory. "I don't know," Cole said.

It was impossible to say how much time had passed when Reif, at Cole's direction, began sawing at the next spear. The chattering outside had begun to fade, and there were long stretches of silence, the crackling of the fire the only sound. But it was never more than a minute before the could hear the crunch of snow nearby. At one point, Greenleaf thought he heard mumbled whispers from just outside the entrance. He couldn't make out the words. He didn't even know if it was words.

"What are they?" Greenleaf and Reif were sitting back to back, the others as close to the fire as they could get, and he kept his voice as low as possible.

"Hmm?" Reif turned his head.

"Outside. They're not really…" Reif didn't respond, and Greenleaf said, "Trijjat aren't real."

"That's a relief," Reif said. "For a moment, I was worried."

"Reif."

"What do you want me to say, Imperial?" There was none of the heat in Reif's voice from earlier. Just exhaustion.

"They're not real." Greenleaf didn't know if he was speaking to Reif or himself.

"How hard are you going to cling to that?" Reif leaned back against him. Greenleaf could feel him shivering. "You came in, assuming you knew everything about us, about who we were, where we lived. Even now, with us hoping that a few pieces of hickory are going to save our lives, even having looked right into its eyes, you're still trying to tell me what is and what isn't."

Greenleaf opened and shut his mouth. He realized that he was shaking his head without realizing it. Finally, he said, "Those are trijjat. They're real."

Reif nodded.

"Why did no one tell me about them?"

"We don't talk about them."

"Why not?"

The big miner shrugged. The temperature was slowly starting to rise in the dugout. Water was beading on the ice crystals adorning his eyebrows. "We just don't. Ever since I was a kid, that's the rule. We know they're real. But they don't come into Lahar, and we don't discuss them."

"But..."

"When we talk about them, things go badly for us." Cole was staring out into the blackness, his back to the rest of them, and he didn't turn around when he spoke, his voice hoarse. "Shipments stop coming. The convoys dry up. The Ministry of Allocation informs us that the Imperial Army needs everything, every bottle of wine, every scrap of fish and meat, and the Gift vanishes, for months on end." He coughed, a wet, deep cough that clawed up from somewhere around his breastbone. "The last time it happened, I hadn't figured out how to shave yet. We had a pair of hunters go missing. Never found anything but a broken sledge, shattered spearpoints, and the remains of two shredded frost suits."

He made no effort to keep his voice down. It was hoarse. He coughed again, and accepted the water skin that Poyel offered. "Thanks." He took a long drink. "The Empire is content with trijjat being stories told to frighten children. The moment we insist that they're anything but, Lahar truly becomes cut off. So we don't talk about it. I never said a word to anyone during my time in the army.

We don't talk about it to traders or visitors. We know, and we teach our children. Quietly, in a dark corner of our homes at night, when no one else is around. We tell them to keep their frost suits on, and to stay outside the border. We teach them to keep a fire burning in the night, and to never, ever let their blood touch the ice." Cole turned his head, his neck popping with a sound like a cracking log in the fire. The hollows of his eyes were dark, his lids heavy. "And we teach them to never, ever speak of it. Not to each other, not to anyone."

***

The sounds faded almost an hour before the sky began to lighten, but none of the five made any movement towards the exit. The hickory spear hafts had served well. There was still a few of the foot-long chunks unburnt, and the fire still quietly crackled. The entrance to the dugout faced west, so they couldn't see the sun peek over the horizon, but they could see the way the warm orange and yellow light scattered off the ice shelf and the distant waves. Finally, Cole rose to his feet. He held the aquasteel spear in his hand, and said, "Let me make sure it's clear."

"Cole, wait." Greenleaf struggled to his feet, and reached out with his left hand. "Let me."

"I have two good hands, captain."

Greenleaf raised an eyebrow. "Left handed and exhausted, but I'll still put money on me being a better hand with a spear than you are now. You disagree?"

Cole frowned. Poyel said, "He is a kaviak."

Reluctantly, the older man extended the haft of the spear. Greenleaf accepted it. "If anything happens, keep the fire burning," he said. "Don't come out after me."

"We won't," Reif said. Greenleaf glanced at the big man, who offered a weary grin.

"Well." Greenleaf walked in the squatting position the low ceiling demanded, stepping past the burning coals until he stood between the twin piles of snow that lined the entrance to their home for the night. As soon as he passed the threshold, he spun on his feet, putting his back to the sea and looking up at the hillside above them. His spear snapped up into a ready position, and if the motion was more sluggish than normal, he hoped the Laharians wouldn't notice.

The light breaking over the hills stung his eyes. He scanned the ridgeline above, looking for movement, but saw nothing. His eyes drifted down to the footprints in the snow. They were long and narrow, split in the center, and he swallowed as he realized how far apart they were. He turned slowly, eyes seeking targets as they tracked over the frozen coast. The neatly piled char was exactly where it had been left, a half-dozen butchered seals a few feet away. There was no trace of the holes they'd bored through the ice. Most of the gig lines were broken, lying where they'd fallen during the sea lion's attack. The place where the bull had burst through the ice was shattered and uneven, but the water had long since frozen over.

Greenleaf opened his mouth to sound the all-clear. Before the words left his lips, snow crunched above him, and he dropped into a combat stance, gripping his spear tightly. The gleaming point extended towards the top of the hill, and his heart hammered in his chest as the footsteps drew closer. When the grey-tufted head of a hound peeked over the ridge, his knees nearly buckled. The dog stood atop the ridge, wagging, and barked several times. Faint voices called out, and as Cole and the others slowly came out of the cave, Odel Deric rose into view, followed closely by Braddock, breath puffing hard from his scarf.

"They're here!" the mining foreman bellowed. Within moments, three dogsleds and a dozen Laharians came clambering over the hill. Braddock slipped as he ran down the hill, but Deric caught his arm.

"How's Braden?" Cole asked as soon as the two were close.

"Resting, at Elif's." Braddock's chest rose and fell as he caught his breath. "She says he should be okay. He went unconscious on the trip back, but she managed to wake him."

Laharians swarmed around them. Someone threw a heavy hide blanket, thick wool stitched on the inside, over Greenleaf's shoulders. If any of the villagers saw the strange footprints in the ice, they said nothing, crushing them beneath the caribou-hide boots they all wore.

Deric looked them over. "Anyone injured?"

Cole nodded towards Greenleaf. "The kaviak hurt his hand, badly. Lost his glove. Definitely has some exposure."

The mining foreman raised an eyebrow. "Is it true you decided to wrestle a Suviev sea lion?"

"Not exactly," Greenleaf said. He realized that he was still clutching the spear tightly, and willed himself to relax his grip. "It was a bit more complicated than that."

"Can't wait to find out what inspired that bit of lunacy." Deric raised his voice, barking at the others. "Get them loaded onto those two sleds! Braddock, Keirnan, you get them back as fast as possible, get our kaviak to Elif. The rest of you, help me load the catch." He clapped Cole on the shoulder. "We'll get it back. Go get patched up."

The sleds had been outfitted with benches, and the Laharians got the hunting party settled into place with practiced efficiency. Someone carefully pulled a new glove, larger than his previous one, over the makeshift bandage, and the gaps in his frost suit were quickly patched. Reif sat next to Greenleaf, Poyel in front of them, and Braddock climbed onto the runners, asking, "All good?"

Reif nodded, and Braddock barked a command, sending the dogs scampering into motion. Without needing to wait for hunters following on foot, the hounds quickly came up to speed, and the rails beneath them hissed as they flew over the ice and snow. The shoreline vanished behind them, and as Greenleaf leaned back and drew the blanket tight around him, he let out a long slow breath, watching wispy clouds drift through a dazzling blue sky.

CHAPTER 11

"**I** just made this frost suit for you," Mistress Elif said as she carefully pulled off the temporary glove. "Took you less than a day to lose a glove. How the hell does that happen?"

Greenleaf gritted his teeth as she began to unwrap Reif's scarf from his hand. "Needed a weapon. Thought it'd be better to pull off the glove, rather than have it shredded when the spear formed."

"Did you get it back?"

"No. I think it fell through the ice during everything."

"So really, you just wasted a few moments."

"Be nice," Braden said. The young fisherman lay on a cot on the other side of the house, close to the trickle of lava heating the interior. He had a bandage wrapped around his head, and his eyes were still a bit glassy, but he was perched up on his elbow watching her treat the kaviak. "If he hadn't done what he did, I'd have been squashed flat."

"Don't get me wrong. Losing the glove was far from the only stupid thing he did," she said. "Doesn't hold a candle to deciding to tackle an angry bull." Elif had nearly finished unwrapping when Greenleaf muttered a curse. The wool was stuck to his hand, and when she tugged, a spike of sharp pain had jolted up his wrist. She picked up a sharp curved blade, and began easing it under the makeshift bandage. It took a few moments, but she finally pulled the ruined scarf free.

Greenleaf's eyes fell upon his exposed hand, and his stomach lurched. His free hand flew to his mouth as he felt gorge rise in his throat. Elif's eyes widened, and she leaned over to grab a bucket, nearly tipping out of her stool as she did. "Here!"

He grabbed it just in time. There wasn't much in his stomach, but he vomited sour water and bile, the room spinning slightly. His face flushed. Wiping his mouth, Greenleaf glanced up at her. "Sorry."

"Why? You didn't sick up on me." She picked up a pair of tweezers. "There's a lot of wool strands stuck to the wound. I need to clean them up. Use the bucket again if you have to."

Every time she plucked a thread from the shredded skin of his palm, a searing needle of pain drilled into his hand. As he'd warmed up, the numbness had faded, and was replaced with a deep, throbbing agony that pulsed all the way up to his elbow. A ragged strip of skin, stretching across his palm, had been flayed away, muscle tissue exposed to the open air. Two smaller patches had been torn loose on the inside of his ring and middle finger, where he'd gripped the frigid steel of the hook. He'd expected that. What he hadn't expected was the state of his little finger.

The entire digit was a deep matte black. The nail was there, but it was as dead as the rest of the finger. The discolored flesh extended down along the side of the palm, giving way to pink skin about halfway between the knuckle and the wrist. He couldn't take his eyes away.

"That should do it for the wool," Elif said, setting the tweezers aside and picking up a needle. "I need you to tell me if you can feel this." She prodded the tip of the frostbitten finger. He shook his head. She tested a few more points, but everywhere the skin was colored dead black, there was no sensation. Sighing, she set the needle down. "I'm sorry, Captain, but the finger and a chunk of the hand... It has to go. It's dead."

"Yeah." He nodded. "Get rid of it. Please." He tried to hold off the tremor in his voice. He failed.

She gave him an odd look, but nodded. Elif hobbled over to a cabinet across the room, and began sifting through bottles.

As she did, Braden quietly said, "Are you all right, captain?"

"I'm fine." Greenleaf immediately regretted the brusque tone as he finished getting undressed. "Sorry. I am, though. It's one finger." *On my spear hand.* He tried to shake off the thought. "It's fine."

Braden opened his mouth to say something else, but they both looked over as Elif opened her front door. A few Laharians were standing outside, Braddock and Cole among them. Standing a few feet back from them, Proudlake's round face tried to peer through the crowd. She scowled at the gathering. "If I didn't ask you to be here, you've got no business crowding my door." She pointed at Cole. "You, come in. Everyone else, go away." She didn't wait for an answer, slamming the door as soon as Cole stepped through.

Gesturing over to Braden, she said, "He can go home. Make sure he gets there, and if he doesn't rest for a few more days, I'll take it out of both your hides."

"Will do." Cole glanced down at Greenleaf as Braden began pulling on his boots. "You going to live, Captain?"

"Yeah." Greenleaf was very aware of the sour-smelling bucket at his feet. "I'm okay."

Cole's eyes flickered over the mangled and frostbitten hand, but he didn't comment. Instead, he nodded. "If she lets you go in the next few hours, find your way over to the Castle. We're butchering the catch."

"You need me for that?"

"No, but it's kind of a community tradition." He shrugged. "Not an issue if you can't be there." He followed Braden out through the door. As it opened, Greenleaf could see Braddock and Poyel peering back through. A sharp word from Cole, and they turned and began walking alongside him as the door swung close.

"Not bad, captain."

He glanced up at Elif. "What?"

"You were in here two days ago, complaining that no one wanted anything to do with you." She arranged several shifted quartz bottles next to an obsidian chip scalpel. One bottle was nearly full of clear liquid. She uncorked it, and poured some over her hands, the smell of wood alcohol filling his nostrils. "Now there seem to be several who look like they'd rather you didn't die. Seems like progress." She picked up the other bottle, which rattled. She peered inside, and frowned. "I really hope they bring more Dezma urchin spines next time. I have four left."

"You don't need to use one on..."

"I'm going to stop you right there, Captain." She pulled one of the six-inch long blue spines from the bottle, careful to avoid the point. Before he could object, she stuck it into his hand, in the fleshy spot just under the index finger, leaving it jutting from his palm. The venom of the Dezma urchin immediately began to work, as the pain melted away, to be replaced with an unsettling tingling sensation as the nerves in his hand shut down, one after another. "If people hear a kaviak screaming like a badly butchered goat from my house, they're going to assume either I don't know my trade, or I've turned Confessor, trying to save your soul with whips and knives. Neither one's going to do well for my reputation."

"You can call me Tomas."

She glanced up at him, raising an eyebrow. "Getting friendly now that I've numbed your hand, aren't you?" Elif picked up the obsidian scalpel, dropping it into the bottle of wood alcohol. "Might not be quite so fond of me after we're done. Numbed or not, this isn't going to be pleasant."

Greenleaf nodded, and turned his head away so as not to look, fixing his gaze on the glowing tendril of lava snaking its way underneath the far wall. A pot was hanging over it, steam wafting gently out from beneath the lid. "Just get it off me."

Elif began working, and he gritted his teeth as he felt the sensation of tugging. The venom of the spine managed to keep the worst of the pain at bay, but hot needles wriggled their way past the numbing. Sweat began to bead on his forehead. "Can you talk while you work?"

"I can," she said. Her voice sounded oddly distant, as if muffled. "You have a topic in mind?"

The heat from the thin trickle of molten rock seemed to be rising, but Greenleaf knew it was a side effect of the venom. He swallowed, his mouth feeling dry. "Uh... Yeah. I do."

"Is it something that I'm going to want to talk about, or is it the one thing I'll wager half my share of the catch that you've been told not to bring up?"

"Please." His words were mumbled, thick between tingling lips. "I've seen them. The blade's out of the sheath." Another spike of pain, and tears sprung to his eyes unbidden. The venom clouded his head. "I saw the eyes. Ice. Lidless ice. They didn't blink. Why didn't they blink?"

Elif paused for a moment, then sighed. "Doped up as you are, I doubt half of what I say'll take root inside your skull. And you're right. Keeping quiet about it to you seems a bit futile."

Something cracked. Greenleaf's vision flared white, but he clung to Elif's words like a lifeline, trying his best to focus through the cloud.

"Was a time that no one'd ever heard of the damned things. No stories, no whispered descriptions between children at night. The ice never lacked in things to raise the hairs on your neck, but wolves and ice bears aren't the same." Her voice was low, quiet enough that he had to strain to hear it. "My momma, may the goddess keep her warm, she remembered the first time the name was spoken, just after the Old Lyceum was abandoned. You saw the spire on the way out, didn't you?"

Greenleaf nodded.

"Before the Lyceum fell, Lahar was different. Connected. There were hundreds of them living in those crystal towers, using the heat of the river to fuel whatever it was they did up there. The Serao made it perfect for their work, but cut them off from the world. If they wanted a change of scenery, they found their way down to Lahar. Wasn't a day that passed without four or five of their sorcerers showing up in town, drinking cloudberry brandy in the Castle or trading with our people. We liked them." She paused, and said, "Well, I liked them. I was young, eight, maybe nine winters? They brought us trinkets. Birds made of quartz, bracelets shifted from liar's gold. They'd sit in the Castle and tell stories. Most of them had traveled all over the Empire. Brought back tales of seven-foot tall Easterners, ships the size of small villages from Vetticci. Few told stories about a ranger sailed up from the Dominion, a slip of a man who could bend rolled steel with his bare hands. We liked that one."

A tug, and the sound of wet tearing, like rib meat being ripped from the bone. A tool clattered in one of the bowls. Greenleaf tried to push the pain aside as he focused on her voice.

"One night, a few dozen came to Lahar. Wrapped in furs, carrying sorcerers catatonic, staring at nothing. My mother knew the trade, helped as many as she could. Me and some other children were set to gathering snow and filling the casks near the Serao to melt. Questions were asked, but there were no answers. The counselor at the time offered to send a hunting party up to help, but the senior Chorale teacher nearly lost his mind telling him that we weren't to go. A few weeks later, the last of the Chorale was gone. They left the crystal towers of their school, and a warning to stay away."

He could feel hot blood running down his wrist, the soft touch of linen as she dabbed it away. The smell of copper and alcohol mixed with the sulfur of the Serao. "When did the trijjat appear?" The room felt a bit colder when he spoke the name.

"My older brother and one of his friends went to run gig lines a few weeks after the last few resonants had left. Nothing they hadn't done a dozen times before. But after a few days passed without seeing them, my da and a half-dozen other went out to haul them back. Found nothing more than bloody scratches in the ice, shredded frost suits, and broken spearpoints. We mourned." Something took a strong hold of the bones below his pinky finger. He couldn't feel the touch of the tools, but he could feel the implacable grip pulling at his hand. "Steady, Captain. This is the last hard part."

The tool twisted, and a crunch was followed by a tearing sound, like someone ripping the drumstick off of the chicken. Red bloomed in Greenleaf's vision, blotting out the house and the orange glow of the lava. The urchin's venom was batted aside like a broken reed by the storm of pain, and Greenleaf screamed through gritted teeth, the noise muffled, transforming in mid-howl from a scream of pain to choked sobs.

"It's done. It's gone." Elif's voice was soothing as she worked quickly, cleaning the edges of the wound. The small pricks of pain that had drawn gasps from him moments before were nothing now. A few more shuddering breaths, and the numbing venom reasserted itself, settling over the pain like a heavy quilt, smothering it.

"There were a few more incidents like that. I don't know who first called them trijjat." She spoke quickly as she worked, trying to distract him. "It's an old Suvievian word, from long before the Empire conquered the Fingers. I don't know what it means. Been so long, not sure anyone does. But we learned. Learned that they don't like the sunlight. Learned to stay away from the oases. Learned that no matter what, we keep our blood off the ice, and if it does fall, we run. Fast as we can, as far as we can. We pieced together understanding from ruined corpses and bloody clothes."

Something cool on his wrist. For the first time since she'd started working, he glanced back over. She was wrapping a wet strip of linen around his hand, the scent of wood alcohol stinging his eyes. The shape of his hand under the bandage was wrong. Where his smallest finger and the edge of his palm had been appeared to have been scooped away, the outline sunken.

Elif kept speaking as he stared and she worked. "But the most important thing we learned was to stay quiet. We tried to tell the Empire. Guardsmen escorting convoys, traders coming in. Marc Edeline, our counselor's father, even traveled to Kaani. First Laharian to willingly go that far in a century. He spent four weeks trying to get someone to talk to him, to hear what he had to say."

She began adding a second layer of bandages. "I don't know what the Chorale did, what they woke up. I don't know how long those things had been sleeping, or where they came from. But if we want to keep that thread of connection to the Empire, see convoys of grain and seeds come in, and anything other than shards and weapons to go out, we've learned to keep quiet. To teach our children what they need to know to stay safe, and to never speak of it away from their hearth. We've learned to do what Laharians have done since we found the banks of the Serao: Survive."

The pain had faded. The dull throbbing in his forearm was still there, but Greenleaf's breathing slowed as he looked up at her. She tied off the dry bandages that covered his hand, and set the linen aside. Looking up at him, she said, "You've seen it now. You know. A more suspicious woman than I might think that's why Edeline didn't argue when you said you were going with the hunters. Maybe he just wanted you to see what we have to do to live, to last through the months of darkness coming up fast. Don't know why." She shrugged.

"I can't tell you what to do. Hell, not a soul in this town has the right to do that. But I'm willing to bet what little I have that if you report what you saw, if you tell the officers and commanders of the Imperial Army that the trijjat are real, they'll cut you off just as fast as they cut us off. You'll be erased," Elif said. "Odds are, you'll never come across one again. So I'd think long and hard about what you gain from breaking the silence."

Greenleaf opened his mouth to speak, but his eyes fell upon a hammered copper bowl sitting on the table. Scraps of ruined woolen scarf lay bloody on the bottom, beneath chunks of blackened flesh. His finger, curled and ebony, sat atop, curled slightly, as if beckoning him to come closer. He stared, transfixed, at the rough black skin, the same skin that he'd seen gripping the side of a hastily-fashioned ice wall, the same skin that surrounded lidless eyes. Lurching to his feet, he grabbed the bowl in his left hand. The room wobbled around him as his muscles struggled to respond to torpid commands. Elif said something, stood up, but he ignored her as he stumbled towards the blazing heat of the bubbling rock.

The tributary heating this building was slender, less than the width of his hand before the ice had claimed its share. The surface shimmered orange and red, heat pouring off like a blast furnace. Sweat was pouring from his brow before he was ten feet away, but he kept going until he stood over the trickle of lava. The toes of his boots were starting to blacken, the skin of his right hand turning red as he extended it over the molten rock, and dropped the bowl in. It didn't splash. It landed on the lava with a dull sound, as if dropped on molasses, and instantly the copper of the bowl began to glow red. The wool inside burst into flames, and what bits of flesh still showed bloody and pale crisped and crackled like bacon on the stove. The metal began to sag and droop, splitting apart as it melted into the Serao, and the smell of scorched flesh and metal filled the house as the frostbitten meat was swallowed up by the hellish molten rock.

As the hissing and spitting faded away, Elif's voice sounded from behind him. "You owe me a new bowl." She didn't sound angry.

He turned towards her, making his way back to collapse heavily into the chair. "Sorry," he mumbled.

"No, you're not. But I understand."

He sat in silence for a bit as she gathered up her tools, dropping them in a ceramic jar filled with that same alcohol. The throbbing in his hand began to worsen as she poured a pale grey powder into a mug. Elif walked over to the steaming pot above the lava, filling the mug with hot water. She handed him the mug before she poured more of the powder into a small paper envelope, handing it to him. "The numbing is going to start to wear off before too long. Willowbark won't keep it entirely at bay, but it will help." She gestured. "Take off the shirt. I can see you favoring your right side."

Between the pain and his heavily bandaged right hand, Elif had to help him get his tunic off. When she did, she raised an eyebrow. "Goddess." He glanced down. From the top of his hipbone to a few inches below his armpit was a mass of violent purple, paling to blue toward the edges. Gently, she probed around with her fingers. He braced himself, but the pain was a flickering candle next to the steadily roaring flame of his hand. "Can you breathe deep?"

He nodded. "Hurts. But yeah."

She pressed over his stomach at various points, and finally nodded. "I don't like to wrap busted ribs. Easy enough to pick up a case of the rasping cough up here without me squashing down your chest. In any case, it doesn't help that much with healing. Just might have to resign yourself to a few weeks of pain."

Lifting his bandaged hand, Greenleaf said, "Think that's likely anyway."

"Stories say a kaviak can walk fifty miles on a broken leg to fight off a hundred screaming Rilskovars."

"Those the same stories that say trijjats aren't real?"

"The very ones." She gestured. "Drink the tea. It tastes like shit, but it'll help."

***

It was a few hours before Greenleaf felt steady enough to leave Mistress Elif's house. The sun had set, and the village was bathed in the dull orange light from the Serao, as well as several oil lanterns burning on the sides of various houses. Drawing the blanket the old woman had given him as he left tight, his painful breaths fogged the air as he began slowly walking towards the Castle. His boots crunched in the snow as he scanned the dark wells between buildings.

After the first few weeks in Lahar, the irony of the building's nickname had faded away. Most of the buildings in town were built for their utility, every choice in their design made in the most efficient way possible. The blocky houses and farms had mottled grey and white exteriors, with few windows and no decoration. The village seat was the only one with the sense of architectural grandeur that characterized the other Imperial cities Greenleaf had seen.

The Castle was a hexagonal building, polished granite columns five feet wide at each of the six corners. Stone brickwork filled in the walls, leading up to the domed roof with a large shifted quartz skylight in the center. The building loomed astride the main flow of the Serao, arches of marble lit from the lava's light as the molten river wound its way through the interior. Greenleaf had seen larger buildings, but as he came to realize the complexity of transporting and building this type of structure thousands of miles from the guilds and quarries, he couldn't help but marvel.

The figure waiting for him outside the double doors had arms folded over his prodigious belly, furred hood pulled up. Proudlake shook his head as he got closer. "I know you wanted to ingratiate yourself with the Laharians, but the stories I've heard seem a bit extreme." He tilted his head. "You're walking, at least. How bad are you hurt?"

Greenleaf held up his hand. "Might be a bit before I can use a spear with this hand. Four fingers are going to take some getting used to."

"Damn." Proudlake winced. "I'm sorry, Captain. Most hunting trips are without incident. When you said you wanted to go, I never thought..."

"Yeah."

"I've heard most of what happened. It must have been a long night, especially hurt as you are," Proudlake said. "I don't understand why they didn't try to bring you back right away. If they'd gotten you back sooner, your injuries might not have been as severe. I intend to have words with Cole about that."

"Don't." Greenleaf shook his head.

"Pardon?"

"Cole did the right thing," Greenleaf said. His words were still a bit sluggish. "We had to get the kid back. That was the priority. And it's my fault. I'm the one who…"

He trailed off. Proudlake tilted his head, and Greenleaf stared at him.

Does he know?

If he did, why didn't he warn me?

Clearing his throat, Greenleaf said, "Uh, I'm the one who gave the order. For us to take shelter so the sled would be lighter." He rubbed his head with his left hand. "Sorry. I'm still a bit foggy."

"It's all right." The commissar glanced around, and lowered his voice. "And the other thing? Were you able to get a chance to look at the cove?"

Greenleaf nodded. "I was wrong. The ice shelf, the icebergs in the water… Any ship big enough to make the trip would be smashed to pieces." He let out a sigh, his breath fogging the air. "I think I've been wrong about a lot of things. The more I think about it, there's gotta be a more plausible explanation than someone trying to actually steal a shard. These people, they…" He coughed, and winced at the pain in his chest. "Gods." Greenleaf took a deep, painful breath of cold air. "I think I've been handling this all wrong."

Proudlake raised an eyebrow. "You did your duty, Captain. You had a theory, and you investigated. It doesn't reflect poorly on you that it didn't pan out." He offered a slight smile. "But I don't think this trip was wasted. If that boy with the lump on his head is to be believed, you fought a bull not much smaller than this building. The rest of the town is doing its best to remain unimpressed, but it's not easy." The wind picked up, finding the gaps in the wool weave of the blanket, and Greenleaf shivered violently. "Gods, what am I doing?" Proudlake exclaimed, pulling the door open. "Get in here."

The interior of the Castle offered immediate relief as they entered the plaza. Tables and chairs were arranged in a semicircle, most full with Laharians sipping drinks from wooden mugs. Even more Laharians stood facing the platform in the center, upon which stood Edeline and Cole, who watched as a half dozen men and women methodically butchered and cleaned the Arctic char and seals the hunting party had brought back. They set thick strips of fish and seal meat upon tables. The room was full of sound, conversation, shouting, chairs scraping along the floor.

There was an empty table near the back with a pair of chairs, set well apart from the others. Proudlake led Greenleaf over, and settled into his seat with a sigh of relief. As Greenleaf sat, he leaned close. "This is your first sharing, isn't it?"

"It is." He watched as Edeline scribbled notes down with a white quill, mouth moving silently as he counted the ever-growing stacks of fish meat. "They log it all?"

Proudlake nodded. "These people do love their records. In any event, they have to. The Agronomic Ministry demands records so they know how much grain to send. He logs it, and when he's done, I'll review it and add my signature. Send it back with the next convoy." The big man shrugged. "Only reason I attend, honestly. I'd rather eat Imperial rations than raw fish." He made a face.

"I tried it, out on the ice," Greenleaf said. "Better than I thought."

Proudlake pulled out a silver flask, toasting the soldier. "A braver man than I." He took a sip, and offered it to Greenleaf, who shook his head. "First few years I was here, half the town spent half the night staring daggers at me during my first sharing. Thought me taking a portion wasn't right. Not too different from what you've dealt with."

"Did you? Take a portion, I mean?"

"I did. Eyes of the Empress has the right." He shrugged. "Worth reminding them that they serve her, even at the frozen end of the world."

Greenleaf frowned. "I think I understand a bit better now. Where they're coming from. They risk a great deal to bring that food back."

"Doesn't mean they shouldn't remember their place," Proudlake said. "It's important, Tomas. Especially here."

Is it?

Greenleaf glanced away, not trusting himself to keep his thoughts to himself. He saw Poyel, Reif, and Braddock leaning against a wall, watching Braden talk animatedly to a group of Laharians. He made thrusting motions as if brandishing an invisible spear. Braddock caught Greenleaf's eye, and the corner of his mouth twitched a bit. Reaching out, he tugged on Reif's sleeve, and pointed. The big miner looked, and started heading to where they were sitting.

"I still think that one's a problem," Proudlake said quietly as Reif made his way through the crowd. "Anywhere else, he'd have gotten caught up with the Brehai years ago."

Greenleaf grunted.

"Proudlake. Here for your hard-earned portion?" Reif asked as he ambled up. "I do know how much you enjoy seal."

"Zdene. Is your father here tonight?" Proudlake's affable demeanor vanished as he spoke in clipped tones.

"He's over at the Freelin house. Checking for a leak."

"A leak?" Greenleaf asked.

"In the walls. Joy Freelin says that it's been colder than it should be. The ice walls are good, but if they crack, the place'll get cold, even with the tributary." Reif raised an eyebrow at Proudlake. "I'll be sure to send your regards."

"Oh, I'm sure that'll mean the world to him."

Turning to Greenleaf, Reif said, "You're in the wrong spot, Imperial."

Greenleaf sighed and stood, wincing at the pain in his side. "I really don't want to argue tonight. You want me to go, I'll go."

"Didn't say you should go, said you were in the wrong spot." He chucked a thumb back over his shoulder. "Hunting party's over there."

The captain frowned, confused. "What?"

"Your ears freeze along with your hand? Hunting party gets first portion. They stand over there. You're in the wrong spot."

Greenleaf shook his head. "I was just the escort. I'm not a hunter."

Reif shook his head. "Don't really care. It's tradition."

"Reif, I'm tired."

"I'm not carrying you, if that's what you're hinting at."

"No, I..."

"Gods. Just follow me, dammit."

Greenleaf looked to Proudlake, who shrugged helplessly. He let out a weary sigh, and nodded. "Okay."

The pair wove their way through the tables. Greenleaf had grown used to the stares of the villagers, but the ones he now received were different. The hostility was replaced by cautious confusion, a strange dissection as if they were trying to determine his species. He could hear murmuring as they passed, eyes tracking the wounded hand he kept tight against his chest to be certain he didn't hit it on something.

"I think you forgot this, captain." Poyel reached behind him, plucking the aquasteel spear from where it leaned against the wall.

Greenleaf accepted it with his left hand. "Thanks. Might have had to answer some hard questions if I lost it."

"Will you be able to..." Poyel gestured at his hand. "You know, make it shift back?"

"I think so. Not until the bandages come off, though. Going to have to get used to the new grip."

"You lost the pinky, right?" Greenleaf nodded, and Poyel said, "Pinky's easy. Less you're trying to strum a harp, you can do most anything short your pinky."

"My da lost three toes to the ice," Braden chimed in, having walked over to join them. "He tilts a bit to the right when he walks, but you'd never know."

"What?" Reif shook his head in disbelief. "After the Sunrise Festival three years back, I found him in the moss by farm two, just walking in circles."

"That wasn't the toe. That was the bottle of Kaani rum that trader with the blonde mustache brought in," Braden pointed out. "Da drank the whole thing. Said it tasted like a song he couldn't remember. Anyway, if Da isn't drunk, you can't tell he can only count to seventeen in bare feet."

"Nose is the worst," Poyel said. "Remember Okair Ceree?"

"He lost his nose to frostbite?" Greenleaf glanced down at his hand. "I suppose I got off easy."

"You wrestled a Suviev bull sea lion, and got away with most of your parts intact," Braden said. "Not sure how you weren't squashed into jelly."

"I didn't wrestle it, I poked it twice and fell off its back. I'm pretty sure it forgot me two minutes after it went back in the water."

"You did your job," Reif said. Greenleaf raised a surprised eyebrow, and the miner said, "Don't get me wrong. Forty-nine hunting trips out of fifty, a kaviak escort is about as useful as a nipple on my right eyeball. But in the once-in-a-lifetime circumstance of an angry bull miles away from any place he had any business being smashing through the ice and trying to sit on Braden, you actually had a purpose."

"That very nearly sounded like a compliment."

"That you're not completely pointless, just mostly pointless?" Reif considered, and nodded. "About as close as I'll get, I expect."

"I still don't get what the lion was doing there," Poyel said, sipping at a steaming mug of tea. "Never seen one in our fishing grounds."

"If we had, it wouldn't be our fishing grounds," Reif pointed out. "Look on the bright side. Even if the three of you had been messily devoured, it would have been too full to eat any of the char."

"How is that a bright side?"

"I'd get more fish?"

Poyel's retort was interrupted by Edeline stomping twice on the platform, his heavy boots thumping loudly on the pine. The chatter around the room fell silent as the village counselor raised his hands. "This'll be the last sharing of the season. We've only got a week or so of daylight left. Three months of night. Three months to come together, reflect on what we have, and prepare for the sunrise. We've had a good year, a bountiful year, much in part to the work you've done. So make sure you've done what you need to do, and I'll stand with you when the sun rises once more."

The Laharians all stomped their feet for a few moments. When the room was quiet again, Edeline bowed his head. Chairs scraped against the floor as every person in the room rose to their feet, clasping their hands before them. Reif, Poyel, and Braden straightened up and did the same, and Greenleaf followed suit, watching from the corner of his eye as Edeline spoke with a clear, loud voice.

"By the warmth of the Serao, we wait out the cold. By the light of the Serao, we wait out the dark. By the warmth of the Serao, we wait out the ice. By the light of the Serao, we wait for the spring." He looked up as people relaxed. "We come together for a sharing. None of us stand alone, and all of us stand together. Seven set forth to provide for Lahar, and seven came home. We name them now to come claim their portion, as thanks for their service. Malachi Cole."

The older hunter was already on the stage. He walked over to the table loaded with long, thick strips of meat, picking up a single large fillet. "I claim my portion, and offer it to Lerric Dunn, who built the sledge that brought our injured home."

A tall man unfolded from his chair, loping over and accepting the fish from Cole's hands, dipping his head in thanks.

"Cailyn Feilenne."

The fire-haired woman looked different out of her frost suit, her hair braided with white bone charms woven in the strands. She walked up to the front. "I claim my portion, and offer it to Seara Feilenne, who will give birth to my niece during the night." A pregnant woman who occupied the seat next to Cailyn's started to stand, but the hunter walked over to her, waving for her to sit back down, handing her the fish.

"Braddock Cenn."

"I claim my portion, and offer it to Malachi Cole, who led us out and home again." Cole scowled, but accepted the fish from Braddock.

"Braden Zenn."

The young man hurried over, and took the fish. Instead of speaking, he bowed his head, and carried it back. Poyel leaned over, whispering, "You can't give up your portion until you're of age. To be certain

they actually have what they need to make it through the winter."
Greenleaf nodded as Edeline spoke again.

"Poyel Feilenne."

Poyel pushed off the wall and headed over. "I accept my portion,
and offer it to Seara Feilenne, in hopes that she doesn't eat the table of
our home in the last few months of her pregnancy before giving me a
daughter." Laughter rippled through the crowd as he walked over to
hand it to his wife, who stuck her tongue out at him.

"Reif Zdene."

The big man didn't move at first, his eyes fixed on the floor in front
of him. Edeline cleared his throat and repeated his name, and Reif
scowled, stalking forward and grabbing a piece of fish. "I accept this
portion, and offer it to Tomas Greenleaf, for an act of monumental
stupidity." He stomped back over and thrust the frozen fish into the
stunned soldier's hands as the gathered villagers murmured and stared.

Once they'd quieted, Edeline said, "Tomas Greenleaf."

He straightened up, looking back at Proudlake, who looked
shocked. The commissar shrugged helplessly, and gestured for him to
walk forward. Greenleaf walked slowly up to the front, feeling the eyes
of everyone in the room on him. He looked over at the stacked fish, and
from the corner of his mouth, muttered to Edeline, "Does it matter
which one?" The counselor shook his head, and Greenleaf picked up
a piece. "I, uh, I accept this portion, and offer it to Roenne Elif."

Looking around, he spotted the older woman at the back, and
began heading forward, but Cole leaned down from the platform,
grabbing his shoulder. "You have to say why," he whispered.

Greenleaf nodded. "For her skill. And her honesty." He walked
through the tables until he reached her, and handed her the fish. She
took it, raising an eyebrow.

"Not really supposed to give it as a thank you," she murmured. "It's supposed to go to those in need, or those who have given to the community as a whole."

"Consider it a down payment on the bowl." Elif rolled her eyes, but a slight grin tugged at the corners of her mouth.

"With those portions accepted and offered, we offer this food freely to all Laharians, in the hopes that it will see you through the night." As Edeline finished speaking, people rose to their feet, some forming a line to the stacked fish, others milling about in conversation. Proudlake took his place in line, considering Greenleaf with a curious expression.

"Well. Not sure if you've won them over, but you definitely have them talking." Elif accepted a piece of undyed canvas offered to her by another villager, and wrapped the fish as she spoke. "Enough of that. Go to bed, now. You need rest."

Greenleaf raised his eyebrow. "I don't think the Imperial kaviak takes orders from you."

"He does if he wants me to patch him up the next time he's an idiot. Bed, now, before I beat you with this fish."

Greenleaf smiled, and bowed. "By your command."

***

He took the steps slowly but steadily. The exhaustion and pain were bearing down on him like a weighted pack, but Greenleaf could feel the eyes following him to the upper level, and he didn't want them to see how badly he was hurting. He was breathing hard when he reached the top, the slight sulfur scent of the Serao filling his nostrils.

When he got to his quarters, he reached out without thinking, and his bandaged hand bounced off the iron handle. In a flash, he stuffed his left fist between his teeth, biting down as tears burst into the corners of his eyes. The pain was brilliant and searing, dancing up his forearm, and he tasted blood as he struggled not to scream. He glanced around, worried someone had seen, but he was alone.

He fumbled the door open, closing it slowly behind him. He stared down at his bed, every muscle screaming at him to collapse, but instead, Greenleaf turned to the desk. He lowered himself into the chair, and slowly began to unwrap the cotton binding his hand. The pain was a constant hum now, but loop after loop fell away until Greenleaf's mangled hand came into view. Dully, he just looked at the stitched skin, black gut sealing away the spot where his finger used to be. He flexed his remaining fingers, just a twitch, and moaned as the stitches tugged at the raw flesh.

Pain doesn't last, son.

He exhaled sharply, flexing his hand a bit more.

Breathe through it, and take the next step. You haven't failed yet. Not until you quit.

Reaching down with his left hand, he opened the wooden box, staring down at the nib and wooden pen inside.

Don't let it stop you. Take the next step. Just one more step.

Picking up the pen, he tried to press it into his right hand, gritting his teeth as he bent traumatized fingers to grip the pen as he'd done a thousand times before.

Just one more step.

His hand felt like he'd plunged it in the river. One of the stitches popped, a scarlet drop of blood blooming where it had pulled free.

Just one more...

The pen clattered to the floor.

Greenleaf stared dully at his broken and bleeding hand, and something inside him gave way. His shoulders began to shake, and his breath came in short, hitched gasps. Words, so soft even he could barely hear them, slipped from beneath gritted teeth.

"I don't know what to do."

In a silent room, filled only with flickering lamplight, Tomas Greenleaf stumbled over to the bed, cradling his throbbing hand to his chest, and collapsed. The memory of blue eyes and broken teeth whispered in his mind, but pain and exhaustion drove him into unconsciousness.

CHAPTER 12

There is a very wide gulf between respect and affection. In the weeks following the ill-fated hunting trip, the residents of Lahar seemed to struggle with finding that balance. The stony silence that had followed Greenleaf around for his first few weeks in town had been replaced by puzzled glances, and muttered acknowledgements when he walked past. Any outright hostility melted away when they saw the bandages wrapped around his hand, but they still didn't seem to know exactly how to deal with him.

Elif wasn't pleased when he came back to see her to get the popped stitch replaced. He was careful to follow her directions, and the wound healed fairly quickly. Once she had reluctantly agreed that he could begin using the hand, he spent every moment clutching a broken piece of hickory spear shaft, clenching over and over as he walked his route. It only took a half hour, but he did it dozens of times a day, silent, his boots crunching against the ice and snow dusting the paths. It was only when he made it through a full day without fumbling the piece of wood that he took his spear back up.

Despite what he had said earlier, Greenleaf hadn't at all been confident that the summoning mechanism would work. Shortly after graduation, Chorale anatomists had numbed his hand with urchin venom, and made a tiny incision in the pads of his index, middle, and ring fingers. They'd placed a metal coil in each one, a delicate thing no thicker than a human hair, inside the incisions and stitched him back up. He knew that the spear had been custom made for him, based on his grip, his height, his reach, but he was still taken aback the first time he held it. It fell into his grip so naturally, the textured gleaming shaft always feeling slightly cool against his skin.

The summoning and dismissal motions had been easy, as if he'd been doing it his entire life. Now, the metal shivered and twitched under his fingers, stubbornly refusing to collapse back to the bracer. It felt as if it was broken, like something was wrong with it. Greenleaf knew the spear wasn't what was broken. It took nearly six anxious, frustrating days before he was sure he'd still be able to use it. He continued repeating his route, but now, he summoned and dismissed the weapon over and over, determined to regain that simple, natural feeling, knowing it would never be quite the same.

Greenleaf was trudging back up the path toward the entrance when Braden came jogging up to him, the young man's breath puffing short-lived clouds. He fell into step beside the soldier. "I think they found the problem."

Dismissing his spear, Greenleaf flexed his hand several times as he nodded. Most of the villagers had become accustomed to the aquasteel weapon, but Braden still remained fascinated, and he watched the metal flow back to Greenleaf's wrist.

"Well, that should make everyone breathe a bit easier," Greenleaf said. "Let's go see."

The convoy had arrived five weeks after the hunting trip. While the Laharians usually were eager to see the bakeries rumble into town, the entire village seemed as if they were holding their breath. To make matters worse, they'd opened the doors to one of the huge wagons to find the three merchants inside huddled close to the stove, shivering violently. While Elif and Corporal Sand treated their minor hypothermia, the caravan master and several builders from Lahar inspected the wagon, trying to determine how the cold arctic air had slipped into the cabin. They knew there was a leak somewhere, but they'd spent five days trying to find it with no luck.

During this time, Sergeant Idar and the rest of the convoy escort had been bunking in the Castle. Greenleaf spotted the sergeant crouched down next to the offending wagon. The legs of two Laharians jutted out from underneath. He could hear muttered curses and the sound of tools on metal issuing from under the wagon. The sergeant spotted him, and rose to her feet, saluting him. "Captain."

"What's the word, Sergeant?"

"I just told the commissar, sir. We should be on the road within the hour." She nodded down to the pair working under the wagon. "One of the smiths figured it out. The steel pinion for the forward wheels came loose, and was rubbing against the floor. Probably been happening for years. Eventually, it gouged a small crack through the floor, under one of the benches. Damn near impossible to see."

"Huh." Greenleaf crouched down, watching the two men work at patching the offending hole. "At least you don't have to abandon the bakery." They had discussed leaving the wagon behind. Greenleaf didn't want the convoy delayed any longer.

"Yes, sir," Idar said, nodding. "We'll have it repaired once we get back to Darun. It'll take a while, but it should be done before we head back out."

Greenleaf nodded as he rose back to his feet. "Braden, could you please go find the commissar, ask him to bring the courier packet?"

The young man's head bobbed. "Sure." He headed back down into the village.

"How's the hand, sir?" the sergeant asked.

"I'll never play the harp again."

Idar frowned. "I didn't know you…"

"I don't, sergeant," Greenleaf said. "It's an old joke my father once told me. I'm fine. Another few weeks, I'll be back to a hundred percent."

"Offer still stands, sir," Idar said. "I know I'd feel a lot better if Corporal Sand and Spearman Pyle stayed in town for the next few weeks to help you out."

"Not much to help out with, honestly." Greenleaf couldn't see the faces of the men under the wagon, but the sounds of their work had paused as Idar spoke. "It won't be necessary. What happened on the hunting trip was a one in a thousand fluke. Besides, no one's leaving Lahar until the sun comes up again. Not going to be much for me to do other than heal."

She looked unconvinced, but nodded anyway. "Very good, sir."

Beneath the wagon, the work started up once more.

Ten minutes later, Edeline and Proudlake came up the path, the latter carrying a flat pouch made of heavy leather. They waved as they approached. "I understand we have good news, captain," Edeline called out.

"That's what they tell me." Greenleaf walked over to meet them. "Braddock and Lavvi are finishing up now. They should be on their way as soon as the shards and weapons are loaded."

"I just signed off on the logs," Proudlake said. "They're bringing the crates up now." He handed Greenleaf the pouch. "Inventory report, requisition requests, and your reports, Tomas. They just need your signature before we can hand them off."

Nodding, Greenleaf accepted the offered pen. Proudlake produced a small bottle of ink, and watched as Greenleaf dipped the pen and scrawled his signature on six different forms. If the commissar noticed the shaky penmanship as Greenleaf struggled to grip the pen, he didn't say anything.

"Did you want to look them over before we seal it?" Proudlake asked, putting away the pen and ink.

Shaking his head, Greenleaf said, "We've gone over it enough." He reached inside his poncho and pulled out two folded and sealed letters. He glanced down at his parent's names written on the outside, and tried to push aside the dismay he felt at the handwriting. He slid them in the pouch, and handed it to the sergeant. "Sergeant Idar, please convey this packet to Colonel Darion, with my compliments."

"Yes, sir."

"There's a request for an Imperial commendation in there, Sergeant," Proudlake said. "Could you please see that it's sent to the capital for approval?"

The sergeant nodded. "If I may say so, Captain, it's well deserved."

Proudlake glanced at Greenleaf. "I agree, our esteemed kaviak does deserve a commendation. The captain doesn't. The commendation is for Poyel Feilenne."

Edeline looked up in surprise. "Poyel?"

Greenleaf nodded.

Over the next two hours, the cargo was loaded, the soldiers and merchants boarded their bakeries, the doors were sealed, and the convoy rattled its way east. Proudlake had begun to shiver after fifteen minutes, and had excused himself back to the warmth of the Castle. Edeline and Greenleaf had remained, and as the last convoy disappeared over the hill, the counselor spoke quietly. "You surprise me, Captain."

"I've asked you to call me Tomas," Greenleaf said, flexing his hand. It had been some time since he had willowbark, and the familiar ache was returning.

"I know," Edeline said. "You do deserve commendation for what happened out on the ice, Captain. You saved Braden's life. Poyel's too."

Greenleaf shook his head. "I did my job." Something cold kissed his nose, and he looked up at the first few snowflakes beginning to drift down. "I'm trained, armed. Poyel wasn't. But he put himself between that bull and Braden just the same. He hasn't gotten the recognition that he should. I'm simply correcting an oversight."

"I appreciate that," Edeline said. "I also appreciate you seeing the records back to their storage." He considered the sergeant for a moment. "I saw your report. Of what happened out there."

"I know," Greenleaf said. "I asked Ayal to have you review it, make sure all the names and specifics were correct."

"You didn't mention..."

"The report detailed everything command needed to know," Greenleaf said, not looking at him. "That's all that matters."

Edeline considered him for several moments. "You're not shivering," he finally said. "I think you're getting used to this place." He tipped his head. "Have a good evening, Capt... Tomas."

***

The sunset celebration three days ago had been a muted affair. The last day with any sunlight was usually marked by a community feast, as well as the distribution of luxury items that had arrived on the last convoy. But the delay of the convoy had put everyone on edge. It felt as if the entire town was holding its breath, relaxing only when the last wagon vanished between the looming cliff faces on either side of the eastern road.

Greenleaf's recovery continued. He'd taken to practicing the basic spear forms for three hours each morning, the once-familiar movements clumsy and painful. Standing on a slab of rough volcanic rock twenty meters away from the glowing delta of lava the Serao formed before it reached the ocean, Greenleaf sweated and cursed as he slowly worked his way through movements he'd mastered as a teenager, movements that now seemed nearly impossible as the heat from the molten rock battering his bruised body.

He'd lost count of the number of times the spear spiraled out of his grip, clattering to the ground with the odd tinny sound that aquasteel made when it struck something hard, as his healing muscles spasmed or his rib spiked in protest. After the spear skittered a bit too close to the drop leading down to the molten delta, he lashed a long leather cord to his wrist, tying the other end tightly around the haft of the weapon.

It was a cloudy morning, dark with no moonlight, as he practiced when a voice startled him to losing his grip once more. Greenleaf cursed as the spear clattered off the rock, and spun to find Reif standing ten feet away, watching with a raised eyebrow. "You scared the shit out of me," he muttered, leaning down to pick up his weapon. He tapped out the pattern on his fingertips, and when it didn't react, scowled and repeated the motion more carefully.

As it melted into the shape of the bracer, Reif said, "Sorry. I didn't mean to... Sorry."

Greenleaf raised an eyebrow. "That's it? You're not going to make a crack about me dropping the spear?"

"If you want, I can point out the concern of having our kaviak be a fumble-fingered drunkard, but it felt insensitive."

"Never stopped you before." Greenleaf walked over and picked up the heavy wool poncho he wore over his tunic, pulling it on over his head. "Aren't you supposed to be at the mine right now?"

Reif shook his head. "It's shut down today. Deric is checking the rigging, and wants to measure the..." He trailed off in mid-sentence, an odd look crossing his face.

"Reif?"

"Hmm?"

"You stopped talking."

"I did." He offered nothing more, and Greenleaf sighed.

"Okay, fine." He flexed his hand, wincing at the painful motions. "What are you doing here, anyway?"

"You didn't tell the soldiers escorting the convoy." Reif gestured towards his disfigured hand. "About what happened." It wasn't a question.

"I told them about the bull, how I got injured." He shrugged. "Didn't feel the need to talk about what happened after. Not sure they'd believe me if I did."

"You sent a report back with them."

"I did. Are you asking if I mentioned more details in there?"

"I don't think you did." Reif shook his head, bemused. "That's something."

"What is?"

Reif didn't answer. Instead, he said, "There's a meeting. At the mine. Starts in five minutes." Before Greenleaf could respond, the miner turned and began walking away. He made it five steps before he turned and glanced back at the kaviak. "You coming?"

"Want to tell me what's going on?" Greenleaf said, grabbing his pack and following.

"I told you. There's a meeting."

"You're just a colossal pain in the ass, do you know that?"

"I do." Reif shrugged. "I'm good with it."

It took them less than five minutes to reach the mine. When they stepped through the doors, Deric, Edeline, Poyel, and Cole were huddled around a table thirty feet from the dipping bridge over the glowing river. Edeline looked up as they entered, and his face fell. "Seriously?"

Reif actually looked abashed, but said, "You didn't say he couldn't be here."

"I didn't think I had to, especially to you."

"Yeah, well..." Reif glanced over at Greenleaf. "He should be here."

"It's too soon. We don't know enough..."

"He's going to find out sooner or later. And he's not going to run screaming back to the capital without reason. We can trust him."

Edeline scowled.

"As much fun as it is to listen to you all talk as if I'm not here, would someone like to clue me in on what's going on?" Greenleaf asked.

The Laharians glanced nervously at each other. Finally, Edeline said, "It's too early to say. We would have come to you if we were sure that something was wrong, but it's too early..."

"We haven't seen a streak for eight days," Reif blurted.

"Dammit, Reif!" Cole snapped as Poyel visibly blanched.

Greenleaf looked back at Reif, frowning. Turning to the others, he asked, "Okay. I'm going to guess from your reaction that's a bad thing?"

No one spoke. Finally, Deric spoke up. "No point in keeping it from him now. I tend to agree with Reif. We can trust him." Edeline still looked unconvinced, but Deric continued. "Yeah. That's a bad thing. Not a drop of raw aquasteel for eight days. Four days before that, we only saw one small one."

"How common is that?"

"I've been foreman for twenty-two years. Never gone more than a day without a streak."

Greenleaf pushed the hood of the tunic back, running his fingers through his hair. "Do you think the aquasteel is tapped out? I know this isn't a mine per se, but could it have run dry?"

"Maybe." Deric looked unconvinced. "But if that's the case, I suspect we would see a more gradual decline in output, over years. Until six weeks ago, we were pulling two, three a day most days. No sign of any issue."

"Tell him the other thing," Reif said.

"There's another thing?"

"There's another thing."

If looks could kill, Edeline's glare would have put Reif on a slab, but he answered. "The level of the Serao is dropping."

Greenleaf raised an eyebrow. "I was just next to the outflow by the delta. It looked fine to me."

"Half an inch, in the last week. Another quarter inch the month before that." Deric shook his head. "I know the Serao better than anyone alive. Trust me, it's low."

"It doesn't rise and fall throughout the year?"

"Despite what we call it, it's not actually a river," Deric said. "The level doesn't rise when it rains, or lower during a drought. It's lava, not water. Comes from the mountains up north. It's geological. Constant. It never, ever changes."

"Except it is," Poyel said.

"Yeah. It is."

"Could something be blocking it?" Greenleaf asked.

"Again, it's not fucking water," Deric said, rubbing the bridge of his nose. "It's molten rock, hot enough that we forge steel over it, and it weighs a ton. Unless you dropped a damned mountain on it, I don't know what the hell could dam it up."

"Except that's exactly what you think it happening," Reif said. "Otherwise, you wouldn't be suggesting this stupid, stupid idea."

Greenleaf looked between the dour faces, finally saying, "Someone's going to eventually have to tell me what he's talking about."

Edeline shook his head. "Deric wants to see if he can go find the blockage. Find out what's causing the lowering level."

"How exactly do you do that with an underground lava flow?"

"The Serao isn't entirely underground," Deric said. "It breaches through to the surface in three different places. Here in Lahar, as it outflows into the ocean, and two other spots between here and the mountains up north."

"But you don't know that the blockage is at one of those places," Greenleaf pointed out. "It could be some place underground."

"If that's true, we're well and truly screwed. But I don't think it is." Deric pointed at the shimmering orange river behind them. "The riverbed isn't silt, or dirt. It's a type of ore called wolfram. Metallic, and with a melting point even higher than the temperature of the Serao. As far as we can tell, it's been in place for thousands of years. The flow of lava underground goes through a tunnel of indestructible metallic ore that's been around since well before the Breaking. If something happened to the Serao, I doubt it happened there. But where it breaks through to the surface, there's the possibility that something fell in."

"Something strong enough to survive the lava?" Greenleaf shook his head. "That doesn't seem very likely either."

"Mark your damn calendar. The Imperial and I agree on something," Reif said. "It's a huge risk for something that's probably not there."

"We have to do something." Deric balled his fist, pounding it slowly against his thigh. "I'm not hearing any other ideas."

"Can't you wait, see if it clears up on its own?" Greenleaf asked. "I can send a report, explain that aquasteel mining needs to be suspended for a bit. They'll want answers eventually, but in the meantime..."

"It's not just the mining," Deric said. "We've had to pull two families out of their homes in this last week. First, Roenne Elif. Then the Freelins. The temperature in their houses has been dropping. It's the tributaries. They're shrinking as the level of the Serao drops. Another week, both of those homes will be uninhabitable without fires, and we're not exactly in possession of an excess of fuel. It won't stop there, either. I've found twelve houses in which the tributary that warms the place has pulled back at least six inches."

"We have room," Edeline insisted. "The Freelins are already set up with the Zdenes, and we've talked about moving Roenne into the Castle for years. Makes no sense, keeping an entire house for one woman, and having her in the center of town works better anyway."

"You still going to sound as confident when those farms of yours start freezing over?" Deric asked. "When the composting piles freeze solid, the seeds die, the irrigation lines burst?" He looked around at the others. "What the hell is the matter with you all? Lahar lives because of the Serao. If it goes away, this village will die. You all know this."

No one spoke for a long moment. Finally, Greenleaf asked, "How far?" Deric glanced over at him. "How far would you need to go?"

"Depends. The first breach is about thirty miles north. The second is six miles past there, at the foothills of the Watchtower."

"Both of which are past the boundary," Edeline said quietly. "Not to mention the very key piece of information you're leaving out." Deric scowled, and Edeline turned to Greenleaf. "The next breach? It's inside the old Lyceum. They built the school around it. Going anywhere near that spot is banned by Imperial decree."

"Well." Greenleaf opened his mouth, but couldn't think of what to say. "Shit."

***

"Are you outside of your gods-damned mind? Absolutely not!"

Greenleaf was impressed. He hadn't thought the commissar could come up out of his seat so fast. Proudlake's legs slammed into the edge of his desk, and he winced, but his wide eyes didn't leave his visitor.

"Ayal..."

"You want me to revoke an Imperial decree. Without direction. On the doomsaying of a miner that's never left the borders of this village." Proudlake shook his head in disbelief. "Really, Captain, I'm surprised at you."

"He makes a compelling argument," Greenleaf said. "The Serao is crucial for every living soul in Lahar. If something's happening to it..."

"It took less than five days after the Old Lyceum was evacuated for the Empress to forbid anyone from setting foot inside. If the Guiding Savant of the Chorale walked in here and suggested the Serao was going to vanish into the ice overnight, if she could show for a fact that was what we faced, this would still be an impossible demand." Proudlake said.

"We have a responsibility..."

"We have a responsibility to the Empire, Captain. I never imagined that I would need to explain that fact to you."

Greenleaf felt his face flush, but stubbornly pressed on. "Since the day I arrived, you and I have been looking for the problem in Lahar. What could be so serious that the Empress would order a kaviak dispatched to the end of the world. Well, we've found a problem. One that legitimately threatens the stability of a strategically necessary resource, not to mention the safety of nearly three hundred Imperial citizens."

"You can't possibly believe that this was why the Empress sent you here," Proudlake said. "How would she even know about it? You said yourself that the mining foreman only realized it was a problem recently."

"You're going to make assumptions about how much she does and doesn't know?" Greenleaf shook his head. "Ayal, this could be it. If I can find the problem, solve it, there won't be any need for me to be here, which will make both me and the Laharians much, much happier." He leaned forward. "You're the only one that can authorize the exemption. I'm not talking about fifty people. I'm talking about five, maybe six, for no longer than we need to verify that the blockage isn't in the Old Lyceum."

Proudlake sank back down in his seat with a slow exhalation. "Captain, do you know why they don't call the current school the New Lyceum? Why it's just the Lyceum? The Chorale doesn't speak of what happened here. The records just show that they moved for a more hospitable climate. Any letter, journal entry, anything that touches on why they left is forbidden. They may have burned it all. Whatever led them to leave, they do not want it spoken of."

"And they'd let three hundred people die just to keep that quiet?" Greenleaf asked. "I can't believe that."

"Don't be dramatic, Captain. No one will die. Even if Deric is right, which I can't imagine he is, the Empire will care for these people. They will find them new homes, new ways to serve their community and the Empress. Lahar is just one village. There are thousands more." He shook his head. "No. I will not revoke the decree, not for so trivial a cause, not for any cause. It's simply not justifiable."

Greenleaf stood. "I disagree."

"Well, then I suppose I should be grateful that the decision is not up to you," Proudlake replied.

"Actually, I don't think that's true."

"Rank notwithstanding, Tomas, all political decisions are deferred to the local commissar." He shook his head. "I understand that you want to help these people, but if you'll just be patient…"

Greenleaf interrupted him. "Political decisions, yes. Strategic and military decisions don't fall under your purview."

"A few villagers needing a few more blankets at night hardly counts as a military situation."

"But a threat to a strategically necessary resource does," Greenleaf said. "Eight days, Commissar. Eight days since they pulled even a drop of raw aquasteel from the Serao."

"I'm certain that's a temporary situation. The Lahar mine has produced reliably for hundreds of years. Eight days isn't enough to take such drastic actions."

"I just spent weeks pouring through over a hundred years of records. You said it yourself: The Laharians are obsessed with them. Never more than thirty-six hours between streaks."

"What about the variance you found? Couldn't that be…"

Greenleaf was already shaking his head. "Nope. Even if something is off about the excessive weapons, it wouldn't change their logs of the streaks in the river. They have someone in that mine every minute of every day. They don't always pull the streaks. Sometimes they're too small, or they can't get the grate in place in time, but they log every one. For three quarters of a century, the Serao has produced raw aquasteel like clockwork. Suddenly, it stops, and you don't think that's alarming?"

"Alarming? Yes. Concerning? Of course. Reason enough to violate an Imperial edict?" He shook his head. "The Empire has stockpiles of aquasteel. Even if something is wrong, there's more than enough."

"For now, perhaps." Greenleaf folded his arms. "But you and I both know that's going to change. Whether it takes them five or twenty-five years, the Chorale is going to complete that bridge. And whatever the official line is, we both know what that means. There are fourteen million people in the Empire. Once that bridge connects to the other side of the Breaking, we'll share a border with nearly fifty million Dominion subjects. Their country is twice the size of ours. We'll be operating with a single supply line, potentially beginning a conquest that could take another quarter century, perhaps longer. The loss of our sole supply of a critical strategic resource, one that made the Unification possible in the first place, is absolutely a military issue." He swallowed. *Gods, I hope I'm right about this.* "Military decisions fall to the highest ranking officer in the region."

Proudlake's jaw tightened. "You and I both know that policy assumes a general staff officer, at least a legion commander."

"I respectfully disagree."

Proudlake shook his head. "Captain, this would be a bad play in the best of times, but now?" He pulled open a drawer, pulling out a sheet of paper. "Have you read the command dispatch yet? I left it on your desk an hour ago."

Greenleaf shook his head. "I came straight to see you after the meeting.

"It's a Ministry alert. The Governesses have been recalled to Kaani for 'consultation'."

Greenleaf frowned. "So? The Empress has the right."

"They weren't recalled by the Empress, Captain. The primarchs unanimously recalled them on her own. The Empress is refusing to see them." He shook his head. "Whatever is happening in the capital, it's happening fast. If Imperial Command gets too concerned, they could issue a hold order. Lock down travel, have on-site Imperial Army assume control of their post." Proudlake pointed at Greenleaf. "That's you. If this mess in the capital gets worse, you need to be here, on site, ready to report that Lahar is secure."

Greenleaf pointed at the paper in Proudlake's hand. "When was that issued?"

"Eight days ago."

"And it's just getting here when, yesterday?"

"So?"

"So, even if they issue a hold order, the soonest we'll see it is six, seven days from now. And that's assuming the bakeries are ready to roll out of Darun," Greenleaf said. "Deric and Reif say that it'll take a day and a half on the dogsleds to reach the Lyceum, maybe four, five hours more to make it to the northernmost breach. We'll be back with news, whether good or bad, days before any other communiques can reach us."

"That's hardly the point!" Proudlake snapped. "No matter what happens, the generals will have their hands full dealing with this. They will have no patience with a twenty-two year old kaviak smashing apart half the regulations he's sworn to obey."

Greenleaf's face flushed with anger. "If things are as chaotic as you say, it makes it even less likely that anyone would send help before it was too late. I'm not asking, Ayal. I'm telling you. This is happening."

The commissar held up a hand. "Even if you wanted to move forward, you'd have to treat it as a military operation. You'd have to go alone."

Greenleaf shrugged. "Not if I conscript whichever Laharians are needed to get this done."

"Tomas..." Proudlake said, his face creased with worry. "Think about what you're doing here. Conscripting civilians without authorization? Leading an unsanctioned military operation into a banned area? Even if you do find the problem, even if you're right, you'll still be subject to a Imperial Command review. They'll order you back to Kaani. Interrogate you, your decisions, every single moment of your time here. If they believe you overstepped your authority, your career, everything you've worked towards... All gone." He shook his head.

"You want to leave. I get that. But look at me." Proudlake tapped the rank signet in his nose. "I haven't been advanced since I got here. Is that what you want? To still be a captain when you have to get up three times a night to piss? I know how much you want out of here, how much you want to prove yourself. But patience is what's called for here," he said. "Continue to take measurements. Make sure this isn't a temporary situation. What if you go out on this lunatic mission and the river stops falling, returns to normal? I'll have no way to tell you, no way to call you back. If you go up there, violate the Imperial decree, it won't matter what your reason was. You'll be lucky if you're not brought up on charges. And the gods know you'll never get near a cavalry unit. You will serve out every day of your ten years right here, and there's nothing to stop them from keeping you in Lahar permanently."

He stood up, walking around the desk to face Greenleaf. "At least send a message back to Kaani. Let them know what's going on, ask for orders. If they order you north, you go with the full blessing of command. Any consequences will be on them. You're just a captain. You must not be the one to make this decision."

Greenleaf gripped the older man's shoulder. "A week. A full week until we have any chance of seeing a convoy," he said. "By the time a message gets back to Kaani, and they're able to send a response, things might be even worse. I'm a kaviak. I'm supposed to protect these people. And that's what I'm going to do." He swallowed, hoping that he sounded more confident than he felt, and trying to ignore the pit in his stomach at Proudlake's words. "I've made my decision. We leave tomorrow."

***

Once the decision had been made, things happened very quickly. Deric issued orders and gathered his team almost frantically, as if convinced that Greenleaf would change his mind. Frostsuits were issued and checked, Mistress Elif modifying Greenleaf's so his spear could be deployed without removing his glove. She informed him in no uncertain terms that he was to return with all of his remaining digits intact. He assured her that he had all intentions of doing so.

In the weeks since the sun had vanished below the horizon for the winter, tracking time had become a matter of watching the moon's path through the sky. It was an adjustment. Terms like "morning" and "afternoon" became subjective. Both were dark. Both were bitterly cold. However, it was technically late in the morning when he met the rest of the expedition at the eastern road entrance.

Cole and Poyel nodded as he walked up, pack slung over his shoulder, breath already fogging through his wool scarf. The malheur sap sacks that Elif had installed in his frost suit were newer than the last ones. They were hot enough against his skin that he had several vents partially opened, allowing the frigid air to balance out the heat from the tree sap. The others had followed suit. Cailyn was crouched next to one of the two sleds, checking the harnesses on the dogs. Her hood was thrown back, her cheeks flushed, red hair peeking out from beneath her grey wool cap. She glanced up and nodded at him.

"I wish I could change your mind." Greenleaf turned to see Edeline and Proudlake walking up. The commissar chewed his lip, worry creasing his forehead. "I know you think this is the only way, but..."

"I know." Greenleaf pulled his bag around, withdrawing a pair of envelopes, both sealed with a metallic wax. Handing them to Proudlake, he said, "Cole's best guess is that we shouldn't be longer than five days. The next convoy is scheduled to arrive in a week. If we're not back by then, give these to Sergeant Idar. The first one are orders."

"Sealed?"

"Not for privacy. More to allow her to verify they came from me," Greenleaf said. "They direct her to remain in Lahar with two men as a garrison, and send Corporal Sand back to Kaani with the other envelope. It's addressed to the Ministry of War. It's a full report on the issues with the Serao, my decision to investigate, and the fact that our status is unknown."

Proudlake's eyes widened. "With all due respect, Captain, are you sure? Perhaps it would be best to wait until you return before deciding what you're going to tell the Ministry..."

"If I'm not back by the time the convoy arrives, something is very, very wrong, and we need to send up a flag." Looking over at Edeline, he asked, "Have you figured out what you're going to tell everyone? About why we left?"

"Hunting trip," the counselor said.

"I thought hunting trips stopped after the sunset."

"We've made exceptions before, when our food supply was a bit tight."

"Are they going to buy that?"

Edeline shook his head. "Not for very long. Hopefully, by the time they start getting too curious, you'll be back."

Greenleaf nodded. "Okay." He shook both their hands, the grips feeling odd around his damaged right hand. "There and back. Few days, we'll have some answers."

"There and back," Edeline echoed. Nodding, he and Proudlake turned and walked back toward the lights of Lahar. When he heard the heavy footsteps behind him, he didn't have to look.

"Still convinced this is a bad idea?"

Reif came up to stand beside him. "I'm not the only one."

"So why are you coming?"

"Deric asked me. Besides, just because I think this is a shit idea doesn't mean I have a better one." Reif took a deep breath. "Can I say something without pissing you off?"

"Our past history would argue no, but go ahead."

Reif's sigh lingered in the air, drifting away on the light breeze. "Things were a lot better before you got here, Imperial."

"If you think I'm going to disagree, you'll be a long time waiting." Greenleaf glanced over at him. "I really, really don't want to go out there."

The miner raised an eyebrow in surprise. "Not exactly fitting the stories of kaviaks. Strangers to fear, that kind of thing."

"Maybe I'm not a very good kaviak."

"Well, you benefit from a lack of comparison, at least." Reif fell silent for a moment. When he spoke again, his voice was low enough that only Greenleaf could hear. "After the last run, I told Cole I was done with hunting trips. Said I wanted to focus on the mine, be ready to take over when Deric retired." He kicked at the frozen path beneath his feet. "Truth is, I think I'm just fine with the nightmares being the closest I get to what we saw back there." He cleared his throat sharply. "Not sure why I told you that."

Greenleaf shrugged. "If either of us calls the other a coward, everyone will just assume it's us being the same bull-headed asses we've been for months."

"True." Cole called their names, and Reif took a deep breath. "There and back, huh?"

Greenleaf nodded. "There and back."

"Okay. Let's get it done."

CHAPTER 13

There was no need for the expedition to line up behind the sleds and walk for this trip. These sledges were larger, each with eight of the Suviev hounds lashed in formation before them, benches affixed to the top. There was space for their packs, as well as two large bundles of gear that Reif and Deric had carried from the mine. In the center of each was a metal sphere, nearly two feet in diameter, suspended between a pair of vertical supports. As he approached, Greenleaf could feel heat pouring off of the metal ball. "Are there fires burning in there?"

"Malheur sap," grunted Cole, lifting a tied bundle of caribou hide into its spot. "Most of the rest of our supply. Should stay hot for at least two weeks." He tied the bundle in place. "You sure you want to join us? Don't think it's going to be as fun as the last one."

"Might be a bit difficult to argue this is a military operation if the only active soldier for hundreds of miles stays behind," Greenleaf said, holding up his right hand. "Long as I don't bring back another souvenir, I'm sure."

"Mmm. No sea lions where we're headed. Wolves, yes. Might be a snow bear or three. But no sea lions," Cole said. "But if you're sure, then we'd best be off."

Braddock took the reins of one sledge, with Cailyn, Poyel, and Deric settling in for the ride, while Greenleaf and Reif climbed onto the benches of Cole's sledge. A series of barked commands sent the dogs straining against the leads, and within minutes, the snow and ice was whispering beneath the long curved steel rails as they left Lahar Valley.

The skies were clear tonight, the moon fat and full over the northern mountain range. Stars spilled over the deep blue sky, streaks of gold and green hanging like luminescent curtains high overhead. The wind was light, but as Cole and Braddock coaxed the teams off of the road to head north, their speed picked up and the cold air tugged at Greenleaf's hood. Ice crystals quickly began to form on his eyelashes, but he left the goggles up on his forehead, unwilling to sacrifice visibility for comfort.

His eyes tracked side to side, straining to pierce the light mist that drifted over the white landscape. A cluster of several malheur trees caught his eye, and at one point, a trio of caribou, their chocolate pelts frosted with a thick layer of snow, burst into motion, gaining distance between themselves and the dogs. The moon offered a fair amount of light, but outside of a few hundred feet, only items in motion registered. Greenleaf's spear was already deployed, sitting across his knees, and he flexed his right hand around the haft, feeling the scar tissue stretch with a dull pain.

He was far from the only one armed. Greenleaf had directed spears pulled out of the latest shipment from the Lahar forges. The black spearhead at the end of Reif's weapon was squared off and nearly a foot long. It lacked the elegant, almost organic sweep of Greenleaf's bladed spearhead, but ripples of gray and silver swirled around the metal, the sharpened point gleaming in the moonlight. Two more spears were lashed to the side of each sledge. Poyel and Cailyn each carried short bows made of horn, strung with tightly braided gut, a quiver of arrows at easy reach on their hips.

After twenty minutes of travel, the sledge bumped heavily, and the sound from underneath increased. The dog's claws clicked off stone. Greenleaf leaned forward, tapping Reif on the shoulder. "Are we on a road?"

Reif nodded, his face obscured behind wrapped wool and snow goggles. "It's the old Imperial road that connected the Lyceum to the Eastern road. Been abandoned for years, but it's the best route there."

Indeed, beneath the ice, Greenleaf could catch glimpses of the unnaturally smooth granite used as paving stones in other cities. He opened his mouth to ask another question, but Reif interrupted. "Ahead!" He extended a gloved hand. Greenleaf spotted the orange flag just before they whipped past, the flame-colored cloth one of dozens that stretched out to either side of the road. "We're across the boundary!" Reif shouted.

Greenleaf's grip tightened around the spear. Visually, the landscape remained the same, but the dark horizon seemed to loom higher. He slowed his breathing, trying to control his heartbeat, which had begun to tick slightly faster as the flag-marked border receded further and further behind them. He leaned closer so Reif could hear him. "The border is for them, isn't it? The trijjat?"

"Yeah. The only times we've encountered them outside the border is if they smell blood, and only at night." Reif gestured gamely at the sky. "Not as much a factor this time of year. Inside the border, they don't really need the blood to come out."

"Think we'll run into them?" Greenleaf tried to keep his voice even.

"I don't know. Never been across the border. Hard to say what to expect."

Greenleaf stared out into the dark ice. "It's a big place. Hopefully, if we're careful and stay quiet, we won't draw their attention."

"You really believe that?"

Once you've made your decision, commit to it. Doubt and second-guessing will shatter the confidence and determination of every man and woman serving with you. They need to look at you and see certainty.

Greenleaf snorted under his breath.

Sounds a lot fucking better in a warm classroom.

Aloud, Greenleaf said, "Look, there can't be that many of them. Not if they've stayed so quiet all these years. We have fuel for a fire, right?"

Reif nodded. "Brought what we had in the reserves. But if we have to burn it all night, it won't last long."

"We're not going to be gone that long. We'll keep someone on watch. Set up the fire, but only light it if there's a threat. No point in advertising our position."

Reif didn't seem convinced, but he nodded. Sitting back, Greenleaf blinked away some clinging ice crystals and stared intently into the night.

Hours passed in cold silence. The terrain changed as it flew past, becoming much more uneven and wild. The road they traveled on wove between large spires of white rock jutting out from the ice, the largest of which were nearly fifteen feet tall. At one point, they'd made their way over a chasm nearly fifty feet across, jagged white walls vanishing into darkness deep below. The bridge was an extension of the road. There were no seams, no ropes, no supports. It was as if the road had simply grown across the gap, joining the other side with no interruption. Greenleaf had seen Chorale-grown bridges before. It was a miniature version of what they were trying to accomplish across the Breaking.

Without a normal sunrise or sunset, they relied on the dogs to determine when they would stop for the night. Greenleaf couldn't tell a perceivable difference, but Cole shouted something, and Braddock nodded his assent, both of them issuing a series of commands while stepping on flaps of wood to drive metal cleats into the ice, helping slow the sleds down so the dogs could come to a halt. The animals were breathing heavily, their chests expanding, their fur now coated in a thick layer of snow. The two drivers walked forward and began uncoupling the dogs from their harnesses.

"Hey, give me a hand with this?" Greenleaf turned at Reif's question, and nodded. He recalled his spear, and as the metal poured into the shape of the bracer, he walked over and gripped one of the rails holding the malheur sphere. Together, they lifted it, grunting with the effort, and carefully walked to a spot about fifteen feet away. "Here's good." They lowered it into the ground, the rails digging deep into the icy terrain. Almost instantly, the ice beneath the sphere began to melt, but the rails held it firmly in place.

The hide bundle Cole had brought turned out to be a portable shelter, which the Laharians assembled with practiced familiarity. Greenleaf watched carefully as the structure came together. Braddock used a steel auger to bore holes in the ice, into which hickory poles were set. The hide coverall draped over the four corner posts, and a taller hickory pole lifted the roof high off the ice, creating a small space for the seven of them, the malheur sphere in the center.

As Braddock and Poyel lashed the hide coverall into place, Cailyn began to carefully pile up stacks of wood and scat in front of the shelter's entrance. Cole walked up to Greenleaf. "Reif said something about you wanting to set a watch?"

Nodding, Greenleaf asked, "Problem with that?"

"Nope. Was going to suggest it myself," Cole said. "Keep the wolves from getting ideas. Two at a time work for you?"

"Should be fine. I'll take the first."

"I'll join him," Poyel said as he tied off the last pole.

Cole nodded. "Take a spear." As the younger hunter walked back over to the sledge, Cole said to Greenleaf, "You're going to see wolves. They've been shadowing us for a while, but I don't think they'll come close, not with the dogs here. If you need, wake us up." He peered up at the moon. "Wake me and Braddock when the moon is overhead. We'll relieve you." He turned to head back to the coverall, but stopped at Greenleaf's voice.

"You haven't said much about this. The mission, I mean," the kaviak said.

"Didn't think I needed to."

"Still. I wouldn't mind hearing your thoughts."

The older man narrowed grey eyes above a dark blue scarf. "Been well over fifty years since anyone came as far as we have. If we get out there and don't find a gods-damn thing, we've taken quite a risk for no reason. I don't feel good about it."

"You think Deric is wrong? About the Serao?"

"Man knows his trade. Hard to see how something could block the river, but if he says we need to look, no point in arguing. But being out here?" He shook his head. "It better be worth it."

Greenleaf watched as Cole went to join Braddock, who was herding the dogs inside the coverall. Soon, the hide flaps fell shut. The kaviak rolled his head, feeling his neck pop, and walked over next to Poyel, who was lifting one of the spears they had brought, feeling the weight.

"Heavier than a hunting spear," he commented. "Be hard to throw."

"It's a pike. Not meant for throwing. It's meant for close up fighting."

"I suppose you'd know." Poyel glanced over at Greenleaf, and said, "Realized that I never thanked you. Back on the shore. It happened so fast, and by the time I collected myself..." He trailed off.

"Yeah. We had other things to worry about." Greenleaf shrugged.

"Not really an excuse. Hadn't been for you, and that insane stunt you pulled, I'd be a smear on the ice." Poyel planted the butt of the spear in the ice, leaning against the thick wooden haft. "Braden, too. Wouldn't have envied whoever told his family."

Greenleaf nodded, his eyes scanning the darkness. The approval for Poyel's commendation had yet to come back. He made a mental note to send a followup when they returned. High overhead, the aurora sent violet light dancing over the ice, glinting off the towering icicles hanging off rock outcroppings. "Know what I've been thinking about lately?"

"Can't say I do."

Greenleaf reached up with the back of his gloved hand, trying to knock some of the crystals from the fur lining his hood. They tinkled down onto the ground. "We took a survival course, back at the war college. Nine weeks, tromping through the woods north of Kaani, learning to start a fire, set snares, evade pursuit, build a shelter, that kind of thing. Master-at-arms who taught the course was an old kaviak from the eastern provinces, name of Googe. Short, foul-tempered bastard. He bragged on the first day that his course would teach us everything we needed to keep alive. Said if we ever ran into a situation that he hadn't covered, he owed us an ale."

"I'm guessing you think he owes you a drink?"

"At this point, he owes me a damned brewhouse." Greenleaf shook his head. "Five years. Twelve hours a day of classes, drills, lectures, all to make sure that we were ready for service. I come here, and none of it helps worth a damn," he said. "This place... It's nothing I expected."

Poyel nodded. "Makes you feel any better, you're not really what any of us expected, either."

"What did you expect?"

Shrugging, he said, "Hell if I know. Whole town was up in arms, everyone coming up with one idea or another to send you packing. Thought you'd have us all reciting the Song of the Empress every morning, poking through our homes each night. Marik Zdene got so hot about it, the commissar dropped threats about reporting him for sedition."

"Reif's father, right?"

"Yup. Source of his sunny disposition."

"Kaviaks don't do that kind of thing. We lead combat teams, patrol highly trafficked areas, investigate serious crimes."

"None of which apply to Lahar. Never made sense to us to dispatch a valuable resource like a kaviak to a cold hole in the furthest corner of the Empire. Can you blame us for worrying?"

"I suppose not." He glanced over at Poyel. "Are people still worried?"

"It's a small town, captain. We've lived for a long time without the Empire's eyes falling on us. So long as we shipped what 's been expected, we've been left alone. You coming here, without any of us knowing why?" Poyel shrugged. "A lot of the distrust has changed to curiosity. Like I said, you aren't what we expected. But we still don't know why you're here. That'll take some time to work through."

"What about Proudlake? He's been here what, twenty years?"

"The commissar?" Poyel said, snorting. "He sits in his office, reading letters from the capital, coming out just often enough that we don't forget that he's here."

"He said that you all still see him as an outsider."

"He's worked pretty damn hard himself to make sure we remember he's an outsider. Tells how different things are in the rest of the Empire, reminds us that we're subjects of the Empress every chance he gets," Poyel said. "We know that. Hell, Reif knows that, despite the grief he throws your way. But it's not the best way to make us feel like he's one of us."

Greenleaf started to answer, but something caught his eye. A shadow, moving through the night, over a hundred feet away from the hide coverall. His spear snapped to ready position as he strained to make out the details. As Poyel turned to see what had drawn the kaviak's attention, the shadow turned, splitting into several smaller shapes. Moonlight glinted off silver eyes, and as Greenleaf's vision adjusted, he could make out the outline of several large wolves, panting silently as they stared across the ice at the pair.

"Is this a problem?" he muttered from the corner of his mouth.

Poyel had brought his spear up, but shook his head. "Cole's right. They can smell the dogs. They're not going to come close, not when we have so many. They're just watching, hoping one of us decides to wander."

"I thought wolves tended to avoid conflict with people."

"Snow wolves don't have the luxury. Not exactly an abundance of rabbits around here. They take meat where they can get it."

Greenleaf dropped his spear to his side, letting out a long breath. He pointed at Poyel. "You're holding that wrong."

"What?" Poyel looked down at his grip on the spear.

"You said it yourself. A field pike isn't a hunting spear. It's heavier. You need to change your stance, widen your grip. Otherwise you're going to get tired pretty damn fast." He demonstrated on his own weapon, and nodded as Poyel shifted his feet and grip. "Yeah. That'll do it."

"Feels awkward."

"You're just not used to it." Greenleaf glanced over at the wolves. The animals were pacing slowly in a long arc that took them around the coverall.

"Easy for you to say. I've handled your weapon. It's got to be a quarter as heavy as this one." Despite his protestations, Poyel tried a few practice thrusts with the new stance.

"I didn't learn with an aquasteel weapon," Greenleaf pointed out. "Three years of spear drills, two hours a day, with practice weapons made of pig iron. Twenty-five, thirty pounds each. I remember after my first day with the sergeant-at-arms, I couldn't lift my food to my mouth at dinner. I had to hunch over the plate."

"Why the hell would you put yourself through that?"

"You have to step with the thrust, turn your hips. Here." Greenleaf traded spears with Poyel, and dropped into the stance. The rippled dark steel spearhead shot forward, coming to a perfect halt at the point of the thrust without a waver or tremble. He demonstrated a few more times, then passed it back, watching the Laharian mimic his example. "There you go. That's not bad. Now do it fifty thousand more times, and you'll be all set."

The hunter made a face. "When we get back, this goes on the pile of spears heading east, and I'll hopefully never pick one up again." Despite his statement, he continued repeating the motion, grunting slightly with the effort each time. "You didn't answer my question. Why put yourself through five years of that?"

Greenleaf watched the wolves lope in the distance, rangy and lean, staring back at him through the white mists. "You ever hear of Skagit? Smallish town, about a hundred miles north of Kaani?"

Poyel nodded as he slayed another invisible foe. "I think so, but I don't know why. Sounds familiar, though."

"Probably heard about it in reference to the Skagit tornado."

"Oh. Yeah." Poyel's eyebrow lifted. "A lot of the convoys talked about that. Bunch of people died, right?"

Greenleaf nodded. "Fifty-five. Out of a town of less than five hundred. Tornado touched down just outside of the village square and barreled right through. It was over and done in less than a minute, but homes, inns, grain silos, farms were smashed apart. It looked as if some giant had dragged a scythe through the center of town."

"I thought you were from Kaani. Why were you there?"

"My father woke me and my mother up, early. Sun wasn't up yet. He told us to pack a few changes of clothes and meet the others outside. Everyone in the district was gathering. They loaded us all on wagons. I sat on top of a crate packed with apples, between my mom and a soldier I didn't know. Hundreds of wagons, coming in from every district in the city. Took us two days to get to Skagit."

Greenleaf reached inside his coat, pulling out his water skin, and took a sip. It tasted stale, but his mouth was dry. "The cavalry got there first, of course. About four hundred of them. They'd set up tents for the injured, and prepared for our arrival. Any of us younger than fifteen were assigned to unload the wagons. Not just ours. They kept coming in. Barrels of apples, casks of fresh water, sacks of sugar and wheat. Lumber, freshly cut. Still smelled like sap. Nails, tools, farming equipment. We spent hours stacking everything up. When we were done, they fed us stew, had us sleep on cots that'd been set up in these long cavalry tents."

"How old were you?" Poyel asked.

"Eleven." He flicked off a few drops that had already frozen on the outside of the spout, pushed the stopper back in the skin, and tucked it back inside his coat. "The next day, we got sent to the village. They needed help digging through the rubble, finding personal belongings, things like that. No bodies. The soldiers had found everyone, already arranged for funeral rites. I was in the wreckage of a house. Wouldn't have known it was a house if someone hadn't told me. I found this doll, one of those cheap ones made of corn husks and scrap cloth?"

Poyel nodded. "My sister had something similar."

"Yeah." Greenleaf leaned against his spear. "Over four days, thousands of Imperial citizens, under the direction of officers like my father, rebuilt Skagit. Houses went up so fast they still smelled like sawdust. Auditors from the Ministry of Cultivation tallied up how much food they'd need, and set up allotments. Families were given what they needed to start recovering. Farmers came from all over to help repair and replant fields."

He straightened up, flexing his hands to keep them warm beneath the heavy gloves. "I get that the experience Lahar has had with the Empire isn't that. But from the time I could walk, I was immersed in a society that made sure I was fed, educated, cared for. When I was sick, I saw an Imperial anatomist. If our home needed repairs, Imperial journeymen came and provided it. And one of my first clear memories is seeing the might and wealth of the Empire brought to bear to help a handful of grieving farmers rebuild. The Empire I saw, the Empire I know, it's one worthy of service and sacrifice. Sore arms didn't seem like a bad trade."

Poyel nodded, weighing his words before he spoke. "Imagine I'd feel the same way, growing up like that." He hefted the spear in his hand. "This is the first that I've ever handled Laharian steel. Since I was a boy, I saw our smiths make some of the best steel in the world. None of it stayed in Lahar, though. For generations, Lahar bled itself white to fuel the conquest of a continent, and tried to survive off what was left."

He gestured back towards the coverall. "Reif started in the mine when he was twelve. He may not have had hair on his chest, but he had heatstroke, burns, coughing from the fumes. We all worked together to build those farms. The Empire didn't send stone, didn't send journeymen. We had to pay for every brick and seed from the Gift." He snorted softly. "The Gift. They take everything we make, everything we mine, hand back a fraction, and call it a gift. They ignore us for a century, taking what they need while we carve out a life between fire and ice, and just as we begin to see a future where we're not clinging to them for life, they send you. A man who lives and breathes the Empire, who grew up in the shadow of the palace, with the authority to command each and every one of us. A stranger."

Looking back up at Greenleaf, Poyel said, "You and the commissar, you spend so much time trying to remind us that we're all the same, all part of the same country. But we're not. You're part of a country that gave everything to you. I'm part of a country that took everything from us." He pointed at Greenleaf's chest. "Imperial." Back to himself. "Laharian. That space between us, it's wider than the damn Breaking. You saved me. You saved Braden. You bled for us, and we're not likely to forget. But you aren't one of us. You can't be."

The wind blowing past them was the only sound for a while. Greenleaf watched trails of snow blow off the stone outcroppings, ephemeral pennants that whirled and drifted in the air before vanishing. The wolves had stopped circling, and sat, ice and snow encrusting their grey fur as they watched. Finally, he spoke. "You're right. I'm not one of you. And I don't think I can change that. All I can do is walk with you, and do my best to give more than I take."

CHAPTER 14

They heard the Lyceum before they saw it.

The crystal spire that Greenleaf had seen glinting from the beach was hidden from the southern approach by a line of hills. As the road began to climb up to the saddle between two of the snow-covered knolls, a sound emerged from behind the ridge, unlike anything he'd ever heard. Both sledges came to a stop, and Reif slowly climbed down from the bench, staring up at the hills.

"What in the gods is that noise?" he breathed.

Greenleaf shook his head slowly. "I have no idea."

A rhythmic thumping vibrated the ground beneath their feet, metallic thunks punctuating each of the cycles, lasting about five seconds each. The sound swelled, a rising pulse of metal sliding against metal, until the crescendo collapsed with a *chunk* that echoed over the hills, rolling past them. The dogs shuffled and whined in their harnesses, ears laid back against their heads. Cole and Braddock walked down the line of animals, stroking their heads and murmuring comforting words as their eyes were fixed on the top of the hills before them, beyond which issued the mechanical heartbeat of a dead and abandoned school.

Cole glanced over at Greenleaf. "What do you think?"

"Not sure." Looking down at the dogs, Greenleaf said, "Will they be okay to continue?"

"Hard to say. I'd rather not push them."

The kaviak nodded. "I'll defer to your judgement. You pull back, a half mile or so, and set up camp. I'll take two others ahead on foot, scout to see if there's any reason to bring the whole party in."

"Splitting the group? Sure that's wise?"

Greenleaf raised a frosted eyebrow. "Anything about this seem wise to you? I want to move quietly and quickly. I can cover these two fairly easily."

Nodding, Cole said, "You're in charge. You should take the miners. If the problem is in there, they should be able to spot it."

"Okay, that's the plan. Reif, Deric, you good with that?" The miners both nodded, and Greenleaf said, "This is a quick scouting. No more than two hours. Any longer than that, come to the top of the hill, see if you can see anything, but do not enter the school. Is that understood?"

At everyone's assent, Greenleaf, Reif, and Deric quickly gathered what they needed from the supplies. Greenleaf left his pack, bringing only his water skin, but took one of the Lahar bows and a quiver of twenty-five arrows, each tipped with a broadhead crafted of that same rippled steel. The miners each took a spear, and split several pieces of equipment between them. They watched Cole and Braddock lead the dogs and the three other Laharians back down the hill, and turned towards the sound.

The ice crunched under their boots as the wind ruffled the fur of Greenleaf's hood. It took them less than ten minutes to reach the ridge line. As he crested the hill, Greenleaf came to a halt, his eyes widening.

The Lyceum had been built as a school, a place in which young people with resonant abilities could be taught to harness them in service to the Chorale and the Empire, but it was bigger than Lahar. Twenty-foot tall walls in the shape of a diamond, each side nearly a half-mile long, loomed over the frozen ground. At each corner, a watchtower added another ten feet. The tower to the north loomed over all the rest, a spiral of crystal stretching hundreds of feet in the air, shot through with a rainbow of color. To the west, the ocean was barely visible, a thin grey line on the horizon, but hills surrounded the Lyceum on every other side. The road they walked on wound its way down the hills to a gateway, which stood open and unguarded.

While the outer wall was built of grey stone, the interior was a different matter. The buildings looked like glass. There were four of them, each arranged around the glowing exposed surface of the Serao. Unlike Lahar, this was not a steady river, curving and splitting off into dozens of scorching streams and tributaries. Instead, the interior of the Lyceum was dotted with a yawning crack in the earth, through which the molten stone of the underground flow could be glimpsed. In addition, three pools, the largest of which was about twenty feet across, bubbled and spit, the same yellowish mud streaked with a rainbow slick as he'd seen in the oasis on the way into Lahar. These were much smaller, lacking the metal grating.

Above the glowing crack in the earth was a device like nothing Greenleaf had ever seen. Suspended on six metal legs that straddled the bubbling lava was a massive metal disk, nearly three feet tall. From the top, a cylinder as tall as a man emerged from the center, and a long piston slowly rose until reaching the top, then fell back down inside the huge contraption. A series of rods and linkages spidered off from the top of the piston, disappearing inside one of the clouded crystal buildings surrounding the breach exposing the Serao to the surface. Two of the three machines ran silently, but one was the source of the echoing sounds they'd heard.

"They have those in Kaani?" Reif asked, eyes wide.

"I've never seen anything like them," Greenleaf said, shaking his head. "But those buildings look a lot like the Chorale's guild hall in the capital. They're definitely resonant-made." His fingers twitched, and his spear formed in his hand. "We stay together, no matter what. No more than an hour, then we head back to regroup and plan our next steps."

The pair nodded. Deric pointed at the machine straddling over the crack in the earth. "I don't know how far below ground level the Serao sits, but I should be able to get a good look. Even if the blockage isn't visible, I'll be able to tell if it's upstream or not."

"How?" Greenleaf asked as they began walking down the hill, his eyes scanning the darkness. A few wisps of clouds had drifted over the moon, diffusing its cold light and shrinking their visibility.

"Aquasteel isn't the only trace material the Serao carries downstream. There's a type of volcanic glass, basalite. It crystallizes on the Serao's riverbed when exposed to air," the mine foreman explained. "We see it occasionally when the dip drops a few loose droplets on the banks. Looks like green flecks. If the level's dropped here, we'll be able to spot it just above the surface, and we'll know the problem's further north."

"How close will you need to be?"

"Closer than I'd like," Deric admitted. "We brought two mining suits. Hopefully they'll offer enough protection that I can get a look."

"Wait." Deric and Greenleaf came to a halt, looking back at Reif, who was peering up at the top of the walls, squinting as he pointed. "I think something's moving up there," he whispered.

Greenleaf turned to look. The black silhouette of the wall loomed against the dark sky, a shadow with no discernible detail. After a moment, part of that shadow shifted slightly, the motion drawing his eye like a magnet.

"Do you see it?"

"Yes." Greenleaf kept his eyes scanning and his voice low. "Deric, keep looking along the wall, as if you didn't see anything. In a moment, shake your head and turn back to Reif. I'll do the same."

"What do you..."

"Whatever is up there, I'd rather it not be certain that we've spotted it."

Deric did as he was told, looking back and shaking his head. "Can you tell what it is?"

"This distance, this light? I can't even tell how many there are." Greenleaf turned his back on the wall, trying to ignore the chill that had nothing to do with the arctic air.

"Do you think it's a..." Reif trailed off, a slight tremor in his voice.

"Don't expect it'd be easy for a wolf to find its way up there, and it didn't look like a bird." Greenleaf weighed their options. "Let's keep moving. It may just be watching us, and waiting's not going to make the odds any better."

"Five years of training, and that's your best idea?" Reif muttered, trying to keep his eyes from flicking upward. Greenleaf didn't answer, but turned and resumed his course towards the gates.

The entrance to the Lyceum was framed in an archway of white marble run through with threads of gold. A pair of heavy stone doors hung about halfway open, each twice the height of Reif. The front of the doors was intricately carved with a stylized key in the center of a sun, the sigil of the Chorale. Greenleaf looked up at the ceiling of the gateway, spotting the slot for a portcullis, the steel-banded teeth of the heavy oak grate suspended inside the wall. "Didn't you say no one comes out here?"

"We're the only ones stupid enough to be doing this," Reif muttered quietly.

"Then why is the gate open? Who raised the portcullis?"

Reif shook his head, and Deric said nothing. Their eyes swiveled up as they walked through the half-open entrance into the courtyard of the Lyceum. The interior was strangely empty. Only the four crystal buildings occupied a space large enough to hold the whole of Lahar. Putrid steam rose from the mud of the geothermal vents, still well distant, the smell of rotten eggs stronger as the walls blocked any breeze. The noise was much louder in here. Greenleaf looked around nervously, fingers tightening around the aquasteel haft. He wouldn't be able to hear approaching footsteps in the din.

"Let's do this quickly," he said, and the miners nodded. The crack exposing the magma lay to the west of the road, next to the first of the main buildings. His eyes tracked up the crystal facade as they approached. The walls looked like countless spun glass fibers, woven together to create a solid surface. Most of the crystal walls were clouded and opaque, but in regular intervals, the wisps of fog trapped inside the clear structure faded away, leaving portals of flawless clarity. The dark interior yielded no clues through the windows as Greenleaf's eyes scanned over the three floors, looking for any sign of movement.

Satisfied, he turned, walking backwards behind Reif and Deric as he inspected the interior courtyard. He made certain to scan every inch before he allowed his eyes to track upward towards the walkway lining the wall. The light wasn't much better, but the grey stone provided more of a visual backdrop. As he looked up at the walkway, he frowned. "Deric."

The foreman stopped, turning back towards him. "Hmm?"

"The walkway. For the guards on the wall. Where is it?"

"It's there... Wait." Deric tilted his head. "I can see the supports, but..." At regular intervals, flat strips of thick metal, set deep into the stone, protruded into the Lyceum's interior, with a long metal strip running parallel to the wall about eight feet out. But there were no planks lining the frame, no surface upon which to walk. "What the hell?"

"No stairs, either." Greenleaf pointed. Metal brackets dotted the wall on a thirty degree incline up to the top, but there was nothing upon which to stand. Without the wooden planks, the steel brackets looked skeletal.

"Come on. Let's keep moving." The pair turned and followed Reif, who had continued towards the massive machine straddling the Serao. Greenleaf looked up at the large construct. The base of it stretched over the crack in the earth, and glowed bright orange. At first, he thought it was reflecting the light of the lava below, but as they closed within a few hundred feet, Greenleaf realized the metal itself was red hot, glowing from the heat that had begun to assail them. The soldier pulled down his scarf as sweat burst onto his brow, muttering a curse and coming to a halt with his companions.

"How close can we get?" he asked, unfastening several vents to allow the cold air to balance the heat.

"In our frost suits? Maybe another twenty, thirty feet." Reif dropped his pack as Deric did the same. They began pulling out pieces of heavy leather, black char marks dotting the surface.

"Gods. Is it hotter here than in Lahar?"

Deric nodded as he pulled off the gloves of his frost suit, and the poncho over his head. "The Serao cools the further from the mountain you get. Lahar's about as cold as it gets, but these northern breaches are pretty intense. Too hot to support any moss or cloudberries. That's why you don't see any here."

As the pair began to don the thick mining suits, Greenleaf raised an eyebrow. "If it's that hot, are you two going to be able to get close enough to check it?"

"Guess we're going to find out, won't we?" Reif glanced up, and pointed at the heavy metal struts supporting the machine. "Those supports. They must be aquasteel. They're not glowing."

"They're huge," Deric said, shaking his head. "Has to be tons of material."

"Might have been the only thing that could withstand the heat," Reif said. He pulled the hood over his head, his eyes barely visible behind the mesh. He and Deric clambered to their feet, moving clumsily in the heavy protective suits. "You good?" he shouted to the foreman, his voice muffled behind the thick tanned leather and wire grating over his face. The older miner gave a thumbs up.

"Make it fast," Greenleaf said. "I'll cover you from here." He dismissed the spear, and as it molded back around his wrist, he strung the bow, struggling for a moment to grip the bowstring in his left hand. Once he'd nocked an arrow, he said, "Don't fall in, okay?" A dry chuckle emerged from somewhere behind Reif's hood, and the two miners began clomping towards the glowing crack.

Their progress was interminably slow. Greenleaf didn't want to take his eyes off of them, but turned to scan the courtyard and the walls above, arrow held lightly between gloved fingertips. He had to satisfy himself with glancing back every ten seconds or so, just long enough to confirm they'd gotten closer to the blazing heat. Thirty seconds passed, then a minute. They were within ten feet of the first massive strut driven deep into the black rock surrounding the crack. From their movements, he could tell they were shouting at each other, waving their arms. Reif shook his head once, then again, then slowly nodded, and he came to a halt.

Tearing his eyes away, Greenleaf resumed his visual inspection. It was made somewhat easier by the lack of any cover on the ground. There were no structures to block his view other than the crystal buildings, and he could see straight to the wall. He looked from the entrance, along the empty wall and skeletal stairway frame, past the steam of one of the vents, to the side of the...

His eyes missed it the first time, but something at the back of his head seemed to grab his eyeballs from the back and wrench them back over to the plume of yellowish steam issuing from the putrid mud. The steam was thick, twisting and coiling through the air in greasy clouds, but through the fog, he could make out a silhouette standing on the other side, between the wall and the oasis. It was humanoid, and hunched over, but details beyond that were impossible to make out.

He began to raise the bow, but paused, straining to make out more. The form was vaguely rising and falling, as if breathing. Greenleaf couldn't determine whether it was looking towards him, and stared intently back. The head moved slightly, the steam parted for less than a moment, and cold blue eyes peered back. The arrow came up to seek out the eyes without conscious thought, but before he could draw back, a shout of alarm brought his head whipping around.

Deric's arm was slung over Reif's shoulder as the pair staggered away from the vent. The mining suit worn by the foreman was barely discernible as leather any longer. Huge sections were charred black, smoke pouring off the cracked and ruined cowhide. Greenleaf could only see one of his gloves, but it was split wide at the seams, the leather blackened and curling back. As they approached, Deric fell to his knees and tore off the helmet. His hair was slick with sweat, his face red as he gasped in the chill air. Around his eyes, countless tiny blisters formed the outline of the eye slit, white dots in a scarlet landscape.

"You have him?" Greenleaf barked. Reif nodded, and the soldier spun back to the vent. It took a moment for him to confirm that the shape he'd made out before was no longer there. He scanned the moonlit courtyard, desperately trying to spot movement. Finally, he relaxed the bowstring, backing up until he could kneel next to Deric. "You okay?"

"No, I'm not okay," the older man wheezed. He coughed, spitting onto the paving slabs at his feet. "Felt like the pig about fifteen minutes into a gods-damned roast." He wiped his forehead, wincing as he did.

"Were you able to tell if..."

"Walls were covered in basalite, almost a foot above the surface," Deric said, prodding delicately at his burned brow. "Wherever the block is, it's upstream from here."

"So either it's at the other breach point, or it's underground, and we're in the kind of bad spot that doesn't get fixed," Reif said. He fished around in his pack, pulling out a small glass bottle. "Here. For your face."

Deric pulled the stopper, and dabbed some of the thick ointment under his eyes. "Shit. Stings almost as much as the burns do." He blinked furiously as tears welled. "I would have bet solid marks the problem would be here. All this shit they built over the Serao, thought something would have busted loose and fallen in."

"Yeah, well, I'd be lying if I said I was sorry we don't get to stay," Reif said. He glanced over at Greenleaf. "When we came out, you had an arrow nocked. You see something?"

"Something, yeah. Not sure what." Greenleaf's eyes never stopped scanning. "You good to move, Deric? Sooner we get back to the others, the better I'll feel."

"I'll need help. Getting back into my frost suit." Deric held up his hands. Several large blisters had already begun to form on the lobster-red skin.

Reif blanched, but nodded, and began to help him. He had to hold the gloves open for Deric to slide his burned hands inside, accompanied by a hiss of pain, but the pair were outfitted fairly quickly considering the foreman's condition. Reif glanced down at the mining suit, piled on the ground. "Do we take it with us?"

"Leave it. Not good for anything other than weighing us down at this point," Deric said, his hands held gingerly in front of him.

"I'm good with that." Reif took Deric's pack as well as his own, and Greenleaf nodded. "Let's move."

The trio moved quicker on the way out than they had in. Greenleaf stayed slightly behind them, rotating several times to see if he could spot the shadowy figure. When they passed under the portcullis, his eyes darted between the open gateway and the top of the walls, but no movement in the shadows hinted at what might be watching them.

Moonlight spilled over the ice, diffusing through the white mist that had gathered in the time they'd been inside. As they clambered back up the hill, Reif muttered, "Can't say that fills me with optimism."

Greenleaf turned his head in the direction Reif was looking. The dark sky was still brimming with stars, but they vanished in the west over the ocean, blocked by brooding clouds towering high above the frozen sea. A brief glow flashed somewhere in the black, and ten seconds later, the faintest rumble of thunder tumbled across the ice, barely audible over the grinding sound of the Lyceum's machines.

"How long before it gets here?" Greenleaf asked, frowning.

"Hard to say. I'll feel much happier with the state of things once we're in the shelter."

Deric had shrugged off Reif's assistance at this point, and was loping up the hill ahead of them. He crested the rise, and came to a halt. Letting out a cry, he looked back at Greenleaf, his blistered eyelids wide behind the scarf. Greenleaf ran up to see what Deric was pointing at. With a muttered curse, he began to run down the hill towards the body lying prone in the snow.

CHAPTER 15

He slowed his pace as he drew closer to the unmoving body, slinging the bow back over his shoulder and summoning his spear to his hands. The fog was denser than it had been, white curls lazily weaving their way through the air, blinding Greenleaf to anything further than fifty feet away, but he spotted nothing close to them. Coming to a halt ten feet away, he stared down at the still form as the booted feet of the two miners rushed up behind him. "Damn it," he said in a low voice as Reif ran past, sinking to his knees with a moan.

Reif reached out and brushed away the snow that had built up on the face. Poyel's eyes stared up at the sky, irises clouded with ice crystals that had formed on the unblinking surface. He still wore his frost suit, but the scarf lay in the ice a few feet away, the heavy poncho was badly torn, and one glove was missing. The exposed skin was a pale white, hoarfrost covering his swollen and split lips. His head lie at an unnatural angle, loose atop a clearly broken neck.

Deric's breathing had quickened as he stared down at the dead Laharian. "Where... Where are the others?" His eyes darted wildly around, staring through the mist. "Where are the dogs? The sleds?"

"I don't see tracks." Greenleaf walked forward, straining to spot any sign of their companions.

"The snow," Reif said dully. Greenleaf looked back. Reif reached out and tried to close Poyel's eyes, but they were frozen in place, and the miner's shoulders sank. "Tracks would be covered by now."

"Maybe they had to run." Deric said. "Had to get away from whatever did this."

"We know what did this," Reif said. "Same thing he spotted while I was dragging you out of the vent." He rose to his feet, voice trembling. "And if they'd run, Cole would have left something, some sign, some indication where they went. They're dead. They're all dead."

"You don't know that," Greenleaf said.

"They wouldn't have just left."

"Maybe they didn't have time to leave a signal," Greenleaf said. "We don't know what happened. All we do know is that we only have one body here. If the others were killed, where are their bodies?"

Thunder rolled through the mist from the ocean. Reif stood and walked over to pull Poyel's scarf from the snow, and gently laid it over his face.

"Whether the others are alive or dead, we've got a more pressing issue." Deric nodded at the horizon. "We have an hour, maybe less, before that storm gets here. We don't have the coverall, the dogs, anything. If we're caught in the open, we won't last an hour."

"The road up to the northern fissure, isn't there supposed to be a permanent shelter built?" Reif asked, still staring down at Poyel's body.

"That's the story, but on foot, it would take us at least two, three hours to get there, and that'd be pushing ourselves harder than I'd like."

"I don't know that we have another option."

"We have one," Greenleaf said.

"That's not an option."

"It might be the only one."

"You're the one who said you saw one of them in there, and now you want to go back in?"

"I don't love the idea, but do you see us having a choice about the matter?" Greenleaf gestured at the clouds. "Even if that shelter exists, even if it hasn't collapsed over the last few decades, we won't make it halfway, and we'll be in the open when the storm hits."

Reif stared back at the hillside. "I don't want to go back in there, Captain."

"I don't either," Greenleaf said. "But those buildings in there? Those are Chorale-grown, shifted crystal. It's nearly indestructible. We got a good look at the closest one. None of the windows even seemed scratched. We get inside as fast as we can. Once we're in, we find a defensible position, something we can lock down. Find some wood, start a fire, and wait out the storm."

Reif looked unconvinced, but rose to his feet. "We should bring his body."

Shaking his head, Greenleaf said, "We can't. It'd take two of us to carry him, and we need to have our hands free until we're secure."

"We can't just leave him here."

"The captain's right, Reif," Deric said. "We need to move quickly."

Greenleaf expected more of a fight, but Reif just stared down, his face blank, his shoulders slumped. Finally, he knelt and picked up the spear he'd let fall into the snow. Reaching out, he squeezed Poyel's shoulder, stood back up, and began walking back towards the Lyceum.

No one spoke as they returned to the gate. The fog had become even more dense, spilling over the hilltops like smoke. By the time the wall loomed before them, there was no point in watching the top. The granite facade vanished into the dense mist, the crenellations completely out of sight.

The walls hadn't kept the fog out of the courtyard, either. As their footsteps crunched in the snow, the sound was more muffled than before. They could no longer see the huge machines towering over the gash torn in the earth, just a diffuse orange glow that pierced through the mist. As they passed under the portcullis, Greenleaf pointed. The bulk of the closest building was a shadow through the fog, a blurred looming bulk that the trio quickly moved towards. As it emerged from the mist, he scanned the walls, looking for a doorway. "It must be on the other side," he said, and they angled toward the left to make their way around.

Something crunched under Greenleaf's boot. When he lifted it, he saw the tattered, scorched remnants of the mining suit glove that Reif had tossed aside, but his eyes quickly slid to the left of the blackened leather. A footprint was impressed in the thin layer of snow and frost that coated the ground. It was long, nearly ten inches, but narrow, tapering down to less than two inches width at the heel, and split. Three toe marks tipped the footprint, each over two inches long, the tip digging deep into the icy ground. He scanned back and found another five feet back, then another, before they vanished into the thickening mist. Neither Reif nor Deric had seen them, and were still moving forward, trying in vain to move silently as their boots crunched against the ground. Greenleaf swallowed, but said nothing, and kept moving, his eyes flickering back to those prints in the snow for a moment before they disappeared behind him.

The cloudy crystal of the Chorale building came into focus as they drew within twenty feet. As they approached the walls, Greenleaf took point, tucking tight against the crystal and making his way around the building. It loomed overhead, nearly thirty feet above. They reached the corner, and Greenleaf leaned around the side as the others came to a halt behind him.

"I see the entrance," he said. "Hold, let me make sure it's clear." He lowered his stance, spearpoint fixed and ready at his side. Without waiting for a response, began to move, carefully placing his feet to minimize sound, his head scanning from side to side. Passing a window, he rose up enough to see over the lower lip. There was no frame, but the cloudy opacity of the walls just simply stopped, giving way to a perfect circle of crystal as clear as a mountain stream. Inside, he could make out a small room, empty except for a series of metal brackets affixed to the wall. A pale white light emanated from the ceiling, but the source was out of his line of sight. There was no motion, no sign of any life, and he resumed his movement until standing just to the right of the entrance.

There were no doors, no gate. A large archway, ten feet tall and eight feet wide, was framed by a scrollwork of the same material that made up the walls, but the space was empty, a gaping maw open to the cold courtyard. His eyes flicked around the frame, and he spotted several steel tabs extending in. He leaned around and looked inside. The entrance opened into a large foyer, lit with that same soft light that he'd seen through the window. The room was empty, save for a pile of ash and twisted metal fifteen feet inside the entrance. "It's clear," he called out, and heard the crunch of footsteps as the others came up behind him.

"Bit austere for what I expected from the Chorale." Deric's voice echoed through the hallway, bouncing off the crystal walls. He reached out and fingered the metal brackets in the entryway frame. "Odd."

"You know what those are?"

Deric nodded. "Hinges. At least half. There must have been a door here at one point."

Reif glanced over them nervously. "Think it got smashed in?"

"I don't think so." The mining foreman crouched down, picking up a pin off the floor. He pointed at several others that lay not far away. "There's no damage to the knuckles, or the pins. It looks like they just disassembled the hinges, took the doors off."

"If that's so, where are the doors?" Reif asked. Deric shrugged.

"Come on, let's get inside." They followed Greenleaf as he walked in, boot heels clicking loudly off the stone floor. As they passed into the foyer, the three turned slowly, looking around. Metal racks stood against several walls, but there were no tables, no furniture that they could see. A wide staircase extended up to a second floor on the other side of the room, and a pair of hallways branched off from either side of the base of the stairs. A second-floor balcony overlooked the foyer from the second floor, wrought iron railings lining the stone tiles.

As they passed the pile of ash, Greenleaf knelt down, sifting through the pile. He plucked out several nails and a metal L-shaped bracket, each twisted and blackened from heat. Deric nudged through the ash with his toe, and something clinked. Reaching down, he picked up a flat piece of metal about the size of his palm. "I think we found the doors," he said quietly. He walked back over to the entrance, and held the metal up to the hinges. The loops fit perfectly. "This must be the other half, the one bolted to the door."

"They burned the doors?" Reif's voice was low, but it still echoed through the vaulted ceilings of the foyer. "Why burn the doors?"

"Same reason we burned the spears," Greenleaf said, shaking his head. "There are no tables, no chairs. I don't see curtains or tapestries. They burned it all."

"I'm guessing it wasn't to stay warm," Reif said.

Greenleaf shook his head. "It's cold, but only from the door. You notice?" He walked over to the wall, and pressed his gloved hand against it. It was difficult to tell through the thick fabric, but after a few moments, he could feel the warmth. "This place is heated somehow." He glanced back at the remnants of the fire. "Come on. Let's see if we can find a place that we can lock up. Let's check upstairs."

By the time they reached the top of the stairs, all three had thrown their hoods back and lowered their scarves. The temperature had climbed at least twenty degrees. At the top of the stairs was a long hallway, punctuated by regular doorways, each wide open. They reached the first one, and Deric pointed. "Hinges again. They burned these as well."

Each of the rooms was the same layout. An elevated stone platform stood at the far end, empty except for a coil of brass tubing, extending out from the ceiling and suspended at head-height. The crystal of the walls had been carefully shaped with long alcoves, bookshelves stacked from floor to ceiling. The shelves were empty. "Do you think they burned the books, too?" Reif asked as he turned slowly in a circle, eyes scanning the room. Neither of the others answered.

"It's a classroom, I think." Greenleaf pointed at the elevated platform. "The Lyceum is where all the members of the Chorale are taught. The layout isn't that different from the classes at the war college. The Chorale built that building, too."

"What's that?" Deric asked, pointing at the brass assembly.

"I'm not sure," Greenleaf said, walking over carefully. As he got within ten feet, he came to a stop, holding up his hand. "It's hot. Really hot." Sweat had begun to bead on his forehead, and he wiped it away as he backed off. "Come on. Let's keep looking."

They made their way down the hall, finding empty classroom after empty classroom. Each had the same brass heater suspended over the lecture platform, and each was barren of desks, books, lecterns, or anything else that might have been crafted from wood. In one, they found a book binding made of brass, but all the pages had been torn out. As they reached a winding spiral staircase at the end of the hall, Deric tilted his head, saying, "Listen." As they came to a halt, they could make out the sound of wind, howling from far away, and the rumble of thunder. "It's getting closer."

"Let's head to the third floor, see what we can..." Greenleaf trailed off as he approached the staircase, and his spearpoint snapped up. A pair of booted feet lay on the stairs, everything above the knee vanishing around the curve of the spiral staircase. He ignored the sharp intake of breath from Reif, and slowly moved forward, climbing the first few steps to bring the body into view. His boot came down on something, and when he lifted it, he saw half of a crossbow bolt, splintered and broken. As he looked back to the corpse, his jaw set and he muttered a curse.

It took Greenleaf a moment to realize that the body wore what was left of an Imperial army uniform. The wool jacket and breeches were scorched, along with the flesh. The skin was sunken and dry, the eyes a pair of hollow pits, blackened and cracked, but there was no sign of rot. The body was curled up into a fetal position on the stairs, the hair burned away, the ears gone. One of his arms was jammed between two rails of the staircase, and the other had blackened fingers clutching at the burned remains of a crossbow. The stone steps of the stairs were charred, black soot covering the column up the center of the spiral staircase, the floor beneath, and the walls to the side, extending out nearly eight feet from the corpse. "Gods." Deric had climbed the first few steps, peering around Greenleaf's shoulder. "What happened to him?"

Greenleaf shook his head, kneeling down. He gently pulled the body's right arm around to see the patch on the shoulder. The fire must have burned quickly. Not all of the pattern had been destroyed. "He was part of the Harmony Brigade, the detachment assigned to protect and support the Chorale. Must have been a guard here."

"Captain." Greenleaf glanced back down at the base of the stairs. Reif was crouched next to the wall, holding something. "Look at this." He passed it over to the kaviak. It was the business end of the broken crossbow bolt, a squared steel head coming to a point. It was bent, the metal crumpled as if driven hard against a stone surface.

"Must have missed what he was shooting at. Hit the wall," Deric said.

"I don't think so," Greenleaf said. "If he had, we'd have found both pieces next to the wall. I think he hit something much closer. The bolt snapped, and the head piece fell down the steps."

"What do you think he hit?"

"I don't know. Some kind of armor?"

"Can armor stop crossbow bolts?"

"Not any I've heard of." Straightening back up, Greenleaf said, "This isn't a good spot to defend. He must have been going up the stairs, turned and fired at something behind him."

"Look." The foreman crouched down, and picked up a charred piece of ceramic on the floor. "There's more over here. Pieces of pottery, maybe?" He sniffed it, and shook his head. "I don't understand what happened. If he shot at something, he either missed, or..." Deric trailed off, staring down at the broken bolt.

"Let's keep moving." Greenleaf pushed the body gently aside, and slipped past, continuing up the stairs. At the top, they found another hallway, directly above the one they'd just come through. That hallway had been empty.

This was a slaughterhouse.

Two dead guards lie in ruined pieces at the top of the staircase. A barricade had been fashioned, several large crates piled between the top of the staircase and the entrance to the hallway. The crates were smashed, several more corpses draped across. One wore white robes stained brown with blood. His head had been torn free, and lay on its side ten feet down the hallway.

Every one of the bodies was dried up, skin sunken in the same fashion as the one on the stairs. Greenleaf knelt by one, pulling a longsword from limp fingers. The blade was cracked six inches from the top, the point of the sword gone. "Why aren't they decaying?" he asked. The sound of his voice seemed obscene somehow, like someone shouting at a funeral. When neither answered, he looked back. The Laharians were frozen at the top of the stairs, eyes wide. Deric's mouth was moving, but nothing came out, and Reif swallowed once, twice, then bent over the railing and vomited. Greenleaf stood to move towards him, but the miner extended a hand, waving him off.

"I'll be okay," he choked out, wiping his mouth. "Just give me a moment."

Greenleaf glanced over at Deric. The foreman was pale, his lips white beneath the salt and pepper of his beard, but he gave a short nod. "They tried to stop them here, didn't they?" he asked, his voice dull.

"Looks like it." Greenleaf looked over the carnage. Some small part of his mind recoiled at the scene, but he pushed that aside to be dealt with at some future moment. "There must have been a lot of them."

"What do you mean?"

"This is a choke point. There's not a lot of room to maneuver, no real escape route. Only reason you pick a position like this is to nullify the enemy's numbers."

"Doesn't look like it worked."

"No, it doesn't." Greenleaf pointed at the white-robed body. "That's a fully qualified Chorale resonant. Probably a teacher or researcher here. If they were using Chorale as part of the defense, things must have been bad. Resonants don't generally fight on their own."

"Do you think the other buildings are as bad?" Reif asked, straightening up. He still looked a bit green, but seemed to have collected himself.

"I don't know." Greenleaf peered past the barricade. The cinderstone set into the ceiling illuminated the other bodies scattered about the hall. These rooms had doors, but all of them were shattered, splintered and hanging drunkenly from twisted and broken hinges. At the far end was a heavy stone circle set into the crystal of the wall. At least half a dozen dead lay in shredded armor and robes, stone stained nearly black beneath them. Greenleaf pointed. "The vault."

"Why does a school need a vault?" Deric asked.

"The Lyceum isn't just the Chorale's school," Greenleaf said. "It's their headquarters, the center of their research and artificing. Archive storage, resonant armories... It's all kept in the Lyceum. This must have been no different."

"They died protecting the Chorale's secrets?" Reif asked, face flushing red.

Greenleaf shook his head. "I don't think so." He glanced back at the other two. "We came here looking for a defensible spot. I think they were doing the same."

Chapter 16

The vault entrance lay at the far end of the hallway, in an open alcove. Large windows looked out into the fog now filling the courtyard of the Lyceum. Greenleaf approached the vault door. "You two watch the hallway. I'll see if I can get this open."

"You happen to bring a key to an eighty-year-old vault with you?" Reif asked, raising an eyebrow. Despite his doubt, he fell into position to the left of the hallway, while Deric stood to the right. Glancing back, he frowned at the large stone vault door. "Even if you did, I don't see a keyhole."

"It's resonant-locked," Greenleaf replied, pulling off his glove from his right hand, and brushing his remaining fingertips over the stone. It was smooth, almost like glass, but he could just barely feel a raised pattern of circles radiating out from the center. "Most are keyed to respond to kaviaks, in the event we have to investigate the contents."

"You can just open any vault door in the Empire? That seems a bit excessive," Reif said.

"It's not any vault door, just those in official Imperial installations. Also, they'll be able to tell which kaviak opened it." He found the outermost circle, and began tracing the path back towards the center with the tip of his middle finger. He could feel a tingling in his finger as the tiny coil of metal beneath his skin began to vibrate. "Plus, these things are usually heavily guarded." Something deep inside the door shifted with an audible thunk, and another moments later. It took nearly two minutes before he found a gently recessed spot in the center, but when his fingertip settled into the shallow divot, a series of rapid clicks issued forth, and the massive stone disc began to roll to the side.

The pair turned to watch as it moved surprisingly quietly for such a heavy object. The air in the room flowed out, stale and dry. They saw the first pair of booted feet after only moments. As the door continued to slide open, they saw the rest, all motionless a few feet above the ground.

"Gods..." Deric whispered from behind Greenleaf as the kaviak slowly stepped across the six-inch gap in the floor across which the vault door had rolled. Nine bodies hung from the ceiling, strips of cloth wrapped around their throats and tied to a heavy oak beam overhead. Two wore the uniform of guards, while the rest wore white robes. The skin was dry, pulled taut against bone as if cinched. Lips had pulled back to reveal grey gums and white teeth. The cloth strips dug deep into the cracked skin of the throat. Greenleaf could see staining around the groin of several bodies, proof of their bowels releasing in the last moments of life, but time had long since robbed the scene of any smell apart from a slight odor that reminded the soldier of moldy bread.

Greenleaf eased his way to the left of the gruesome display, stepping past into the vault. It was about thirty feet square, with shelves lining the walls. Wooden and metal boxes of various shapes sat upon them, and in the center of the room was a heavy oak table with a large tome on top. Two chairs were toppled beneath a pair of the hanging bodies. The floor beneath the corpses was stained, from what exactly not a single member of the trio cared to consider.

"Should we..." Reif swallowed as he looked up at the bodies. "Should we cut them down?"

"They've been there for eighty years," Deric said. "Eighty years, and no one came for them." He looked past them to Greenleaf. "Do you think the other buildings are like this?"

"I don't know." Greenleaf weighed the options for a moment, then nodded. "We'll cut them down, drag them into the hallway before we shut the door. We need to move quickly, though."

They worked wordlessly, their need to put the dead out of sight evident in the rapidity of their efforts. The razor edge of the aquasteel spearhead whispered cleanly through the old cloth, and the miners eased them down, carrying them out and laying them in a neat row outside the vault. Reif took a moment with each to cross their arms over their chest, murmuring a quiet prayer over them one after another. Finally, they all stood inside the vault as Greenleaf pressed his fingers against the inside of the door, and it rolled back into place.

Several large slabs of cinderstone were set into the ceiling. It had been long enough that the luminescence had begun to fade, but it was still more than enough light to illuminate the room with a ghostly glow. Deric picked up the chairs, and dragged them as far away from where the bodies had been as possible, falling into one of them heavily before burying his head in his hands. Reif stood and stared at the door for a long while. Neither of them spoke as Greenleaf walked over to look at the book.

It was locked shut with a thin brass clasp riveted to a heavy leather cover. There was no title, no markings of any kind. A quill stood in an inkwell next to it, the ink inside having dried to a caked powder long ago. He fidgeted with the clasp. The rivets pulled out, the lock coming free from dried leather, cracked and faded. Carefully, he opened the book.

"Are you sure we'll be able to get out of here?" Reif's voice echoed in the small space, and he winced.

Greenleaf nodded as he scanned the handwritten lines on the first page. "As long as the mechanism is intact, it's easily opened from the inside." He pointed at a lever built into the right side of the vault. "Right there, that's the release. It's not a cell."

"If it's so easy, why didn't they open it up?" Deric asked. His voice was dull and exhausted. "Why did they stay in here until they..." He trailed off, shaking his head.

"This should tell us." Greenleaf tried to turn the page, but the paper cracked under his fingertips. He winced, and slid his belt knife out of its sheath. Delicately as possible, he slid the blade beneath the page, and eased it over. It cracked near the spine, but it was still legible. "It's a log, written up by one of the Chorale members after they were locked inside."

"It says what happened?" Reif said, glancing over. He walked over to stand behind Greenleaf as the soldier nodded.

"It does." Clearing his throat, the kaviak began to read.

***

This was a bad idea.

Not that we had many good ones left. We had three bakeries. Loaded them up, mostly with students. A few preceptors. Don't know if they made it. We made sure none of them were cut. Hoping that they ignore them if they're not bleeding.

We've been barricaded in the seminar building since they left. Burned the furniture first. Probably should have made it last more. We piled it high. Smoke filled the lobby. Made it really hard to breathe. But it kept them back, far enough that we couldn't see them. We could hear the screaming from the Provisor and Aritificing halls. Didn't last very long. They must not have gotten the fires lit before the things broke through.

Once the furniture was gone, we starting tearing out the doors on the classroom level. Bookshelves, too. They're heavy oak, so we hoped that it would burn for a while. I suppose it did. The fumes off the burning paint made my head hurt. We had everyone clustered on the first floor. The classroom and dormitory levels had too much smoke in them. Caoulin convinced us to slow down, burn the fire a bit lower. Kept them back, but they were able to crawl around the entrance. Watching us. Waiting for us to run out of wood. We can hear the chattering. It echoes when they make it into the hallway. The chattering is so loud, but it's preferable to the whispers. They go away in the daylight, but there's little enough of that this time of year.

Books went next. That was hard. A few argued, but they were quickly overruled. They burn fast, though. So do the tapestries. Faster than we expected. We were running low on food, not that there was all that much here in the first place. We'd found whatever scraps students had squirreled away under their mattresses or in their trunks. Never thought we needed to stockpile food when our pantry and dining hall are a quarter mile away. Didn't think we needed to stockpile water, either. Doesn't rain here, but melting snow and ice always seemed the obvious solution. Hard to do when you can't go outside.

I'd like to say it was the students who started panicking first. Think they had it easier, though. Hungry, thirsty, but they still looked at us like we had answers. As if we were going to pull some resonant technique out of the air that would send these things back to the nest. They did what they were told. Slept when they could, conserved energy. The preceptors, though. That was different. I'm not sure when I knew for certain no one was coming. I hung on to that delusion far past the bounds of logic and reason, like it was a buoy in the midst of a storm-tossed sea, but every hour that went by, hearing those whispers outside the walls, seeing those eyes peering in past the fire at us, made it more clear. Even if the bakeries make it to Lahar, no one there can do a thing for us.

The guards tried shooting them. The bolts don't penetrate. Don't think spearheads or those side swords they carry do either. If they did, it didn't help the group that tried to go help the artificers working by the nest. Not as if the preceptors have been able to do much more. We have a few students here that are fairly strong spacers. We linked with them, pulled everything we could from the coils. They threw a few horseshoes hard enough to split an oak. Knocked one of the things down. Thought for a moment it was dead, but wasn't more than three or four seconds before it was back on its feet. Left two students and a preceptor shorted out, and not a damn thing to show for it. If our translocator was still breathing, she could get at least some of us back to the capital, but I can see what's left of her from the third floor windows. She always insisted we all needed to learn the technique. Guess she was right.

Anyway. The panic. Caoulin kept insisting we needed to keep the fire low, burn it slower. Got into an argument with Hayes. The fire was low enough that a few of the creatures had crawled into the doorway, still keeping their distance, but crouched. Watching us. Hayes didn't like that. Insisted the fire needed to be bigger. They started shoving each other, Hayes yelling. We separated them, and Hayes stormed off. Thought that was the end of it. Few minutes later, he comes running back with that tapestry from Elder Rashamov's office, the one with his family sigil. We'd been tearing the tapestries into strips, feeding the fire slowly, but

Hayes didn't want us to stop him. Ran up, and dumped the whole thing on the fire.

I know he didn't mean to smother it. He wasn't thinking straight. None of us were. Didn't matter. Soon as the flames were covered, they came at us. They're so fast. Don't move like anything natural. They were on Hayes before he had a chance to scream. Just the two at first. We ran. Not really proud of that, but it's not like there's anything we could do. Made it to the classroom level, headed up to the third floor. That corporal with the lisp - can't remember his name - tried to hold them off. Lit one of the oil jugs on fire and smashed it. Bought us a few minutes, anyway. The guards dragged some crates out, started building a barricade. Told us to get into the vault, lock ourselves in. Caoulin stayed with them. I wanted to. I really did. I always thought I'd be the kind of man that stood between the nightmares and the innocents. But when the door closed, I was in here, and Caoulin was out there.

Couldn't hear anything once the door closed and the vault sealed. We built this to be airtight, to preserve any artifacts we kept here. The stone's not easy to shift, but there are places that I was able to open up some holes for air. As soon as they formed, we could hear them. Eating, I guess. It didn't sound like chewing. More like slurping, like someone trying to drink honey through a reed. And the whispers. Their teeth stop chattering when they feed, but the whispers get louder. When they're close, you can always hear the whispers. At one point, they were so loud that I was certain one of them had its mouth pressed against the hole. I could smell... like rotting meat mixed with burning copper. Something came through. Couldn't see it well. We all pressed our spines against the back of the vault. It came further in than it should have. Thin, curling. I don't know if it was a finger or a tongue, but it stretched nearly a foot into the vault. Waved in the air back and forth, like it was looking at us.

They're waiting for us. One of the guards that came in with us, he fell on the way in. Scraped his wrist on the floor. That's all it takes. Once they smell blood, they won't stop. We waited past sunrise, but I guess they can stay out during the day if they're inside. They just whisper, waiting for the door to open, for curiosity to overwhelm us and one of us to peer through the holes. I don't know what would happen, but none of us will find out. We were curious before, when we hit the barrier. We were curious enough to break through. But blood and screams and sightless eyes are cauterizing. They burn the curiosity right from you. If I could wrap myself in ignorance, blot out the memories of everything, forget what I know, die slowly in here oblivious to what we woke, I wouldn't wait. I hope when my heart stops that everything I know dies with me, that the images blow away like a sand mandala in a storm. I hope they don't linger, that I don't linger.

It won't be much longer. I don't know how many days we've been here. It's hard to think. My lips are cracked. Head is splitting. I think it's dehydration. Can't remember the last drink we had. Kelsea, one of the students, can't stop crying, but her tears are dry. None of us want to wait much longer. I'm afraid I'll pass out, fall and hit my head. Bleed. I don't want to bleed. I don't want to draw them to me. I don't think they can get through, but I can't die that way, find out what that sound was. I don't want to know, not ever.

If you find this, leave now. Leave while the sun is out. Don't look back, don't come back. And don't bleed.

This isn't the only nest. We woke them all.

✳✳✳

"Is that what's going to happen to us?"

It was the first words spoken since Greenleaf had fallen silent, the last scribbled words trailing off on the page in a blotch of ink. Near the end, the script had been barely legible. Reif had stood behind him, reading silently along over his shoulder, but Deric had not moved from his seat, had not lifted his pale face from behind his gloved hands. When he spoke, his words were hollow and dull, his eyes staring at nothing.

Greenleaf took a long breath before he spoke. "I hope not." He eyed the holes in the stone door. Outside, he heard only the faint howling of the wind. No whispers, no footsteps. "We came back to the Lyceum, ready to fight or run if we were attacked by a trijjat. We spotted a few, but they didn't approach. Didn't follow us inside that we could see. We're not going to see daylight for a few more months, so the only thing I can figure is that for some reason, they're not interested in us."

"He's right," Reif said quietly. "If our weapons can't hurt these things, there's no reason that they would hold back. We don't have a fire."

"Didn't stop them from taking the others." Deric looked up at them, his eyes red. "Didn't stop them from killing Poyel, leaving his body in the snow."

"Maybe they made a mistake."

"Like what?"

Reif swallowed. "Maybe one of them bled. Cut their finger, something. Enough to draw the trijjat." He gestured at Greenleaf, then at Deric. "None of us are bleeding."

"You think Malachi Cole made a mistake?"

"No, but Cailyn, maybe. Hell, one of the dogs could have gotten a scrape," Reif said. "I don't know, Deric. I don't know what happened to them. But we're still here, and we still have a job to do."

"A job to do?" Deric stared balefully at Reif. "There were seven of us. Four are dead. The dogs are gone, the coverall is gone. We have no food, no water, and we're sealed in a tomb. The job is over."

"No." Reif shook his head. "It's more important than ever. It's not about the aquasteel anymore. It's about keeping these things away from Lahar."

Greenleaf nodded. "I think you're right."

"What are you talking about?"

"You and I have lived here our entire lives," Reif said. "Until that night on the coast, neither of us had ever laid eyes on a trijjat. The only thing we know for sure that keeps them back is fire."

"If fire keeps them back," Greenleaf said, "the Serao definitely would."

"The footprints we've seen. All of them, every one, was next to the wall. As far as you can get from the breach. I'll bet not a one strays close to that crack in the earth." Reif walked over, crouching in front of Deric. "That's why they don't come into Lahar. The Serao is everywhere. Under every house, in every farm, the mine, the forge. The entire valley is lit with the light from the river. If the level keeps dropping, if the tributaries dry up..."

"Gods." Deric ran his fingers through his thinning hair, blinking his burned eyelids rapidly.

"How long before it's not enough to keep them back?" Greenleaf asked quietly. "Even if they're only drawn to blood, there are nearly three hundred people in Lahar. Children. People working the forge. I promise not a day goes by without someone spilling a few drops, and if the Serao isn't high enough to hold them back, there's no guard force. No garrison. No place to go." Shaking his head, he said, "We have to keep going. We have to check the last breach."

"And how are we supposed to get there?" Deric asked. "The dogs are gone."

"You said the northern breach is six miles north, right?" Greenleaf asked. Deric nodded. "Can we make it that far on foot?"

"Assuming one of us doesn't get a nosebleed and get us all devoured?" Deric shook his head. "I don't know. Cole's the expert in this." Glancing up at Reif, he said, "What do you think?"

Reif leaned back against the desk, considering. "We'd need to wait out the storm. No way we'd make it more than a mile in a blow like this." He swallowed. "We should also go back out to Poyel."

"Why?"

"His malheur sacks. He doesn't need them, but he'll have six extra sacks. With two extra each, it might be enough to keep our temperature up for a day or so." Reif shook his head. "I don't know. I think so." He turned to glance back at Greenleaf over his shoulder. "It might get us to the breach. But there's no way we can make it back to Lahar on foot. That distance would take over a week on foot during the summer. In winter, it's impossible."

"Doesn't matter," Greenleaf said. "We don't have any food. We can melt snow for water, but…"

"You're saying we're not going home," Deric said.

"We won't make it back to Lahar, even if we head back straight from here," Greenleaf said. As the truth of his words settled in around him, he felt a surprising weight lift from his shoulders. "If we stay in here, we'll die in a few days from dehydration. We won't survive this. But we can decide how we die. If there's a possibility, even a small one, that we can figure out what's blocking the Serao and fix it, we can give everyone in Lahar a chance."

Deric took a deep breath. "A lot of our gear was on the sleds. But we still have one mining suit, and Reif's gear." He looked over at the other miner, and shrugged. "It's probably not enough. But maybe, if we're lucky, we might be able to figure something out."

Reif nodded. "I'm not lying down and giving up yet. Maybe we can take a caribou, or figure something else out. Hell, the convoy should be arriving any day now. Maybe the guards will wonder where their commanding officer wandered off to, come looking for us."

"Doubtful," Greenleaf said. "I left orders telling them specifically not to do that."

"There really is no point in having you along, is there?"

Greenleaf allowed the ghost of a smile to cross his lips.

Chapter 17

The sound of the wind drumming against the looming walls of the Lyceum had faded hours ago by the time Greenleaf climbed to his feet. Reif had slumped against the wall, and despite the strain of their circumstances, had dozed off. Greenleaf nudged him with the toe of his boot. "We should head out."

Reif blinked bleary eyes, and nodded. Deric was already standing, testing the point of his spear with his thumb. "Is there a point to bringing these along?" he asked. "Doesn't seem like they're all that effective."

"Trijjat aren't the only things out there," Reif said as he stretched, popping his back. "Spear'll still work pretty damned well on wolves or snow bears. Besides, if we have any hope of bringing down an animal for food, we'll need them."

They listened at the small holes in the vault door. Now that the storm had passed, silence filled the hallway outside. Taking a deep breath, Greenleaf glanced at Reif and Deric in turn, each nodding silently. Reif tightened his grip on his spear, Greenleaf extended his hand as the aquasteel flowed into place, and Deric reached up and gripped the handle, pulling it down. Several loud thunks issued from somewhere in the wall as the stone door rolled aside once more, revealing an empty hallway. The bodies lay untouched where they had placed them.

"All right. Let's move quickly and quietly, make our way out the gate as fast as we can," Greenleaf said. "I'll take point. Reif, you bring up the rear."

Despite their efforts to keep the noise to a minimum, their boots echoed off the stone and crystal of the Lyceum building. Stepping over the corpse in the stairwell took a moment, and Deric nearly stumbled as he overextended to not touch the charred remains. Reif paused every thirty feet or so, wide eyes darting to peer through missing doors into empty rooms, but if they were being watched, there was no indication. When they reached the foyer, they came to a halt. "That could be a problem," Greenleaf said.

When they had first entered the Lyceum, the courtyard had been dusted with an inch or so of snow, which had already begun to harden into the layer of fragile ice that coated the long-frozen terrain. That inch had since been buried under nearly two feet of white powder. The snowfall spilled into the open entrance, illuminated by moonlight.

"Damn." Deric dropped his pack off his shoulder. "We'll need the snowshoes."

The Laharian packs they carried each had a pair strapped between the pack and their spines. The wooden frames with a carefully woven rawhide lattice gave the packs some structure, but each of the three unfastened the snowshoes, separating them out and unfastening the bundled straps. Reif showed Greenleaf how to put them on, redoing the bindings after Greenleaf made an attempt. As he knelt in front of him, pulling the leather straps tight, he asked, "I don't suppose walking on snowshoes was part of your training?"

Greenleaf shook his head. "It's not considered 'combat effective' to fight in snow this deep."

"Wonderful." He cinched down the straps over the toes of his boot. "It's going to slow us down, especially until you get the hang of it." He looked up at Deric. "If we run into heavy uphill slopes…"

"I know." Deric straightened up, lifting one foot then the other.

"Any idea what the terrain's going to be like?"

"No more road, I know that. We'll be going cross country. Other than that…" The foreman shrugged. "No one went up towards the source even when this place was occupied. No real reason."

Greenleaf wiggled his feet, trying to get used to the awkward footwear. "Six miles, right?" The toes of his boots were tight against the lattice, but a joint installed at the toe allowed the heel to lift away, the snowshoe swinging freely. The bottom of the snowshoes had dozens of small metal nails driven from the top, the points jutting down against the stone floor.

"Long way on foot. Even longer through deep drifts."

"Well, maybe it'll help keep us warm," Greenleaf said. The Laharians exchanged a glance, but Reif just nodded.

"Let's go."

Any plans of a quick and silent escape out the walls of the Lyceum were dashed with the first few clumsy steps atop the packed snowfall. The buildings were blanketed in white, large drifts of powder piled up against the exterior walls, giving the sharply angled structures a muted, blobby appearance. The wide expanse of snowfall sank in around the breach, orange light glowing off the powder, as well as around the oasis. He could see the sulfurous steam wafting up, marking the spot of the thermal vent. As he attempted to clamber his way up the hill, Greenleaf struggled as the snowshoes sunk a few inches into the snow.

"You have to kind of kick forward," Reif said, demonstrating. The front rim of his snowshoes sent a spray of flakes ahead of him, but he moved up the slope smoothly. Greenleaf attempted to imitate him, and made his way up.

"I'm beginning to understand why they said we wouldn't be combat effective," he muttered as he tromped slowly over the snow. "If we get attacked while I have these canoes on my feet..."

"Please don't finish that sentence," Deric said, eyes darting around. "We wouldn't even be able to tell if they'd been out here. Any prints would be buried."

The snow compressed with an audible whispered crunch every time they took a step. Greenleaf quickly fell into the pattern of lifting his knee, swinging the shoe forward, and planting it to sink a bit before the compressed powder could hold his weight. As he learned to better match the duck-like gait of the Laharians, their pace began to improve, but it still took nearly fifteen minutes to reach the gate. His eyes constantly shifted between the snow in front of him and the walls high overhead. The white fog that had preceded the blizzard was gone, the sky clear and speckled with thousands of twinkling stars. He saw nothing move among the crenelations.

By the time they stepped outside the walls of the abandoned Lyceum, Greenleaf had opened several of the vents in his frost suit, his heart thumping in his chest. He turned and looked back at the short distance they'd traveled, and let out a long exhalation, his breath fogging in the cold air. "Six miles."

Deric nodded as Reif adjusted his straps. "I know you said we should go find Poyel, get the malheur sacks, but..."

"I know." Reif stared up at the ridgeline rising in front of them. "Getting up there is going to be a bastard, and there's no guarantee we'd be able to find his body under two feet of snow. Even if we did, we'd have to come back up the ridge to make our way north."

"Can we make it without the extra sacks?" Greenleaf asked.

"I don't know."

There was a few moments of silence, the world quiet around them, no wind, no motion. Finally, Deric said, "Gotta be honest. I think I'd rather freeze to death out here than go back into that charnel house." He pointed. "If we follow the walls, we should be able to see the Watchtower. Waiting's not going to improve our chances."

"I guess he's right." Reif took a long breath. "Feel like going on a stroll, Imperial?"

Beneath his scarf, the corners of Greenleaf's mouth twitched. "Why not."

An hour later, the three men came out around the north side of the diamond-shaped walls of the Lyceum to find themselves at the foot of a slight rise. While not as high as the hill they'd come over from the south, Greenleaf's chest was still heaving when he reached the top. All three had begun using the butts of their spears to dig into the snow, leaning on them to lumber up the slope. The slender haft of the aquasteel spear wasn't as effective, stabbing deeper into the powder before giving him any support, but it was better than nothing.

As they all stood to catch their breath, the arctic terrain spilled out before them. Several large ravines sent dark cracks splintering across the ice, and massive slabs of grey-streaked ice, broken from the shelf, jutted up in the air like jagged hills. In the distance, the Terminus mountains loomed over the continent, sharp teeth of stone and ice stabbing up through the broken ice at the end of the world, and at their center, the Watchtower, high enough that its peak was wreathed in clouds. Even from where they stood, the base of the massive peak glowed with the fire of the Serao bursting forth into the world.

***

He didn't know how long they'd been walking when the moon slipped back below the horizon, plunging the frozen world back into darkness. Ribbons of amethyst and sapphire light danced high overhead in the cloudless sky, the surreal colors flickering over the snow and ice. The soft crunch of their snowshoes sinking into the powder seemed the loudest thing in the world. Following the storm, there was almost no wind, nothing to disturb the vista except the steady march of the three men.

No words were exchanged for a long time. Scarves were tight around the face as they drove the butts of their spears down to help them move forward. Greenleaf had checked and rechecked the cuffs on his wrists and ankles, sealing every possible gap. His eyelashes were thickly frosted with ice crystals, the skin around his eyes already beginning to go numb. He blinked fast, fearing that the moisture on his eyeball would begin to freeze. As he did, he could feel the frost cracking at the corners of his eye. His breath condensed on the fibers of the scarf, icing over and chilling the woven fabric.

Any hope they'd had of following a straight line vanished the first time they reached one of the chasms in their path. None of the cracks in the ice stretched more than a quarter mile or so before they found a path across, but every detour slowed them down. If the aurora hadn't been overhead, Greenleaf didn't know if they'd be able to move safely over the ice, not that they would have stopped. They pushed inexorably forward, the looming height of the Watchtower ahead.

When they reached a slab of granite the size of a building that had burst through the ice, Reif came to a halt. "We'll take a few minutes here, catch our breath." Puffs of fog marked each of his words.

"I don't know if we should stop," Greenleaf said, leaning on his spear. "We're fighting against time as it is."

"Wasn't asking," Reif said. "If we push ourselves too hard, we're going to start sweating, and cold as it is, venting isn't an option."

Greenleaf nodded, not pushing any further. The truth was, his chest was heaving like a bellows, and he could feel sweat along his armpits and thighs, near the warm spots of the malheur sacks. He said nothing, but turned and pretended to be looking up at the aurora as he eased one of the vents on his breeches open. He'd loosened only the first toggle, opening the vent up less than a millimeter, when he had to bite down hard on his lip to keep the gasp of shock from slipping free. The cold air was like a dagger, a shard of pain as if someone had driven an icicle deep into his thigh. He fumbled to close the vent, shivers already beginning to radiate out. It slowly faded as he tied it shut, but Greenleaf knew he'd lost valuable heat in the experiment.

"I warned you not to do that." He turned to find Reif watching him with a frown. "You're sweating, aren't you?"

Reluctantly, the kaviak nodded. "You aren't?"

"Beginning to, yeah," Reif admitted. "Snowshoeing is challenging under the best of conditions." His hand rose to his midsection as he winced. "Hungry, too. Stomach is beginning to cramp."

"Me too." Greenleaf looked over at Deric, who was leaning against the side of the granite outcropping. "How are you doing?"

"Never thought I'd miss spending hours sweating bullets in the mine," he mumbled. Waving his hand, he said, "I'll be fine. Head hurts, but I've had worse after testing the brandy."

"Don't suppose there's any way of knowing how far we've come," Greenleaf asked.

Reif shook his head. "I don't know this area. The few expeditions I've heard of that came up here traveled up the coast, followed the foothills of the Terminus east. No one's stupid enough to go cross country like this, especially not on foot. Don't know that it's ever been mapped. Best I can say, we're closer than we were." He gestured at the cloud-shrouded peak in the distance. "Hard to miss the landmark."

Greenleaf nodded. "Well then. Best get to it, I suppose." The miners straightened up in weary agreement, Reif taking point as the others fell in behind him.

The three men made their way across the ice. The night was silent, the only sound the crunch of their snowshoes and the heavy breaths that fogged the air in front of their scarves. The arctic seemed to go on forever. It felt as if they were the only people in the world. Greenleaf focused on each step, on trying to keep his breathing steady.

Just one more step.

Then do it again.

The outcroppings soon became nearly as big a nuisance as the chasms. Several were large enough that they couldn't tell which way was the best path around. Once, they spent twenty minutes huffing to the west only to find a splintered crack in the ice, yawning nearly ten feet wide, blocking their way. Their progress was maddeningly slow. As they made their way between an angular slab and a ravine, Reif slowed down to allow Greenleaf to catch up. "Tell me a story, Imperial."

"What?" Greenleaf didn't look up as he carefully maneuvered around the narrow end of the chasm. "Is this really the best time?"

"Feeling a bit sleepy," Reif said. "Just need something other than my foot placement to focus on."

"You okay?"

The miner came to a stop, turning to look at him. There was no anger in his voice, just weary resignation. "No. I'm not okay. I'm walking through temperatures miles below what my frost suit is designed to deal with. I haven't eaten in days. One of my best friends is dead and buried under feet of snow, and people I grew up with are somewhere dying or dead. I spent the night in a slaughterhouse that resulted from the last time Imperials came to Lahar, I'm possibly being hunted by the same thing that killed all my friends, and I know gods-damned well there aren't any caribou up here, or anything else that's going to keep us alive. I'm going to die up here, and I'm scared, and cold, and I just want to sit down and shut my eyes. But I can't do that, so I need you to help me keep my mind off of all of the many reasons that I'm not fucking okay."

Greenleaf met his eyes, and took a deep breath. "Reif, I..."

"Forget it." The miner turned, and began tromping forward again.

"I tried to cheat my way out of coming here."

That brought both of them to a halt. Deric and Reif turned to look at the kaviak. "What?"

The deep breath Greenleaf took felt like needles in his chest. He resumed his path forward as he spoke, not wanting to meet either of their gazes. "The arrogation came down a month before our graduation. It didn't take long for word to spread. Whoever graduated at the top of the class would be given the honor of answering the Empress' call. I'd worked for years to be at the top of my class. Normally, available postings are awarded in order of class ranking, and all I wanted, all I ever wanted, was to serve in the cavalry."

Kick the right foot forward. Watch the snow fly. Plant the butt of the spear. Slowly transfer your weight, see if the powder holds.

"I learned to ride when I was five. My father taught me, brought me to the garrison's stables to practice. Hours a week, before I was old enough to shave. I even had a lance, some wooden model he'd had made for me." The scarf was now frozen solid. He had to reach up to press on it, breaking the ice and letting his exhalations pass through. He couldn't feel his lips. "When I was admitted to the war college, I knew that only one or two kaviaks would be assigned to the cavalry. I stayed up late practicing forms and studying strategies. I didn't have friends. Never slipped out to go drinking or visit the brothels like some of the others. I stayed for the harvest holidays instead of going home to see my parents. Everything I did was focused on the goal of being top in my class. Four and a half years, I gave everything to that school."

Another step, then another. He no longer tried to watch the horizon for threats. The night swallowed everything but the glow of the Serao against the Watchtower over the horizon, and the glimmers of jeweled colors from curtains of light overhead. Reif walked next to him, Deric behind them.

"I knew. I knew I was at the top of the rankings. Another candidate, Oriana Halfsdotir, was close. Maybe a few points behind me. She'd done better on strategy and theory, but I had her beat on drills. I knew there was a chance she'd get higher marks on our final exams. I didn't know if it would be enough to put her at the top, but I knew it was her only chance to beat me. I'd studied. Worked with a tutor, made sure I knew everything backwards and forwards. Before the arrogation, I was desperate to finish first. But when they announced it, when people started asking me if I was disappointed about going to Lahar..." He swallowed. There wasn't much saliva in his mouth. He tried to lick his cracked lips with a tongue dry as sandpaper. "I couldn't imagine it. Couldn't imagine years of my life, of devotion to everything the Empire is, everything it's done, putting me at the end of the world, guarding people who hated me. Being alone. Discarded. Out loud, I said all the right things. What an honor it would be to answer the call. But alone, at night, as I lay in bed, I was angry."

They came around the edge of an outcropping, and found themselves at the bottom of a rise. Slowly they began to make their way up, walking at an angle to minimize how steep the climb would be. His breath became more labored, and he fell silent as he felt his heart thumping in his chest. His armpits were now icy cold, the malheur sack a searing hot point in the middle of a growing numbness. Greenleaf didn't know how long it took them to reach the top, but it felt like hours. He came to a stop, not moving for a moment, his shoulders rising and falling as his chest heaved. He blinked his eyes rapidly, trying to knock away some of the crystals that blurred his vision. In the distance, an orange flare glowed, bright in the darkness, the molten river of the Serao visible at last.

"It's close," he said, his voice hoarse. He pulled his waterskin from inside his poncho. Even that motion allowed the cold air to slip in. Greenleaf made no attempt to hide his grimace. The cork was frozen to the mouth of the waterskin. He worked it back and forth, breathing on it to loosen it. When he went to drink, only a few icy drops came out. As he squeezed the leather, he could feel the ice inside cracking. He let his arms fall to the side, kneeling down to scoop up a handful of snow. Tugging the scarf down over numb lips, he pushed the powder into his mouth, feeling it melt and swallowing what little water it yielded.

"Don't," Reif said, gripping his shoulder as Greenleaf grabbed another scoop. "You're losing heat to melt the snow."

"Dehydration'll kill me just as fast as hypothermia," the soldier grunted, but he let the snow fall back to the ground. Reluctantly, he accepted Deric's help back to his feet. "Looks like a few miles, unless we hit another chasm."

Reif nodded. He pulled his scarf down to take a drink. Greenleaf's eyes widened at the black patch on the tip of his nose, but he said nothing as the miner shook out the few unfrozen drops between his dried and reddened lips. Deric's bottle yielded nothing, but his face was blank from exhaustion. He tugged the wool back over his mouth.

"We can warm up when we get there. Melt enough snow to drink and recover, then see what the problem is." The older man's voice was thin and weak, but he stuffed the waterskin back into place. "Let's get to it." As Greenleaf started forward, he said, "Finish the story."

"Yeah." Greenleaf nodded. "You can guess what I did. The last stage is Elevation. It's a huge event. People from all over Kaani come to watch. Every candidate that qualifies for graduation has to face a different set of opponents, a different challenge. I wasn't sure that I was still in the lead, but my supervising instructor was fairly sure that I was." Going downhill was trickier. The spikes on the bottom dug into the snow, keeping him from sliding, but he had to drive the heel deep, leaning back to maintain balance. "In the middle of the fight, I had a chance. I'd dropped two of the three opponents, and the other was right there, right in front of me. Nothing he could do to stop me, and I..."

His voice cut off as the spikes struck something hard beneath the snow and skidded off to the side, driving his right leg painfully out from the body. Greenleaf tried to shift his weight to compensate, but his muscles were sluggish, as if the commands from his brain were fighting through molasses, and he pitched forward, spear flying from his hand as he smashed down into the snow, tumbling, numb fingers grasping at nothing. The snow proved worthless as cushioning as the hard and frozen ground leapt up to smash into him again and again, his hipbone hitting a stone with an audible smack as his limbs twisted into agonizing positions, thrashing wildly. He came to rest in a heap at the bottom of the hill.

Greenleaf lay motionless, staring up at the black sky, taking deep lungfuls of freezing air. The furred hood had been thrown back, one ear exposed as the wool cap was shoved up to the side. The pain in his nose drove past the numbness, bringing tears to his eyes, and a flash of panic ripped through him as he brought gloved fingers up, dabbing to check for blood. To his relief, no scarlet dotted the leather fingertips. He glanced up at the scraping sounds of Reif and Deric trying to stay upright as the skidded down the hill towards him, relief plain on their faces as he struggled to a seated position.

"Gods," Reif breathed as he reached him, gripping his arm and hauling him to his feet. Greenleaf gasped at the spike of pain in his hip, but it faded quickly. "Anything broken?"

The kaviak carefully brought weight onto his right foot, shaking his head as the dull pain throbbed up his side. "I don't think so." He spotted a glint thirty feet away, and struggled painfully over to where his spear had fallen, snowshoes dragging as he limped. Leaning down, he picked it up. His fingers ached as he gripped the haft, and he realized that his teeth were chattering as he shook snow from his sleeve, which had pulled free of the glove in the fall. The skin of his wrist was burning from the cold.

He took a moment to check his frost suit, his fingers fumbling as he tried to reseal the cuffs. After a moment, Reif pushed his hands aside and adjusted the fastenings for him. Greenleaf couldn't feel his fingers or toes any longer. Part of him wanted to pull off the gloves to inspect for the black flesh that had devoured so much of his right hand, but a much larger part reminded him how disastrous that would be while simultaneously quailing at the idea of seeing. As Reif tugged his collar back up, snug around his throat, he muttered, "I'm feeling numb. Fingers, toes. Might have compromised the frost suit. I don't think it's working."

"It's working fine," Reif said. "Haven't felt my toes since we passed that larger crevasse." His eyes flicked up from Greenleaf's collar to meet the kaviak's stare. "It's just cold. Too cold for the suits."

"Even if we found food…"

"I know."

Greenleaf took a deep breath. Every inhalation sent shivers through his body, but it helped clear the fog that seemed determined to settle over his thoughts. "Let's go. If we're going to die, I want to die warm."

Their progress was slower. While he believed his assertion that he hadn't broken anything was true, his hip throbbed, and the ribs he'd broken back on the coast were aching again. His muscles seemed reluctant to move, every lift and set of a snowshoe feeling like a herculean effort. He gripped the haft of his spear as tightly as possible, afraid that if he dropped it again he'd not be able to pick it back up.

"We must be close." Reif and Greenleaf turned at Deric's slurred words. The mining foreman sounded drunk, his syllables running together, and had come to a halt, leaning forward, hands braced against his knees. "Getting hot. I can't see it, but maybe we're close to a vent or somethin'."

Frowning, Greenleaf leaned down, bracing against his spear to keep from falling over. He held his hand close to the ground, but felt nothing. "Reif, do you feel it?"

Reif shook his head. "I think we're still too far to feel anything from the Serao."

"The hell you two talkin' bout?" Deric leaned up, eyes wide. "It's getting hot. It's really gods-damed hot."

"Come on," Reif said, shooting Greenleaf a worried glance. "We're close. Not much further, and we can warm up."

"I am warm." Deric began fumbling at his poncho. For a moment, Greenleaf thought he was trying to reach his water bottle, but to his horror, the older man began to drag the heavy woolen poncho over his head. He threw it to the ground, pulling his hood back and tugging the woolen skull cap off of his head. Sweat was beaded over his brow, his skin flushed. They reached him just as he tore the scarf from his face. Reif grabbed his hands as Greenleaf picked up the poncho. Deric tried to shove Reif off of him, but his movements were slow and jerky. "Get off me! It's hot!"

"What the hell is wrong with him?" Greenleaf shouted. Deric's head lolled over in his direction, eyes wide and wild, ice already starting to form at the corners of his blistered eyelids. The big man threw a clumsy blow at the soldier, less a punch and more of a weak slap. In his current state, Greenleaf knew he'd be hard pressed to avoid a blow from any healthy opponent, but Deric was far from healthy, and he managed to snag his wrist and twist it behind the foreman's back, holding him in place.

Tears began to form in Deric's eyes as he struggled, freezing moments after forming, tiny jewels glittering in the meager starlight on ruddy cheeks iced with frost. "Please," he said, his voice reedy and weak. "I'm burning up. Please." His salt-and-pepper hair was growing hoarfrost as if the tiny ice crystals were alive, crawling across his head and skin like something organic. The edges of his ears were already a deep, angry red, and Greenleaf knew they would soon darken further to the black, dead flesh devoured by the frigid cold.

"We can't fight him like this!" Reif tried to shove the skull cap back on his head, but Deric was thrashing back and forth, head swinging drunkenly in protest. "Gods-dammit, Deric, stop fighting me! We're trying to help you!"

"What's happening?!" Greenleaf demanded again. He cinched his grip up, and Deric wailed with pain, an eerie, childlike moan that echoed across the frozen ground.

"He's dying, that's what's happening!" Reif gritted his teeth, and drove his fist as hard as he could into the older man's belly. The air burst from Deric's mouth and nose in an insistent cloud of fog, his eyes bugged, and he gagged. If Greenleaf hadn't been holding his arm, he would have fallen to his knees, but instead, he sagged forward, gasping bitterly cold air between blackened and cracked lips.

Ducking down, Reif slung Deric's arm over his shoulder, taking the man's weight. "Get his other arm."

Greenleaf shook his head. "We're moving slowly as it is. If we have to carry his weight…" His voice trailed off, and he muttered, "Fuck it. Hold him for a second." He released Deric's arm, and did his best to drape the poncho back over his shoulders. It hung wrong, bunched up, but Greenleaf shoved the cap back onto his head and tugged the hood over. Deric wept something that might have been a protest, but his voice was so weak and quiet that the kaviak couldn't make it out. Greenleaf dismissed his spear, and as it settled back around his forearm, he ducked under Deric's left arm. "Let's go. Fast as we can."

Reif nodded, and they began shuffling over the ground, the icy tundra creeping past them. There was no kick and lift of the snowshoes, just a dragging motion. Deric stopped fighting them, and when Greenleaf glanced over, the miner had slumped forward, slight puffs of air drifting from his ice-covered nostrils, mumbling something under his breath. He felt as if he weighed as much as a draft horse.

It was no longer about the glow in the distance. It was no longer about navigating around the next chasm, around the next slab of frozen rock. It was just the next step. He just kept planting his foot, dragging the snowshoe forward to crunch down on the ice, and doing it again, gasping frozen air with each painful step.

Foot by foot, they shuffled over the ice. Several times, one or both would stumble, dragging all three to a heap on the ground. Each time, it took several long and painful minutes to stand. Every breath seemed to drag more of the rapidly vanishing warmth from Greenleaf's chest. Every step drove the sensation out of a bit more of his body. He could no longer feel his arms. His legs were leaden posts, heavy things he had to twist his body to swing forward, snowshoes plowing long furrows in the powder. His vision was so blurred he could barely make out the orange glow before them.

The pain of walking vanished, replaced with a horrible numbness that had nibbled away at more and more of his flesh. His muscles no longer cramped, they simply felt like lumps of raw clay, dead and unwilling. An image swam into his mind, muscles white with ice, cracking with every step, falling apart to hang from bones brittle with crystals of frost.

Greenleaf could no longer tell how far away they were. There was no end, no beginning to this ordeal. There was only the next step, the war between the weaving momentum of his dull and dying body and the drag of the frozen earth beneath them. Every lurching stumble forward was a battle, any sense of victory driven from their minds by the every-present horror of another impossible step to come. There were no words. He was certain that if he opened his mouth to speak, his jaw would crack, tumbling to the ground to shatter like an icicle. The only sound was the huffed exhalations of him and Reif, punctuating the wheezing weak gasps from Deric's unconscious form. The dark night was bearing in, swallowing up the vista, wrapping his world in the cold black. He stared, unblinking, at the ground before him, the only thing left that mattered.

He had no concept of how long they'd stumbled forward, how long they'd dragged their snowshoes through powder undisturbed for centuries, for surely nothing living had ever walked here. Minutes, hours, days. Through the icy fog that had crept into his mind, filling every space to bury his sense of self under that thick layer of white, a thought taunted him. This was death. His corpse lay somewhere in this dead and abandoned corner of the world, a place any creator had made impassable and forbidden. As punishment for his trespass, they would spend eternity in the dark: cold, numb, forever trudging forward to a warmth that would never touch their skin. He could not remember being warm. Could not remember the sensation of hot tea trickling down his throat, chasing chills away from his warm breath and heated blood.

In a flash, his body reminded him. The sensation of liquid fire bloomed in his hips and shoulders, pouring down his limbs, a searing heat that filled his veins. He gasped, his eyes wide, and nearly stumbled as sweat burst upon his cheeks and brow. It felt as if he'd thrust his arms and legs into a steaming tub, and while the heat was so joyously welcome at first that he nearly wept, it kept building, kept climbing, until he felt as if he'd been thrown into a sauna. The frost suit clung to him, stifling him, strangling him. The poncho hung on him like a burning tarp, choking him with the heat.

Greenleaf had never felt anything quite like this. His thoughts, so torpid and sluggish, were all shrieking at him to cool down, that his body was cooking. His hands and feet howled in pain, nerves deadened in the arctic chill waking to screaming life. He reached for his hood, just to push it back for a moment to vent some of the heat, but as he did, he caught Deric's face out of the corner of his blurred vision. The miner was barely breathing. Thin trickles of fog slipped from his nose, which was angrily red with a coal-black tip. Every bit of his face was covered in hoarfrost. Past him, Reif stared blindly forward, his face slack, his chest heaving as he broke into a deep wracking cough.

You haven't failed yet.

His father's voice clawed its way up through the panic and the delirium.

Not yet. Everything can go wrong, everything can fall apart, but until you stop, until you turn back, until you lay down and die, you haven't failed the mission yet.

"So hot." He didn't know if he'd said the words aloud or just imagined them. Neither Derick or Reif reacted. Another step.

Bloodied, broken, bruised. None of those are failure. You haven't failed yet.

Greenleaf reached up and took hold of the voice, clinging to it like a preserver in wind-tossed seas. Desperately, he poured everything he could into that thought, winning another step.

Don't think about how far. Just take another step.

He did.

Now do it again, Tomas.

Captain Tomas Greenleaf couldn't imagine the moment when the ice gave way to dry pumice slabs, each the size of tables. He and Reif Zdene couldn't possibly drag the mining foreman of Lahar Valley from the ghost-filled corpse of an abandoned school to the shores of fire, where the blazing heat pouring off the glowing surface of the Serao drove back the chill of an entire arctic wasteland. The distance was too far, the cold had wroughbt too terrible a toll on their starving, exhausted bodies.

Instead, they fought for every step. Every shuffled lurch forward was a victory in itself, every time the two men decided to go a bit further instead of laying down a triumph. There was no surge of motivation, no period of relief that let them finish the journey, just one agonizing step after another, an impossible odyssey of pain. When they sank to their knees, bathed in the warmth of a burning river, there was no joyful shout of victory, but just the shuddering sighs of two men at last granted leave to fall.

CHAPTER 18

He wasn't sure how long they'd laid there. Greenleaf drifted in and out of consciousness. Every time he fell asleep on the steaming warm rocks about fifty feet from the Serao, another part of his body would cry out in pain as the heat drove the numbness from his bones. His discomfort warred with his exhaustion, but it wasn't until a hand gripped his shoulder that he managed to blearily and painfully struggle to a seated position.

"Here." Deric offered him a waterskin. The foreman's face was a wreck. One eye had swollen completely shut. The majority of his nose was dead black skin, as was his right ear. His upper lip had cracked so badly that it looked like someone had taken a razor to it. There was no blood, just raw red flesh. When the foreman offered a weak grin, the effect was ghoulish. "Yeah, figure if I look half as bad as I feel, it's not a pretty sight. Drink."

Greenleaf tipped back the waterskin, and gulping gratefully at the lukewarm water. His mouth was so painfully dry that the first swallow seemed to be absorbed into his tongue and cheeks, like long-abandoned sponges sucking up any moisture they could find. "Reif?" he croaked. His voice was a ruin.

"Still unconscious. But he's breathing. I managed to dribble a bit of water into his mouth."

Nodding, the kaviak climbed to his feet, unable to keep the moan from slipping past his dry lips as his muscles screamed in protest. He slowly turned, stretching his limbs as he took in their surroundings. His eyes widened as they fell on the Serao. At its widest point in Lahar, the river of molten fire was about sixty feet across. Compared to the hellish mouth of the river, Lahar was a trickle. In the distance, a cascade of lava poured from a gaping cave a hundred feet up the slopes of the Watchtower, which vanished in the clouds overhead. The glowing orange lake at the base of the firefall was massive, easily a thousand feet across, and a river poured forth, a thick blaze of liquid rock wider than a city block, carving a canyon through the glittering pumice and basalt lining its banks. It was so bright it hurt to look at, and despite being over fifty feet away, the heat poured off in unrelenting waves like a blast furnace.

The heat had driven the ice back, holding a eon-long front against the arctic about seventy feet from the banks of the Serao. As Greenleaf looked back out in the direction they'd come, he could see the white fog over the frozen landscape, their dragging footprints leading to this point. Reif lay curled up a few feet away, Deric's poncho folded up and tucked under his head. About two hundred feet to the east, he spotted a plume of steam, and pointed. "Is that..."

Deric nodded. "An oasis. There's another about three hundred feet past that, and I think I can make out one on the other side of the river."

Greenleaf nodded. "I don't suppose there's anything near there worth seeing."

"Doubt it. Nothing lives near oases. The fumes coming off are pretty nasty. I did find those, though." The miner pointed, and Greenleaf saw a neat pile of pale brown eggs between them and the banks of the river. His eyes widened, and Deric said, "Found five or six tern nests. Probably more, but I didn't want to stray too far. Got as close as I could and let them sit in the heat. Figured after a bit, they'd be cooked through. It's something, anyway."

They both turned as Reif stirred, the motion drawing a wince from Greenleaf as his hip howled in protest. Reif had pushed himself up on his arms, but his eyes were still shut as he groaned. Deric limped over. "Don't try to stand up, not all at once." Glancing back at Greenleaf, he said, "I have the other two waterskins melting over there. Grab one, will you?" Moments later, Reif was drinking greedily, draining the skin in half a minute.

Wiping his mouth, he looked up at Deric. "Gods. You look like hell."

"Lost some of those boyish good looks yourself," Deric said.

"Yeah." Glancing to Greenleaf, Reif said, "If I might suggest a new Imperial policy, can we make that shit we just did illegal?"

"I'll write the Empress." Reif extended an arm, and Greenleaf took it, helping the miner to his feet. Deric stepped away for a moment as Reif leaned against the soldier until his head stopped spinning, returning moments later with several eggs in his hand.

"Take these, will you? They're hot."

Several of the eggs had a small red spot on them, but no one cared. Greenleaf shoved his gloved thumb through the shell, peeling the small egg and stuffing it into his mouth. It was overcooked and rubbery, the yolk so dry it fell apart like powder between his teeth. It was the most delicious thing he'd ever eaten.

"There are more," Deric said.

Reif and Greenleaf were already moving. As they approached the pile of a dozen or so eggs, the heat began to build astonishingly quickly. The air was heavy and dry, and they quickly gathered up a handful of eggs and backed away. "Gods," Reif said, shaking his head. "That's so much hotter than home."

"Closer to the source." Deric glanced over at the gargantuan firefall. "Much closer. By the time it gets to Lahar, it's been cooled by almost fifty miles." He grimaced as he spoke, prodding his cheeks with his fingers.

"That's a problem," Reif said. "You could barely get close enough back in the Lyceum to look for the basalite."

"In the Lyceum, the Serao was nine feet down inside a crack." Deric pointed. "No need here." Along the banks of the Serao, clusters of tiny crystals glittered red-green in a thin line above the surface. "The blockage is upstream."

"That probably means it's in the mountain," Reif said, pushing his hood back as he stared towards the base of the Watchtower. "I don't see any landslide or avalanche. Doesn't look like anything's blocked it at the surface."

"If that's the case…"

Reif finished Greenleaf's thought. "Then we came all this way for nothing. Cole, Poyel, Braddock, Cailyn, they all died just so we could come up here and realize there's nothing to be done."

The three stood silent for a long while, the low rumbling sound of the Serao flowing smoothly past the only sound. There was little wind, and the sky was as clear as glass. Greenleaf was already wholly exhausted, but the weariness that settled over his shoulders had nothing to do with the physical toll their journey had taken. He let out a long, slow breath, feeling an odd sense of relief despite their failure.

"I guess that's it, then." Deric pulled the cap off his head. "We're done."

"How long can we survive on eggs and melted snow?" Reif asked.

"How long do we want to survive on eggs and melted snow?" the foreman shot back. "We have no shelter, nothing to protect us the next time a storm rolls through. There's nowhere to go."

"Any chance Edeline will send someone to find us?" Greenleaf asked.

"Doubtful. Without knowing what happened, it's too big a risk, especially after losing two miners and several of our most experienced hunters," Reif said.

"Fine. Then let's be sure."

"Be sure of what?"

"That the blockage is actually in the mountain, where we can't get to it."

"Imperial, use your eyes," Reif snapped. "There's no hidden dam, nothing blocking our view. We have a clear view from here to the mouth of the mountain. Even if something had fallen here, the Serao is too hot, too strong. You could drop a gods-damned hill into the middle, and it'd burn away in minutes."

"I'm sorry, do you have a pressing engagement?" Greenleaf shot back. "Something keeping you? We've come this far, walked through the frozen cellar of hell. We're dead. We're beat to pieces, half eaten by frostbite. Today, or tomorrow, or a week from now, I'm going to lay down, and that'll be my story. Succeed or fail, makes no difference to the three of us. But I followed you two out here on the idea that it makes a hell of a difference to everyone back in Lahar." He glared at the pair of them. "I may have wanted nothing to do with Lahar, but I'll be damned if I give up before I make absolutely certain we're done."

Reif returned the glare, but finally looked to Deric. "Is there anything, anything at all you can think of that could block the flow above ground that we wouldn't see?"

Deric shook his head. "Nothing." He paused, then offered a half-shrug. "But I never thought anything could block the Serao anyway, so what do I know? We can follow it towards the firefall, get as close as we can. Make sure the basalite is visible the whole way. If it's not, we at least know where the problem lies. Mark it or something on the off chance Edeline isn't smart enough not to throw good money after bad."

***

They refilled the water skins with snow, leaving them to melt, and dropped their packs before making their way upstream. It didn't take long for Greenleaf to realize how narrow the band of comfort that existed in this place actually was. Ten feet closer to the Serao, the heat became constant and intense, battering any bits of exposed flesh like roasting meat. Drawing any closer than thirty feet was impossible. However, outside of a certain distance, the temperature didn't drop, it cratered, the chill of the arctic eager to gobble whatever heat they'd managed to recover.

In single file, the trio walked across the rough surface. The ground here was hot enough that all moisture had long ago been driven away. Oddly regular octagonal chunks of basalt were interspersed with swells and clusters of pumice, making for irregular and treacherous footing. Their progress was deliberate to avoid rolled ankles and abraded knees, but after the slog across the open ice, it felt almost as if they were sprinting.

The surface of the river back in Lahar was a dull reddish-orange, blotched with large sections of darkness, throwing a dull flame-colored light over the buildings. Next to the hellish mouth of the Serao, it was a weakly burning coal. The lava here was the searing color of a flame's heart, flowing at nearly twice the speed. A few bubbles surfaced, but very little discoloration marred the surface. The light pouring off hurt the eyes, sending shivers through the air above, leaving everything on the far side a dancing visual wobble. The longer he peered at it through squinted eyes, the more Greenleaf doubted anything could dam up this torrent of fire. It was a gushing wound in the very flesh of the world, and the blood pouring forth had done so for thousands of years.

The bright light was what kept them from seeing until they were right on top of it. A large chunk of basalt had long ago been shoved up from beneath the ground, jutting up at a drunken angle, looking like a ramp from which some crazed priest would hurl sacrifices. The slope climbed at a forty-five degree angle, nestled in the crook of a gentle curve of the Serao, the top about thirty feet above the surface. As they drew closer, Reif stopped, squinting. "Do you see that?" he asked, pointing.

At first, Greenleaf saw nothing. But as his eyes struggled to make out detail among the fiery light, he spotted a thin dark line, extending from the top of the outcropping at a slight angle down to the river. "What is that? A rope?"

"That lava is twice as hot as back home," Deric said, shaking his head. "Not a rope in the world that could get even close before bursting into flame."

"Let's try to get a closer look," Greenleaf said.

They made an attempt to approach from the base of the outcropping, but gave up immediately. There was no way to get close enough on the ground without the heat beating them back. Finally, they moved to the base of the incline, and began to climb. The bulk of the formation did a good job of blocking most of the Serao's heat, but the rock beneath them was getting hotter and hotter as they climbed. Greenleaf could feel it radiating through the soles of his boots. About halfway up, Reif, who was in the lead, came to a sudden stop. Greenleaf nearly bumped into him from behind, saying, "What?"

"It's a chain."

A steel spike, blotched and pitted with rust, as wide around as Greenleaf's forearm, had been hammered down into a crack in the stone. It had been driven through a chain link nearly six inches across, a loop of bright metal that connected to a long string of smaller links. The chain extended up to the edge of the outcropping, disappearing over the drop into the Serao itself.

Deric made his way further up, frowning. "That's not... Where the hell did this come from?"

"I thought you said no one came up here."

"No one does. There's nothing to hunt. The coast is twelve miles to the west." Deric struggled to keep his footing on the steep slope as he stepped to the side, tilting his head as he inspected the spike. "But someone put this here."

"Can't have been long," Reif said. "Doesn't matter how good that steel is, the Serao'll melt it away eventually."

Deric reached out to grab a crack in the slope, and hissed in pain, drawing his hand back. "Gods, that's hot." He'd removed his gloves at some point, but pulled them back on, testing the ground through the thick leather before nodding. He pulled himself closer, making his way inch by inch with the others watching.

"Careful," Reif said, eyes wide as he watched, his hands coming up every time Deric's feet skidded over the slope as if to catch him. "It's a long tumble down."

"I know, I'm just trying to..." A chunk of pumice Deric had braced his right foot against snapped off, clattering back down the hill, and he threw his hands out without thinking, his fingers grabbing the third link of the chain, his other hand seizing the spike. He cried out, releasing the spike. "Shit's like a cooktop!"

"It's metal, you idiot!" Reif began scrambling up after to help him.

"I know it's metal. I didn't mean to..." Deric trailed off, and stared down at his left hand, still holding the link. "Reif, this isn't hot."

"That's impossible," Reif huffed, coming alongside him. Greenleaf made it up to their level just as Reif touched another link, this one closer to the spike. He frowned, and pulled off his glove. Greenleaf started to cry out an objection as the miner pressed his fingertips on the metal, but Reif's eyes widened as he said, "He's right. It's not even warm. Not cold, either."

"There's no rust." Deric's one visible eye was wide, the bloodshot whites staring down at the thick chain. "The spike has rust, but the chain..."

"Gods." Reif reached down to touch another link with his right hand, a link that matched the color and texture of the bracer on the kaviak's arm. "It's aquasteel. Refined fucking aquasteel."

Greenleaf shook his head. "Each of these links is almost as much material as my spear. This would cost a fortune. Why would some-one..."

"It's the only metal that could survive the Serao," Reif said. "If you wanted to lower something into the lava, it has to be aquasteel. Nothing else could last more than a day or so."

"How long has it been here?"

"There's no way to know. It's not going to melt, or rust, or weaken."

"Whatever's on the other end, it has to be the source of the block, right?" Greenleaf asked.

Deric shuffled his way to the north side of the outcropping, squinting as he stared down into the burning river. "It's hard to say, but I can't make out any basalite. No glittering, no green." He turned to stare at the chain, his face slack. "And it's not what's on the chain that's the problem. It's the chain itself."

Greenleaf shook his head. "But we don't even know what's on the other end."

"You asked. On your first day here, remember?" Deric ran his fingers through his hair. "Why we didn't use aquasteel sieves to mine the Serao."

"I did?"

"You did." The foreman's jaw tightened as he spoke. "Raw aquasteel bonds with refined on contact, hardens immediately. It can't be removed, can't be shifted, can't be melted, not ever again. That chain has been dipped in the Serao for gods only know how long. Every drop of raw aquasteel that brushes against it solidified instantly. Every drop made it bigger, made it fill more of the river. Every drop turned that chain into a fucking dam."

"Who would be stupid enough to do this?" Reif asked in disbelief. "This chain would cost a fortune."

"Could someone have stolen shards?" Greenleaf asked, carefully watching both for their reaction.

"Not from Lahar. Every ounce mined is logged, every shard measured and documented," Deric said. "Edeline verifies my count, and Proudlake has to sign off on everything moving into storage, and everything going out. He does the inventory, sends all the records back with the shards."

"Besides, we don't have any shifters in Lahar," Reif said. "Even if someone stole a shard, you need a trained shifter working with a smith to set aquasteel in its final form. This chain couldn't have been made in Lahar."

And Laharians would know how disastrous this would be. "So it's Imperial." Greenleaf shut his eyes, his stomach a hollow ball despite the eggs.

"Has to be."

"The Empire hasn't been up here since..."

Greenleaf interrupted Deric. "Since the Chorale abandoned the Lyceum. This thing has been in the Serao for almost a century. No wonder it's blocking it up."

"Why would the Chorale do this?" Reif asked.

"I have no idea. That journal, it said they were researching the Serao and the oases, right?" The Laharians nodded, and Greenleaf said, "Maybe it's some Chorale artifact, something to measure whatever the hell they were interested in. Maybe they fully intended to come back, pull it out before it was a problem."

"But the trijjat came, and they had to run," Reif said, his face clouded with anger. "They dumped this, left it, and a century later, it's choking us to death."

Greenleaf felt a numbness wholly different from the chill of the ice. "Can we get it out?"

Deric reached over, gave the chain an experimental tug. It didn't move. "I don't know. If it's big enough that it's choking off the flow of the Serao, it's really damn big. Aquasteel is light, but it's not just pulling the aquasteel up. It's the weight of all the lava on top of it. If we had a team of yaks, a dozen more people, maybe."

"Not that we have any way of letting Lahar know," Reif said. "Even if it could be moved, there's no way of getting the help we need to move it."

Greenleaf struggled to his feet, his boots skidding slightly on the terrain. "Come on. Let's get back to the gear."

"There's nothing in our bags that can fix this, Greenleaf," Reif snapped.

"No, there isn't, but there's nothing here that can fix it either," Greenleaf shot back. "You're angry, and I get it. The Empire is still taking from Lahar, even decades after they left. But we know what the problem is now. Let's get back, eat something, and think about how to deal with this. We're not done yet."

Reif surged to his feet, eyes flashing. Before he could say something, Deric's hand shot out, grabbing the back of his poncho and dragging him back down to the incline. Reif lost his footing, and slid a foot or so before stopping his descent. "The hell is your..." He fell silent as he saw the foreman's finger on his lips.

"Shut up." Deric's voice trembled. "There's something next to our packs."

Greenleaf spun, the spear sprouting from his bracer to fall into his hand. The distance and the distortion in the air from the heat made it difficult to make out, but he could make out a figure, in a crouch, next to the trio of packs they'd left. It started to move, and after a few moments, he realized it was approaching them. "Stay here," he muttered. He eased his way down the slope, trying to make as little sound as possible, skidding over loose chunks of pumice.

As the figure drew closer, moving directly towards them, he slowed his breathing, ignoring the pangs of stiffness in his legs as he lowered into a crouch, the gleaming spearpoint coming to the ready position. He tensed, preparing to strike, but as the creature came closer, the distortion faded and the spearpoint dropped. Behind him, Reif and Deric released strangled sounds of joy, and the three stumbled and ran across the baked stone shores until the running sled dog reached them, tail wagging furiously.

"How…" Greenleaf stared in disbelief as Reif sank to his knees, burying his face in the soft grey fur. "Where did she come from?"

"There." Deric nearly wept as he spoke, staring out into the ice. Greenleaf turned to see the three figures approaching, several more dogs padding along beside them, and his breath flew from his chest in a sharp exhalation. He barely kept his feet, relief turning his legs to water, as Braddock, Cailyn, and Cole, wrapped tightly in their frost suits, approached from the ice.

CHAPTER 19

As Reif pounded Braddock on the back and Deric clasped Cole's hand, Greenleaf held back, letting the Laharians have their reunion. When Cole looked over at him, Greenleaf grinned, saying, "You weren't lying: you are a good tracker."

The old hunter shook his head. "Not exactly the stuff of story-books. Spotted your prints headed north. Only one place you could be heading."

"What happened?" Greenleaf asked. "When we found Poyel, we thought something had happened to you."

"Honestly, we thought the same thing," Cole said. "I wanted to set camp a bit further back than we agreed, find better shelter in case the storm rolled in faster than we thought. I sent Poyel to wait for when the three of you came back, show you where we'd settled. Two hours passed, best I could tell, so we tied off the dogs and went to find Poyel on foot. When we did..." His eyes dropped to the ground, and he swallowed. "Figured whatever did for him must have taken the three of you as well. Storm was hitting about that moment. We made our way back to camp and hunkered down, waited it out."

"So you didn't see? What happened to Poyel?"

Cole shook his head. "I shouldn't have sent him to wait alone. Should have sent Braddock with him."

"Not sure it would have mattered," Reif said, reaching out to grip Cole's shoulder.

"Still. My fault." Cole rubbed the bridge of his nose. "We went back and forth as to whether we should go into the compound to look for you three. I'll be honest, I didn't think it was a good idea."

"Probably wasn't," Greenleaf allowed.

"But, didn't feel right heading back with a question mark like that. Thought that even if the worst had happened, we should at least bring your bodies back." He shrugged. "Saw your tracks following the outer wall north. Wasn't hard to reason where your head was at. Still, I wouldn't have bet on the three of you actually making it up here."

"Not something I'd want to repeat," Reif said. Deric said nothing. Cole's eyes traveled over the frostbite and blisters over the men's faces, and he nodded.

"How were you planning on getting back?"

"We weren't," Greenleaf responded. "Thought we might be able to find the problem, do something about it. But we barely survived the walk north. Going back was never a possibility."

Cole looked over the three of them, lifting an eyebrow. Braddock was leaning on his spear, bow strung and slung over his shoulder, while Cailyn had lingered back. She offered Greenleaf a nod when he glanced over. Finally, Cole said, "Well, I'll expect you're hungry. We've got the sleds staked out next to the oasis. Stinks like week-old eggs, but it's warm, and there's plenty of food. Once you feel strong enough, we can head back."

"Not sure the last time I heard something I liked better than that," Reif said. "Let's go grab our packs first."

"Don't worry about them," Cole said. "We'll come get them once you've recovered a bit. Not like they're going anywhere."

Reif shrugged, and they began walking back to the column of yellowish steam hanging over the ice. The chill began to reassert itself as their distance to the Serao grew, but the damp and heavy heat of the oasis took hold very quickly, the scent of sulphur crawling up Greenleaf's nostrils. Through the thick clouds of steam, he could make out the bubbling rainbow-colored mud, the pit nearly fifty feet across, a pond of thick boiling sludge. The sleds waited at the far side.

Twenty feet minimum.

The words bubbled up at the back of his tired mind, and Greenleaf frowned as the stained ground beneath his feet squished. He gave his head a brief shake. Cole glanced over, seeing the soldier's expression. "How long's it been since you slept?"

"Slept, or passed out from exhaustion?" Greenleaf asked, giving a weary chuckle.

Cole nodded. "While you eat, we'll set up the coverall. Let you get a few hours before we head back."

"When you say few, do you mean ten?"

"Wish we could, but I'd rather not be caught out if another storm front comes through. I'll give you as long as we can, but we need to get back to Lahar."

Greenleaf nodded. "I get it. We can always rest on the..." He trailed off, tilting his head, coming to a stop. *Twenty feet. No less.* He struggled to remember where the voice came from, and slowly turned, looking back towards the Serao, trying to find what was itching at the back of his neck. Reif and Deric hobbled forward behind him, with Braddock and Cailyn bringing up the rear. He couldn't see anything behind the Laharians. Braddock saw him turn, and tilted his head curiously.

"Something behind us?" the big man asked, turning his head to glance back. His words were difficult to make out, between the mask and his distance.

Twenty feet.

"No, I don't..." Greenleaf trailed off, glancing between Braddock and Cailyn, who had come to a halt as he did. The voice kept repeating the same words, trying to shout through the fog of exhaustion in his head, and he turned back to Cole, frowning. "You didn't ask us what we found."

"What?" Cole tilted his head.

"We told you that we came up to check out the Serao, see if we could find the blockage. You didn't ask."

"Figured there was time for all that," Cole said.

Greenleaf didn't respond, but he kept Cailyn in his peripheral vision as he spoke to Cole. "Twenty feet is the rule. What they taught us."

Frowning, Cole said, "I don't understand."

"I think you do," Greenleaf said. He spotted Reif come to a halt, staring back in confusion between the two. "Cailyn. There a reason you have that bow strung?"

The woman glanced at Cole, but said, "It's dangerous out here, Captain. You know that."

"You have an arrow nocked, too." Cailyn glanced down at the feathered fletchings clutched between her fingers as Greenleaf turned slowly to eye the bow in Braddock's hands. "Twenty feet is the distance you maintain between you and a prisoner." He kept his hands clear of his body, and finished turning to stare at Cole. "I'd really appreciate it if the three of you would stow those arrows, Cole."

"Gods, Imperial, what the hell are you..." Reif's mouth shut with a snap when he saw the expression on Greenleaf's face. He looked over at Deric, who was staring wide-eyed at Cole.

"I don't want to repeat myself. Stow those arrows, and let's go have a chat."

Cole took a deep breath, his brown eyes mournful above the scarf. "No need to repeat, Captain. Heard you just fine. But I'm afraid we're going to keep them nocked. I do need you to go ahead and summon that spear of yours. Slowly."

"Why do I need my spear?" Greenleaf asked, trying to keep his voice even.

"Not so much that you need it, but more that I really need you to toss it into that mud over there."

"Malachi, what did you do?" Deric's voice trembled.

Greenleaf made no motion to summon the spear.

"Cole, what are you doing?" Reif stepped forward, and froze as Cailyn and Braddock's broadheads came up sharply to train on him. His eyes were almost bulging, darting between the two. "What is this? You're not going to hurt us! We're Laharians, you're not going to hurt another Laharian!"

"They already did." Greenleaf's voice was hard and cold as the ice. Reif shook his head a few times, then paled as realization dawned. "What happened? If Poyel didn't know what was happening, why didn't you send him with us?"

Cole drew his own bow, nocking an arrow. "He knew. Just had a change of heart. Didn't feel right, you having saved Braden and him. Pushed Cailyn off the sledge, tried to make it back to the Lyceum to warn you. We caught up with him before he made it."

"You killed Poyel?" Reif's voice was barely a whisper. "Why?"

"Same reason they meant to abandon us. Same reason he doesn't need to ask us what we found." The kaviak might as well have been carved from stone, his eyes locked on Cole. "You already know what we found, don't you?"

"It's not personal, captain." Cole blinked slowly as the wind blew ice crystals across his brow. "I tried to talk you and the others out of this. But we had to be sure you didn't interfere."

"You put the aquasteel in the Serao," Deric said. It wasn't a question.

"Few months back. Hunting trip."

"Cole..." Reif shook his head. "Why would you do that? You know what it's doing."

"I know." Cole gestured at Greenleaf. "The spear, captain. I won't ask again."

"And if I don't?"

"There wasn't a kaviak assigned to my legion during the war, but I did come across a few. I hold no illusions about how dangerous you are. But you're exhausted. Doubt you're at a hundred percent. At least one of us'll feather you before you move ten feet," Cole said. Greenleaf could hear the creak of bowstrings tugging against bone behind him. "I'd rather not do that. Toss the spear. You have my word, we'll see you warm and fed before we come to what's next."

Greenleaf still didn't move. "You sure you understand the damage you're bringing to Lahar? It's not just the aquasteel. You heard Deric. The level of the Serao is falling. People's homes are freezing. The forge is going to fail. And if you'd seen what we'd seen back at the Lyceum, you'd know that's nowhere near the worst of it." He tilted his head. "That chain is going to kill everyone you know."

"I doubt it. We'll lose Lahar, but the people will find new homes. Build a new life," Cole said. "They'll start over, but they'll start over in a country that's still at peace. Have a chance to see their sons get married, have kids. That bridge reaches the other side of the Breaking, and all that goes up in smoke."

"The bridge? What the hell does leaving Laharians to freeze and die have to do with the bridge?" Reif asked. "That's thousands of miles away!"

"Thousands of miles tends to draw really damn close when the army needs people." He stepped forward, pointing vaguely south. "There are fifty million people in the gods-damned Dominion. Fifty million is a hard, long war if you have a steady supply of aquasteel to outfit your cavalry. Fifty million is impossible if you don't. I love Lahar. I do. But between Lahar and seeing the world catch fire again? That's not a gods-damned choice."

"You think stopping the aquasteel is going to keep our soldiers from crossing the bridge?" Greenleaf shook his head. "How many shards have been mined in the last century? How many soldiers are already wearing liquid armor, carrying spears like mine? The Imperial army seized the Fingers. They crossed the Greymare Peaks. They have the Chorale at their back. You think an empire that wills its way across the Breaking is going to turn back because they don't get more aquasteel?"

"I do."

"Then you're a fool."

"Others say different. Anything that gives pause before slaughter is worth trying," Cole said.

"Says the man who snapped his friend's neck and is leaving women and children to face the trijjat," Greenleaf shot back.

"What are you talking about?"

"The Serao is the only thing holding those things back. We saw it. In the Lyceum." Greenleaf pointed back to the molten river. "If that blockage keeps growing, if it chokes the Serao off, Lahar will face the same nightmare that the Lyceum did. They had a trained force of soldiers and dozens of the most gifted resonants in the world. They lasted days. How long do you think a few hundred undefended villagers will last?"

"He's right, Cole," Deric said, stepping forward. His hands were up in front of him, as if trying to soothe an angered horse. "Help us. I don't think it's too late. We can bring up more men, all the dogs. Get the yaks from the next convoy. We can get the chain out before it chokes off the river, get the Serao to rise back to where it should be."

Cole shook his head. "No."

"You want to save lives. I get that," Reif said. "Here's your chance. You had us burn our spears to hold the trijjat back on the shore because you knew how important it was to keep them back. Help us keep them back now."

Cole didn't speak for a long moment. The wind drifting over the ice whistled, and the sulfurous mud of the oasis bubbled quietly next to them. Overhead, the aurora had burst into stunning scarlet and purple life, throwing an eerie light over the old hunter's shrouded face. Finally, he said in a quiet, flat voice, "I am saving lives." He met Greenleaf's eyes. "You get to save Braden twice. Once, by standing between him and danger. And now again with your silence. Take some solace in that."

"Little chance."

"I hope you feel different before the end." Cole's voice was tinged with regret. "Braddock, Cailyn. If the captain's spear isn't in the oasis in the next ten seconds, shoot him."

"You're not going to shoot him," Deric said, his eyes narrowing.

"I will."

"No, you won't." Deric began walking towards Cole, his big fists clenched at his side. "You just want him unarmed so you can snap his neck. Snap all of our necks."

"Deric, stop." Cole raised his bow, training the broadhead on the miner's face.

"Shoot me, shoot him, there's blood." Deric drew within ten feet. Greenleaf lowered slightly into a crouch while Reif looked around frantically. "Broken neck doesn't spill blood. And you really, really don't want to spill blood, do you?" The mining foreman was shaking with anger. "Did you even look Poyel in the eye when Braddock killed him like you would a chicken?"

The blackened steel of the broadhead was only three feet from Deric's face. "You said the Serao holds them back," Cole said, his voice hard. "You sure the oases don't do the same?"

"You shoot me, you'll find out," Deric snarled. "You willing to take that chance?"

Cole opened his mouth, but closed it again. The arrowhead drooped slightly. His eyes fell for a moment, and when they rose to meet Deric again, they were mournful. "Yeah, Odel. I guess I am."

At this range, the arrowhead slammed through the foreman's eye and drove eight inches out the back of his skull before it stopped. The wet crunch was deafeningly loud in the quiet arctic night. Blood sprayed from the ruin of Deric's skull in a scarlet arc, falling in crimson drops over the mud-streaked ground at their feet. Reif screamed, a wordless howl as his mentor dropped to his knees, his one remaining eye unblinking in the sea of blisters next to the feathered fletchings sprouting from his head.

Before Deric's knees struck the ice, Greenleaf was already moving. There was no conscious thought, no concrete awareness of the moment the switch in his brain flipped. There was no anguished expression on Reif's face, no cries of shock behind him.

There were only targets.

One ahead, temporarily unarmed. Not an immediate threat. Two behind, momentarily distracted.

He sprang off his heels, spinning as he leapt backwards. The spike of pain in his hip was an irrelevance, to be dealt with later.

Cailyn reacted faster than Braddock, loosing her arrow with a shout of surprise. The razor edge of the broadhead neatly sliced across Greenleaf's hood, catching his ear as it flashed past his vision. He felt the sting and the heat of the blood as he rolled, coming up five feet away from the hunter. His hand came up as if in a punch, and as it did, the bracer erupted into liquid motion, flowing into the shape of a spear, the point of which neatly intersected the hollow of Cailyn's throat. The keen aquasteel edge parted skin, muscle, and cartilage with a whisper, and as Greenleaf spun to face Braddock, he tore her throat out as the spearpoint whipped around to address the other hunter.

There was still nearly twenty feet between the two of them. Braddock sighted down and fired, but the spearpoint flashed, and the arrow was knocked aside as Greenleaf darted forward, the distance between them vanishing in a heartbeat. Braddock was fumbling for another arrow in his quiver when Greenleaf whipped the leaf-shaped blade in a flat arc, slicing cleanly through the grip of the bow. The tension of the string ripped the weapon apart, and Braddock screamed as the aquasteel blade sliced off two fingers in the process. The spear spun in the kaviak's hands, and when it flashed forward again, the point exploded through the huge hunter's kneecap, pinning his leg against the muddy stone beneath their feet. Braddock's eyes bulged as he shrieked, falling backwards, his weight tearing what little remained of the joint apart. Greenleaf ripped the spear back, dismissing Braddock as a threat as he turned back to Cole.

Cole was on his back, arms up to shield his face from the blows raining down. Reif had tackled him to the ground, and was sobbing as he drove his meaty fists into Cole's head and face. The hunter's hood had been knocked back, and his nose bent under Reif's knuckles. He howled, spraying blood from the ruin of his nose, and his stiffened fingers shot up into Reif's Adam's apple. The miner gagged, jerking back and falling against the ground, coughing and choking as he scrabbled at his throat. Cole struggled to his feet, then froze as Greenleaf's spearpoint kissed his cheek.

"Stop." The kaviak's voice was void of emotion. "You're done."

Cole's chest heaved, his shattered nose making an odd whistle every time he exhaled. His scarf was soaked in red, and his eyes fell on Cailyn's body. Her sightless eyes stared up at the ribbons of light overhead as blood pooled beneath her, a slowing waterfall spurting from the ruin of her throat. Braddock writhed on the ground, leg and hand a scarlet mess, moaning in loud, choking sobs. Back by the sleds, the dogs were barking frantically, straining at their leads.

"Reif. You with me?"

Reif had risen to his knees. He was still coughing, but between hacks, he took long, reedy breaths. Dismissing him, Greenleaf returned his attention to Cole.

"You're going to harness the dogs, and we're going back to Lahar. Now."

"Gods." Cole's shoulders slumped, and his hands were beginning to tremble. Blood bubbled up on his nostrils. "You killed them."

"Cole." The hunter dragged his eyes up from the carnage to meet Greenleaf's. "You're going back to Lahar. It makes no difference to me at this point whether you're breathing or not when you do. The choice is yours, but I will not ask again."

Cole shook his head. "It doesn't matter. Not anymore."

"Maybe not to you, but how about to him?" Greenleaf jerked his head back in Braddock's direction. "You get to decide if he comes back with us or not."

"You're not going to leave him here."

"Look at my face." Greenleaf reached up and pulled his scarf down, revealing his bloody face and hard stare. Cole recoiled. "Listen to my voice, and believe me when I say that if you don't follow my orders, I will leave him here, alone, bleeding, and crippled, for whatever's out there to find."

The dogs were still barking, letting loose the occasional howl as they tried to pull free of their rigging. Cole tried to hold the kaviak's gaze, but something gave inside him, and his shoulders slumped as his eyes fell back to the ground. "All right. I... just, all right. Just help him, okay?"

"Reif. Can you stand?"

Reif looked up at Greenleaf, a strange expression on his face. "Yeah," he croaked.

"Go see to Braddock. Put a tourniquet on that leg. He's going to lose it, so tie it tightly."

Reif nodded, a quick jerk of the head, before stumbling to his feet and staggering over towards Braddock.

Greenleaf gestured with his spear. "Move." Cole turned, and slowly began walking back towards the sleds. Greenleaf stayed behind him, keeping the spearpoint leveled at a spot between the old hunter's shoulder blades. The dogs were nearly frantic now, thrashing. Greenleaf stopped, and said, "Where are the others? The dogs you had untied?"

"Huh?" Cole looked around slowly. "They were probably frightened by the fighting. Ran."

Greenleaf stared at the dogs. The steam billowing off the oasis made it difficult to tell, but after a few moments, he spoke again. "The dogs aren't trying to get to us."

Cole turned to look. One of the sleds had fallen over. The anchor they'd driven into the ground to keep the sledge and dogs in place was still deep in the ice, but the frenzied pack had yanked it so hard it had tipped. They were pulling away. "They aren't hunting dogs. They get frightened. You just butchered two of their handlers. They're scared."

Greenleaf shook his head. "They're not pulling away from us. They're pulling away from the oasis." His stomach clenched, and his eyes darted over to the steaming mud, trying to make out the surface of the geothermal vent through the yellow clouds. At this distance, the heat was a soaking blanket, smothering and humid. He lowered back into the crouch, spearpoint coming up. One heartbeat passed, then another, and something broke the surface of the boiling liquid.

It was a hand, fingers like brittle branches, long and grasping, steaming mud dripping off. It clutched the muddy rock by the side of the oasis, gripping a crack in the ground, and pulled. The rest of the arm followed, dragging a flat head with closed eyes behind it. As the mud oozed off the face, the eyelids parted, bright blue on a sea of white. The mouth was shut, a wide line slashed in the coal-black skin, and as the trijjat pulled itself free of the oasis, those lips peeled back to reveal broken teeth drumming out a staccato rhythm, a chatter that replaced the baying of the hounds, who had fallen completely silent. A slender tongue, long and red as raw beef, snaked out from between the lips as boiling ooze dripped from the long, spindly limbs. The knees bent the wrong way, a hand splaying out over the ground as the trijjat leaned forward on inverted legs, tongue tip flicking and darting in the steaming air.

The sound that emerged from Cole's throat was not a human one, a guttural moan of terror. The trijjat crawled towards them in languid movements, weaving from one canted leg to another as it crept over the rock, and Greenleaf felt his bladder let go. The panic that bubbled up from deep inside him was not a thing of memory, but something instinctive, primal, and this terror slammed into military discipline like a battering ram. He could feel his focus cracking as the tip of his spear swung to face the new threat. He didn't dare blink, and as the trijjat approached, another flat head broke the surface, than a third, chittering teeth echoing over the stony ground.

Cole backed away, hands up, and Greenleaf followed suit, the two men side by side, retreating from the oasis as the three creatures slowly crept in their direction. The first trijjat reached the point which Cole had stood, and paused. Lowering its head to the ground, the tongue flicked out to a drop of scarlet on the rock. As the tip touched the blood, the chattering stopped. The trijjat's pupils instantly dilated, bulging eyes flooding with sapphire blue, and its gaze snapped up to Cole. With terrifying speed, it skittered over the ground, darting straight towards the hunter. The bent and canted legs coiled beneath and exploded, driving it forward in a leap that crossed the last ten feet in an eyeblink, and the trijjat slammed into Cole just as the hunter threw up his arms. The pair went tumbling down, the momentum carrying them out of the thawed ring surrounding the oasis and onto the cracked ice.

Long fingers encircled wrists, bending Cole's arms back and pinning them to the ground. The hunter thrashed, bucking his hips and trying to bring his legs up to shove the trijjat off. His knee came up hard between its legs, but the creature ignored the blow. Its lips peeled back, revealing black gums with broken teeth, and the trijjat yanked Cole's right arm upward, pinning it beneath his head. The tongue slithered into his armpit, the tip slicing through leather and wool like a scalpel. An amber fluid spilled out, and the trijjat recoiled for a moment, staring down at the malheur sap leaking from the sliced sack. The tongue flicked against the sap once, twice, and then slashed wildly at the area with quick, bloody strokes, ripping through the sack and the fabric beneath, slicing deep into the wall of Cole's chest. Blood fountained, steaming in the air, and where it touched that undulating tongue, it was sucked in, like water into a dry sponge.

Cole shrieked as the tongue slipped between ribs exposed to the frigid night air, the flesh that once covered them ripped and torn. His back arched as more and more of the snaking tongue burrowed deep in his chest, absorbing blood into its mass, the tongue swelling obscenely, like a leech at the end of a long and luxurious meal. Greenleaf saw the trijjat's other hand trace a path down to Cole's groin, finding the inside of his thigh, and with the claw at the end of a long, slender finger, it sliced deep, neatly cutting the thick pulsing artery inside. The blood fountained out, and the other two trijjat silently darted forward, crashing down upon Cole in a frenzy. The hunter's cries changed to a gurgling choke as clawed fingers wrenched his jaw open with the sound of cracking ice, and a tongue was forced down his open mouth.

This was the only chance they would get. "RUN!" bellowed Greenleaf, breaking into a sprint back toward the orange glow of the Serao.

CHAPTER 20

Greenleaf didn't know how long the trijjat would be distracted by Cole's corpse. He didn't know how fast they could move over the open ground that stretched far between them and their packs on the banks of the Serao. He didn't wait to find out. Reif stood next to Braddock, eyes bulging, frozen in place, and Greenleaf seized the miner's upper arm, yanking him out of his paralyzed state and nearly off his feet.

"Braddock!" Reif shouted. "What about him?!" The injured miner lay at their feet, barely conscious, his leg a bloody ruin.

Greenleaf turned back to shout at Reif, and his eyes widened. Two more of the creatures were clambering out of the oasis, eyes fixed on Cailyn's unmoving form. With that same skittering motion, they were upon her, tearing and digging deep. Greenleaf saw one slip its fingers into the hollow above her collarbone and tear it out with a wet crack.

"We can't carry him! Reif, we have to go! NOW!" Reif blanched, but broke into a stumbling run, feet skidding on the muddy stone before they found purchase.

Adrenaline drove them forward, but Greenleaf knew neither was as fast as they might have been. His hip was now a screaming knot of agony, every impact of his right heel sending burning spikes through his body. Reif began to outpace him. When he realized they weren't running next to each other any longer, the miner slowed, offering his hand. Greenleaf waved him off. "Go! Get to the packs!" Reif hesitated, and the kaviak roared, "GO!"

As soon as Reif had increased the distance between them, Greenleaf shifted direction, heading at an angle away from his companion. He'd only been able to glance over Reif's form as they started running, but he hadn't seen any blood on the miner. He could feel the sticky warmth on the side of his face. The bleeding had stopped, but there was more than enough soaking through the fabric of his hood. Half-limping, half-running, he stumbled forward, the ice crunching under his boots, the cold creeping over his exposed face. His toe struck an outcropping, and he fell, reflexively keeping the point of the spear away from his body as he slammed hard into the frigid ground. He rolled, lifting his head to look back at the bloody scene they'd left.

He couldn't count how many trijjat had emerged from the oasis, but at least four were piled atop Braddock's unmoving form. Several more were finishing off Cailyn, and the three that had taken down Cole were starting to lift their heads. Their tongues wove lazy patterns in the air, but the long slender muscles that had flicked at the air before were now obscenely swollen, a deep red color, almost too big for their mouths. In all the carnage, the only sound they'd made beyond the crunching of bone and tearing of flesh was that whispering. Strange, unnatural syllables that had faded as Greenleaf and Reif had run, but swelled once more as two of the trijjat fixed their ice blue eyes on the kaviak, and charged.

They were fast, faster than he could run. By the time he'd clambered back to his feet, they'd covered nearly all of the distance between them, their broken-looking legs springing off the ice in bursts of speed, front claws digging deep and dragging the spindly creatures forward even faster. His grip on his spear was awkward after the fall, and as one of the trijjat coiled its legs and drove forward in a powerful leap towards him, he wasn't in position for a thrust. Instead, he sidestepped the attack, slipping out of the trijjat's path as he whipped the base of the aquasteel shaft around to smash into the creature's jaw. It was a perfectly executed strike.

It may as well have been a light tap.

It was all Greenleaf could do to keep hold of the spear as the creature's bulk knocked it aside, the trijjat flashing past his face, the scent of blood and decay filling the kaviak's nostrils. It crashed into the ice, tumbling uncontrollably for a moment, and Greenleaf spun on his heel to meet the other one, throwing his spear up just in time to block the swipe of long, slender claws. The trijjat's talons screeched as they dragged over the aquasteel, and reflexively, Greenleaf stepped forward and snapped his foot up to kick the creature in the chest.

The trijjat tumbled backwards, landing on its back, but in a flash, its arms and legs twisted unnaturally, driving down into the ice without flipping over, pushing it back up onto its feet. Those whispers poured from its maw around the swollen tongue, which thrashed around like a headless eel. The syllables rang discordant in Greenleaf's ears, insane and yet somehow horribly familiar to some deep part of his brain.

He tried to spin his spear back to a ready position as the trijjat lurched forward towards him. It opened its jaw, and the tongue burst forward, at least three feet long, emerging from the black hollow of its toothless mouth. Something flashed in Greenleaf's peripheral vision, and the trijaat's head jerked to the side. Thick, almost gelatinous blood, nearly black, sprayed in a torrent from where the arrow had pierced through the thickest point of the tongue. The trijjat reached up, grasping at the arrow, and yanked it free, but the barbs of the broadhead ripped the last foot and a half off. The severed tongue fell to the ice, and where the oozing blood spattered on the frozen ground, it hissed and steamed.

There was another *zip* of an arrow flying close to him, and Greenleaf heard wood crack and splinter. He whirled to find the other trijjat back on its feet, staring intently towards the Serao. A broken arrow lie in pieces next to it, and another came hissing in, striking the trijjat just below its right eye. The arrow bent and snapped, the steel point of the arrowhead skipping off the creature's hide as if it were stone. Its sapphire gaze fixed on Reif, who knelt sixty feet away next to their packs, nocking another arrow, and gathered its legs beneath it to charge. It never got the chance.

The aquasteel spearpoint slammed through the side of the trijjat's chest, the gleaming razor edge neatly slicing into the hide. Greenleaf's thrust was perfect, in, then out, twisting the haft as he withdrew, and that same black blood sprayed over his face as he ripped the trijjat's chest open. The entire time, the creature was silent, despite thrashing around. Unblinking eyes stayed locked on Greenleaf as the trijjat's legs failed it, sending it crashing to the ice, and Greenleaf drove his spear straight through one of those sapphire pools and out the back of the creature's head.

He whirled to face the other trijjat, ripping his spear back out, and found the second one stumbling away, shredded tongue waving weakly in the air, whipping black blood in all directions. Greenleaf looked back to Reif. The miner was sighting down again, and the kaviak looked where he was aiming. At least six trijjat were charging towards them, and Reif screamed, "MOVE!" as he nocked and loosed, nocked and loose.

Greenleaf sprinted up alongside the miner, feeling the heat of the Serao lash against his face. He brought the spear up to meet the charging creatures, which were less than fifty feet away. Most of Reif's shots were landing, but none were penetrating, and Greenleaf shouted, "Back! Get as close to the river as you can!"

The pair fell back to the Serao, Reif firing his last two arrows, one of the bags slung over his shoulder. Even through the back of his frost suit, Greenleaf could feel the heat building faster than he thought possible. His boot heel crunched on something. Cooked egg sizzled under his foot. The leather on the back of his neck was burning hot, scalding the back of his neck, and still they came.

The first leapt straight on, eyes fixed on Greenleaf, and the aquasteel blade flashed in the frozen air, slicing from the corner of the mouth up through the eye, then back down to slip with a black spray through the trijjat's throat. The others skidded to a halt, fanning out to either side, the whispers pouring from their mouths, loud enough to be heard over the rumbling of the river. Another step back, and still they advanced. The heat battered Greenleaf like a physical force. He could hear Reif throw down the pack.

Two of the trijjat darted forward, one from the left, one from the right, and Greenleaf spun the spear in his hand, stumbling clumsily through forms he'd thought automatic. He didn't land a blow as the creatures danced nimbly out of range. Their black hides danced with the orange light of the river, the air shimmering between them from the heat boiling from the rock underfoot, the same heat that was burning the kaviak's feet through the thick hide boots. Sweat mixed with blood blurred his vision and poured down his face, but he didn't dare take an instant to wipe it away.

Each time, the trijjat danced forward, whispers dribbling from toothless mouths, and each time the spear drove them back, but every thrust and slash was slower than the last. Desperately, he took two, three more steps back. This time, the trijjat came to a halt, all stopping three feet away from where the kaviak crouched, bloody and sweating, chest heaving like bellows, spear gripped tight. They stood, a line of horrors watching them, blue eyes lit bright with the fires of the river, and the discordant, chaotic whispers settled into a chant, whispered words in unison, syllables that crawled like a spider over his eardrums.

Every breath burned hot, air searing down his throat. Greenleaf smelled smoke, and when he glanced down, the arm of his frost suit was smoldering, leather curling and blackened, wisps of smoke issuing from the seams in the sleeves. The pain in his back and thighs was overwhelming, the heat hammering through the leather and wool to curl and burn leg hairs as the skin beneath began to cook. His heart hammered in his chest, and his vision began to blur. The point of the spear wavered once, then fell to the ground as he released it, falling to his knees, the spear clattering to the ground with an oddly musical sound. He screamed as the heat from the ground poured up through the leather of his breeches, and he could feel big, fat blisters, like rotting overripe fruits, swell up on his skin. Still the whispers continued. Still the blue eyes watched.

Reason was boiled from his brain, caution burned away like chaff in a flame, and he began to crawl forward, towards the trijjat, desperate to get away from the gently flowing incinerator behind him. The light was brilliant, his body throwing a long shadow towards the waiting tongues, and he crawled towards hungry mouths, some part deep inside him having judged that pain lesser than being cooked alive. The closest trijjat lowered onto its forelegs, leaning in, that tongue curling and extending, snaking its way through superheated air towards bloody burning flesh. Those eyes seemed to loom larger than a moon, so fixated upon him that they didn't look up until the thick hide gloves seized ahold of the tongue.

Reif Zdene roared like a lion from behind the woven steel mask of the mining suit, hauling back on his wriggling prey as the trijjat thrashed and writhed. The miner seemed to tower above Greenleaf like a fiery god, the light of the lava bathing over the heavy cowhide. Smoke poured from the ever-blackening leather, but the protection held as he heaved, dragging the creature past their point of no return, towards the searing orange river of molten stone. The wire mask began to glow. Flames curled along the thread of the heavy apron as the trijjat battered frantically, claws digging deep furrows in the thick hide. The miner was implacable. He stomped over searing stone, hauling the trijjat every inch of the way.

The black hide split, ripping open along the back, the throat. The wide lidless eyes were bubbling, and one burst. The end of the tongue stopped thrashing, and began to blacken and curl. Ten feet away from the bank of the Serao, Reif stopped. Gripping the back of the creature's neck with one hand and its back leg with another, the miner lifted the trijjat over his head, and pitched it towards the burning river.

It was too far for him to reach. The trijjat landed five feet away, on stone glowing from the incandescent heat which had battered it for eons. It was enough. The trijjat split wide open, black blood and organs hissing and spitting as they cooked, flames bursting into dancing life at a hundred points, crackling fire drowning out the dying whispers.

Reif turned as the trijjat burned, stomping forward, his suit scorched and crackling, wreathed in smoke and backlit by the flickering pyre of the trijjat. He stooped, picking up the spear, and stalked directly towards the remaining trijjat, which had fallen silent. Reif extended a gauntleted hand, reaching for the now-motionless tongues, and the creatures broke, fleeing back towards the oasis. The whispers had never stopped, fading into the distance as Reif grabbed Greenleaf's collar and dragged him out of hell.

CHAPTER 21

Reif released Greenleaf's collar once they reached the packs. The kaviak collapsed to the stone, sucking in great lungfuls of cold air as he tore off his poncho. With trembling hands, he peeled off the other layers until bare chested, sweat soaking the underclothes as if they'd been plunged into a river. He fumbled for a water skin, draining it in desperate gulps as Reif stood there, watching the trijjat disappear back into the clouds of sulfurous fog rising from the oasis. His back was screaming in pain, and as he raised his fingers to brush the back of his neck, he could feel blisters bubbled up, each a bright needle of agony when touched.

The spear fell to the stone with a clatter. Reif was weaving gently back and forth, as if drunk. He turned to face Greenleaf. The soldier was about to ask if he was all right, but the words died in his throat. The steel mesh on the front had drooped from the heat. The heavy hide was split and blackened. The miner raised his hands slowly to the helmet, but his motions were sluggish. Greenleaf struggled to his feet. "Let me," he said, and lifted the helmet from Reif's shoulders.

Something caught and tore, but the miner didn't respond as the ruin of his face came into view.

The left side of his face was a mass of reddened skin, dotted with the patches of frostbite. Where the dead frozen skin met the rest had split, leaving raw chasms across his cheek. That side of the face had clearly been facing away from the lava. The right was charred, like a steak left too long on the coals, dead white skin curling up against roasted black pockets of flesh along a ruined eye and ear. His hair was melted and smoking. His remaining eye blinked several times, and in a slurred voice, he said, "Doesn't hurt. M' arms hurt. Belly hurts. But m' face doesn't."

"Gods," Greenleaf whispered. He quickly began to strip the remains of the mining suit off of Reif, wincing every time flesh burned to the leather hide stuck and tore. The worst burns were limited to his face, with a nasty patch on his right shoulder where the hide had split open. The rest were large patches of red and blistered skin. "What do I do? What can I do?"

"Nothin'." Reif tried to shake his head, but the best that he could manage was a weary wobble of his shoulder back and forth. "Just gotta get back. Back home. Please."

"Yeah. Yeah." Greenleaf nodded. "The dogs. How do I…"

"Three whistles to call 'em back." Reif leaned on Greenleaf as he lowered down to a seated position. "Use the reins. They know the way home."

Greenleaf pressed another waterskin into the miner's hand. "Okay. Just rest. I'll be back."

"Not goin' anywhere, 'mperial."

It took nearly five minutes for Greenleaf to pull the dirty, scorched remnants of his frost suit back on. When the fabric hit his burned back and neck, he clenched his teeth so hard to keep from screaming that he feared they might crack. He leaned down and picked up the spear. The head was smeared with black gore that had burned to the metal.

Slowly, he began limping away from the Serao and across the ice. It didn't take long for him to realize how damaged his frost suit was. Despite the short distance, he was shivering, the trembles sending waves of pain over his blistered back. He clutched the haft of the spear tightly as he approached the oasis, eyes fixed on the bubbling geothermal vent. There was no motion.

Braddock's hand sat on the ground, the wrist a mass of torn flesh. The bone jutting out was shockingly white against the mud-spattered ground. Of Cailyn and Cole, nothing remained by some shreds of clothes, and one boot, mostly intact but empty.

Greenleaf's boots crunched as he crept past the oasis, the humid warmth battering his face, the stench of rotten eggs filling his nostrils. He knew as a fundamental truth that the spear in his hands was less than worthless. The aquasteel could punch through the creature's hide, but the man holding the weapon was no longer capable of wielding it. It was all he could do to hold the exhaustion and pain at bay. The spearpoint drooped down towards the ground. If they were going to come, they would come. His fate was no longer his own.

By the time he reached the sled, he had stopped watching the oasis. The large sledge was tipped on its side, the long steel runners spattered with mud. The malheur sap sphere was still lashed to the center, and as he reached out, he could feel the heat pouring off the dull metal surface. The leather gangline had dragged the front of the sledge to point away from the oasis, with only the metal anchor holding it in place. At the end, the eight dogs huddled together, pressed tightly against each other, their chests rising and falling. One raised its head to look at Greenleaf, and whined.

"It's okay," he murmured, walking slowly forward with this hand extended. "It's okay."

The dogs slowly rose to their feet. They moved carefully back towards him, tails tucked between their legs, ears tight against their skull, each sniffing the air as they reached the soldier. It took a few moments of stroking their head before they calmed down.

There was no sign of the other sled. Greenleaf could see a chunk of ground torn out about thirty feet away, runner tracks vanishing into the distance. "Hope they just go home," he said quietly as he scratched a furry head. Limping over to the side of the sled, he grasped it and strained, struggling for a few moments, but finally tipping it back rightsize with a gasp of pain. Slowly, he moved to the back, climbing up on the footboards. Seeing him take his place, the dogs eagerly fell into line, glancing back and whining.

"Okay," Greenleaf muttered to himself, gripping the handle. "I can do this." He raised his voice, calling out, "On!"

The dogs burst into motion, and the runners scraped noisily over the muddy ground surrounding the oasis. Greenleaf glanced fearfully over at the bubbling surface, but nothing emerged. When they hit the ice, the cold air rushing past his face, he shouted, "Lee! Lee!", and the lead dogs leaned against their neckline, pulling the sled in a wide circle to the right. Their path back to Reif was less direct than he would have liked, but within five minutes, he shouted for the sled to halt, stepping on the claw brake twenty feet away from Reif, who was slumped against the packs.

Greenleaf leapt off the footboards. His foot skidded on the ice, and a needle of agony darted up from his hip, but he recovered and limped over to Reif, whose eyes were shut. "Reif!" Greenleaf grabbed the miner's shoulder, and Reif's eyes burst open as he gasped in pain.

"Gods, don't fucking do that," he moaned. "Hurts."

"Well, don't scare me," Greenleaf shot back. "I have the sled."

"Oh." Reif's remaining eye blinked several times as he stared at the sniffing dogs. "Okay. Can we go home?"

"I don't know the way," Greenleaf said, carefully helping the miner to his feet.

"Dogs do. Command's *huebsh*." Reif had to repeat it several times. Greenleaf wasn't sure if the slurring was due to the damage to his face or something more serious.

"Come on." The two limped over to the sled, and Greenleaf eased Reif down on one of the short benches lashed to the frame directly behind the malheur sphere. It took a moment, but Reif managed to curl up on his side on the bench, almost wrapped around the warm sphere. After a moment's consideration, Greenleaf took a coil of rope from his pack, and began tying it around Reif's waist to the frame of the sled.

"You 'resting me?"

"For being a general pain in my ass," Greenleaf said, checking his knots. "Don't want to have to lift you back on the sled every damn time you fall off."

"Mmm." Reif laid his head back down against the worn wood. "What about you?"

"I'm not burned."

"Bullshit."

Greenleaf shrugged, feeling the scalded skin between his shoulder blades tug painfully. "Not burned as bad as you, anyway." Satisfied that Reif was secured, he took a long breath. "Do the dogs need someone steering?"

Reif didn't answer. Greenleaf looked down, and saw that his eye was shut. He checked Reif's pulse, trying to find a good spot on his throat that wasn't dotted with watery blisters, and finally found a steady heartbeat. Greenleaf looked over the dogs, which were sitting patiently on the ice. "Gotta be honest, don't know if I can stand for too long. Can you handle getting us back?" he asked. The two lead dogs looked back and wagged. "I'll take that as a yes." The kaviak released the claw brake, and settled into the bench in front of the sphere, gritting his teeth against every movement.

"Okay. Okay." He let out a long breath. "Let's go home. *Huebsch.*"

The dogs perked up, and he repeated the command. The large black striped lead dog barked several times, and burst into motion, his pack mates following suit. The sled slewed back and forth for a few minutes, but the pack settled into a direction, and soon the runners were singing over the ice, gliding through the dark night.

Greenleaf had his spear sitting across his legs, his eyes scanning the horizon. Every few minutes, he struggled to turn enough to make sure Reif was still breathing. A few bundles were lashed to the sled in front of him. He fumbled at the knots holding them in place. The second bundle he searched had strips of dried seal meat wrapped in greased canvas, and Greenleaf devoured four long strips, chasing it down with water from his skin, the burn of the ice peppers a shadow of the rest of his body. His stomach still growled at him, but he counted out sixteen more strips, and reluctantly wrapped them back up.

Overhead, the aurora shimmered in pinks and greens. The moon peeked up over the horizon in front of them, a sickle of golden light casting long shadows over the glittering ice as the sled wove between rocky outcroppings. There was no movement, no sapphire eyes watching from the darkness. Greenleaf didn't stop watching. Deep down, he knew that he never would.

There was no way of knowing exactly how much time had passed, but the crescent moon had clawed its way into the sky by the time Reif moaned. Greenleaf turned a bit too quickly at the sound, and gasped as something popped on his back, warm liquid trickling down beneath his left shoulder blade. He tried to shove the pain aside. "You with me?"

"Mmmm." Reif brought a pair of gloved fingers up to his charred cheek, and before Greenleaf could stop him, prodded the grey and blackened flesh. "Think so." His cracked lips curled slightly in what might have been a frown. "This doesn't hurt. Doesn't feel like anything. 'S not good, is it?"

Greenleaf briefly debated lying, but said, "Probably not. Flesh is dead."

Reif nodded slowly. "Hungry."

"Can you chew?"

"I'll give it a shot." Greenleaf passed a strip of meat back along with the water skin. For the next few minutes, Reif slowly gnawed on the food. He took drinks every few bites, dribbles of water slipping from the corner of his mouth. He didn't seem to notice. He finished the strip, but waved off a second when offered. "Hard to chew. Mashed potatoes 'n brandy, please."

Greenleaf let out a dry chuckle. "I'll let the chef know."

"Serving the 'mpire is your job, right? Serve some food I don't have to chew." Reif took another drink. He didn't meet Greenleaf's eyes as he asked, "You think Edeline knew?"

Greenleaf shook his head. "I don't know. Hard to imagine he didn't."

"Yeah." Reif stared out into the dark for a while. Finally, he glanced back in Greenleaf's direction. "Not because of you."

"What?"

"What they did. Blocking the flow." Reif took a deep breath, and began coughing. It took him a few moments to stop. "Wasn't cause you showed up. Cole and Braddock went on a hunting trip, 'bout month 'fore you got here. Gone close to a week. Came back empty handed. Said they just had bad luck, but..."

"It'd be enough time for them to get there and back," Greenleaf said, nodding. "I found something. In the records. Looked like someone was hiding a missing shard. I couldn't prove it, but that's why I was pressing you, trying to get you to lose your temper, make a mistake. I thought you might be involved." He shrugged, the movement sending shivers of pain through his blistered back. "I was wrong."

"So I'm in the clear?"

Greenleaf cracked a slight grin. "Yeah, I think I can cross your name off."

Reif shifted, fidgeting with the rope on his waist. "You never finished. Your story. About coming here."

"I didn't?"

Reif gave his head the smallest shake. "Just said you were mad."

"Oh." Greenleaf waited for the shame of the memory to hit, but it was gone, buried under layers of exhaustion. "I slipped. In the final combat assessment. Had the last archer dead to rights, but I spotted some loose soil, and before I could think better of it, I placed my foot in the worst possible spot. What should have been a clean finish ended up with me scrabbling in the dirt. I was terrified they saw, knew I slipped on purpose."

"Did they?"

Greenleaf shrugged, the tiniest twitch of his blistered shoulders. "If they did, they never told me. Instead, my final assessment report deemed the error 'not representative of my performance history'. They ignored it."

A wet, bubbling chuckle issued from Reif's throat. "They knew. They knew what you were trying to do. Just didn't want to let you."

Nodding, Greenleaf said, "You're probably right." He looked up at the curtains of light undulating overhead, throwing ribbons of pink and emerald glittering over the frozen ground that flew past. "My father was there. He knew."

"He told you?"

Greenleaf shook his head. "He didn't have to. I had a week after the Elevation before I left Kaani. He didn't speak to me, not one word. Made excuses about being busy, but I knew." He rubbed his forehead, feeling the blisters under his fingertips. "I keep writing him. He hasn't written back."

Reif nodded slowly. "You think he told anyone?"

"Doubt it. Don't think it would have mattered," Greenleaf said. "Might not have been anything that I could have done to keep from coming here."

"If you hadn't..." Reif trailed off, shutting his eye. He kept it closed as he spoke again. "You have to investigate, don't you. Find out who else knew. Who else was involved."

Greenleaf turned to face the front of the sled, watching the puffs of fog from the dog's muzzles as they scampered over the frozen ground. "It won't be me. That's the commissar's job. He'll make sure we know everyone who knew what they were doing."

"Keep wondering. Why they never asked me," Reif mumbled.

"Because you never would have helped them."

"Sure about that?"

"They wanted to sabotage the Empire's military. They were willing to sacrifice anything to do that, including Lahar." Greenleaf glanced back at him. "There are many things I could say about you. Many things I have said about you, repeatedly and with relish." Reif loosed a rasping chuckle. "But you love your home. Everything you've ever said, everything you've ever done, it's always been about preserving Lahar."

Reif was quiet long enough that Greenleaf turned painfully around to see if the miner had fallen unconscious once more. He was watching the stars overhead, the light from the aurora dancing over his face. When he spoke, his voice was low enough that Greenleaf had to strain to hear it. "Nothing's going to be the same."

"We'll find a way to remove the aquasteel, get the Serao flowing again," Greenleaf said. "It might take a bit, but the Empire won't rest until it's done. Hell, they'll send a few dozen Chorale members down to make it happen."

"Not what I'm talking about." Reif's eye shut as he kept speaking, his voice cracked and broken. "Lahar isn't the Serao. It's not the aquasteel, or the forge. It's everyone. My family. Friends. Never looked at them in doubt. But that's over." He took a deep breath. "That's why I didn't want you here. Never knew what drove you, what you were after. Now I know. But I know that the people I love aren't who I thought they were. Not a fair trade. Not one I wanted."

Greenleaf turned back to face forward, looking away from the miner's ruined face. "I'm sorry."

"Not your fault." He trailed off, and Greenleaf listened to his wet, rasping breathing slow once more as Reif fell mercifully unconscious.

The endurance of Suviev hounds was legendary. Greenleaf didn't know how much time had passed when the dogs finally began to flag, flecks of foam blowing back from their muzzles. He struggled to remember the command to bring them to a halt, but after a few failed attempts, he convinced the pack to slow and stop, pressing on the claw brake to ease their deceleration.

They'd left the rocky area and entered the wide open stretches of the open ice. A pair of malheur trees dotted the horizon to the east. The aurora had faded, but the stars and crescent moon splashed white light that glittered on the frozen expanse. Greenleaf clambered down from the sled, but moving more than ten feet away from the dull metal sphere sent horribly familiar icy tendrils creeping into the many gaps of his damaged suit. He scanned the dark horizon, looking for yellow steam or figures creeping against the empty white, but saw nothing.

He turned back to Reif, who lay curled around the back of the malheur sphere, his chest slowly rising and falling as he slept. Greenleaf took his wrist, pushing back the miner's sleeve to find his radial pulse. It was still steady. Slowly, he settled back onto the bench, dismissing his spear back to the bracer. His intent was to maintain watch, but the exhaustion never left him the option. His eyes blinked heavily, and he jolted upright. He didn't know how long he'd been out, but the moon had leapt in a shallow arc across the horizon. Most of the dogs were still sleeping, curled up next to each other, but one of the lead dogs lifted its head and looked back at him, its black eyes blinking slowly.

Greenleaf took the last of the dried seal meat, and used his belt knife to cut it into smaller chunks. He tossed one piece to the lead dog, who rose to his feet as he gobbled it up. Within moments, the rest of the pack was stirring. He did his best to make sure that every dog got at least a few bites, but there wasn't much. The dogs licked at the ice after finishing the meager meal, their tongues lapping melt. Once they'd finished, Greenleaf croaked out, "*Huebsh,*" and the dogs resumed their path south.

He kept drifting off. The only thing keeping him awake was the pain of his raw throat and his collection of injuries and burns. He'd drained the last of the water from his skin hours before, but he didn't want to risk stopping to gather snow to melt. There wasn't much to gather in any event. The ground was a sheet of hard packed ice, white and glimmering beneath the stars. When the sled bumped with a sharp jolt, he started awake, and immediately summoned his spear. His eyes fixed blearily on the red flapping cloth twenty feet away, and for a moment he was confused at the change in sound beneath the runners. "Reif," he said, coughing at the cracking in his voice. Reaching back, he shook the miner, who moaned at the motion. "Reif!"

Reif leaned upward drunkenly. "Mmm."

"I think we reached the road."

The miner looked at the flag, then pointed to the west. "Look." A greasy smear of black smoke blotted out some of the stars. Greenleaf couldn't make out the source.

"Lahar?"

"No. Too small."

In the darkness, it was difficult to make out the bulky shape in the distance, but the sounds of metallic squeaking and wood scraping echoed over the ice, growing louder. Greenleaf clambered down, squinting into the dark, and stepped back at the sound of a snort. The spearpoint came up, and he realized that he had dropped into a combat crouch. When the broad curled horns of the first yak head emerged from the night, he let out a sharp exhalation. "It's a convoy. It's a gods-damned convoy out of Lahar."

He started to rush forward, but the cold immediately drove him back into the warm radius of the sled. Reif gestured weakly. "The dogs. Cut the dogs loose."

Greenleaf did as suggested, and the hounds leapt forward, barking loudly at the yak, which snorted and tossed its head in confusion, coming to a stop. The massive wagon on the back jerked to a halt, the capped iron chimney on top belching dark smoke. There were two other wagons lined up beforehand, all three stopping in the face of the excited pack. From the first wagon, a series of loud thunks issued, and Greenleaf heard the squeak of iron hinges. Four figures in belted Imperial Army coats jumped down to the ice, moving around each side with spears out, faces wrapped in wool masks. The tallest glanced down at the dogs, then spotted the two figures slumped against the sled, barking an order. The three others spread out, spears held ready. The figure tromped forward, boots crunching with each step.

"What the hell are you doing, blocking the road? You need to..." Her voice trailed off, and the pale eyes behind the mask widened. "Captain?" Stepping forward, Sergeant Idar tugged down her mask, staring at her commanding officer. Once certain, she broke into a run towards the pair, screaming, "Sand! Get Sand out here, fucking now! It's the gods-damned captain!"

Greenleaf nearly collapsed when she reached him, another spearman following close after. They threw Greenleaf's arm over their shoulder to hold him up. Behind them, the healer was running towards them. His feet skidded on the ice, and he fell onto his ass with a curse, but clambered back up and was with them in moments. Sand's eyes widened as he saw the blistered skin of Greenleaf's face. "Get him back to the wagon, now!"

Greenleaf dug in his heels as they tried to move him. "Reif. See to Reif."

"Sir, I need to make sure you're..."

Something inside Greenleaf bubbled up past the exhaustion, and he narrowed blistered eyelids at the patcher. "That's a gods-damned order, Corporal. See to the Laharian, now."

Sand glanced over at Sergeant Idar for an instant, but nodded. "You two. Help me." Moments later, they were carrying the Laharian miner back to the wagon, while Greenleaf limped back over, leaning his weight on the spearman.

"Sir, what the hell happened?" Idar asked, glancing over the tattered frost suit. "You get attacked by animals?"

Greenleaf shook his head. "Not animals." They reached the back of the wagon. Pyles was shoving crates aside, giving Sand room to work as the patcher used a sharp knife to cut away Reif's hood. The field anatomist was barking orders, demanding supplies that Pyles passed over to him as they winced at Reif's face. The heat from the iron stove in the center of the wagon battered against Greenleaf's face, and he pushed his hood back. "Report, Sergeant."

"Report..." Idar shook her head, confused. "Sir, we did our scheduled drop off. We left Lahar two hours ago."

"I need the orders," Greenleaf said. "I need to change them."

"Sir?"

"The orders, sergeant. The ones Proudlake gave you."

"Sir, you need to sit down." A spearman whose name he couldn't remembers pressed a flask into his hand, and he uncorked it, draining the contents in several quick swallows, gasping between gulps. He accepted an outstretched hand, trying not to cry out as they pulled him into the wagon, his burned back screaming in protest. Idar and another helped him take off the poncho of the frost suit as he watched Sand work on Reif.

"We don't have a lot of time, sergeant." He took another long drink. "How long to get the convoy turned around?"

"Pyles!" The private glanced back, and Idar said, "Go see the caravan master. Tell him we need to be heading back to Lahar within the hour."

"Aye, sergeant." The young man scampered forward in a crouch, slipping behind the front curtain into the driver's bay.

"An hour?" Greenleaf asked in dismay. "Why so long?"

"Sir, these yaks aren't bred to be steered. They learn one route, and follow it back and forth their entire lives. We can do it, but they're not going to be happy."

"Only two." Greenleaf coughed, spitting up a bit of water. "We need to send one on to Darun with the orders once I've clarified them. Notify the local legion commander. We found the blockage, but it's going to take a lot of men and animals to clear it. Give me the orders, and I'll amend them to include what we need. Do we have ink here?"

"Captain!" Idar gripped his shoulder, and yanked her hand back as he hissed in pain. "Sorry! Captain, you're exhausted and hurt. We'll get you back to town, let you rest before…"

"We don't have time, sergeant!" Greenleaf shook off her hand. "The longer we wait, the harder it's going to be to clear the blockage."

"Sir, what blockage?" Idar asked. "What orders?"

"The orders the commissar gave you," Greenleaf snapped. "If we don't have ink, I'll need someone to relay my verbal orders as accurately…"

He trailed off at the baffled expression on Idar's face. She shook her head. "Sir, I saw the commissar three hours ago. I had to brief him on everything that's happening, give him the orders that the new provisional Imperial council issued to you."

Greenleaf rubbed his eyes. His head felt as if it was stuffed full of cotton batting. "What? Provisional Imperial council? What are you talking about?"

"I think it's better if Commissar Proudlake explains…"

"Corporal, I'm starving, exhausted, burned, and have no time. What is the provisional Imperial council?"

"The governesses, sir. The four governesses are in control of the government. They formed a provisional council to establish order during the transition."

"What transition?" Greenleaf asked, staring at the sergeant in confusion.

Idar hesitated, and Greenleaf saw Sand and a spearman exchange a glance. "The Empress has stepped down, sir. She abdicated. The governesses have taken over until they can figure out what comes next."

"What?" Greenleaf felt light headed as he blinked slowly. "I don't understand."

The sergeant spread her hands. "Neither do we. Couriers have been flying everywhere, bringing orders and letters. Half is rumor, but we think it happened about two weeks ago."

"Why would the Empress abdicate?"

"The governesses say that she's having health issues." Idar trailed off, looking uncomfortable.

"Sergeant. Say what you want to say."

"Sir..." She swallowed. "Most everyone says it was a coup. That she's either dead or imprisoned, and the governesses took control. No one has heard from her brother, either."

Greenleaf sat back, the pain in his back momentarily forgotten as his head reeled. It was as if someone had told him that two plus two actually equaled six, thank you. None of it fit. "That's impossible."

"Like I said, sir, most of it's rumor. But the Chorale is following the provisional council's orders. They suspended construction of the bridge over a week ago, and the entire Chorale is heading to Kaani. So are the Fourth, Eighth, and Ninth Legions. The generals are recognizing the council's authority."

For a long few minutes, Greenleaf sat in stunned silence. He couldn't wrap his head around what the sergeant was saying to him. When Sand rose from Reif and headed over, the anatomist had to try several times to get his attention. "Hmm?"

"Can I look you over now, sir?"

Greenleaf looked down at Reif. "How is he?"

Sand shook his head. "He's lucky wounds don't go septic easily up here. Third degree burns on his face, shoulder, arms, and hands. Second degree burns pretty much everywhere else. Maybe frostbite too, but it's hard to tell. He's stable. He needs a Chorale healer. A good one. The dead flesh will have to be removed, with carrion beetles if possible. I treated his burns with aloe liniment. If the burns sour, I don't think he's strong enough to survive." He gestured at the kaviak. "Can you remove your tunic, or do I need to cut it off?"

It took Idar and Sand helping him to ease it off, and then he sat silently for a long time as the patcher fussed over the blisters on his back. As Sand dabbed a cooling ointment between his shoulder blades, Greenleaf asked, "You said we had orders?"

Idar nodded. "As they were, yes. We're to hold station. Make sure our route is secure until things settle. No one seems to know what's going to happen next. Most of the Imperial Army and the Chorale seem to be following the governesses, but it feels like the whole country is holding its breath."

"If the Chorale and the legions fall in line, no one's going to make too much noise," Greenleaf said. "Any word from Kaani?"

"Again, rumors only," the sergeant said. "We hear they locked the city down, that the Home Guard took control to prevent rioting."

"Has there been?" Greenleaf hissed as Sands prodded a sensitive spot. "Rioting, I mean?"

"Couldn't say, but not in Darun," she said. "The Brehai had everyone whipped up in a frenzy the last few months, but now that the bridge construction has stopped, they've gone quiet. Just kind of feels like everyone's waiting to see what happens next."

Greenleaf swallowed, and shook his head. "Whatever's happening in the capital, it doesn't change what we need to do. Do we have ink? If not, I'm going to send you back with one of the wagons while I take the rest of the garrison to Lahar. You'll need to let them know the changes to my orders."

"Sir. I tried to tell you earlier." Idar shook her head. "I don't have any orders. I spoke with the commissar. The only thing he gave me to send back was his usual sealed state packet for the Ministry of Dedication. He didn't give me any orders from you."

"No, I left him sealed orders for you, and another set to take back..." Greenleaf trailed off, frowning. "What did he tell you? Where did he say I was?"

Idar glanced at Sand, then Pyle, confusion written in her expression. "Sir, Commissar Proudlake said you were escorting a hunting trip. That you wouldn't be back for a few days. That's it. He didn't say anything about a blockage, and he definitely didn't give me orders."

Greenleaf's head dropped, his eyes shutting for a moment. In his mind, he saw two ruby teardrops.

I didn't see it. Why didn't I see it?

Idar began to lean forward when the kaviak spoke again, his words flat and dead.

"Sergeant, get this convoy back to Lahar. When we arrive, deploy the garrison throughout the town immediately. Search every building. They are to find and detain Commissar Proudlake, and have him brought to me. Alive. Do you understand?"

His tone brooked no argument. "Yes, sir."

CHAPTER 22

Concepts like "day" and "night" were somewhat ephemeral during the long period in which Lahar didn't see the sun, but the rhythms of the village continued even after sunrises were a few weeks in the past. At the moment that the wheels of the first bakery rolled over the bars to chime the convoy's early return to Lahar, Greenleaf knew that the majority of Lahar would be asleep. He also knew that the unexpected chimes would let the villagers know something was wrong.

With the exception of Sand, who was crouched in the back of the wagon over Reif's unconscious form, the rest of the soldiers were gathered around Greenleaf and Idar. Once she'd received her captain's order, the sergeant wasted no time gathering the handful of soldiers traveling with the convoy. "Stay in pairs, and work slowly. There's nowhere to go, nowhere really to hide. I don't want anyone kicking in doors or causing a riot," she said. "There's seven of us, and hundreds of Laharians. Do your jobs, and report back to me or the captain immediately if you find the commissar."

"Edeline, too," Greenleaf said, cinching the wrists shut on his frost suit. The fabric was charred and damaged beyond usefulness on the ice, but it would do quite well in Lahar. "I don't think he was involved. But I want him detained until I know for sure."

"Could be others. Likely, even," Sergeant Idar said.

"I know."

The bakery lurched to a halt, and steel whispered against leather as short swords came out of sheaths. Idar had ordered spears stowed in favor of the thirty-inch gently curved blades favored by Imperial forces fighting in city environments, and the greasy light of the wood stove glinted off dark oiled steel. The doors swung open, revealing a quartet of Laharians, including Braden, standing behind Roenne Elif.

"Captain?" Her voice was uncertain as she watched the bakery disgorge hard-faced soldiers with steel in gloved fists. "We heard the chimes. I thought someone might be hurt. What's going on?"

Greenleaf jumped down, stumbling as pain rippled through his injured hip. Elif started forward, but one of the soldiers immediately moved between her and the kaviak. Greenleaf waved him off. "It's all right. Go, start your search." Straightening up, he nodded back to the bakery. "Reif's in there with Sand. He's in bad shape."

Sand leaned out of the door, and spotted Elif. "Mistress. Is your house still set up for the injured?"

"What? Ah, no." She shook her head. "My house has gone dark. They moved me and my gear to the Castle. What happened to Reif?"

"Captain, permission to take Reif to the Castle?" Sand asked, ignoring her question.

"Do it."

Roenne snapped instructions to four other Laharians, who moved to help Sand carry the stretcher carrying the unconscious miner.

Greenleaf said, "Idar, you lead the search. Sand and I will escort them to the Castle, and find you after."

"Yes, sir."

Greenleaf's spear fell into his hand as he followed the Laharians. Sand's sword was still sheathed at his hip as he marched next to his captain. The village was silent. The forge had shut down for the night, and virtually everyone in town was sleeping. The only sound was the dull rumbling and cracking coming from the Serao. Greenleaf's eyes found the burning river as they walked over the grey paving stones. It seemed dull after the searing fire at the base of the Watchtower.

By the time they'd reached the door to the Castle, the lights in some windows had come on as Laharians woke to knocks on their door. Greenleaf could hear raised voices from somewhere, but couldn't make them out. Inside the building, the glow of the Serao threw orange light over them as Elif directed them to a long table.

The river was noticeably lower than the first time Greenleaf had visited this room, the green crystals glittering along the eight-inch banks that dropped down to the molten surface. They carefully set Reif down as she opened her bag. Greenleaf began to head to the stairs that led up to Proudlake's office and quarters when the door to the Castle opened once more, and a voice said, "Captain? Captain!"

Greenleaf looked up to see Edeline gaping at the scene before him. Limping towards him, Greenleaf snapped his fingers, and Sand stepped forward to take hold of the counselor's arm. Edeline tried to jerk away, only to find the corporal's grip unyielding. "What is this? Captain, explain yourself!"

"Where's the commissar?" Greenleaf said, his voice hard and flat.

"Ayal?" Edeline shook his head. "As far as I know, he's upstairs. What's going on?" He spotted the unconscious form of Reif on the table, and his voice jumped an octave. "Who is that? Where are the others?"

"Sand, I have him. Go see if the commissar is upstairs."

"Sir." The corporal took the stairs three at a time, drawing his sword. Edeline took a few steps towards Elif, and stopped.

"He's bad." Greenleaf walked over to stand next to him. "Burns, frostbite, both extremely serious. Sand got him stabilized, but he's not sure if he'll survive."

Edeline looked down at his hands, which were shaking. He swallowed. "Cole? Braddock? The others?" Greenleaf gave a short shake of his head, and the color spilled out of the older man's face. "What happened?" he whispered.

"Did you know?" Greenleaf asked.

"I don't understand."

Elif pulled back the linen Sand had wrapped around Reif's skull, revealing the charred and blistered ruin of the miner's head.

Edeline let out a choked sob. "How could this happen?"

Elif muttered a curse, barely audible over the rumble of the river before raising her voice. "I need to move him. To my room. Easier than bringing everything here." Without waiting for permission, she barked instructions, and the Laharians lifted Reif's body and carried it away. Braden glanced back, his face pale with fear and confusion, and Elif looked at Greenleaf for a brief moment before shaking her head and following the others around a corner.

Edeline watched wordlessly until Greenleaf placed a hand on his shoulder, gripping it firmly and turning the village leader to face him. "Counselor, I need you to answer me. Did you know what they were doing?"

"He didn't know, captain." The two of them turned to look up at the second floor balcony. Ayal Proudlake stood looking down on them, the light of the Serao bathing his face in a hellish glow. Sand stood ten feet behind him, and followed him as the commissar made his way across the high bridge arcing over the river and down the stairs. Sweat beaded on Proudlake's face as he reached the bottom, but he met Greenleaf's hard eyes without blinking. "He didn't know."

"Sergeant." Sand looked over at Greenleaf, who said, "Go find the sergeant. Tell him I have the commissar in custody. I want the mine and the forge secured, and I want two men posted at the gates of this building."

"Yes, sir."

Proudlake looked over at Reif, his face betraying nothing. "The others?

Greenleaf tugged off his gloves, passing the spear from one hand to the other as he did. The Serao bubbled and rumbled thirty feet away, and the heat was perfect at this distance. He flexed his hands, feeling the stiffness in his remaining fingers. "No."

"You, or the ice?"

"Does it matter?"

"No, not really," the commissar said. "For what it's worth, I find myself relieved that you're all right."

"All things being equal, it's not worth all that much."

Edeline swallowed, and said, "Ayal." The commissar turned to look at him, and he whispered, "What did you do?"

"I listened, old friend," Proudlake said, smiling sadly as the lava danced in his spectacles. "All those dinners, years and decades worth. I listened."

Greenleaf shook his head. "The blockage. It was him. Him and Cole. The others, too, except for Reif and Deric. They dropped an aquasteel chain in the Serao." He didn't wait for Edeline to respond. "Why?"

Proudlake took off his spectacles, folding them carefully and placing them in his pocket. "This could be where I ask you if it matters."

"If it matters?" Edeline blurted. "Is this true?"

Proudlake nodded slowly. "We waited. Until the farms were sustaining, until they were producing enough that you didn't need the shipments." He shrugged. "We didn't think it would effect the level of the river. Didn't think anything could."

"Five people are dead," Greenleaf said.

"I did try to stop you. I told you not to go."

"Does that make it better? Absolve you of your part in all this?"

"I don't need absolution, captain," Proudlake said. "What I've done was necessary. You're young. You've never known anything but peace, never had the chance to watch the people you love devoured by a conquest that was meant to bring an end to that kind of loss." He tilted his head. "Do you know who has? Malachi Cole. He wore the uniform, fought for ten years in pursuit of a dream, came home believing the horrors that followed him all the way to the banks of the Serao to wake him in the middle of the night were a price worth paying. He believed, just like I believed that my sons died for a purpose. But it was all a lie."

The commissar extended a finger, pointing south. "How long did it take her? Four, maybe five years? An eye-blink compared to how long we spent at war. Generations after generations bled white to unify everything north of the Breaking, and once we finally had it, finally had the peace she and her family had promised for years? She marshaled all our resources, the great Chorale itself, for the purpose of reigniting the fire we'd spent centuries putting out." He turned his stare to Edeline. "How many weapons have we counted, Dhrez? How many thousands have we shipped off? Every inch that bridge crawls over the Breaking is a day closer to those weapons ending up in the hands of a boy like

Braden, a scared child who will either come home with nightmares, or won't come home at all."

He shook his head. "If that bridge finishes, Lahar will trade its sons and daughters for teardrops, along with every other village and town in this country. You know what the Empire is, Dhrez. You know what they've done." Proudlake spread his hands, smiling sadly. "Like I said. I listened. I heard you."

Edeline opened his mouth, but no sound came out. Instead, he ran his fingers over his balding head, a shudder rippling through his body. "Can it be reversed?"

Proudlake's smile faltered for a moment. "I don't..."

"Not you." Lahar's counselor looked over at Greenleaf. "Can the blockage be reversed, can you restore the Serao? The aquasteel?"

"I don't know," Greenleaf said. "If we get word out, help will come. Men, yaks, even resonants. If there's any way to clear the blockage, they'll do it. The aquasteel is too important."

"The aquasteel. Not Lahar," Proudlake spat. "He's telling you the truth. They won't come to save Lahar. They'll come to save their war. If he and his soldiers are allowed to leave this village, everything Cole and the others died for will be for nothing."

"Allowed to leave..." Edeline's eyes widened. "Ayal, what are you saying?"

"My sons died for nothing, for a lie. But Braddock, Cole, Poyel, Cailyn? They can die for a future, a real future. We have a moment here, a chance to bring actual peace, to strangle this war in its crib before it can set fire to the world. Against that, what sacrifice is too much?"

"The empress is gone!" Greenleaf exploded, his anger burning through his exhaustion for a moment. "You talked to the sergeant, you know what's happened! The bridge has stopped! You want to flood the streets of Lahar with blood to stop something that's never going to happen! You put everyone in this town at risk, and now you're willing to see more death, more violence."

Proudlake straightened. "I've only done what had to be done."

"The bridge is stopped," Greenleaf said again. "The Empress is deposed. Let it be done."

"It will never be done," the commissar said. "You think a nation goes to war because one woman thinks it's a good idea? The Empress has a river of blood flowing through her fingers. For months, years, maybe even decades, we'll be able to point to her, say, 'Wasn't it terrible, all the awful things she did? Thank the gods we're past that', as if she held every spear, burned every house, led every step of a conquest that started centuries before she was born." Proudlake shook his head. "We'll wrap ourselves in the new lies. Admire ourselves in a mirror, see heroes where butchers once stood, and tell all who will listen that the cruelty and greed is part of our past. But it will fester and grow. It's part of us. If the aquasteel continues to flow, the Empire will march south."

Greenleaf opened his mouth to respond, but before he could, Edeline took four quick steps forward, and struck Proudlake across the face with an open-handed slap. There was little force to the blow, but the commissar staggered a few steps back, sweat bursting on his brow from the heat of the river as shock bloomed on his face.

"You sanctimonious bastard," Edeline hissed as Greenleaf rushed forward to grab his arm, pulling him back. The heat was intense, but Greenleaf barely registered it. "How could you do this?"

"I..." Proudlake's expression raced from confusion to dismay in a heartbeat. "Dhrez, I knew that you couldn't be involved in this, but you have to see what I was trying to do. The Empire's taken everything from Lahar. Your life has been dedicated to distancing your home from Kaani and the Empress." He shook his head sharply. "You *hate* the Empire."

"You said you listened." Edeline wiped sweat from his face. "You didn't listen, you only heard what you needed to hear to justify this madness. You think I hate the Empire more than I love Lahar? You think I hate the Empire enough to send our sons to die on the ice, to see everything we've worked towards torn to pieces?" Tears brimmed in his eyes. "Weeks, Ayal. Weeks to get word back to the mainland. Still more time for them to send help. The tributaries are already shrinking. The soil is freezing. Even if they can restore the Serao, the farms are dead. It will take years to grow back what we've lost. Everything we've worked for, everything my father believed in, ruined."

"I..." Sweat beaded on the tip of the commissar's nose as he licked his lips, searching for words. "You wanted them gone. Wanted me gone. You never said as much, but I could see..."

"I wanted them to stop taking from us, to stop using my family and neighbors!" Edeline moaned. "We built a foundation that could have carried Lahar into whatever future was in front of us, to build something they couldn't take. I thought you understood, but you..." He coughed, his hands clenched into fists. "You're no gods-damned different. You used us, used my people. Convinced people I loved to choke their home to death to satisfy your anger."

Tears fell down his ruddy cheeks as he stared at Ayal Proudlake. "At least the Empress never hid what she took from us. You called me friend while you put a noose around our neck, and call it righteous." He turned to Greenleaf. "Captain. Am I free to go? Your soldiers probably frightened a lot of people. I need to calm things down before..." He trailed off.

Greenleaf slowly nodded.

Edeline looked between the two of them, his hands trembling. Wordlessly, he turned and left.

Proudlake watched him go. His face was pale, his eyes lit with the orange glow of the river that rumbled behind him. Reaching into his pocket, he withdrew a clenched fist, opening it to reveal a pair of glittering ruby teardrops. Staring down at them, he said, "Nothing changes, does it?"

The kaviak summoned his spear. "Ayal Proudlake, by the authority of the Empress, I bind you for tribunal."

Proudlake shook his head. "No Empress. No authority." He turned and took four steps. The heat flushed his face red, and smoke began to issue from the strands of thinning hair that curled in the face of the Serao's rumbling glow. Greenleaf just watched as the commissar extended his hand and opened it. Ruby glittered in orange light as the teardrops fell, tiny flames burping as they sank beneath the molten surface.

He turned weary eyes to Greenleaf, tears burning streaks between blisters emerging on his reddened cheeks. "I hope you get to hold on to your lies, Tomas. I hope you can live with what comes next."

Greenleaf was certain he was going to reach out, grab a fistful of the rich padded silk tunic before it vanished over the short drop. He knew that part of his mind sent the signal to his hand to save the commissar of Lahar Valley, as certain as he knew that another part made sure his arm didn't move. The screaming was bad. The smell was worse. He didn't know how long he stood there, staring down at the wisps of smoke that were the only gravestone Ayal Proudlake would ever have.

Chapter 23

Five weeks later

"You can wait in here, sir. The general will be with you in a moment," the young yeoman said.

Greenleaf gave a short nod, and the soldier fled back through the door to the desk that had been set up just outside. It was less of a desk and more a small pub table that had been moved to the third floor of the Castle for his use, but in the two weeks since it had been put there, it had gathered an impressive collection of paperwork.

Once the door shut, Greenleaf could no longer hear the rumble of the Serao three floors below. He glanced around the room that had once been Ayal Proudlake's office. Crates were stacked along both the east and west walls, making the office feel smaller. Black streaks on the outside betrayed the contents, though Greenleaf had never really doubted. The Imperial army had brought cartloads of coal with them when the company had arrived.

Any trace of the office's former occupant were gone. A wrapped leather bundle sat on the desk, a command seal securing the flaps shut. There were a pair of chairs facing the desk, but Greenleaf didn't take a seat, despite the twinge in his hip. The Chorale anatomist that had looked over his wounds reluctantly admitted that Elif had done an excellent job. He also agreed with her that the pain would take months to fully fade, if it ever did.

Boots tromped along the walkway outside, and Greenleaf came to attention as the door opened. "Tea, also. The green tea I brought, not the local brew," General Anatoli Brehev said to the yeoman as he stepped into the office. "That stuff makes my damn teeth itch." He turned to Greenleaf. "Captain, you want tea?"

"No, thank you, sir."

The general gave a nod, closing the door behind him. Brehev was a big man, with the blonde hair and the bright green eyes of the Greymare regions. He towered nearly four inches over Greenleaf, his chest nearly as big as a keg of ale. He waved his hand towards one of the chairs. "Sit, sit," he said as he shrugged the heavy wool coat off of his shoulders. Beneath, he wore a knit sweater over his uniform tunic. "Never thought anywhere could get colder than a Rilsko winter, but this place..." He shook his head as Greenleaf settled gingerly in the chair.

"Yes, sir."

Brehev settled his bulk into the chair behind the desk, and tugged off calfskin gloves, tossing them down next to the folder. "How are your injuries healing, Captain?"

"Quite well, sir. I was lucky."

Grunting, the general said, "By all accounts, that's an understatement. Few things to go over, and I'll let you get back to your convalescence."

"I'm good, sir," Greenleaf said. "I'm ready to get back to duty."

"Captain, I brought eighty soldiers and two dozen Chorale resonants with me. I feel quite confident that we can maintain order in this village while you fully recover."

"Of course, sir, I didn't mean..."

Brehev waved him off. "I know you didn't." The door opened, and the yeoman came in bearing a steaming mug on a tray with a small pitcher of milk. Wordlessly, he set it down and withdrew.

The general took a drink, and nodded. "Better. All right, Captain. I wanted to update you on the progress up north."

"They've made some?" Greenleaf asked, raising an eyebrow. The last two weeks had been an exercise in frustration for the crews making the long trek up to the mouth of the Serao. In the light of dozens of coal fires, teams of yaks and dozens of men had struggled to haul the tangled mess of solid aquasteel out of the Serao. They'd managed to shift it several times, but nothing more.

"It's done." Greenleaf raised an eyebrow in surprise as the general continued. "The Chorale group got there last night. They had several spacers with them. Don't ask me how, but they gave the teams enough of a boost to get the blockage hauled out." Brehev shook his head. "Apparently, it's bigger than a stovewagon. Light enough, being aquasteel, but they're lashing it between two carts to get it back here."

"What are they going to do with it, sir?"

"The Empresses have requested that we send it to Kaani. Some talk about it being displayed as a monument." He blanched for a moment. "Dammit. The provisional council. It's catching."

Greenleaf could sympathize. After centuries of talking about the Empress, many of the soldiers and Laharians had begun referring to the four governesses who had taken control of the government as Empresses. The provisional council had pushed back against the name, but it seemed like a losing battle. "If they really want people to stop calling them Empresses, it's not going to be easy, sir."

"No, but as long as we wear this uniform, we need to set an example." Brehev shook his head. "Might not matter. Even money says they just assume the title anyway." He dismissed that line of conversation with a wave. "Anyway. The Chorale group is going to stick around long enough to make sure that the blockage is indeed fully cleared. Once they do, they'll head back to the mainland."

"Will the company be escorting them?"

"Not all of them." Fishing a small key from a chain around his neck, the general unlocked the command seal, throwing the leather flaps back to reveal several stacks of paper tied with black thread, as well as several folded sheets. He picked one up. "New orders. We're to leave a permanent garrison in Lahar. Twenty-five soldiers. Make sure nothing like this happens again."

"Twenty-five…" Greenleaf's eyebrow raised. "Sir, that's a lot of soldiers. I don't know that the Laharian farms can produce enough food for that many extra mouths, especially with the recent… loss of experienced hunters." He tried to keep his voice even at the last point.

"We're increasing the convoys as well. Weekly, and double the number of bakeries. Enough materiel for the entire garrison. They won't siphon off the village's resources."

"Would I be in command?"

Brehev shook his head. "No one would justify putting a kaviak in command of a town garrison. Yeoman Liand is working up orders for my signature now. Sergeant Idar will be Lieutenant Idar tomorrow morning. I assume you don't have an issue with that?"

"No, sir. She's an excellent choice. Knows the area better than most."

"Glad you agree."

Greenleaf leaned back in the chair. "Sir, may I ask... Even with everything that's happened, I don't see how Lahar needs both a full garrison and a kaviak."

"They don't," Brehev said. "You're going to be reassigned."

"Reassigned?" Greenleaf blinked, stunned. It was what he'd been working for, but instead of relief, he just felt numb. "I thought..." He cleared his throat, trying to collect himself. "I was under the impression the arrogation was for ten years."

"That arrogation was issued by an Empress who has since abdicated. No one in Imperial command ever could justify posting a kaviak here. A garrison's a better choice, anyway. More flexibility, more manpower."

He took a deep breath. "Do you know where Imperial command intends on sending me?"

"They've left that choice up to me." Brehev pulled out the two bundles of paper, setting them side by side. "And I'm leaving the choice up to you."

"Sir?"

The general tapped a meaty finger on the stack to the right. "Do you know what this is, Captain?"

Leaning forward, Greenleaf immediately spotted his signature on the front, just below his signet seal. He swallowed. "Yes, sir. It's my report on the investigation and discovery of the blockage."

Brehev nodded. His fingers rested atop the report, but his eyes never left Greenleaf. When he spoke, his voice was even, betraying nothing. "Captain, I've spoken with Corporal Sand, that Elif woman, and the anatomist from the Chorale. You suffered second degree burns over close to a third of your body. That was after enduring advanced hypothermia, and severe frostbite. I can only guess at how many contusions and bruised bones you have." He leaned forward, folding his fingers together. "Elif and Prefect Zhukov both agree that you were showing signs of malnutrition, dehydration, and exhaustion. You were in exceptionally dire condition, and yet you still insisted on writing your report within three days of your return to Lahar."

"Yes, sir. I wanted to make sure that I didn't forget anything important," Greenleaf said.

"It might have been best if you'd waited until you recovered somewhat," the general said. "As it was, it would not be unreasonable for me to believe that you were not entirely of sound mind when you wrote this. Exhaustion, hypothermia, and dehydration can all cause hallucination and memory issues, I'm told."

Greenleaf was already shaking his head. "Sir, I promise you, I reviewed it several times to be certain. It's as complete and accurate as I can make it."

Brehev held up his hand, and Greenleaf fell silent. "As I was saying, captain. If you were to request permission to revise this statement on the grounds that you were not mentally fit when you wrote it, no one would think twice about me granting that request. And considering the ordeal you've endured, I wanted to make this as simple as possible." Reaching out, he tapped his finger on the other stack of paper, which was about a quarter of the thickness.

"This is a revised version of your report. All it needs is your signature. It explains that upon discovering that the level of the Serao was falling, you took command of a detachment of Laharian miners and hunters in order to investigate. You proceeded directly to the base of the Watchtower, where you discovered the sabotage, at which point you were confronted and attacked by the conspirators. You were forced to defend yourself, as well as the loyal Laharians who had accompanied you. You killed the conspirators, and managed to carry Reif Zdene back to Lahar. Upon your arrival, you discovered that Ayal Proudlake was a Brehai sympathizer, and had orchestrated the sabotage. He chose suicide rather than arrest." Brehev paused. "Captain, did anything I just describe not happen?"

Greenleaf stared at the general. "Sir, that's not..."

"I asked you a question, Captain Greenleaf. Does this report contain any direct falsehoods?"

"No, sir." Before the general could continue, Greenleaf said, "But it leaves out..."

"It leaves out nothing of importance. Nothing that I can't easily dismiss as a figment of a mind worn thin from trauma and exhaustion," Brehev said. "And Captain, let me be very clear. It is exceptionally important that those omissions are indeed figments. It is exceptionally important that your report not contain multiple references to fairy tales told to frighten children. It is exceptionally important that your official, legally binding report not describe your decision to violate an Imperial quarantine. It is exceptionally important that a report bearing the signature of a kaviak not leave this office with insane ramblings about the fate of a facility abandoned decades ago, quoting the last rantings of a suicidal man."

Greenleaf was stiff with anger, his hands gripping the end of the chair. When he spoke, it was with a clipped venom. "Are you calling me a liar, sir?"

"I am calling you a gods-damned hero, Captain, and I'll overlook your tone," Brehev snapped. "You endured a horrible ordeal, pushed yourself past any rational point, and suffered because of your commitment to defending a key strategic resource. That's why we're having this discussion. This?" He rapped a pair of fingers on the signed report. "This would erase all of that. What happened here would no longer be the story of a hero kaviak, braving the ice of the Suivev arctic and uncovering a conspiracy. It would be proof of someone that can no longer be trusted, either because he's dishonest, or because he's no longer stable."

He leaned forward. "You have a choice to make, Captain. I want you to stretch your legs, take a walk. By the time fourth bell rings, you will be standing back before my desk. That's a bit less than two hours. When you do, you will either sign the revised report, or you will not." He tapped the blank signature space on the thinner stack. "If you sign, I will immediately carry out Imperial Command's recommendation of your field promotion to Major. In addition, you'll be on the next convoy east, with orders to assume the position with the Second Cavalry Regiment as General Findlay's aide-de-camp, and you'll be doing it with the Order of Kaani pinned to your uniform." Brehev tilted his head. "I don't need to tell you what a huge step in your career that would be."

Anger heated Greenleaf's cheeks as he eyed Brehev.

Do you know?

Do you know what they woke up?

"If I don't sign?"

"If you insist on this being your official report, you'll still be on the next convoy east," the general said, his voice growing cold. "But you'll be going to Kaani, to report to Imperial Command for an immediate assessment of your suitability to continue to serve as a kaviak of the Imperial Army. This?" he rapped his fingers sharply on Greenleaf's signature. "This will make it an absolute certainty that you will be deemed unfit. Stripped of rank and privilege, and ejected from the Imperial Army. This report will be buried, dismissed as a work of fiction."

Greenleaf leaned back as if struck, eyes widening. "Sir…"

"I do not want to do that, Greenleaf." Brehev shook his head. "You've done remarkable things here, and losing you would be a blow to this new nation we're trying to build. There will always be room for courage, determination, and the kind of iron will you must have drawn on out on the ice. There will never be a place for ghost stories and slander."

He gritted his teeth. "Even if it's the truth?"

"If it is the truth? No one wants that truth. No one will listen," Brehev said. He gestured at the revised report. "Everything this report describes happened. It's not a lie. It's the truth, and It's a truth you deserve to have heard."

Greenleaf sat, jaw working, flexing his mangled right hand to feel the scar tissue tug.

Brehev rose to his feet. "Take a walk, Captain. Get your head right, come back here, and sign this gods-damned report."

Greenleaf stood stiffly. His four-fingered hand came up in a salute so sharp it could cut through rice paper, and he walked wordlessly from the room.

As he stepped through the doors of the Castle out into the frigid air, the pair of soldiers flanking the door came to attention, saluting Greenleaf, who nodded in acknowledgement as he pulled his coat tighter. After months in Lahar without seeing another uniform, it was unsettling to see so many in the small town. Lahar wasn't big, and a few dozen guards scattered throughout the town, bundled tight against the cold, stood out like an ugly scar.

The guards were the only ones he saw outside. The Laharians had withdrawn inside their homes, only coming out to work and visit one another. They greeted the uniformed Imperials with a stony silence that was all too familiar to Greenleaf, but the confrontational glares were gone. The community had been rocked by the loss of so many of their people, and while the precise details had been kept as quiet as possible, the rumor mill in a town this size ran more efficiently than any machine an artificer could produce.

The sun glimmered over the horizon, just peeking up to scatter buttery light over the ice walls of the village. The night had ended a few days prior, but they still saw no more than a few hours of sunlight between long stretches of starry skies. Greenleaf's heels thumped against the stone of the walkway. The moss was dotted with cloudberry buds, all glittering with a layer of hoarfrost. He'd been looking forward to seeing the buds flower in a few weeks.

When he arrived at the large doors of the mine, he wasn't sure if he'd intended to walk there or not. Four guards had already come to attention as he approached. Pyle was one of them, but his rigid posture betrayed no familiarity with the kaviak. "The foreman inside?" Greenleaf asked.

"Yes, sir," Pyle said. "He's taking those measurements again."

"Good." Greenleaf nodded at the door, and Pyle hesitated.

"Ah, sir, the general's orders state that only essential…"

"If you want to report it, that's fine, spearman," Greenleaf said. "I need to speak with the foreman. Consider it essential."

There was a brief pause, and Pyle nodded. "Very good, sir." He and a guard Greenleaf didn't know pulled the large doors open, and Greenleaf stepped through.

The burst of heat upon opening the doors didn't seem quite as oppressive as it had. His eyes went to the bridge over the glowing orange river. A man in a mining suit was pulling up a steel sounding rod. The tip was dripping lava, scorched deep black where the molten rock had kissed the metal. Once the last few drops had fallen free, he made his way down the stairs, holding the sounding rod ahead of him, and walking over to a heavy wooden table, covered in char marks. The wood smoked where the glowing tip of the rod touched it, and Reif pulled off his hood, setting it aside. He glanced over at the kaviak. "Don't think you're supposed to be in here, Imperial," he said. "You're going to get yourself in trouble."

"Bit late for that, as it turns out." Greenleaf walked to a rack of tools, plucking a long strip of metal with regular markings on it off some pegs. He handed it to Reif, who took it with a nod. Greenleaf kept his eyes on the miner. It was difficult at times. Nearly everyone had trouble looking the young man in the eye. His face was a mass of mottled scar tissue, a patch over his missing eye. His nose ended about a half inch before it should have, and on the right side of his head, his missing ear was surrounded by bubbled scarred flesh instead of deep brown hair. The instinct was to look away, but Greenleaf knew it mattered that he didn't.

"Thanks." Reif laid the strip next to the sounding rod, marking the length of blackened metal with a charcoal pencil.

"Working alone today?"

"Mine still isn't producing. Not much reason to have anyone else here. Sent them to help Edeline clean up the farms. They have to clear all the dead plants away before the new shipment of soil comes in." Reif nodded down at the marking. "Looks like that may change, though. Level's up an inch and a half since yesterday."

"I didn't know if anyone had told you."

"Last night. That general came by to ask me to take soundings for the next few days." He offered a cracked grin at the kaviak. "Didn't stay long. Don't know that he could handle just how pretty I am. Plus, he seemed in a bad mood. Asked me a few questions about things in your report. Don't think he liked my answers."

Greenleaf nodded. "Yeah. He's not too happy."

"I did warn you."

"I know." It was true. Greenleaf and Reif had eaten dinner together nearly every night for three weeks. Most nights, they ate in silence, but the few times they'd broached the topic of what had happened out on the ice, the miner had been clear on his opinion. "I just thought the truth was best."

Reif shook his head. "That's not a truth they want."

"That's not supposed to be an option!" Greenleaf snapped, pounding his fist against the table. "Truth is truth. It's what happened. There's no angle to it, no agenda, it's just what fucking happened."

"When people have lied to themselves for that long, the truth feels like an attack." Reif tilted his head. "How much trouble are you in?"

Greenleaf scratched a rough spot on the table. "Depends. He gave me a choice. Sign a heavily modified report, one that leaves out everything with the Lyceum, the trijjat, anything they don't want to talk about, and I get a medal, a promotion, and a new assignment."

"New assignment?"

Greenleaf nodded. "Aide-de-camp for a cavalry general."

"I don't know what that is, but it sounds important."

"It is." A piece of charred wood flaked off, and he flicked it to the floor. "It's the kind of posting you give to someone being groomed for command."

Reif attempted to arch an eyebrow, but he had none to arch. Instead, his scarred eyelid just kind of twitched. "That's what you wanted, right?"

"It was. Yeah."

"It's not anymore?"

"I don't know. Maybe." Greenleaf shrugged. "A lot's happened."

"You think?" Reif handed the measuring strip back to the kaviak, who replaced it on the wall. "What happens if you tell the charming general to shove it?"

"I still get a new assignment, but it's back to Kaani, where I'll most likely be judged unfit for duty, stripped of rank, and ejected from the Imperial army."

Reif chuckled. "And you're struggling with this decision why?"

Greenleaf flushed with irritation. "They want me to pretend like none of it happened."

"Of course they do." Reif shook his head. "Haven't you been paying attention? They won't listen. If you go back to the general, all indignant and blathering about truth, that report's not going to open people's eyes to the reality of what happened out here. He's going to ship you back to Kaani, and your report that you're so eager to throw your life away to protect is going right into the river. They'll burn it, and you alongside if you keep trying to shove this down their throats."

"It's the truth…"

"Gods, this is what pissed me off about you from the beginning," Reif sighed. "Self-righteous is never a good look." He tugged off his glove, rubbing at the patch of scar tissue where his ear used to be. "Fucking itching's going to drive me crazy. Look, you have to understand what you're asking. It's not just asking them to believe in trijjat."

Despite himself, Greenleaf felt his fingers twitch at the word, as if looking for a spear. He gave his head a quick shake, trying to dismiss the unease. If Reif noticed, he didn't say anything.

"You're asking them to acknowledge that the Chorale, the most celebrated group in the entire Empire, did all of this. Stuck their nose where it shouldn't be. Tried to force what they wanted on a place that had no use for them, and woke up something they were helpless against. You're asking them to change a story they've clung to for nearly a century. If they were wrong about the Lyceum, about what they released, what else are they wrong about?"

"Isn't that the point of this new era? Call it a transition, call it a coup, but everyone who was shouting for the Empire to change direction, aren't they trying to acknowledge the mistakes the Empire has made?"

"Are they giving back any of the territories seized during the Unification?" Reif asked. "Making compensation to families they killed, rebuilding towns they burned?" He shook his head. "It's hard enough to get a person to say, 'I was wrong and you were right'. You want an entire nation to do just that, to face up to the stain they left on a tiny corner of their Empire, but once they start looking too closely at their story, they're going to find so much more. They'll never do that. They can't." He shrugged. "Momentum is a terrible thing. You try to force them to change, and you'll be buried."

Greenleaf clenched his fist, but there was nowhere for his frustration to go. It settled into his gut, and he knew it would be quite comfortable there for a very long time. "Hey, if they throw me out, I could always come back and settle here."

Reif offered a ghoulish smile. Not unkindly, he said, "Even if they let you, Tomas, you know there's no place for you here. Everyone in Lahar knows the truth. We know what you did, what you did for us." He reached out and gripped Greenleaf's forearm. "For me. But you're a reminder. You killed people they knew, people they grew up with, shared meals with, loved. They can either see you as a murderer, or they can acknowledge that those people who they thought they knew betrayed us all. Which do you think is easier?"

The bitterness was thick in Greenleaf's voice. "That's what it's always about. Laharian, Imperial, it's about what's easier to believe. No matter what I did, what I tried to do."

"Braden's alive because you were stupid enough to stand between him and that bull," Reif said. "Every Laharian is alive because you were stupid enough to walk all the way to the mouth of this river, and I'm alive because you were stupid enough to carry me all the way back. I hope that's enough for you, because it's all the thanks you'll get."

He turned to pick the sounding rod up, dropping it in a quench barrel with a loud hiss. Looking down at his reflection, he sighed, and turned back to Greenleaf. "Can that be enough?"

Greenleaf shook his head. "I don't know."

"Honesty's always been your least appealing trait."

"I thought it was my uniform."

"Yeah, well..." Reif shrugged. "Maybe that doesn't fit you as well as I once thought it did."

They stood quietly for a moment. Finally, Greenleaf pushed off of the table. "Okay." He took a few steps towards the doors, then paused. "Dinner tonight?"

Reif nodded.

Greenleaf turned away from the fire, and stepped out into the cold.

EPILOGUE

Idar crunched through the snow towards Greenleaf as a cluster of Laharians heaved the last crate into the back of the wagon. "Any final orders, sir?"

Greenleaf shook his head as the villagers shut the bakery doors and made their way back down the hill. None of them looked at him as they walked past. "Lieutenant's stripes suit you."

She offered a thin smile. "Thank you, sir. Not exactly what I had in mind for my first command." She watched the Laharians leave. "They're not happy to have us here."

"No."

"Any suggestions?"

He glanced up at the ribbons of light in the dark sky. It had begun to lightly snow. "You're here to protect these people. Make sure your men remember that." He shrugged. "You'll do fine."

Lieutenant Idar nodded. "Safe travels, Major." He shook her hand, and she turned to walk back into Lahar.

Taking a deep breath, Greenleaf walked back to the last open bakery. The general and his staff waited inside. He hauled himself up, and said, "Fully loaded, General. We're ready to move out." Brehev nodded, and Greenleaf reached out to pull the doors shut. As he did, he spotted Reif, watching them from fifty feet away.

Their eyes met. Greenleaf raised his hand, waving. Reif nodded, and turned back home.

"Shut the door, Major," Brehev rumbled. "It's gods-damned cold out there."

No. It's not.

He shut the door.

Acknowledgements

Twelve years ago, I published my first book, and set forth into the world brimming with confidence that I was at the beginning of a long and successful writing career. Instead, I was at the beginning of ten years of writer's block. The reasons behind this are many and varied, and not worth delving into here, but the reason that I found my way back to the keyboard are the people listed here. Without their support, love, enthusiasm, and the occasional kick in the ass, this book wouldn't exist, so if you didn't like it, blame them.

The continent of Alddarri was created not with a book in mind, but in a desperate attempt to come up with something unique for my first big D&D campaign in which I served as DM. During the insane and headache-inducing antics of my players, this world settled into shape, and gave me a solid (if often disturbing) foundation to begin telling these stories. To Juliette Vincent, Josh Abel, Chris Norman, Quentin White, and Kaylah Brown, thanks for dropping exploding sheep on some zombies. Nothing I write will ever quite match that, but it's a bar I'll always try to reach.

There was a sixth player in that game. We'll get to her.

My developmental editor, Cameron Montague Taylor, did a heroic job of helping me disassemble and reassemble what I'd written into an actually interesting story. She never once lost patience with my neurotic and paranoid emails, and was fully committed to making sure that I told my story in the best way possible. You're the best, Cee. Thanks for not using your venomous spines on me.

To the many deranged elves at Gamers With Jobs, thanks for always supporting me.

I had the privilege of earning my degree under several teachers that did yeoman's work shaping me into someone who wasn't an embarrassment every time they sat down to the keyboard. Leon Alligood, Deborah Gump, and Jennifer Kates, thank you for everything you taught me and all the support, even after I graduated.

To Shannon Black: thanks for helping me find my way back.

While at school, I met a lot of gifted and talented journalists and writers, but several became some of the best friends I will ever know. Christopher Merchant constantly inspires me to embrace the weird and swing for the fences. Becca Andrews is fearless, brilliant, and we all knew she was going to change the world long before she published a book that really can change the world. I love you both, and let's drink irresponsible amounts of coffee very soon.

Josh Mauthe has been the first person to read just about everything I've written since we met in college, and has always been willing to gently point my errors with gentle and sensitive comments like, "You sly dog! You got me monologuing again!" He's not only one of my closest friends, but he has a fundamental understanding on what makes a story work that rivals anyone I've ever known, and he also happens to be one of the best writers I've ever met. Thanks for being patient with my bumpy first drafts, thanks for always being there for me, and here's to twenty more years of annoying everyone else in the room with our book conversations.

Fifteen years ago, I scared the absolute shit out of a coworker with a card trick, and ever since then, she's been one of my closest, dearest friends. She's also believed in me with a simple certainty that kept me afloat all the times I didn't believe in myself. Bennett, I love you, and thank you for everything you've ever done for me.

Someone once said you need a person who thinks everything you write is amazing. I would argue that having someone who threatens you with physical harm if you don't keep writing is even better. Having a best friend to road trip with, be terrible at PUBG with, get spectacularly drunk with, and watch terrible movies would be enough. But you've been there for me every step of creating this world and telling these stories, and I know you'll be there for a long, long time. Thanks, Toni. Love you. Enjoy the cheese.

I firmly believe that no story worth telling can be told without dogs by your side. Don't argue with me, I've done the research. Patton and Pickle, you're both very good boys. Shelby, you were the best dog, and I miss you. Thanks for the unconditional adoration when I needed it.

To my sister Owen: you're a superhero. I love you and I'm in awe of you every day, and I'm so very proud of you.

To Nephi: Your life is incredible, and no one deserves it more than you. I'm proud to be your brother.

Mom and Dad: Thanks for being the first to read my stories. I love you both.

Emi. Being your dad is the best thing I will ever do, and I plan to do it for a long, long time. You're kind, determined, and I will spend the rest of my life being grateful for you. Thank you for helping me learn how to be a dad. I love you so much, legal daughter.

Hannah. Since the moment I failed to impress you with a card trick (the first time), I've watched in awe as you've grown into a formidable, extraordinary woman. You could do anything, and you've chosen to help others, and I'll never stop being amazed that I get to be your dad. I am so proud of you, and I love you.

And to the sixth player at that table:

You're the best, kindest, funniest, most loving person I've ever known or will ever know. More of your love has gone into my writing than anything else, and everything good in my writing came from you. You're the love of my life, and I wake up every day bewildered that you chose me and fall asleep grateful that you did. I love you, Jen. Thanks for being my wife. Thanks for being my person.

About the Author

Dietrich Stogner lives in Smyrna, Tennessee with his wife, two daughters, and two dogs. He's a veteran of the US Navy submarine service, attended journalism school at Middle Tennessee State University, and can be found prowling around BookTok offering book recommendations and spectacular dancing videos (one of those is wholly false). He's also a pretty damn good cook.